Praise for C.C. Humphreys

'[A] truly moving masterpiece'   *Daily Express*

'Excellent sense of time and era, great and realistic characters who
stay in the mind, full of action: what more could any historical
fiction fan want? . . . Highly recommended'
                                        Historical Novelist Association

'C.C. Humphreys is one of the very best historical novelists
around. This is a great tale, finely woven with action, romance,
palpably real characters and terrific twists of fate'
    Simon Scarrow, *Sunday Times* bestselling author of *Centurion*

'An accessible, fast-paced, narrative-driven . . . historical thriller'
                                        Globe and Mail (Canada)

'Vigorously imagined, dashingly done espionage adventure . . .
thoroughly gripping, intensely readable'   *Literary Review*

'As swash-buckling as a young Errol Flynn, languidly escaping
death with the ease of a teenage James Bond, this is a roaring
adventure whose pages are remorselessly consumed'
                                        Good Book Guide

C.C. Humphreys was born in Toronto and grew up in Los Angeles and London. A third generation actor and writer on both sides of his family, he is married and lives on Salt Spring Island, Canada. To find out more visit www.cchumphreys.com

BY C.C. HUMPHREYS

Novels
The French Executioner
Blood Ties
Jack Absolute
The Blooding of Jack Absolute
Absolute Honour
Vlad: The Last Confession
A Place Called Armageddon
The Hunt of the Unicorn
Shakespeare's Rebel

Writing as Chris Humphreys
The Fetch
Vendetta
Possession

Plays
A Cage Without Bars
Glimpses of the Moon
Touching Wood

SHAKESPEARE'S REBEL

C.C. HUMPHREYS

An Orion paperback

First published in Great Britain in 2013
by Orion Books
This paperback edition published in 2014
by Orion Books,
an imprint of The Orion Publishing Group Ltd,
Orion House, 5 Upper St Martin's Lane,
London WC2H 9EA

An Hachette UK company

1 3 5 7 9 10 8 6 4 2

A CIP catalogue record for this book
is available from the British Library.

ISBN 978-1-4091-2027-8

Typeset at The Spartan Press Ltd,
Lymington, Hants

Printed and bound in Great Britain by
Clays Ltd, St Ives plc

The Orion Publishing Group's policy is to use papers
that are natural, renewable and recyclable products and
made from wood grown in sustainable forests. The logging
and manufacturing processes are expected to conform to
the environmental regulations of the country of origin.

www.orionbooks.co.uk

To John Waller
Swordmaster, mentor and friend

The British Isles in the 16th century

N E S W

Orkney

Hebrides

Atlantic Ocean

Scotland

North Sea

Dundee

Edinburgh

Alnwick

Londonderry

Ireland

York

Dublin Castle

Manchester

Cork

Much Wenlock

Celtic Sea

Wales

Cambridge

Stratford upon Avon

Cardiff

Oxford

London

Nonsuch Palace

Zennor

Plymouth

Portsmouth

Dover

Penzance

English Channel

—Hemesh Alles—

ACT ONE

Nor have we one or two kind of drunkards only, but eight kinds. The first is ape drunk, and he leaps and hollers and danceth for the heavens. The second is lion drunk, and he flings the pots about the house, calls his hostess whore, breaks the glass windows with his dagger, and is apt to quarrel with any man that speaks to him. The third is swine drunk . . . the fourth is sheep drunk . . . the fifth is maudlin drunk . . . *the sixth is martin drunk, when a man is drunk and drinks himself sober ere he stir . . .*

Thomas Nashe, 1592

I

The Martin Drunkard

February 1599

John Lawley lay in a haypenny bed, in the lowest tavern in Wapping, musing on fleas, on Irishmen and on drums.

Did the fleas that feasted on him so vigorously die once they had gorged?

Had the Irishmen who had just, for the third time, stolen the whole of their shared and threadbare blanket ever slept between rich linens, as he oft had?

Also – and this was his most pressing concern – did the drum that beat so loudly exist, or did it strike only within his head?

It was important to know. For if it existed, then truly he should answer its summons. Waking, though, meant taking action; the first of which, surely impossible, the lifting of his forearm from his brow. Yet even were he to accomplish such a feat, prove himself that Hercules, what then? To what task would the drum drive him next?

Nothing less than the forcing of his gummed eyelids.

That was too much. Furies hovered beyond them. Some were even real. Rouse and he would be forced to distinguish between them. Rouse and choices would have to be made. Whither? Whom to seek? Whom to avoid?

There were too many candidates for both.

No. Even if every drum stroke, imaginary or not, beat nausea through his body, until he was forced to do otherwise it was better to just lie there, and utter prayers for the beat to fade. And while he was about them, pray also that in its fading the sweats would begin to warm, not chill.

He shivered. He'd have liked his paltry share of blanket back. To reclaim it, though? That required the same effort demanded for arm, for eyes . . .

Impossible, he concluded. Sink back then. Seek warmth in memory. Illusion could sustain him. Indeed, in circumstances far worse even than these, illusion was all he'd had. Among all the things he was, was he not a fashioner of dreams?

Was he not a player?

He was. So make the drum real. Place it beyond, not within, his head. Make the heat real too, not the little transferred from men's rank bodies.

Where had he been hottest? Under a Spanish sun. Yet temper its fierceness with a breeze over waves. Conjure other sounds to drown the rising mutters of his bedfellows.

The plash of oars? The boatswain's call to each beat?

Thump.

'Pull!'

Thump.

'Pull!'

Thump.

'Pull!'

Truly, John Lawley thought, settling back, eyes still sealed and forearm yet lolled, this morning can wait. That other was better.

For a time, at least.

Three years earlier. 30 June 1596. The Bay of Cadiz

Thump.

'Pull!'

Thump.

'Pull!'

Thump.

'Pull!'

John lowered his forearm, closing his eyes to the sun's sharp bite. He had seen enough. The beach they were making for, some three

4

miles south of the town, was undefended. He had made landings under fire before and it was not something he sought to repeat. If his boat was sunk, his three primed pistols would be soaked, while swimming in breastplate and helm while retaining his sword was hard, made more so by the fact that he *could* swim. The majority of his companions couldn't, and experience taught that they would try to use him as a raft, with every chance of drowning both themselves and him. He would be forced to kill them. And, truly, he was only there to kill Spaniards . . .

. . . on behalf of the man who spoke now. 'Do you pray, Master Lawley?'

There was no need to open his eyes again. 'Aye.'

'You do? Yet I did not see you at the deck service before we embarked,' the voice continued. 'Soft! Perchance you were with the Catholics in the hold, celebrating a secret Mass? I always suspected you for a Papist.'

'I was not.'

'Then what were you about, while other men sought forgiveness and heaven's blessing?'

'About?' John smiled. 'Good my lord, I was about the sharpening of my sword.'

The bark of laughter made him open one eye. His questioner stood at the prow of the flyboat. 'A soldier's reply,' said the man, smiling wide. 'Though I have often wished that you cared as much for your soul as you do for your steel.' Separate red eyebrows, like hairy caterpillars upon white oak, joined to form a frown. 'You are not devout, Master Lawley. You are not devout.'

'Nay, faith, I am so.' John assumed his pious expression, one he'd use when playing clerics in the playhouse. 'For I most fervently believe that since God already has my soul in trust, he only asks that I do not part it from my body until he is quite ready to receive it. So I sharpen my steel and heed his commandment, both.'

General laughter came at that, though several men crossed themselves. 'Well, John,' cried Robert Devereux, Earl of Essex, 'if you ward my back in what is to come as well as you have ever done, then I will undertake to pray enough for us both.' He squinted up into the burning sky. 'He well knows that I have worn out the knees on a dozen stockings on the voyage here, to give us His victory this day.'

Not those stockings, though, thought John, eyeing them where they peeked above the boots. These were new and saved for the occasion. Tangerine, the earl's own colour, and a match for the sash that girdled the shiniest of breast and back plate, that burnished shine spread through other items of armour – vambrace upon his arms, greaves upon his shins, gorget at his throat. Beneath these, the rest was swathed in finest black cambric.

Should the Lord choose to ignore his entreaties, thought John, young Robbie will make the comeliest of corpses. Yet not only his apparel would distinguish him. The face brought aboard the ship in Plymouth, bloated with excess and worn by cares, had been transformed by four weeks of sea air and exercise into the handsomeness that so inspired the balladeers. Essex had commanded John to fence him daily, and stripped to the waist the two of them had duelled, gripped and thrown upon the quarterdeck of his vessel, the *Due Repulse*. If during the first fortnight John had held back, while his pupil shrugged off the life of both indulgence and ceaseless, sleep-sapping intrigue he lived at court, in the last two weeks the earl had regained both strength and many of the skills John had taught him over the years. Another week and perhaps he'd not have bested his protégé. Essex was ten years younger after all, a bare thirty, half a head taller, lithe for his height. It was a good time to be turning their skills upon a common enemy – one who would perceive them as twinned furies, with John dressed near identically to the earl, if less sumptuously, being in his hand-me-downs. It was a noted subterfuge of war, to have two leaders to confuse the foe.

Yet they were not the only ones with trimmed beards, styled hair and lean shanks. Others had joined in the training. One spoke now. 'And what steel he raises for your cause and God's, my lord!' the man cried. 'A hardy broadsword, note you all. None of your foreign fripperies, your "rap-i-ere"' – he exaggerated the French sounds – 'for John Lawley. A yard of English steel to carve two yards of soil for any Spanish hidalgo he meets.'

Jeers came, from more than one man, while John smiled. His friend George Silver was a fanatic for all things native – especially the nation's traditional weaponry – and deplored the foreign blades that several of their comrades bore. In the face of their jeering, he grabbed

John's arm. 'Come, Master Lawley. Help me convince these fools of the virtues of true English weapons.'

John reclosed his eyes and turned his face once more to the sun. 'George,' he drawled, 'the only virtue I subscribe to is in an old proverb: "It is good sleeping in a whole skin."'

'Nay, John! Good my lord . . .' began Silver loudly, as other men entered the quarrel.

'Peace, all.' The earl's voice silenced the hubbub. 'And know only this: I care little how you kill our foes this day. Spit them with rapiers, hew them with backswords, smash them with staffs . . . or pluck me their eyes out with a three-tined fork!' He laughed. ''Tis one to me. Only so long as yon citadel of Cadiz is mine by nightfall.' All men looked north-west, to the ramparts of the city. 'Mine, not my effing Lord of Effingham's or, worse, that popinjay Raleigh's!'

All now looked back to the men-of-war, where the fleet's guns still smoked from the havoc they'd wreaked upon the enemy. 'For my part, I know only this,' the earl continued, his voice softer as he drew two inches of steel above his scabbard, 'this English blade was bequeathed to me by another hero of our land. And for him and that land it shall this day be lodged in some Spanish breasts – or lodged beside me in my tomb.' He shoved the weapon back. 'And now, master boatman, double time if you please. Some other vessels seem eager to beat us to the beach. Impudent dogs! Do they not remember that I must be first in everything?' He waved the helmet he held above his head. 'And I will begin by being first on enemy sand,' adding with a roar, 'Stop me if you can!'

He was echoed from his own boat and from those nearby. Theirs surged ahead, at the boatswain's speeded cry, the drummer's increased beat. Silver, flopping down again beside John, leaned in. 'Ah, Lawley,' he said, 'you may fool some with your veteran's ennui.' He mimed a yawn. 'But I know different. Know that you are as ardent for glory as any man here.'

'I am ardent for gold,' John grunted, 'and the pickings of the sack of Cadiz could be rich indeed. Now let me sleep.' Closing his eyes again, he wondered if Silver was right. What were these twitchings about his heart? There was only one other place he'd had similar feelings – in a theatre with a new play to give and too swiftly conned lines to speak. Yet this, of battle? It had been eight years since he'd last drawn a sword in more than playhouse anger. Different commander, same enemy, the one he'd fought near all his life and across this wide globe.

Spaniards, he thought, taking a breath. There is always something about fighting Spaniards.

A concerned cry opened his eyes. Their vessel, which had drawn initially ahead, was starting to fail. They had fewer men at oar than some of the others, carrying Essex's close companions as they did, and some of those oarsmen were flagging now. John knew that Robert needed to be first ashore, first to the gates, first through them; that he cared little about plunder though he was probably more debt-ridden than any. All he wanted was the glory – and Queen Elizabeth's hand tugging his red curls, calling him once again her 'sweet Robin'.

He saw the earl's shoulders droop – from their first meeting ten years before, John knew the young man to be prone to a sudden melancholy that could be brought on by just such a reverse. 'To oar, lads!' he cried, seizing the one from the puffing sailor beside him. 'Let we yeomen of England disdain nothing in giving our lord his first triumph.'

The cry was taken up, the challenge. Essex himself dropped down to grasp oak. After an initial slip of momentum as one man replaced another, the oars dipped again, the vessel surged. They may not have been sailors, but the Bay of Cadiz was calm and the trick one they had all learned before.

The boat grounded, the man at the prow launching himself with the sudden stop. Water lapped his boot tops but did not halt him. Five strides and he was on dry sand. And for a moment, Robert Devereux, Earl Marshal of England, had sole possession of that foreign shore.

'Cry God for her majesty!' he shouted.

But another name was on the lips of those who spilled over gunnels to follow him.

'My lord of Essex!'

8

'Will ya stop kickin' me, varlet?' the voice said. 'Me shins are already as black as a negro's bollocks.'

'Sure now, give him blow for blow,' a second voice suggested, before lowering to a whisper. 'Or have you sought other recompense in his purse?'

John did not try to open his eyes. They were still stickily shut beneath his forearm. Besides, he wasn't disturbed by the question. He already knew the answer – the one the first man gave now.

''Tis as barren as my da's fields these last three summers. So if he kicks me one more time, or tries again to steal back his cloak – the least he owes me, mind, for the night he's given me! – I'll pay him with that blow. You'll see.'

John ceased writhing. He didn't want rousing just yet from his reverie of warmth. Especially as he had just come to the part where it had all gone so well.

Until it hadn't.

'What's he moaning about now?' the other man asked. 'Is that Spanish? He's dark enough for a dago, ain't he? A pox on him if he is. I'll join you in giving the dog a beating, you can be sure.'

You'll be one of a crowd, thought John, drifting back . . .

Cadiz. 1596

It had been too easy. The unopposed landing, the three-mile march on soft sand to the plain before the city gates. Five hundred mounted dons had attacked an advance party sent for the very purpose of luring them on, bait for a trap, duly sprung. At Essex's command, the main body had erupted from their concealment, pincering the Spanish. A volley from musket and pistol and the proudest hidalgo fled, pursued by Englishmen shrieking like fiends. The defenders had shut the gates so fast, half their number were trapped outside. Yet rather than surrender there, or, more likely, be slaughtered by the charging enemy, they had shown that enemy the swiftest way into their city – through walls under repair, scaffolding up against it and holes still full of tools.

'On! On!' screamed Essex, red-stained sword aloft and running at the widest hole, through which a cloak, emblazoned with the Star of Seville, had just disappeared. Yet even as he reached the gap, its edges exploded, mortar blasted out by shot, fragments of stone and metal whining off his breastplate and helm. To the horror of all, the earl fell, but immediately scuttled to the hole's side, joined there in moments by his closest companions.

John was among the first. 'How fares my lord?' he said, reaching out to the blood that daubed the tangerine sash.

Essex glanced down. 'Not mine, I think,' he said, brushing aside the reaching hand. 'Or if it is, it's mingled with a few others.' He laughed. 'God a mercy, John, that was a good first roll of die. But what's within?' He jerked his head at the hole. 'Can we storm this, think you?'

John thrust his head into the gap, noted the inner wall that faced this outer one, saw flintlock flashes there, withdrew just before bullets nipped the masonry. 'A wall defensible about fifty paces off and a killing ground before it,' he said. 'Hard to tell the numbers. Not many, I'd hazard, since they chose to relinquish this wall' – he slapped the one they sheltered behind – 'to defend that. Still, enough to pin us here, for we can only go through this gap two at a time. If we wait for numbers . . .'

But Essex had stopped listening. 'You'd hazard and so would I, Johnnie. All we need is to buy a moment.' More of his advance guard were arriving, weaving to avoid the fire of snipers in the turrets. Some of these newcomers bore muskets, others grapple and rope. 'Silver?'

The swordsman slid across. 'My lord?'

'Take you these dozen musketeers to the scaffold above. Tell me when they are primed.'

'My lord.'

While he scrambled up, followed by his men, Essex took out a pistol. 'Load all. When Silver calls, be ready to move.'

'My . . . my lord, a word.' The tremulous voice that came was that of the earl's steward, Gelli Meyrick. On a nod, the man continued, his Welsh tones heightened by the strain. 'You have oft asked me, look you, that I counsel you when . . . when impatience rules your honour. Even at the risk of your displeasure' – he swallowed – 'I so counsel now.' He pointed back the way they'd come, across the valley dotted with the bodies of Spanish cavalrymen and riderless mounts, to the slight rise beyond where forces were mustering. 'I see my lord of Effingham's standard there. He brings the main body. If we were to wait, look you . . .'

'Wait?' roared Essex. 'Is that your counsel? Wait for my lord Charles to march up and steal my glory? I piss on him and any waiting.' He finished loading the pistol, snapped its steel down, thrust it into his cross belt, began loading another. 'What say you, Master Lawley?'

John looked up from his own loading and into the younger man's eyes. They were maddened, within the streakings of black powder. Yet somewhere in the heart of them was also the misgiving Essex ever had. He gave every man's doubts an ear and could be swayed by them. Or woman's – a queen's slight would send him to his bedroom for a month. But John also knew this well enough: Essex would rather be dead than cede an ounce of glory to any other.

John glanced around at the other men, clutching pistols, hefting swords. While blood was up, they may as well act. First glory – if they survived – but first pickings too in a town as rich as Cadiz. His share would solve a lot of problems back home. Rich enough, it might even persuade Tess to marry him. 'I am game if you are, good my lord.'

'I am. Oh, I am!' Essex looked around at other expectant faces. 'And you, stout hearts? Are you with us?'

'Aye,' came the shout.

Pistols loaded, armour adjusted, a man, one Robert Catesby, leaned forward. 'Master Lawley, I heard a strange rumour of you: that you are, as well as a famed warrior, a player of some note. Is it true? Have you strutted the platforms of England?'

Plus a few on the Continent, thought John. But it did not feel like the right moment to detail his curriculum vitae. So he simply nodded and said, 'I have.'

'Well, sir, in my experience of 'em – and I am particularly fond of Edward Alleyn's performances at the Rose.' John rolled his eyes. 'Well, sir, could you not give us some speech of fire from the repertoire. Some warrior's words to see us through the wall and among the enemy? Tamburlaine's, perhaps? Or even our majesty's illustrious grandfather and his words at Bosworth?'

Marlowe or Shakespeare? John thought. He had played them both, of course. He had his loyalty to the brother of his soul, William, and his preference. Yet truly, he cared little for recitation unless there was coin in it. So now he glanced at Essex, just finishing the loading of his last pistol. With his red beard stained with black powder, some-one else's blood on his cheek and a dancing light in his eye, he looked like the youth John had first met ten years before.

John leaned forward. 'Nay, lads, why hearken to some false and foreign hero from the playhouse when you have a true and native one before you? And when our commander writes verse as inspiring as any?'

Essex shrugged, entirely failing to look modest. 'Aye, good my lord' and 'We pray you, do' rang out.

The earl looked slowly around, then nodded. 'Then see here,' he said, rising to one knee and drawing his sword. 'This weapon that I carry is the very one carried beside me into battle ten years since by my brother in arms, the brother of my heart, Sir Philip Sidney.' A sigh came. 'That was a day, Master Lawley, was it not?'

It was not the hour for memory but for myth, so John simply gave the nod required and the earl continued. 'At Zutphen in the Nether-lands it was, and three thousand Spaniards marching to relieve the town while I . . . I had but three hundred mounted Englishmen to stop them. Yet I did not hesitate. With Sir Philip on my right arm, and John Lawley on my left, three times we charged, and rallied, and charged again.' He paused, and his eyes filled. 'Yet on that final charge, his blade becrimsoned in foemen's blood, my brother took the musket ball that gave him his quietus.'

He looked around at all the faces, those nearest, those others who'd drawn nearer as he spoke, and raised his voice to reach them. 'He died in my arms two weeks later. He gave me this sword ere he did, and these words: "Never draw it without reason nor sheathe it without honour."' He nodded. 'I never have and I never will. And I will not on this day.' He focused on one man. 'So do not counsel that we wait for others, Gelli Meyrick. Do not seek fellow travellers on the path to glory. They will only get in our way.' He looked around the circle. 'This honour, and England's glory, belongs only to us,' he added, and holding the sword by the blade, he raised it up before him like a crucifix.

Men reached out and placed their hands upon it, as if it were indeed the true cross. John only hesitated a moment, remembering well where that particular path of glory had led – to Philip Sidney's tent, and the foul-sweet stench of gangrene as the poet-warrior died. Yet Essex had not only inherited the sword, he had inherited the mantle of the dead hero. Men would follow it, like a banner. Follow him.

A voice from above. 'All's ready here, my lord,' George Silver called.

Essex stood, lifting the sword high. 'For honour! For England! For St George!' he cried.

'Honour! England! St George!' came the shout from two score throats.

Smiling, Essex tipped his head back and shouted up, 'Fire!' drew one of his pistols, half cocked it. John did the same, readying himself.

Above, the musketeers laid their weapons on the ramparts; a ragged volley was discharged. 'Now, Goodman John?'

'Now, my lord.'

Both men went to full cock. At a nod, they thrust their pistols through the hole, pulled their triggers. Then, through the gunsmoke and side by side, they entered the city of Cadiz.

The two who followed them died, Spanish gunmen rising from the crouch. But more Englishmen charged through, while others swung down on ropes from above. Briefly it was backswords and bucklers against rapiers and pike. Some of the enemy fought bravely. Most broke and fled down the narrow streets that gave on to the wall.

'Follow! Halloo! Halloo!' cried Essex, giving the hunter's call. Somewhere a bugle echoed him – Lord Howard, Raleigh and the rest of the English army approaching fast. The chase was on along the path, and glory was the prize.

'There's something hard diggin' into me.'

'I thought he was too sottish for that. Foul bastard!'

'Not in his breeches, ya simpleton. Higher up, about his chest.'

'Dagger?'

'Too small. Feels like . . . like a locket, mayhap.'

'A locket?' Fingers rasped on an unshaven jaw. 'Let's have it out. Perhaps it'll fetch enough to pay us for this wretch's thrashing that so marred our sleep.'

'Do you stand by with your cudgel then, though I doubt he'll stir. I'll delve. Christ's guts, but don't he stink?'

John heard the words, felt the fingers questing for the locket Tess had given him on a happier day. He should have sold it three days since, bought one last bottle of the water of life. Was her cruelty not the reason for the debauch, after all? Should she not share the cost? And yet he'd found he could not.

It would take a better picker than this oaf to pull the jewel from him. So he had some moments to linger still, where the land was warm, and the cause clear.

Cadiz. 1596

They'd pushed too far, of course. Blood in their ears, its taint in their nostrils, fleeing backs, feeble stands brushed aside. They'd chased as far as the town's central square, where someone had rallied the last of the defence. Too few, too late for the English army, whose bugles were sounding even then from the town's main gate. Too many for Essex's band, down to twenty, dwindled now by casualties and those who'd slunk off to loot.

A volley of sorts. Two more of their band on the cobbles and fifty of the dons running from the ranks, screaming, '*Por el Rein! Por Dio. Por España!*'

'Back!' shouted Essex, and it was the Englishmen's turn at quarry. Down the alleys they'd stormed up, making for the walls again, John in step with Essex, Silver and the rest speeding ahead. No one was panicked. Bugles everywhere showed that the town was fully breached and would soon be theirs. Now, if they could only keep alive till that happened.

'This is more like it, Johnnie,' Essex cried, laughing as he ran. 'Let's lead these dons into a hot English welcome, then turn hound and chase them back again. I want to be the one to take their general's sword.' He laughed. 'Though it will probably be a rapier and Silver will mock it.'

John laughed with him . . . until they turned into another alley, a rare straight one, short enough for the rest of the party to have cleared its end as the earl and he were entering it. Yet just as they did, from a house halfway down stepped a half-dozen swordsmen. They had been waiting for the larger party of Englishmen to run past before emerging from their shelter. Seeing only two left, with a shout they drew their weapons and advanced.

Boots on the cobbles behind. Their pursuers coming on fast, the two abreast that the alley allowed. There was but a moment to stand back to back, calculate the odds, note that they were poor, and act. 'Here!' John yelled and slammed his shoulder into a door to their side. The earl joined him. Under double assault the wood splintered then gave and they were falling into the front room of a house. A woman screamed, a child snatched up into her arms.

'There!' cried Essex, running for the doorway beyond. As their pursuers surged in, delayed by a bench John threw, the fleers took the stairs two at a time. But near the top, John slipped, a triumphant cry telling of an enemy close behind. He braced against a step, kicked back hard with both feet. Shod boots connected and a body was falling, blocking the stairwell. The earl reached, jerked him up. Together they leapt the last few stairs.

Into the bedroom, mostly occupied by the large bed, posted in each corner and curtained. There was a window on to the street, large enough to squeeze through – but a glance showed John more dons below trying to push in. There was one other way out – a ladder rising to a shut trapdoor. 'The roof!' he called.

Essex had his foot upon it when the first Spaniard ran into the room. But the moment he took to look around was a moment too long, John reaching him in an extended lunge, his backsword thrust straight, a slight turn of wrist guiding the Spaniard's rapier over his

15

own shoulder, while his point pierced the man's throat. He reeled back with a choked scream, dropping his weapons, hands raised to clutch and fingers failing to stem the blood that ran between them. His fall was taking him to the door and John accelerated it, hitting him with his buckler, slamming the small round shield into the man's spine. He tumbled out, into the man who was trying to get in, and for the moment the doorway was blocked by blood, body and scream.

John turned. The earl was only halfway up the ladder, paused there. 'Go!' John yelled.

'And leave you? Nay, I'll stay.'

'Then both of us will be ta'en, my lord. Let me hold them awhile and you escape.' He saw the hesitancy on the younger man's face, heard the shouting on the stairs, his victim's heels thumping down 'em as he was cleared away. His comrades would be coming in moments.

He made his voice softer. 'When you have made good your escape, I will yield. When we hold the town, you can have me back for a small price. But if they take the real Earl of Essex, not his substitute' – he gestured at their deliberately similar apparel – 'the bargain may be harder to strike. And you would be in Lord Howard's debt for ever.'

The concept worked. The hesitancy vanished. Essex began to climb. 'True words, Honest Yeoman,' he called over his shoulder. 'I will return in arms.'

His boots vanished and thumped swiftly overhead. 'Nay, good my lord, you are most welcome,' John muttered, a brief smile coming then leaving when two dons came through the door. These were ready for him, rapiers and daggers thrust before, tips close like steel gates before bodies held well back. The brief thought came: that Silver should be there, expostulating on the situation, lauding the superiority of short English blade and shield over foreign technique and fancies. It was a matter of some debate still among the fight masters of London.

Yet he was not in London but in a bedroom in Cadiz, and technique could go hang. Principle was the key with this his sole one: stay alive long enough to make good the earl's escape. Live himself afterwards.

As the Spaniards came for him, he set about doing so.

In the small part of his brain that was not focused on survival, he was aware of an irony here; for in his other life, the life he preferred, the life of the playhouse, one of his tasks had been to arrange the fights that occurred in most plays. And so, like players upon a stage, he set about organising his enemies' moves. There were more of them crowding the top of the stair and, in good conscience, two were as many as he could handle, so he was determined to hold the combat near the door, and prevent entrance.

As always, he watched their weapons. For all the firmness of their guard, he could see the men's hesitancy – and that was not just because of the constant shiftings of their feet, a trait of your Spanish swordsman, forever dancing as they fought. Perhaps the sight of their comrade's body thumping down the stair, gouting blood, made them pause. Perhaps being chased like rabbits through their own town. Whatever caused it, John could use it.

And did. Raising his hilt above his head, blade angled down and diagonal across his body in true guard, he did not leave it there, but swept it in a tight circle, using only the wrist, the fastest form of attack. His weapon gathered theirs, rapiers and daggers, all four knocked aside for the moment John needed. As they stumbled sideways under the force of the heavier blade's strike, John vaulted off his front foot, spinning around, using the pivot to bring his buckler sweeping across, smashing into one opponent's cheek. With a cry he was down, sprawled across the doorway, John's whole desire.

But the other had leapt clear, regained his weapons, while the force of John's spin, the buckler strike passing to the left, his sword out right, left his belly and chest wide. The Spaniard thrust with his rapier before he could withdraw that invitation, and only a leap back, and a rapid sucking in of waist, saved his life at the cost of a button. Parrying hard with a circling flick of sword, he gave back again as the man's dagger went for his eye, deflected the swung sword over his head with his buckler. As it clanged into a bedpost, he thrust forward hard, like a pugilist punching, but the Spaniard eluded him with a slip of shoulder, then came again.

John lost every thought save two: keeping the man before the doorway, and deflecting his assaults. All became blur, blows and thrusts given, warded, redoubled. The bedposts blocked both of them, the curtains snared blades until they were shredded by slashes. In but a few moments steel met steel twenty times or more and there was not time to consider anything but that. Until John became aware of life beyond the whirling blades, of movement again at the door-way, another opponent finally stepping through it . . . and behind him, the creak of rungs on the ladder.

It would be typical of Essex, changeable as quicksilver, to come back. Forcing his opponent back with a whirl of blows, John risked both a look and words – though 'My lor—' was as far as he got. It was a Spaniard on the ladder, he'd just flung a cudgel and John had only enough time to turn his head so it did not strike him in the face. Yet it struck his temple well enough, and his helmet only made the blow ring louder.

It did not send him entirely to oblivion, or at least not constantly. His eyesight was taken, sure, and what his other senses gave him was mixed. He heard an English bugle near, low-voiced commands, felt his body being lifted. There was street air and scents, blood in his mouth. Then a cooling breeze in the heat, salt tang, the sudden shock of his face on floorboards awash with seawater. The part of him hanging on to consciousness wondered if he was being taken back to the *Due Repulse*, felt gratitude at the thought. Until he heard the language the oarsmen were speaking. He understood few words of it, knew only that it was Spanish.

'*En nombre de Dio*,' he muttered.

The haypenny bed, Wapping. 1599

'What's the dago bastard sayin' now?'

Enough, thought John. Further in memory and I will have too much of heat. It may be as cold as a nun's tit in this Wapping tavern, but I would not trade it now to be warmed again beside the Inquisition's fires.

Besides, he could sleep no more – not when delving fingers had finally fastened on the locket. It was all he had left and he might still need to pawn it; though he'd rather keep it, as token of woman's faithlessness. Either way he was buggered if he was going to let some amateur cutpurse have it.

His eyes were still hard to open. When he finally managed it, he saw, silhouetted against the wooden slats of the tavern's attic, the same object that had lately entered his reverie – a cudgel. Its wielder was not looking at his face but at his companion's hand and what was emerging from within John's doublet.

'Bloody thing's on a chain,' the thief was saying. 'Can't . . . prise it . . . loose . . .'

'Snatch the bloody thing off!'

John wanted to say, 'Can I help?' But his throat was as gummed as his eyes and issued only a groan. It was enough to make the cudgel wielder look up, see his eyes were open, pull back the club to strike . . .

Which took too long. John shot one hand up, grabbing the wrist, twisting, causing pain and the dropping of the weapon. His other hand wrapped around the thief's head and he pulled the man's face hard into his chest.

He had them both – but he could not hold them long. The cudgel man was large and the cutpurse wiry, and both were jerking like hogs on a rope. Releasing them by flinging them back, John rose unsteadily from the three-man mattress. At once his head spun in concert with his stomach and he had to lean down, hands on his knees, taking breath.

It gave the other men time to recover their courage, and the one his club. 'Right, you whoreson,' he declared, 'give us that locket.'

'You cannot have that,' replied John, swallowing back his nausea, slowly rising, reaching up, back. 'But you can have this.'

There was only one other thing he possessed now, truly the last thing he would ever part with. It rested between his shoulder blades, in a sheath designed for the purpose. Drawing the six-inch blade now, he took guard.

Its appearance punctured the men's bravado like its point would have an inflated bladder – to John's considerable relief, since both men, though stationary, refused to stay still to his sight, and more-over had each acquired a glowing yellow and green carapace. 'Now, now,' said the wiry one, swallowing, 'there's no need for that.'

'Is there not?' asked John. It was a real question; yet before either man could answer, boots sounded upon the stairs. Keeping the knife before him, John shifted it slightly towards the attic door. Spaniards might be about to burst through it.

They didn't, but the landlord of the Cross Keys did. 'Out, swine,' the three-bellied man bellowed. ''Tis past nine. Do you think I keep a bawdy house and you the Earls of March? The nightmen want your bed.'

He seemed oblivious to knife or cudgel, just shooed them while a boy entered, swept a filthy cloth over the more soiled of the floor-boards and left bearing the teeming bucket. The two thieves followed with a few brave mutters and dark looks at John. Fumbling his knife back into its sheath – he nicked himself doing it, adding a future scar to the ones already there – John bent, repossessed his cloak and lurched towards the stairs.

The landlord delayed him with words. 'Someone looking for you. In the yard.'

'Me?' It was a surprise. He didn't know anyone in Wapping, an outlying district far from his usual haunts. It was why he had chosen it for the climax of his month-long debauch. 'Who?'

'A boy.' The man put a hand on his shoulder and pushed. 'Now be off.'

A boy? For a moment, John's heart lurched. Ned, he thought. His first two steps were quick at the happy thought, slowing thereafter. He might want to see his son. He did not want his son to see him. Not like this, the way he looked, the way he stank. It had been a year since the last drunk, and he'd given Ned some cause for hope that it would not be repeated.

Still, he peeped into the yard, hoping to at least get a glimpse of the heir to all his nothing, ready to run out the front once he had. It was not Ned there, though, but a dark-haired younger lad, maybe ten years of age. John did not know him, though he thought perhaps he had seen him somewhere before.

'You seek me?' he said, crossing the slick cobbles with as even a gait as he could manage, making for the butt of rainwater in the yard's corner. It had a crust of ice on it. John broke it; then, taking a breath, he plunged his whole head in, gasped at the shock and pain, plunged deeper.

He stayed submerged as long as he could stand. When he rose, he discovered the boy had come closer but not close. 'Well,' he asked, through dripping water, 'who sent you?'

The boy did not reply. Perhaps he did not wish to open his mouth. Instead, he held out a scrap of paper. The moment John took it, its deliverer turned on his heel and fled.

Some of the ink smudged under what ran from his fingers. But the brief message was clear enough. He scratched at his wild beard and beneath his doublet. He was flea food again.

What, John thought, sucking soured rainwater from his moustache, did London's most famous actor want with him now?

Southwark Ho!

He had fortune on the riverbank. No wherryman came so far from London for fares and he had no coin for one if he had. But a skins trader was bound thither with a full load and was in a good enough mood to allow John – who requested it with little more than a few grunts and gestures – free passage with him; as long as he didn't mind riding on his wares.

'As comfortable a bed as you've slept on for a while, I'll warrant ye – if you've slept in a bed at all,' said the man, eyeing John's stained clothes and scraggled beard before gesturing to the mound of cow hide. He and a labourer sang hymns while they rowed, and did not seek news of the world, the usual fee for a free ride, allowing John to sink back with a groan and consider how, indeed, it was a far better bed than he'd had in many a week – fewer fleas, a soft pillow not a log, most of all no flatulent, kicking, thieving fellow occupants. Better too than the walk he'd thought he'd have to make. The fields of Mile End and Whitechapel had started to be encroached upon by those who could not squeeze within the City's walls or sought freedom from its controls. That meant businesses of every kind – taverns, ordinaries, brothels, shacks and tenements – and it also meant people, some of whom would be watching for the unwary traveller.

Him, John thought. He was amazed that he'd seen off the bed-sharing thieves.

Yet if he believed the comfort would make him doze again, he was wrong. He ignored the banks, the jostling humanity in the wharves and warehouses. The river better suited his mood, drew him eye, ear and nose. Streaked with daubs and paints of different hues, sheened with effluent from the tanneries, dotted with spars of wood and broken rafts twined with rope on which perched gulls and gannets. Carcasses floated, a bloat sheep here, a piebald dog, a cat; once, a human, gender rendered indeterminate by long immersion and the pickings of fish and bird.

So much flotsam was a match for the jumble of his mind. It was always thus, after a month's debauch, detritus swirling around his head, with him unable to alight on any item for long. Yet settle he must. This summons from Richard Burbage? Did opportunity lie in it? Would he be sober enough to seize it if it did?

A harsh cry drew his eyes from murky surface into the air. More a bark, for ravens did not call like other birds. He knew this for he had spent months listening to them, when he had little else to do but learn to distinguish between their voices. He had even befriended one, a blue-black brute he called Jeremiah, in the time when they'd shared the dwelling.

He raised his eyes to that dwelling now. The Tower rose like a stone mountain from the water, dwarfing every building nearby, the weight of its stones pressing upon the city and upon himself. It appeared almost as a continuation of his dream from the morning, for his capture by the Spanish that day in Cadiz, his imprisonment in Seville afterwards had led, within a year, to imprisonment there. It was what the English authorities did with prisoners who had, by whatever means, escaped the clutches of the Inquisition. For many had been released only on the promise to return to London and assassinate the heretic queen, and that John had reported this mission on arrival had not led to the hailing of a hero and the rewards he'd expected but to three months of close examination.

'A foul place!' exclaimed the skin trader, seeing the direction of John's gaze. 'Gives me the fears each time I pass by.'

John grunted agreement.

'Well, to happier thoughts, eh?' the man said, leaning on his oar against the current, swinging the prow of his boat away. 'And fairer prospects.'

Fair was not a word oft used to describe what was before him now, but for once John thought the description more than apt. It wasn't the vista, the usual huddle of riverfront warehouses, many with the fug of industry rising from them, slaughterhouses alongside fish smokeries, tanneries beside glue factories. It wasn't the byways beyond which would be the same twisting, narrow, gloomy, cess-filled alleys and streets that were upon the opposite bank.

It was the people who thronged them. It was the life upon them. It was the pleasure that could be had along them. It was the Liberty of the Bishop of Winchester, and contained more taverns, more brothels, more cockpits and bear bait rings, more gaols and more playhouses than any other square half-mile in the known world.

'Southwark ho!' the trader announced. 'It's where we're stopping, so unless you want to ride back to Wapping on the next tide, you'd best alight.' The prow nudged into a wooden wharf and the labourer leapt off to make the vessel secure. 'Pickle Herring Stairs. Will they suit?'

John rose from his hide bed, wobbled to the gunnel, paused there to get his balance. He inhaled, filling his nose with the acrid, sweet, rancid scent emerging from the warehouse that gave the stairs their name. For the first time in a long time, he tried a smile. Words accompanied it. 'They suit well. And I thank you for your kindness.'

The man reached out a steadying hand and braced John as he stepped on to the wharf. He looked surprised. 'You're English?'

'I am.'

'God's teeth, I thought you was, you know . . .' He shrugged. '. . . foreign. On account you're so dark and you don't talk much.'

John shrugged as well, stepped away. The man called after. 'You sounds like you could be a bit of a gentleman too. So I'd watch myself in Southwark if I were you, sir.' John turned to look back. 'Know any people 'ere, do you?'

John found he still had a smile on his face. It went on the man's words. 'A few,' he replied, and climbed the stairs. More than a few, he thought, as he pushed through a crowd of labourers seeking coin to help unload the cargo. And very few of those do I wish to see. But Richard Burbage is certainly one.

Should he go there straight? He bent his head to his chest, sniffed his doublet, winced at an odour so strong it even pierced the fug of pickled herring. Peg Leg, he thought, and turned, not along the route to the playhouse. but down the High Road.

*

The inn was called the Castle upon the Hope, and was run by a former comrade from the wars, Jack Tanner, known as 'Peg Leg' Tanner for what he'd given for his country. Peg Leg kept a bathhouse, a taste for which he'd picked up during his time as a prisoner in Granada. There was hot water to be had there – and if John was to meet with London's premier player it was probably better not to be stinking like a stallion at covering time.

The reason he was called 'Peg Leg' and not 'Legless' was down to John. He'd arrived in the nick and managed to prevent the four Spanish soldiers sawing off the other limb by the neat device of killing them all. Today, though, he could see in the man's eyes that his gratitude was not, as he had blubbered at the time, eternal. In truth, thirteen years of presuming upon it appeared to have worn it thin.

John observed this through rising steam. The water was quite clean, scarce in its second or third use, a state he was, however, changing rapidly with his occupancy. Though it seemed that even this was not the main cause of Peg Leg's plaint.

'You were here a week ago, John.'

'I was?' It was news, and especially alarming as he remembered nothing about it. He always avoided Southwark during a debauch – for reasons that his old comrade began to enumerate.

'You were. And most . . . distraught, I would say. You demanded your sword. There were men you had to kill.'

'What men?'

'You did not say.'

John thought back. Nothing came. 'You did not give it to me?'

'I did not. You had made me swear, a month ago, when you embarked on this latest . . . voyage . . . that under no circumstances was I to let you have it until you were sober.'

'Quite right. You did well in refusing me.'

'I did, John. But my inn did less well. You were lion drunk.' He looked mournful. 'You broke things.'

'What things?'

'Chairs. A door. Several tankards. You boxed young Harold's ears, then took a bottle of whisky and ran off.'

'Ah.' John contemplated the greying foam on the water's surface. 'I will pay you for it all, Jack.'

'You have money?'

'Oh. No. Not now. But soon. I have hopes.' He saw the doubt in the other's man's eyes. 'Burbage has sent for me today. Perhaps he has a role in mind.'

'Are you not still . . . exiled from the stage?'

'Exiles end. Grudges cannot last for ever.'

'Some men's can. Just like their obligations.' Peg Leg sighed. 'Have you clothes to meet him in other than . . . ?' He pointed to the discarded and reeking pile.

'I do not. Might you . . . ?'

Another sigh. 'I will see what I have. This time though I will want them back. Unholed.'

'Of course.' The man turned to go, and John called after, 'And, Jack, one other thing . . .'

'John, truly, I cannot bring you whisky . . .'

'Nay. I have foresworn it. Ale only passes my lips, as it has done for three days now. It is my . . . method, as you know. Speaking of, a pint will further my recovery.'

'I will send a boy with it. Would you like a crust and some pottage?'

John considered his stomach, then shook his head. 'It is yet a little early for food.'

The man did not turn, spoke over his shoulder. 'Anything else?'

'My sword. Nay, do not fear, old friend. I ask it now for protection, not vengeance. No man should go unarmed within the Bishop's Liberty.'

'*You* shouldn't.' Peg Leg nodded. 'I will fetch all.' He turned, paused, turned back. 'The day after you were here, two men came seeking you.'

John, who'd begun to hack at his vast beard with some shears, stopped. 'Who?'

'They did not vouchsafe their names. But they seemed most keen to find you. And . . . they wore tangerine sashes.'

He hopped off. John raised the shears above the water. His hands shook, worse than a man with the palsy. 'I'll wear a sword this day,' he murmured, 'and pray God and all his angels that I have no cause to draw it. Not for myself' – he shuddered – 'and certainly not for my lord of Essex.'

Peg Leg's lendings were the innkeeper's third-best wear – the beige woollen doublet had holes under the armpits; the breeches, a poorly contrasting green, had been made to accommodate a leg removed below the knee. The netherstocks beneath were wool, threadbare and baggy over the ankles. Still, his long black cloak, as deloused as the attentions of the tavern boy could achieve, covered the worst of the clothing, and a wide-brimmed hat pulled down concealed the poor job he had made of trimming his beard. Anyway, he doubted that any would be looking to judge him for fashion.

Burbage's note had said only to meet him, but not when or where. He wondered again how the player had tracked him to Wapping when John had thought himself invisible there. Like his return to Southwark and his breaking of Peg Leg's door, it was a mystery lost to memory. He wondered if anyone else knew of his debauch. Especially . . . she. He would not have it so.

He was making for the Globe, thinking that the most likely place to find the actor would be in his place of labour – the playhouse he owned, ran and barely left. Yet something nagged at him as he walked, set off by his surroundings. What was it about this day? Southwark rarely slept, yet it seemed twice as busy as any other noontime. Higglers lined the main thoroughfares. 'Humble pie! Lovely braised cow tail! Rich saveloys! Cock and bull puddings!' came the competing cries; most seemed to be purveying some kind of meat. And it was that fact, combined with a crowd of blue-aproned apprentices who should have been at labour but instead were running shouting down the roadway, that finally pierced the fog in his head and told him what day it was.

'Shrove Tuesday,' he muttered, the thought halting him. The day before Lent, the four-week period when meat must be put aside – so this day all consumed excess of it. Excess of everything. One fact lodged unleashed many more, enabling him to see – the whores already out upon the streets or leaning to whistle from windows; the doormen bellowing from taverns, urging entrance for cheap ale; the boys calling people to bear-bait or cockfight.

But not to the Globe, John remembered, this final fact penetrating. For the Lord Chamberlain's Men played this Shrove Tuesday at the palace, by royal command. And John had ended his debauch three days before to be as sober as possible for the event. For it was not every day that a Lawley appeared before her majesty.

Not he. His son.

Ned, he thought, the name smashing another dam in his brain, flooding him with thoughts he'd pickled these four weeks. For it was not the news that his son, newly apprenticed to the Chamberlain's Men, would be treading the platform John himself longed to retread that had set him drinking again. It was the news that came almost concurrently, the bad with the good, as news so often did.

It was the boy's mother. Her plans for Lent's end.

John stepped forward again, his bent no longer for the Globe. Burbage would be across the water, rehearsing in the Palace of Whitehall. Ned would be there too, nervously preparing for his debut. He would join them. He had no coin for a wherry, so he must take the bridge and make the long walk to Whitehall.

Yet almost without willing them, his feet did not keep straight. With the bridge's gatehouse ahead, the traitor's heads spiked upon it in plain sight, his feet turned him left on to Long Road.

He was making for another inn, the Spoon and Alderman. Not to drink – even if he had the coin, he had long since been banned from doing so within those premises. No, all he wished was a glimpse of the proprietress. Maybe the briefest of conversations. Enough to ascertain if what had been true was no longer so . . .

. . . and that on the third Sunday after Lent in the parish of St Mary Overies, Tess Morton, Spinster, would not be marrying Sir Samuel D'Esparr, Baronet.

III

A Garden

His scheme to walk in the front door for a quiet word was thwarted in his first glance.

The two men at the inn's door were not the usual cut of doorman retained by Tess to keep out the excessively drunk each Shrove Tuesday. These two were bigger, leaner, with a martial way of resting their hands on their pommels. Yet the most disturbing thing about them was that each sported a tangerine sash across his chest.

Stepping deeper into the shadows of the alley, only now did he hear the sounds of traded lust further up it. 'Tangerine,' he muttered. 'A plague on't. Why does it have to be tangerine?'

He'd worn it himself. He'd been unaware that his rival for Tess had – for those had to be D'Esparr's men at the door. A new convert to the cause, perhaps? Not surprising with Essex's star waxing again. John may have been drunk for a month but not so far gone – at least until the last week – that he had not heard the rumour that the earl, down so long, was up again at court. And with Essex up, two things were certain: the dogs of war would soon be unleashed; and the earl would be looking for his old comrade to ward his back, as he had done in the Netherlands, in Calais, in Cadiz. Those other two men, sent to seek him at Peg Leg's tavern, spoke to that.

'I'll meet him in hell first,' John muttered as, behind him, business concluded in a prolonged squeal. Shortly, a grinning apprentice staggered past, fiddling under his blue apron, followed a moment later by a woman old enough to be the lad's mother, the paint on her face scarcely concealing the pox marks beneath. She was tucking a coin up beneath her skirt so did not see John until she bumped into him. She yelped when she did, staggered back a pace. 'Peace, punk,' he said, holding up his palms to show they were empty of cosh or blade.

'Oo you callin' a punk, you bull's pizzle?' Her accent located her birth within a few hundred paces of where she laboured.

'I meant no insult,' he replied, 'seeing as I am a bit of a punk myself.' He smiled. 'Can you tell me, fair one, if those orange men yonder have fellows within?'

She squinted across the street, then up at him. 'What's it worth ya to know?'

'My undying love, sweet maid.'

She laughed. 'Well, no skin offa my teats.' She nodded across. 'One more inside, just as ugly. They stopped me going in, not 'alf-hour since. Spurned me favours too.'

'I am astonished. My thanks.'

As he stepped away, she called after him, 'Come on, Romeo. You can thank me better'en that. A last one before you lay off for Lent? 'Alf price, 'cos yer 'andsome?'

John did not pause to answer. Two very drunk men were trying to enter the inn and being roughly refused. The distraction covered him across the street. Slipping into the alley opposite, unoccupied for once, he ran between two high brick walls. Though its air was rich with piss and other savours, he knew he would not have to hold his breath long. For the wall beside him concealed one of the finest gardens in the realm and so one of the sweetest-smelling. He knew, because his Tess had made it.

One glimpse of her. One word. One of each, and then I'll seek out Burbage and watch my son make his debut before the Queen.

He tried the door – bolted within. But its lintel had handholds which he knew because he had gouged the bricks himself for the purpose. The wall was topped by shards of broken pottery because this was Southwark; but when he'd placed them there at Tess's behest, he'd left himself a passage through. He found it now, put one leg across; perched there, swinging his other leg over. Readying – a mound of raked leaves below would break his fall – he saw movement. Steadying, he saw her.

He had chosen not to breathe in the sour alley; here, he had no choice. The first sight of her always stopped his breath and it mattered little whether they had been apart for a year or for a month, as now. Each renewed sight a link in a chain of breathlessness back to that first sight of her thirteen years before. In another garden, this one belonging to the house they both served, the Earl of Essex's, and the countess's youngest lady-in-waiting looking back with a combination of bewilderment and desire that was a mirror for his own.

Forbidden, of course. However much the earl valued him and his sword, John Lawley was merely a soldier, with Tess a gentleman's daughter. Forbidden . . . and thus all the more impossible to resist. The courtship was brief; the passion, due to the necessities of war, briefer. A single night that created one life and changed several.

He only discovered he was a father on his return from war a year later. Discovered too that, fleeing the shame she'd brought on her family, Tess was already mistress of the Spoon and Alderman, purchasing the lease with the aid of the Countess of Essex, who had always loved her. Over the years since there had been some nights when that passion had again been impossible to resist. But on each subsequent morning, his proposal was declined. 'I will never marry,' she'd declare, steel in voice and eye. 'What is good enough for our sovereign is good enough for me.'

I will never marry, he thought, as he watched her move to a different raised parterre, bend again. 'Tess,' he called, as he dropped from the wall, landing on the wet leaves, rolling off them and on to his feet a few paces from her.

She gave a cry, swiftly suppressed. She clutched snowdrops to her, vivid white against the damask gown she was wearing, one he'd never seen. He thought that strange, her attire. As proprietress of the tavern, she wore an apron to protect her from spilt food and ale. In the garden, she wore a smock against the dirt. This new dress was rich crimson-dyed wool, a brocaded front studded with river pearls. And her thick russet-brown hair, usually poorly gaoled within wooden combs, was held now by tortoiseshell brevets, not a hair astray.

Her eyes, however, were the same. Green as springtime meadows, widening now in shock, while eyebrows that usually shaded the meadows like summer hedgerows had been thinned to a line.

'John,' she cried, those eyes moving from him to the wall behind. 'Are you pursued?'

'Not this time.'

'No?' Her brow contracted. 'Then why did you not enter by the front door?'

'Because there were men at it, preventing entrance.'

'Only of drunks.' She looked at him more closely. 'Are you drunk, John?'

He was not . . . but neither was he entirely sober. So he just shook his head.

Her gaze moved over his borrowed clothes, his rough-hewn beard. ''Tis a miracle then – for rumour had you drunk as a lord from Twelfth Night till the eve of Lent.'

Rumour? When he'd striven to keep his debauch discreet by seeking the perimeter taverns? 'Well, I am not sho now,' he slurred. 'So. Now.'

'Indeed?' She walked past him, turning along one of the gravel paths that ran between the parterres, stopping before the brick wall that faced south-west. 'Yet if you desire to be so again, may I suggest that you suck upon the neck of your cloak?'

He sniffed, caught the sour hop of beer, an undernote of whisky, was briefly perplexed as to how he'd managed to spill any of that precious liquor; wondered, even as he scented it, if she might consider standing him a tot. *No!* He shook his head. 'Tess . . .' he called, stepping after her.

She was leaning forward. Against this brick wall that the sun caught and heated she conjured fruits that should not grow in England. Certainly not in the garden of a tavern in Southwark. He had seen pomegranates there; while the cloth she tugged aside now protected a lemon tree. She'd wash in lemon juice in the season, to remove the taint of the tavern – a perfume he preferred to any of Araby.

Without looking up, she spoke, gesturing to a barrel nearby. 'There is water there, if you wish to drink.'

He gave a weak smile. 'I do not drink water, Tess. Do you know what fish do in it?'

She did not smile, nor look up. 'Not in this water, I warrant, for it falls from heaven.'

He glanced over. A gutter ran along the wall, beneath a sheltering jutty, a pipe running down. He licked dry lips. 'I'd prefer a beer.

Small beer,' he added hastily, seeing the line of eyebrows rise. 'One of your sweet, light brews.'

'Then why did you not enter the inn by the normal way and purchase one?' Still she did not look at him.

'Because the men at the door wear livery. Its hue is tangerine.'

'Which signifies?'

'Which signifies that they are of the camp of the Earl of Essex. Or of one of his followers.'

He emphasised these last words. 'Ah.' She unstooped, looked at him. 'And what do *you* signify from that?'

'Only this.' He felt the fear surge within him and, as usual, converted it into anger. 'That a certain bankrupt knight, poor in everything but fat, of which he has excess, has attached himself to the Earl of Essex's cause and, emboldened, has then presumed upon a lady's innocence to woo her, dared to think he has won her. And falsely won, dares to rule her in her work, in her life . . .'

His voice had lowered. Hers dropped to match it as she interrupted. 'You are the one who dares! Scaling my wall like a thief, reeking from your debauch. You the one who presumed upon my innocence, took it without a thought to consequence, took me from my gentle life, from the love of my family, from all respectability with your attentions . . .'

'Nay, Tess, it was not like that.'

'Aye, John, it was!' she stormed. 'You swear to your great love. You borrow sentiments and verse from your playwright friend Shakespeare. You weep into your whisky *of which you have excess!*' She paused, glaring. 'You are a player, John Lawley, not just upon the stage where they will no longer allow you, but in everything. You play at war, you play at love, you play at fatherhood. You'd have played the husband if I had let you and you would have failed in that as in all these others. You are as sudden and brief as these,' she said, flinging the snowdrops into his chest. 'Well, I want something else now. Someone. One who can give me all you took with your . . . playing.'

Unusually, his anger quailed before hers. Looking down to where some snowdrops clung to him, showing even whiter against the beige doublet, he mumbled, 'You said you'd never marry, Tess.'

'Well I changed my mind!'

He looked at her, the colour in her cheeks, the plucked eyebrows raised in fury. Saw, most especially, those eyes that had first bewitched him. Lines radiated from them that cares had worn. He had carved many of them himself. Yet he saw a sadness there too, that she was failing to entirely mask with her anger. Not just regret for the life he had taken from her, nor for all the times he had failed her since. The sadness lay in what she was doing now. In this furious rejection of him. So beyond the rage, he saw a tiny hope and his voice, when it came, was gentle. 'Then since it is settled, what can I do but wish you joy?' He could see she had not expected this. They'd had arguments that had lasted days before, not moments. He continued, as gently, 'What will you do with the Spoon?'

She looked away to the building, her voice still vibrating. 'Samuel says we will let it, and use the rent for a part of our income. The brewery and various other properties I have nearby we will sell. He mortgaged his all to accompany his lord to war and these sales will redeem it. We will restore his estate and live there.'

John thought it unwise to mention that her knight had mortgaged his all to fund his ineptitude in cards. He had taken some of it himself, off Cadiz, three years before. Instead he asked, 'And where is his estate?'

'Finchley.'

Finchley! A village half a day's ride to the north of the city. He had mustered with the army there once, knew it for a dreary rural stew, with inhabitants dull and more inbred than most peasants. Again he did not say it, but looked around. 'And this garden? You have worked such magic here. Any tenant will return it to the yard and stables it once was.'

She glanced around. 'Well,' she said softly, 'there will be a garden in Finchley too.'

He saw more sadness. It further fuelled his little hope. She had regrets; doubts could follow. He needed time – and an answer to his next question. 'When are the nuptials?'

'The wedding will take place in springtime, at the D'Esparr family chapel.' She pronounced his name the French way. It sounded better than in English.

His hopes rose. Spring was the other side of Lent. He had a month to break this. He stepped close, took her right hand, lifted it. She did not pull away, as he studied the glitter upon it, a splay of emeralds around a single ruby. 'A fine token, Tess.'

'It is. Sir Samuel has exquisite taste.'

'Did he buy it for you?'

'He chose it, I . . .'

She broke off, tried to withdraw her hand, but he would not relinquish the prize. 'You paid for your own ring?'

She shrugged. 'Aye.'

'At least I bought you one. A finer ring than this.'

'And then you pawned it.'

'Because you refused it.'

'Because you were thirsty.'

'Aye.' He laughed. 'They still sing ballads of that week on the Isle of Dogs.'

She couldn't help her smile. 'Oh John,' she murmured. 'What do you want here?'

What do I want, he almost shouted, tipping his head back. I want you. I want our life as it could once have been. I want . . .

And then he saw it. Movement at the attic window, a face pressed out. One he recognised despite the bottle thickness of the glass. He dropped the hand he held.

'What's Ned doing here?'

He saw her hesitation, which she swiftly covered up. 'He lives here.'

'Aye. But e'en now he should be in Whitehall Palace, preparing for his debut before the Queen.' He flushed cold. 'Has he the fever?'

'Nay. He . . .' She hesitated again, then went on swiftly. 'With the announcement of our engagement, Samuel did not feel . . . *we* did not feel it . . . appropriate that Ned should continue . . .' She reached for his hand again, her voice softening. 'You must know that it is for Ned, as much as for myself, that I do this. I can give him the life a son of mine should have had. A gentleman's. Not . . . not . . .'

'A player's?' He snatched his hand away, fighting the fear and instant fury that sought to overwhelm him again. 'But that is his greatest desire.'

'I know that it is yours for him.'

His voice rose. 'No, Tess! No! His for himself! Since he was breeched, 'tis all he's ever talked about.'

She kept her voice even. 'It matters not what he desires, John. He is not of age. It only matters what is best for him.' She turned from his glare, gestured to the inn's rear door as if to someone within. 'He will go to Samuel's school at Westminster Abbey. Then on to Oxford. Samuel will adopt him, give him his name . . .'

His restraint was swept away by a word. 'He has a name!' he shouted, seizing her hand again. 'Lawley! Ned Lawley!' She tried to pull herself free, but he held tight. 'Do not do that of all things, I beg you,' he cried. 'Leave him his name.'

'And what name is that, pray?'

The new voice that spoke was querulous, nasal and too high-pitched to emerge from such a frame – yet it did. For at the top of the back stairs, making the wide doorway look narrow, stood a very large man. He was dressed, sumptuously, in tangerine. And when his name was pronounced the English way, it came out as . . . Despair.

IV

Fathers and Son

He hadn't lost any weight, from what John could see – the struggle his three followers had to squeeze past him showed that. They managed it eventually, contriving to slouch menacingly in the little space they were allowed, hands resting on the pommels of their rapiers and poniards. Sir Samuel D'Esparr was quite tall for a wide man but he obviously did not like peering through shoulders. 'Down,' he commanded, and his hounds obeyed, descending the stairs and forming a half-circle at their end while their master remained above, and spoke. 'Why, if it isn't an old comrade! I did not recognise you at first. That beard. Those . . . clothes. Still, Time will have her way with us all.' He patted his swelling stomach. 'How fare you, Master Lawley?' He did not wait for a reply. 'Yet beshrew me for asking such a civil question when I have caught an intruder. More – caught him alone with my *wife*.' He glanced over. 'Has he frighted you, my dear?'

'Frighted? No. Surprised, but—'

'Surprised, eh? Surprised my *wife*.' Again he overemphasised the word. 'Can a gentleman allow such an affront? Nay.' He leaned over the railing. 'Tomkins, some correction may be required.'

John had been studying the men-at-arms. Two of middle years like himself, and one younger, they looked capable. At his best he would not wish to take on three capable men – and with a head like a forge, a throat like a lime kiln and his hands imitating St Vitus, he was far from his best. Besides all, he must not brawl – not now he'd learned that Ned was above an inn when he should be across the river in a palace.

Yet if he had sized up his men, they would have done the same for him. They did not rush to obey. There were ways to end this without blows. Bravado had worked in the past . . . at least half the time. 'I have already had dogs set on me for her,' he said, his hand settling on the pommel of his backsword. 'I will not suffer it again. So know this, Despair: once I have done with them, I will also do for you today . . . and dance the Tyburn jig happily for it tomorrow.'

The men looked up at Sir Samuel, who shifted, spoke. 'Od's heart-lings, but what a man of violence it is. Whatever did you see in him, dearest chuck?'

'I forget.' Tess took a pace closer, putting herself a little between the armed, undrawn men. 'And I see nothing in him now but a memory. Yet for that, I would not see him corrected. He meant no harm . . . and he was *leaving*.'

This last was directed straight at John. He relaxed his grip on his weapon, as did the men before him. 'Well,' drawled the knight, 'if you say he offered no affront. And I can afford magnanimity, can I not.' He beamed. 'As I retain possession of the field, eh?'

It was tempting, to act. He could have done so too, with the dagger between his shoulder blades. Yet once again his new-found near sobriety saved him – and he had other weapons to cut with. So he let his gaze fall on to the scarves the louts wore, then their fuller expression in the tangerine that strained the buttons of the knight's doublet. 'Still, I wonder what my lord of Essex would say if he heard you'd assaulted his master of fence.'

'Rumour says that unlike his true and loyal servants e'en now rallying to his standard, John Lawley skulks in taverns to avoid his duty,' Sir Samuel sneered.

John smiled. '"Skulks"?' he echoed. 'Well, rumour is just that. Whereas the earl will likely remember who was at his right shoulder when he stormed the walls of Cadiz . . . and who was in a ship's hold, shitting in a bucket.'

It didn't help that Tomkins, the eldest lout, tried to conceal a laugh within a sneeze. The blow struck, and the high-pitched voice pitched higher. 'I had the flux,' Sir Samuel squealed. 'All know that!'

'All know that flux wastes a body. And that you returned to England fatter than when you set out.'

Sir Samuel's face had gone a strange colour, and he reached for his neck folds as if he did not have enough air. It was Tess who spoke for him. 'Enough, John. Go now.'

'Not until I have seen my son.' He took a step towards her, lowering his voice. 'Tess, for pity's sake. He plays before the Queen in a few hours. If he must assume the rank of gentleman, let him do so tomorrow at the least. Do not let the name of Lawley—'

The choking man had recovered enough to bleat. 'His name will be D'Esparr,' he said. 'D'Esparr, I tell you. And he will not disgrace it in consorting with scum.' He gripped the railings before him. 'Her majesty will have to be disappointed – as will Master Burbage when he has to find another pair of buttocks to plunder!' His voice rose higher to little less than a shriek. 'The son of Sir Samuel D'Esparr will not a base player be! And you, sirrah' – he jabbed a finger down – 'I will not insult the earl whose man you profess to be by giving you the thrashing you deserve. But I will call the Bankside Watch and have you placed in the stocks for trespass! Call them! Call them!'

Froth was falling on to the men below, as if the vast and pallid orange fruit Sir Samuel had resolved into was being squeezed. At Tomkins's nod, the youth ran up the stairs and passed the raving knight into the tavern. 'Go, John,' whispered Tess. 'Think of me and not him. If you have ever loved me, go now.'

It was a sharper weapon than any man there possessed. John looked at Tess, sighed. She was a battle he would fight another day. There was a more pressing need now.

'I go, lady,' he murmured. 'But I vow I will return.'

'Do not . . .' she called, but to his back, for he was already slipping the bolts on the garden gate. Without a backward glance he was through, pursued by insults, which faded as he ran down the alley, turned right onto the street and sharply into the first doorway – of a well-known brothel, Holland's Leaguer. He had done the abbess a few favours in the past and so was known, and admitted by the doorman without question. Some lolling trulls called to him but he ignored them, took the flights to the upper floor, climbed the ladder into the attic. There was only one reason he frequented the house, and he made use of it now.

Pushing open a hinged wooden casement, he looked at the one opposite, only a long arm's reach away in the eaves of the Spoon and Alderman. 'Ned!' he called softly. 'Are you there? Ned?'

A latch was lifted. John smiled. It was fortunate he did so with his mouth closed, for it was not a face that appeared but a bucket; flung, or at least its contents were. Failing to dodge anything that came his way hardly mattered on that cloak. 'And good to see you too,' he said, keeping his eyes shut as liquid slid over them.

It appeared that his son was displeased with him.

'Oh, is that you, Father?' Ned replied. 'Alack, I thought I heard a familiar rat in our gutters that will ever be gnawing at them.'

No apology, no true attempt at a lie. On that angel's face, caught between his parentage, her green eyes under his black thatch, there was a studied innocence, one that would read in the playhouse galleries but his fellow players would know to be false. This close to, and even in the gloom under the jutties, John could see what backed it: rage, scarcely suppressed. It was the savage blood, passed down from his own line, prone to break out under certain provocation – or none. Counting himself lucky not to have taken the bucket as well as its contents, he wiped the stinging liquid from his brow and said, 'Well, Ned, this is a fine stew we are in.'

'We?' his son echoed. 'I have heard of the one *you* have been swimming in. Dived in, as I heard, the very night I was accepted into the Chamberlain's Men. Did you not think, Father, having taken me thus far, to stay around and see how I progressed? Or did jealousy put you to it?'

Jealousy? Aye, it was so – though not of his son but of a knight named Despair. Ned's elevation and the news of Tess's betrothal had blended into a session at the cockpits, some successful birds, a full purse – and a tankard of double double brought to him in a moment of triumph. That one pint of strong ale had become seven, rendering him helpless to resist the bottle of Ireland's finest aqua vitae when it was produced by all his new friends.

Still, the causes of his debauch – or his excuse for it – mattered not. Nor that here he was a month later reeking of piss – his son's? His love's? His rival's? And indeed there was little to be gained now in trying to counter the moral judgement of a twelve-year-old. Only one thing concerned, and he spoke to that. 'Ned, you are to play before the Queen in less than three hours.'

'Oh, that!' The shrug was as studied as his look. 'I am, of course, sorry to disappoint the Queen, who no doubt will weep not to see my Welsh princess . . .'

'Welsh?' John frowned. 'What is it you play?'

'A tired old work, some three years gone. *The First Part of Henry the Fourth*,' Ned replied, then raised a hand against his father's interruption. 'However, I am sure her majesty will forgive me my absence when she hears that I am to be a gentleman.'

It was the least convincing of his deliveries. Ned was trying to be insouciant and failing. John looked closer. There was a bruise on his son's cheek, a fresh one judging by its colour. His eyes were red-rimmed. He . . . vibrated with passions. It was not every day that a young man performed before a queen – especially when it was the first step in a career he'd dreamed on all his life. So John asked, quite casually, 'And is it your desire, Ned, to be sent away to school, and thence to university?'

Another shrug. 'It is my mother's. And the wish of the man who is to be my father. I am not of age and can do little against it.' He leaned closer, his expression softening. 'You know she was never happy with my course. You thought to keep your training of me secret, but she knew. And . . . acted.'

The pun was intentional. Ned was versed in them, the trade of the player. And John cursed himself now for not realising how he would force Tess to act – not only for her son, but for her whole life.

Nearby a bell tolled the quarter; across the river the players would already be readying another – though learning a role in Welsh would be hard at short notice. Yet, however pressed, John knew he could not rush here – his son had been coerced enough this day. So he asked, cautiously, 'You did not answer me, Ned. We know your mother's thoughts. What are yours? I will not force you to something you do not wish to do.' He raised his hand. 'I know! I cannot *force* you. But you stand at a crossroads now, lad. I can help you if you choose a direction. Help . . . or leave you to your choice.'

He had leaned a little over the alley. Needed to see what was in his son's eyes. Saw there a doubt he recognised – and recalled. For he'd had it too, had stood at this same crossroads, at near this same age. He had chosen to leave the town of Much Wenlock where he'd been born; chosen to join the players. And despite all it had led to, and

41

every crossroads choice since, he had never regretted it. That one, at least, he had never regretted.

He watched the struggle in his boy's eyes. Then saw them flick behind him, and panic enter them. 'They call me,' he hissed. 'Sir Samuel's man is at the bottom of the attic ladder and says I am required to attend below.'

'Then I fear the choice must be swift. The gentleman awaits below, the player above,' John said and, slowly, reached out his arm.

Ned hesitated. He turned again, to the commands John could now hear. The knave had to be climbing the ladder. Then Ned looked again at his father, and a different expression came into his eyes, a different accent to his tongue. Not the future gentleman. The youth, raised on the streets of Southwark. 'A poker up 'is arse,' he said. 'Stand by, I'm comin' over.'

Relief gave John strength. He reached, grasped, hauled, there was a moment of dangling and then Ned was across and in his father's arms. They hugged briefly, his son's nose wrinkling when pressed against John's cloak.

A shout broke them apart. 'Heya!' yelled D'Esparr's lout, Tomkins. 'Give 'im back!'

Neither Lawley needed prompting. They took the ladder and then the stairs three at a time, the younger only slowing when a half-open door showed a couple carnally entwined. Seizing his collar, John dragged him on. As it was, they emerged from the brothel just as the first tangerine-scarfed man burst from the inn.

'Paris Garden Stairs, and by the swiftest route,' John said.

'This way,' cried Ned, running down an alley. John let his boy lead, keeping one ear on their pursuers, one hand on his sword . . . and half a mind on his stomach, which was protesting in lurches at this sudden exercise.

They burst into a small square, packed with stalls and the people attending them. It being the day before Lent, many were selling meat, for it was the last day that the fish laws – three times a week – would not be strictly enforced. Men and women crowded around braziers, gorging, and John's mouth flooded with saliva. He had not eaten much for too long. Yet there could be no pause, with his fleet-footed son ahead and pursuit close behind. 'Here,' Ned cried.

The alley beyond was thick with folk and thickened further when the pursuing cries changed from 'Stop!' to 'Stop, thief!' Ned's progress was halted by two burly apprentices, offal pies in one hand, cudgels drawn in the other.

John drew too, reached Ned in two strides. Whirling his sword above his head, he bellowed, 'Stop, thief!' as well. Dividing the apprentices with a slice of his blade, he shoved his son through the gap – into a stall of dead animals, feathered and furred, directly before them. 'Under,' Ned yelled, dropped and rolled on to the cobbles, disappearing instantly.

John, whose knees lacked the springiness required, was stooping to follow when a yell turned him back. A flash of tangerine bore down on him with all the speed of youth.

'Gotcha!' the youngest of D'Esparr's louts cried, which he shouldn't have because he hadn't. His reaching hand was bent sharply against its inclination, the youth drawn down till his face was level with John's, who drove his head sharply forward, planting a Southwark buss on the bridge of the nose. The youth screeched, fell back, leaving John to sheathe then crawl beneath a fringe of dripping carcasses, as more tangerine burst through the crowd.

A different colour confronted him on the other side – the stallholder, a huge negro, who jerked him up by his collar. John was not small and yet his toes scraped. Clutched in his other hand, Ned's feet did an imitation of the Tyburn jig above the cobbles.

'Who thief?' the man demanded, shaking them both.

'Them.' John nodded to the front of the stall. Tomkins and his fellow had arrived, drawn, and were flicking hares and pheasants aside with their swords in an attempt to see. A bird fell. 'Desist!' the stallholder roared, dropping his burdens to protect his wares.

John and Ned were up and running in a moment. Judging from the angry shouts behind them, D'Esparr's men were being detained, at least for the nonce. But pursuit had driven them into a maze of alleys and narrow avenues, and though father and son both knew Bankside well, there were areas where few ventured by choice. Warehouses leaned in, though many had been converted into tenements, judging from the lines of clothes hanging between jutties, the doorways crowded with ragged children, faces smirched, bare knees covered in sores.

Another crossroads, and not a hypothetical one. 'Child,' John called to the nearest group, 'where is the river?'

The one addressed, a little girl no more than eight, stared at him blankly, then thrust out a hand, the gesture clear. Some child behind her cried something, and John recognised the accent if not the word. Dutch, he realised, refugees from the never-ending war. He had fought in it himself, knew a few words. Certainly this one, because he had near drowned in one during the siege of Zutphen.

'*Rivier*?' he asked, and though several more children had begun to crowd around, filthy fingers thrust forward for coin, one did point down the middle alley ahead. Just in time too, for the cries behind them were getting closer. 'On!' John yelled and ran, Ned following close.

It was a good choice. The alley's end led to a small wharf and a gate that gave onto Paris Gardens. Before him John saw men grouped on the lawns, despite the February chill, playing bowls. To his right, the Thames glimmered, reflected in the bow lights of wherries and skiffs, the bulk of St Paul's on the far bank. Paris Garden Stairs were about two hundred paces away. But to run through the playing fields, with their pursuers hallooing the chase, and join the crowd bound to be there . . . ?

John peered at the river traffic. Most of the boats were laden, passengers headed to the delights of Southwark or returning sated from them. But some boatmen were just commencing, and others sought easier fares than in the turmoil at the Stairs. He spotted one, placed finger and thumb to his mouth, whistled loud. The man looked up from his oars and both he and Ned waved frantically. They watched the bow put about, the vessel driven swiftly towards them. On the thrust-out jetty, a ladder went into the water and Ned sprinted to it – just as boots thudded on to the wooden platform behind them.

John turned back. Tomkins was bent holding on to his knees, breathing hard. The youth was upright, head tilted back with his now besmirched tangerine scarf raised to staunch the blood flowing from the nose. Only the third fellow was unwinded or unbloodied, and he now drew his dagger to pair with his rapier.

John heard the crunch of wood on wood as the wherry slid against the stanchions. 'Board, Ned,' he hissed, drawing too. There was no time to untie his buckler. It would be two weapons to one – to six when the others recovered. He cut air as he took a high guard, the sound causing his drawn assailant to pause. Yet behind him, Tomkins had got his breath back enough to draw in his turn, while the bleeding youth dropped his scarf, let his blood flow, and drew as well. 'Stay back, you curs,' he bellowed, hoping a touch of bravado and another slash would delay them. When he heard Ned's cry, 'I am aboard,' he swished again, turned and ran the few steps to the dock edge, saw the wherry at the ladder, its owner regarding the scene above him with alarm. 'Cast off!' John yelled, just as he heard the approach of boots, swept around, sword cutting at eye level. All three men were before him. 'Diavolo!' he cried, jabbing his point hard at the meeting of steel, splitting dagger and sword point, causing them to ring. 'Did I not bid you bide? Come then, braggart, and swallow your death.' He lunged, knocking the blades aside with a great sweep. On their ring, he ran for the ladder, knowing it for a sorry chance with men on his heel. He saw the boat a yard out, oars in the water, felt the rapier's point driven at his back, noted the one other option that had been in his head like a trace of yesterday's ale: the crane and its dangling ropes . . . and took it in a leap, clearing the dock side, eluding the thrust, swinging out beyond more of them. In the fraction of a moment of stillness at swing's end, he looked – to the dock and the three men upon it; to the boat. If he fell into it, he'd sink it and his son with it. There was but one other choice. Sighing, he let go.

The Thames was as cold as he expected it to be – skin-puckering, bollock-shrivelling, head-pounding freezing. Sinking as far as his velocity took him, he kicked up, broke the surface with a gasp that fuelled his cry of 'Christ's balls! Get me out!'

He dumped his sword in, grasped the gunnel of the wherry. The boatman yelped and dived for the other side as Ned dragged his father up. Somehow the vessel did not founder and when John slipped in, he spat out water and said, 'Wh . . . Wh . . . Whitehall Stair.'

As the men on the dock cursed and shouted threats should he fail to return, the boatman plied his oars lustily. Ned bent over him. 'Father. What can I do?'

'L-l-little enough, I w-warrant.' John sniffed at his chest. 'W-well.

Many have c-complained about m-my savour lately. My s-swim has at least cleared the smell of your piss.'

The youth smiled. 'I am sorry about that, Father. But you were not there when I needed you.'

'Aye. Well, I am here now. A p-piece of me anyway. Though I am not sure how long I may re-re-remain. How far till we dock?'

Ned looked. 'The Fleet disgorges its filth to our right.'

John groaned. 'S-so far yet? I'll be d-d-dead before the Temple, let alone Whiteha-ha-hall.' He sneezed violently. 'For mercy's sake, talk to me, boy. Distract me from my woes.'

Ned grinned. 'And what would you talk of, Father?

John felt it, the tiniest flash of heat in the iceberg his body was becoming. 'Tell me of that cur, Despair. Your mother and he are b-b-betrothed?'

'Aye, 'tis so. I was called to witness the hand-fasting.' He shivered, not in sympathy but in distaste.

'But was it . . .' John glanced at the boatman, who, despite his labours, was taking an interest in the conversation. 'Was it *de praesenti*?'

Like John, Ned had attended the grammar school. 'No, they will not marry in haste. Mother wants a full ceremony and at Despair's estate.'

'So it is only *de-de-de futuro*?' John nodded, enjoying the little warmth he could have. 'Good. Such an engagement may be broken off at any time.'

'Aye. Unless of course there is *copula carnalis*.' Ned scratched his chin. 'In which case, of course . . .'

'Enough!' The chill had returned with the Latin. He wasn't going to discuss *copula carnalis* with his son. Especially to do with his mother. And he also knew her. All would be conducted correctly. She would fulfil her obligations as a wife – but only in their pre-scribed time. 'W-well,' he chattered, 'I have some hopes, then.'

'Few enough, sure,' replied Ned. 'Not that you had many before, but this last debauch . . .'

'No m-m-more!' John held up a hand, shivered twice as hard as a sluice of water ran down his armpit. 'I have prospects now to back my hopes. Burbage has sent for me. Perhaps a re-recall to the company?' He saw the doubt clear in his son's eyes. 'Or perhaps he wants you for apprentice and would talk terms.'

The light came into Ned's eyes, then fled as fast. ''Twould be an honour, but . . . but my mother would never allow it. My' – he ground his teeth – 'my new father will not either. They would have me a gentleman and there is little you can do.'

'We shall see about th-th-that,' John growled. But angry thoughts were no longer sustaining him against the chill, and blue lips could no longer frame words. His mind froze and his ears nearly didn't hear the boatman's call of 'Whitehall Stair'.

'Father!' Ned shook him. 'Coins. 'Tis thruppence for this distance.'

'Ah.' John made a small show of fingering at his leather girdle. 'I forgot. My p-purse, Ned. Cut in some low . . . low place. Could you . . . ?'

His son stared at him a moment, shook his head, before reaching to his waist to produce the required silver coin. Then he helped his now near frozen father disembark.

Players entered Whitehall Palace the same way as offal traders, cess pit cleaners and scullions – via the stables. Yet in the suddenness of escape, Ned had left behind the token showing him to be one of the company. 'We have our orders,' said the corporal in charge of the guard. 'There are threats against her majesty. Spies. Spaniards. Papists.' He spat into a pile of hay beside him. 'So unless you have someone to vouch for you, you are not coming in.'

John opened his mouth, but words could not be mustered amidst the shaking. 'Wuh . . . wuh . . . wuh . . .' was the most he could achieve towards the name he wished to speak. Yet fortunately for him, and for Ned, who had begun to bluster, the possessor of the name he sought decided at that very moment to appear.

'Lawley – *pater et filius*!' came a familiar voice.

The semicircle of guards opened, and into their middle stepped a man. 'Sir!' cried Ned, sweeping into a bow.

'Old f-friend!' managed his father. 'Well m-m-met.'

'That, Master Lawley,' replied William Shakespeare sternly, 'remains to be seen.'

V

The Bard

'Is there a problem?'

The playwright addressed the corporal. The officer tipped his pike towards Ned. 'Boy says he's one of your company.'

'He is so. He is late but in the nick. And there is a lad in rehearsal now who will be most relieved to see him, and spare his tongue the mangling it is receiving from Welsh vowels. Will you admit him?'

The guard grunted, raised his pike. Ned darted under it and the pike came down again. Shakespeare held his arm and pointed. 'Across the yard there. We are in the horse stalls. Be swift.'

With one backward glance, Ned sprinted off. 'And this one?' the corporal asked.

The playwright turned back. 'This? This . . . is a frozen version of an old colleague.' He hesitated a moment, then continued. 'And a player too. Admit him, if you please.'

The corporal nodded, swung his pike up again. Reaching, his friend took John by the sleeve, frowning at its wetness. 'Come, man. There's a fire close by. Let's get you before it and out of these.'

In the centre of the stable yard a brazier blazed. The playwright led John to it, left him raising his chapped hands, returned in a moment with a couple of men and an armful of clothes. Between them they had him stripped and redressed in moments, swift changes being one of their practices. 'This is Augustine's costume for Don Pedro in *Much Ado*. He plays it in Bath next week, so pray do not soil it. You can smell by the urine that is has only just been cleaned.'

'I will endeav . . . endeavour not to,' John replied, lifting his arms to allow one of the costume men to bend and tie the dark red

48

breeches to the maroon doublet. A pewter mug was shoved into his hands and he burned his tongue on the mulled ale within it. Nevertheless, he managed to quaff some, returning life to his mind if not to all his extremities. There was a box before the brazier, and when he was dressed, his boots emptied out and replaced, he sank upon it. 'I am g . . . grateful, Will.'

'While I am surprised. Even you were not wont to swim in February' – Shakespeare smiled – 'unless it were in a butt of beer. For I heard you were . . . about it once more, John lad, eh?'

From Burbage, no doubt, John thought. It was a harsh world within which a man could not get drunk and keep the fact unknown to friends. 'There's a story to it all, William,' he mumbled.

'As ever with you. And stories are my delight, as you know. But swiftly now, for I fear I will soon be summoned. Begin with the end – with Ned here despite a curt note of unknown hand saying he would not play. And with your concluding swim, of course.'

John swallowed hot ale, nodded and began, studying his friend, who settled beside him on the box, even as he spoke. It had been only six months since last they'd met . . . yet something had altered with the playwright. But what? Not the eyes, still contrastingly gentle and sharp, beneath the arch of the brow; nor the auburn hair, teased forward even under the soft cap he wore – vain in that, his hair having begun a retreat that threatened to turn rout all too soon. Though John was the elder by some seven years, his own hair was still thick and as black as the coming night, a fact Will often commented on with envy. Was the change in the mouth then, the full lips within the beard?

Will's mouth, John thought, even as he began to speak of Tess and Despair. It was what he had first noticed – God's mercy, thirteen years before in Stratford-upon-Avon. Unframed by whiskers then, the lad had marched up to the tavern table where John and the two other remaining players in the Admiral's Men sat disconsolate – for one of their fellows had killed another over a woman, the dead one's wife. Now they were two short, one in a grave, t'other in gaol. Two short was two too few to give *The Tragedy of Medea* upon the inn yard stage – especially when the dead actor was Medea. Then that mouth had formed those words: '*I* play,' and John had looked on William Shakespeare for the first time.

No, thought John, concluding his story with swordplay and swimming and his study with a nod. The change is not physical, nor in the several parts. It is in the whole. For despite the soft smile, the amused questions, his friend looked sadder than John had ever seen him. When he got the chance, he would find out why.

'Well,' said Shakespeare, ''tis a tale to rank with some of your worthiest japes. Alas, I believe I must wait to question you further on't' – he gestured to a boy John had not noticed approach – 'for I am summoned to rehearsal, am I not?'

The boy bobbed. 'Yes, master.'

Will rose and John did too, buckling on his sword belt. 'What do you play?'

'The first part of *Henry Four.*'

'I knew that. But you within it?'

Shakespeare sighed. 'I am doubling Westmorland and Bardolph. Old men's roles. 'Tis what my fellow players consider me suited for.' He tugged at his diminished forelock, laughed, as he followed the boy.

John fell into step. 'And who arranges the fights?'

'You do. That is, Burbage and Sly, as Hal and Hotspur, believe they mostly remember your moves.'

'Mostly?' He shuddered. 'So do I get paid for them again?'

Will smiled. 'You know you do not. As I do not get paid for the words. Fight arrangers and playwrights, John. We are fee'd, not waged.'

'But you are a sharer in the company. It is different.' They had halted by the half-opened door of the stable. Lines were being bellowed within. 'I could look at them once, if you liked. Gratis, of course.'

'You know I would like it. Would like you to do more than set the fights. But there are those within who do not.'

'Those? You mean one. Kemp.' John spat the word.

Shakespeare shrugged. 'You punched him.'

'Which he deserved.'

'He often does. I'd punch him myself when he mangles my lines – were the oaf not twice my size and handy with his fists.' Will grinned. 'But on stage? During a performance?'

'I had a speech,' John grumbled, 'an important one. He was above me on the platform, pretending that an invisible dog was biting his leg.'

'But as we both know, man, when you punch someone, they stay punched.' Will sighed. 'He couldn't jig for a week. Now I may dislike his cavorting but the mob doesn't. Some come only to see him, more's the pity. Our takings dropped.' He shook his head. 'You just said it: Dick, Gus, I – and Kemp – are sharers as well as players. That punch took money from all our purses.'

John grunted. It was an argument he'd had before, could not win. Though the company had formed a gauntlet to applaud him when he'd come offstage, he'd still found the tiring-house door closed to him when he returned the next day. Now he thought of it, that was the start of his last great debauch – the one before this one, one year back. Both had been prompted by disappointment. Then it had been theatre. This time it was love.

His friend must have noted the sadness in his eyes. 'Do not despair, old friend. Time heals even old grudges. Or players leave.' He glanced through the open door, at a shout. 'And Kemp is not content. He does not like all these new words I keep giving him. He's for a jig and a lewd tale, or he fears the audience will sleep.'

'Still, the Queen loves his Falstaff, does she not? Isn't that why she requested this piece tonight?'

Will looked back. ''Tis strange you say that. We thought the same. But the Master of the Revels revealed that it was not she who requested it. She asked for us to play what we will. Someone else called for *Henry the Fourth*.'

'Who?'

Will lowered his voice. 'The Secretary of State.'

'Cecil?' John frowned. 'Strange indeed, when all know that Sir Robert hates plays and players. They offend his Puritan soul.'

'So why this play now?' Will shook his head, his words still given softly. 'Indeed, the Master Secretary even sent a letter asking that certain aspects of the piece be . . . emphasised.'

John frowned. 'Have a care, William. You'll be writing in lines next.' He smiled. 'Though it could be profitable – advertising the wares of this linen merchant or that goldsmith – yet what price the liberty of the playhouse then?'

'What liberty do we have now? Our betters dictate what we play, with every new work submitted to the Master of the Revels for approval.' He stared above John's head for a moment, his eyes narrowing. 'I yearn to write something that will do more than entertain. To hold the mirror up to nature and show our nobles who they truly are.' He glanced towards the palace. 'Or perhaps who they could be.'

'You already have done that, and oft,' John said as softly as his friend.

'Nay, only here and there. I would do it more. And I have something in mind. A play that would transcend . . .' He broke off, his gaze returning to John. 'For tonight? Aye, I believe there is meaning in Cecil's choice, beyond the entertainment it gives. Something afoot in the realm. Perhaps you'll be able to tell what that is, from your perch in the minstrels' gallery. Speaking of ' – he dug into his cloak's pocket – 'here's a token. It shows you are one of us, and can sit above with the musicians.'

He passed over a brass token. John studied the stamp upon it – Atlas bearing the globe of the world upon his shoulders. It was the symbol of the new playhouse for which the company had just broken ground upon the south bank. Will continued, 'We will speak later and you can tell me what you've observed.' He smiled. 'Just avoid Kemp, will you? We need him unpunched – for this one night at least.'

A line was shouted from within, in that way that showed a player had missed his entrance. 'Mine,' said Will. 'I must go.' He turned, turned back. 'Here,' he said, holding up another coin, silver this time. 'I suspect your purse is as empty as your stomach. Buy yourself some food. You have some hours yet. Nay, do not demure. *Food*, John,' he emphasised, pressing the coin into John's palm.

It was a crown. It would buy a fair amount of food, not to mention an unshared bed for the night. It would also buy a single glass item . . . John shoved the thought away, replacing it with another that had hovered for a while in his still cloudy head, tangerine-tinged. He reached out, gripped his friend's arm, delaying him. 'William, do you know of anyone else who might be attending the revels tonight?'

'Well, it is the last great festivity before Lent . . .'

John squeezed. 'You know what I mean. *Whom* I mean.'

Will's eyes narrowed, his voice dropping. 'Indeed I do. And I cannot believe, now that he is both back in her favour, and recently appointed to command her majesty's armies against the Irish rebels' – he paused while John took in as news what he had heard as rumour – 'that the Earl of Essex would miss this evening for the wide world.'

With that, his friend slipped into the stable, leaving John alone – and disturbed.

He'd known, of course. Though he'd never acknowledged them, reports had eventually reached even the lowest taverns where he'd seen out his debauch. Also he had a vague feeling that his visit to Peg Leg's tavern to demand his sword the week before, though he could remember nothing of it, must have been connected to this news. He would want his sword if Robert Devereux was raising his war banner. Not to draw it beside the standard. To fight off any who would drag him into its shade.

John tucked coin and token into his doublet – players' costumes, unlike workaday clothes, had pockets to hold properties that might be required upon the stage. He listened to the voices within – Will greeted, mocked, mocking in return; a short silence that ended when Will Kemp's Falstaff gave Bardolph his cue for the third time: 'Banish plump Jack and banish all the world!'

He turned away. He was the one banished from the world he loved, and it hurt. At least this night, though, he would see one Lawley upon a platform . . . and perhaps observe the mischief his friend had said was afoot within the court and so within the realm. Safely above it, certain of only one thing . . .

Whatever it was, he would never, ever again be drawn into the madness of Essex.

VI

Command Performance

It was a fine perch from which to view a play, sharing the minstrels'
gallery with the three musicians, revelling in returning warmth. By
the end of the second act he even had to undo a button or two on the
borrowed velvet doublet for the rising heat in the hall.

It was the flames. The banqueting hall of the palace was lit like
midsummer's day. A vast chandelier dangled above the platform, its
candles glimmering off thousands of cut-glass facets. The spectators
sat in three ranks along both sides, each raised dais studded with
candelabra, while every column sported a rush torch in a sconce. The
last court gathering before Lent had drawn the highest in the realm.
They had spent enough on their clothes and, players in their own
way, they would be seen.

Most light, however, was concentrated on the central dais that
fronted the stage, bidding all eyes when the action slowed or when,
as now, the principals resumed their places – for unlike in the
playhouse, there were breaks between acts in the palace, for refreshments, for the renewal of candles . . . and for other necessities. Well,
thought John, even if there are rushes upon the floor here as at the
Rose, you can hardly expect the Queen of England to piss on them
like any groundling.

As if summoned by his thought, she returned, in a rush, through
an arras, laughing at something the man beside her – an ambassador,
John guessed, he knew him not – had said. The court rose as she
walked to her seat, and when she reached it, the two men who had
hung back till that moment charged forward, elbowing aside the
emissary in their haste to offer their hands.

As before the previous three acts, the court held its collective breath . . . until Elizabeth placed her fingers into the hand of the Earl of Essex and all there exhaled as one.

'Twice,' John muttered. Twice to Robert Devereux, and twice to Robert Cecil, with one act to go and suspense for the final judgement. Perhaps she will bring out a golden apple and award it, John thought. The Queen flattered herself a classical scholar and had oft been likened to Helen of Troy in many a sycophant's ode.

'Still beautiful, is she not?' the musician beside him said, picking up his pipes.

'Indeed,' John replied, but thought, you need new spectacles, my friend. His own eyes were good enough to see white lead paint that had been put on by the trowelful, while the red curls of the wig were studded with gems to draw the eye away from a closer, lower scrutiny. Sixty-three years old, yet still wearing a dress slit near to her navel, the skin between no doubt pulled taut by her dressers, who smoothed its folds with powder.

She did not sit immediately, held Essex's proffered hand, pulled the man close, bent to whisper in his ear. The smile on her face found echo on his. He placed his lips, turning her hand so he kissed her inner wrist. She snatched her hand away with a delighted cry of outrage, then sat, allowing the rest of the court, whispering like starlings now, to finally settle, and the play to recommence.

As Giles Tremlett, leader of the consort, tapped three times with his bow, then applied it to his viola, John switched his gaze from kissed to kisser. The Earl of Essex had aged too, in the two years since he'd last seen him. Even at this distance John could detect grey now amidst the red of that distinctive square-cut beard. 'Cadiz style' the earl had named it, after one of his very few military triumphs. Yet he had not changed its style on returning from the disaster of the following year, the failed raid on the Spanish treasure fleet near the Azores. Rumour had the Queen boxing his ears when he'd tried to blame everyone for the fiasco – even her! Rumour also whispered that he'd made to draw his sword on her after the blow, was only narrowly restrained from such treason. He had lived in disgrace on his impoverished estate ever since.

Yet here he is, John marvelled, acting the role rumour reassigned him: sweet Robin to her sweet Bess. Kissing the hand that had struck him. Striving again for favour against the man now limping back to his place on Elizabeth's other side. What a contrast he provided to the gangling Essex. For Sir Robert Cecil was a crouchback, and the story was that Burbage had modelled his walk as Richard III on the diminutive Secretary of State, earning his enmity for the players ever since. Dressed entirely in sombrest black, he was a crow to Essex's lilac-, yellow- and tangerine-swathed parrot. Yet tonight Cecil, for all his oft-expressed puritanical distaste of theatre, seemed to be enjoying himself, laughing loudly at Falstaff's antics. While his rival, after the kissing of the Queen's wrist, slumped into his chair and returned to the state in which he'd watched the previous three acts – a gloom that shrouded him like a one-man cloud. The Earl of Essex was barely looking as the music swelled and the first players marched out.

Melancholy again, Robbie? John wondered. What had set him off this time, now he was back in favour and had received what he always sought – the command of an army in war? And he was known to like the playhouses, oft accompanying his friend – and Will's patron – the Earl of Southampton to them.

Perhaps it was this play? John knew it well, having appeared in the first staging at the Theatre, the Burbages' playhouse, in '97, after his return from imprisonment in Spain and his emergence from the Tower. *Briefly* appeared. After the reality of his ordeals, it had, he now realised, been a little early to be returning to a life of illusion. He had also been drinking too much in the joy of freedom. Both factors had led to his punching of Kemp. Truly, he did not regret the punch, only its consequence: exile from the world he loved as more than spectator.

One day, he thought, and returned his wandering mind – only somewhat restored by mutton pottage, maslin bread and an hour's doze upon some hay – to the observations Will had set him. What *was* afoot here? Why Essex so gloomy, Cecil the cock of the walk? *The First Part of Henry the Fourth* was largely that mix of patricians speaking sentiments in verse and plebeians telling jokes in prose. Well balanced in the end, with the drunken sot Falstaff the centre of the laughter. Many of the knight's flaws and several of his sayings John knew to be drawn from his own life, for his friend the playwright was a shameless pillager of both the times and the people around him. Yet there were politics too – especially in the contrast of the two ambitious young men. Essex had oft been likened to, had indeed been nicknamed, 'the fiery Hotspur'. And tonight, in broad style, Dick Sly was speaking the role not with the usual blunt northern vowels but with more than a tinge of the Welsh borders that, notwithstanding his years at court, Essex had never quite eradicated from his speech. His renowned bravado was also mocked and the biggest laugh of the night so far had come on Prince Hal's description of Hotspur: 'He that kills me some six or seven Scots at a breakfast, washes his hands and says to his wife: "Fie upon this quiet life! I want work."'

Yet the players were ever licensed fools – at liberty to mock their betters up to a point, and those betters taking it in good spirits. Essex should have been laughing with the rest, laughing it off even if the barbs stung, to show his good humour. That he could not was perhaps to do with what else was new this night – for it had become quite clear to John that Cecil was identifying himself with Prince Hal, the future hero of England, Henry the Fifth. Not physically, of course – Cecil was ever the small and twisted hunchback. Yet by this, the fourth act, Hal had thrown off the gaudy colours of dissolute youth and donned the sober black of the Puritan – not unlike the suit Cecil himself wore – along with the responsibilities of the prince.

Is that what is afoot this night, William? John asked himself. Is it that your play is being used as a weapon in the ceaseless war around the throne?

The music crescendoed. The actors took their positions, Sly's Hotspur began to speak. Then, in moments, Ned appeared as a messenger. John leaned over, held his breath. It was a relief to hear his son speak English, for his previous appearance had been as a Welsh princess who spoke only her own tongue. He had gotten laughs for it, though, to John's joy – the lad clearly had his father's bent for comedy. Here, he dispatched his few lines clearly and without gilding, and John could settle back, still proud. Ned had made his debut with the Chamberlain's Men and before her majesty – let Sir Samuel D'Esparr try to turn him into a gentleman after this taste of glory!

The play proceeded – on and off the platform. For where the fourth act ended, no interruption came, the actors continued, the audience remained seated – and Elizabeth's concluding choice on whom to bestow her hand was unresolved. Few would notice; John did, and wondered briefly what her withheld favour signified, before the action took him on.

The plot sped up. The scenes got shorter, more filled with the wind of martial vigour – except when Falstaff punctured it like a bladder inflated for a game of football with a speech John did not remember from the original, that asked: 'What is honour?' and answered, 'Air,' as if expelling from that same deflating ball. It was another sentiment John had expressed to his friend before a tavern's fire, its glow reflecting in eyes that looked back on too many battles fought, too many fallen comrades. Honoured? Maybe. Dead? Without doubt. 'Good, Will,' John murmured. His friend had complained that all he did was entertain. John had always known him to do much more. As now.

Bugles sounded. Leaning forward, resting his forearms on the balustrade, he felt his first true excitement of the night, noting also that the earl at last sat up. It was the call to war, and men in armour now took to the stage. There were alarums and excursions and one knight, dressed to counterfeit the King, fell to a Scottish lord's sword. John glanced down, wondering if Essex was, like him, remembering how they'd stormed Cadiz looking the same, ending so differently.

The early skirmishes were brief and functional. Stock moves, basically executed. Those who knew the play knew the main bout was to come. Those who did not could guess where the climax lay: in two rivals confronting each other in trial by combat, with power and glory going to the victor alone. And when Sly and Burbage stepped upon the stage, John could not know how much of the spectators' buzz was for the fight itself and how much for its significance that night. What he could see was Cecil leaning forward as eagerly as Essex, and Elizabeth's knuckles paling as she gripped her chair.

Lines spoke to the mood in the palace as they never had in the playhouse.

Two stars keep not their motion in one sphere
Nor can one England brook a double reign
Of Harry Percy and the Prince of Wales.

Yet the gasp that provoked was lost in the first clash of weapons, in music so different to the previous thuds of iron blade on shield or pike shaft hitting shaft. That past dispelled now in this present: for Harry fought Hal with rapier and dagger, and their steel rang out like silver bells.

John held his breath. No matter that he had set this fight two years before. No matter that few there would know or care that anyone had set the fight at all. This was his contribution to the evening, his tiny remaining place with the Lord Chamberlain's Men. They would know whose work they performed, as they knew they spoke Will Shakespeare's words.

If, as with words, the trick of it was to make the audience believe that the players were making them up, so here in this . . . argument continued by other means. With the added complication that while few men performed, most men fought – and considered themselves experts, ready to applaud, readier to condemn.

Though he'd set it a while ago, it reappeared to John now, piercing the fug in his brain as nothing else had since the ending of his debauch. A fight consisted of moves so practised they appeared the opposite, and he looked first to see if the combatants were antici-pating the timing and placing of blows or seeming to react to them. The latter, in the main, moving fast and vigorously. And while in a battle a warrior looked to the weapons and where they were moving, here upon the platform the players trusted themselves to each other's eyes, seeing the moves there a fraction before they happened, part-ners in illusion.

Burbage and Sly each held the other's gaze; there were few slips he noted – one misplaced parry, a blow astray covered with a wider vault to the side, making it a part of the whole. And they had clearly practised hard, for the fight was as punctuated as the music had been from the consort beside him, progressing not in one even wash but in staccato exchanges like pistol shots, in legato movement flowing like silk.

It ended too soon for John, the fact that even he was carried away by it showing that it was well done. Especially the superbly executed kill, moving from what John's Bolognese master would have termed *coda lunga e distesa*: dagger forward and taking Sly's two blades, sword stretched back so that the audience could see it travelling the longest distance, see and anticipate the blow that ended Hotspur's life, safely placed in the player's side. Sly's reaction was perfect, making it seem real and horribly painful, yet contriving also to die nobly – and with a length and calmness of speech John had seen no one manage when expelling their guts upon an actual battlefield.

The applause was long, sustained and John took it for his fight, though he did not rise, simply nodded to himself – and to Burbage, who acknowledged him with one swift salute of his rapier. Others took it differently – Essex slumped back again, Cecil grinning and staying forward, remaining so through the short scenes that follow-ed, through further laughs for Falstaff, to the play's conclusion and more applause.

The players were bowing. Yet most of the eyes were upon that other stage, and its actors, the foremost of whom waited for the clapping to fade, but not die entirely – she was a gifted player too, rising to build on the applause for herself, then silencing it with a gesture. 'Well, Master Shakespeare,' Elizabeth called, summoning him from the throng. He approached, bowing low, the carbuncled wax nose he'd donned for Bardolph already off and in his hand. 'You and your company have once more richly entertained us.' She smiled. 'I am intrigued how an old play on such an old theme can have such . . . fresh meanings. An interesting choice for our times.' She paused, teeth gently pulling at her lower lip before reaching behind her. The Master of the Revels placed a purse into her hand. 'Here,' she said, 'is your reward.'

Will took the purse, bowed still lower, before retreating back to his company, who bowed once more then swept out to more applause. John had time to note Ned's delighted grin before the doors closed and the Queen, opening her arms to the court, spoke again. 'And now, to our further delight – does any here crave dancing a coranto or a galliard as much as I?'

There was an immediate hum as people rose from their seats. Elizabeth cut through it. 'Come! Who shall be my first partner?'

John, who'd half risen with the intention of leaving with the musicians, sank back. There'd been another drama performed this night – and he might as well see the end of it.

Elizabeth had turned to the men behind her. Both who had so sought to offer their hands before now shrank back, discomfort on the contrasting faces – Cecil, with his high forehead, carefully groomed brown hair and long, pointed beard, Essex with his thatch of reddened gold and Cadiz-cut facial hair, both kept stylishly unruly to signal the man of action over the courtier.

'My Secretary?'

Cecil took a step forward. His voice, especially after the strength of the actors', was nasal and thin. 'Your majesty, I . . . I believe those players once said of a crippled king, "I am not shaped for such sportive tricks."' He sniffed, bowed. 'So I fear I will only trip the Queen, and my clumsiness could be perceived as treason.'

A little laugh came, which Elizabeth joined. 'I hope you do not have the malice of a Richard Crouchback. You are excused, Master Secretary.' She turned. 'But you, my lord of Essex? Your shape *is* fitted for sports, is it not?' Another titter came. All knew that Elizabeth was not referring to his reputation as a jouster.

'Some, my lady,' he grunted. 'The galliard is not one of them. However' – he raised a hand – 'as my Queen commands.'

'Nay, my lord!' Elizabeth lightly struck the earl's fingers. 'I offer a dance, not to lead you to a scaffold.' She turned to the court. 'Odd's faith, I hope his lordship is bolder in Ireland, or how shall he make that arrant rebel Tyrone dance a jig or two?' More laughter came, which Elizabeth acknowledged before turning to the third man who had always exited and entered with her party. 'Monsieur de Maisse, perhaps the French ambassador can teach these English lords some courtesy?'

The man stepped forward, bent to kiss the proffered hand. 'It would be an honour, *majesté*,' he replied. 'There is a new dance that our sovereign Henri is most taken with. It is like the galliard . . . *mais plus vite!*' He bowed. 'It is called the lavolta. It would be my delight to show you the steps should you desire it – but it will be required that I lay hands upon your majesty.'

'Lay hands upon me? I warrant I am glad that someone wants to!' Withering the two courtiers with a look, she turned to the crowd. 'Bravo for the courtesy of the French. And bravo for their wine. Let us drink some of it while the floor is cleared.'

A squadron of servants appeared, some to bring refreshments, others to expertly dismantle the dais and platform. In the gallery, the musicians collected their sheets, stands and instruments, making way for the far larger Queen's Consort coming in. Taking a last look at Essex, head bent and ignored in the mayhem, John went to seek the players.

In the stable yard, the company had gathered around the brazier, for full darkness had come in the time of the playing and the February night was chill. Burbage had the purse and was conjuring with the silver before handing over each player's share. On receipt, several of the actors began juggling with the coins, passing them back and forth. John remembered many such Shrove Tuesday nights – a London season's end and no performances until they reached Bath in a week's time. No lines to learn for the morrow, no rehearsal to rise for. Tonight all could celebrate with a good conscience – and accept the foul head it would give in the morning.

Among the jugglers he spotted Ned, laughing as he caught and dispatched the coins. It would be his first such celebration, his 'blooding' as it was called. John remembered the occasion of his – but none of the events of it. Just the day groaning abed that followed. Well, he would leave Ned to it.

Unless . . . the thought froze him – unless Despair would try to reclaim him now? He could not believe the knight would simply accept Ned's abduction. Tess would not allow him to allow it! And if he did appear, what then? Would John have to take on the knight and his louts?

He raised his sword hand – still shaking as if he had an ague. Truly, he thought, this is all too much for a man who's been drunk for a month. Sighing, he turned to his most pressing need – he needed a piss! He made for a stable that was flush to the brick walls of the palace garden. But within, just as he was seeking to free himself before a pile of rushes, a voice called, 'Oy! Not there, ye dog! I sleep there!'

John looked at the scowling guard. 'Then can you suggest a place, friend. My need is urgent.'

'Back in the yard, or' – the soldier jabbed a thumb – 'through that door. There's a garden that gives on to the palace. It will be un-occupied since, as you hear, our betters are cavorting.'

The distant sound of stamping came. They must have begun with some country dance, for the nobility liked to fancy themselves peasants in a field. Free of the dung and the rickets, of course. 'For this relief, much thanks,' said John, and passed into the garden.

Not much light spilled from the banqueting hall's tall windows. But he did not need much to do the business. As long as he could avoid the rose briars that garlanded the ash arbor hard by, and spare his cock a scratching.

He groped forward, found a wall. Don Pedro's breeches were cut in the Spanish style and so demanded an elaborate unwinding, requiring him to take off his sword, lean it against the brickwork. When he was at last freed, it took a while to come, such was his need; when it finally did, it came in a gush that would have disgraced no stallion.

'Ah,' he sighed, closing his eyes.

The voice came from right beside him. 'Do you mind,' it said. 'You are pissing on my leg.'

John Lawley jumped so hard that he sprayed the wall, his hand and Don Pedro's breeches. The shock wasn't so much in the voice itself but in the fact that he recognised it instantly.

He was pissing on the Earl of Essex.

VII

My Lord of Essex

As John stood, mouth open, cock in hand, held in midstream, unable to speak or piss further, that voice came again from the dark. 'No, no, fellow. Continue, pray. Everyone else in Whitehall is doing it, so you may as well join them.'

'I th-thank your lordship,' John stammered, cursing himself for using a title, moving a few paces down the path, flooding again. *Christ's blood!* He was tempted to run, venting as he did. But his deluge was furious, and near endless; besides, the other's tone had been full of the melancholy for which he was renowned. He would take to his bed and not rise for weeks. So he would perhaps remain in the arbor long enough for the business to be concluded and a quiet exit made.

John's hopes lasted until the moment he was tucking himself away – when the gravelled path crunched and the voice came again, almost at his shoulder. 'Ha! I thought as much. I'd know those Cornish tones anywhere. God a mercy, if it ain't John Lawley.'

Despite the years they'd known each other, John had never been able to persuade the earl that his tones came from Shropshire and the deep dark of his hair from the father he'd never known, dead before his birth. He would forever be a 'black Cornishman' – and now was not the time to renew the argument. ''Tis I indeed, my lord,' he replied, fumbling at his groin.

'Do you know, as I watched the fight above – the only good aspect of a dismal evening – I wondered if you had had a hand in it. Then fell to thinking how I could not find you, though I have had men searching for you this little while.' He nodded. 'Your appearance is the first good omen I have had in an age – I can only guess at the evil conjunctions in the horoscope that Magister Simon Forman is drawing up for me e'en now. Like the hunter of the heavens, the hound Sirius gambols at my heel. Dog days indeed, Master Lawley. Dog days!'

Like many – and John was not of their number – the earl set much store by the movements in the heavens. 'Indeed, my lord? Well, I am certain you are wanted above, while I . . .'

Essex stepped forward, grabbed John's arm, halting his motion away. 'Still, here you are, at least. My lucky token.'

'Good to see you also, my lord. And looking so . . . well.'

The other man had stepped into the faint torch spill that came from the banqueting hall. And what John had guessed at from his vantage in the minstrel's gallery was confirmed close to. The liquor fat, stripped from him by custom of exercise before Cadiz, had returned all the heavier, jowls drooping behind a jaw on which the beard was now half grey ash, not all fire red. The tawny curls no longer needed forever flicking back, lying limp instead upon the high, damp forehead; while the eyes were bruised and bloodshot, vessels for the melancholy that had been clear in the earl's sprawl during the play.

He did *not* look well. The last time John had seen Essex was over a year before, on his release from the Tower, after his imprisonment there and in Spain. It had not been the happy reunion of old comrades. Neither man had been at his best – John with his prison pallor and thinness, Essex newly returned from the disaster of the Azores voyage and his failure to capture the Spanish treasure fleet, and thus far out of the monarch's favour. Reacting as he always did, alternating frenzied bouts of drinking and drabbing – the lower the class of whore the better, it was rumoured – with weeks of fanatical prayer. John had encountered him in the latter phase, and had endured a rambling sermon on the salvation to be found in Christ's mercy, with nary a mention of John's salvation of Essex in Cadiz. He had been dismissed with a plea for abstinence and the reward only of a beautifully bound book of prayers – which John had sold straightway in St Paul's Churchyard, getting heroically drunk on the proceeds.

John had not born the man a grudge – as worthwhile hating a fox for his desire to eat chickens. He had simply kept from his way . . . and would remove himself swiftly again if only he could tuck himself back in his breeches and plead an excuse.

'I look well?' echoed the earl, as John fidgeted. 'I? Man, I am beset with more maladies than Job.' He scratched at the beard that thrust down from his face, stiff as a lath brush. 'Yet I have risen from my sickbed to serve her majesty – and witness how she and her pygmy Cecil treat me!' He jerked a thumb to the windows above. 'They dub me "Hotspur" and laugh at me behind their hands. Mocking me within a play by your friend Shakespeare.' He laughed, a mirthless sound. 'Yet if they picked one, surely it should be his tale of Romeo. For have I not, within this mockery, been handed a poisoned chalice to drink from, its contents mixed for me by that same mountebank, that hunchbacked dwarf?'

This rant, ending on a shout, had given John time enough to put himself away – and to calm his initial urge to flight. The earl had spun a web of spies near as wide about the realm and near as thorough as Cecil's. That John had not been found, and blind drunk when so, was by fortune's grace alone. He could hide no more. Best to deal with the inevitable here, and avoid its consequence later.

'What is this poison, good my lord?' John asked softly.

The earl turned back. 'Its name is Ireland,' he replied, his voice as low, repeating the word like a keen over a gravestone. 'Ireland. Ireland. It killed my father and, by God, it will kill me.'

He gave a small sob, stepped away, his black cloak dissolving him again into darkness. After a moment, creaks came from the arbor bench, Essex falling upon it. John did not follow straight, just spoke. '*Must* you go, my lord?'

'How can I refuse? I am the Queen's Champion, Earl Marshal of England, foremost soldier in the land.' The proclaiming voice lowered to a whisper. 'Though the truth is also this: I must venture or I am ruined. I am impoverished, with debts too vast to number. I've spent my all in the Queen's service and am no nearer her favour for it. Others are,' he growled, 'jackals who crowd her throne and prevent my drawing near. Keeping me away from my sweet Bess! Cecil, Raleigh and their packs of mangy curs.' Suddenly he appeared in the light again, standing facing the windows where shadows

66

shifted to lutes and tabors. 'By the cross, I should charge up there now and cut my way through 'em all. Spit the bunch-backed toad on my rapier! It is he who offers this poisoned draught! Wanting me to drink. Willing me to fail. By Lucifer's balls . . .'

As long as John had known the man, he was ever like this – one moment so enervated he could barely rise from his daybed, the next so agitated he would charge a hundred men and mourn that he could not kill them all alone. But John *had* known him long, so now he stepped forward and carefully placed his hand over the other's. 'My lord,' he said gently, 'I warrant there is a better course.'

'What course?' The earl's eyes rolled white, down to John's hand on his, pressing blade back into scabbard. 'Let me go! You dare to touch—'

'The course, Robbie,' John continued as gently, 'is not to drink the poison. It is to go to Ireland . . . and return with the traitor Earl of Tyrone's head upon your lance.'

The soft tone, the name used only in the most private of moments, the command he'd once had on the younger man, all had their effect. The eyes ceased rolling, settling at last on John's face. 'The better course! Yes, Johnnie, yes. To return with victory's wreath upon my brow.' He snapped his fingers. 'Let the hunchback try to bar my way to my Bess's sweet lap then. With the people hailing me in the streets as a returning Caesar? As Henry the Fifth of glorious memory?' He stared above again, seeing his glory, then looked back at John. 'And yet,' he said, his voice softening again, 'so many others have failed before me. Not only my father, who left his bones there. Every commander since.'

John smiled. 'The greater glory yours then, my lord, when you do what even Sir Walter Devereux, of illustrious memory, failed to do. And meantime, avenge his death in rebels' blood.'

He watched the face transform again. Father and son, he thought. Honour and revenge. A mixture for a chalice more potent than even Sir Robert Cecil could concoct.

'By the helm of Mars,' the earl exclaimed, 'you have hit it there, John Lawley.' He reached up to scratch his beard, now with vigour. 'Yet Ireland is a quagmire, and its inhabitants barbarous. It is not like fighting the hidalgos of Spain, who live in cities they would defend and whose honour bids them fight you face to face. The Irish have no honour, nor any city worthy of the title. We have the only one, Dublin and the smallholdings around it, a few fortified places beyond. The rest is a wilderness of moor and mountain, swathed in the foul mists from which they slink to attack a patrol here, murder a sentry there, bleeding the army drop by drop. Waiting for the foul contagions of their bogs to sicken every second soldier.' A huge sigh shook him, and then the voice grew stronger. 'Yet if I were to march into his heartland, lay waste to his land, ravage it and his people till they cry out for relief – and force Tyrone to a pass of arms? What then?' He gripped John's hand. 'S'wounds, what if he would meet me alone and armoured under our armies' eyes, to try the cause in single combat? Nay, he is older than me; aye, and I *am* Champion of England.' Essex tipped back his head and laughed. 'Then let him send five champions, one after the other or all at once, I care not. I'll take them on, yea, and beat each one too!'

The colour of his beard might have changed – but the man himself had not. Give him a sniff at blood and solitary glory, John thought, and he will take on the armed world and damn all odds, just as at Cadiz. 'My lord, that is the spirit that wins wars.'

'It is. Yet Tyrone is known to be as cunning and as devious as . . . as that crouchback who stands between my Bess and me.' He nodded up to the lights of the hall, then turned back. 'I will need a force equal to its task. I will need an army worthy of the name. Not a rabble of . . . what was it that Falstaff said tonight? Something of . . .' Essex stood straight, one arm aloft, in the pose of the player, ' "of slaves ragged like Lazarus, revolted tapsters and ostlers, trade fallen"?'

'He did indeed, my lord. And may I say, well spoken!'

The arm chopped down, then flew up again. 'Out on such rogues!' he yelled. 'For I will have the cream of England's warriors! The noblest captains that e'er drew steel.'

'Drawing only for you!'

'The gunners who sank the Great Armada . . .'

'Storming again!'

'Musketeers who shattered the legions in Cadiz.'

'Rallied once more to your standard,' John called.

The earl stepped forward, his hand dropping on to the other's shoulder. 'And I will have you, John Lawley. I will have you.'

When hell freezes over, John thought, but said, 'Yours in the ranks of death as ever, good my lord.'

He was grasped, hugged. Essex was as tall as he, which was tall, and that blunt beard prickled his ear like a blackthorn hedge. The voice was moved by tears. 'John, Goodman John. We march together again to war!'

'Yes, my captain.' John unclasped, stepped away, took a breath. 'Indeed I yearn for that hour when I will, with all speed, follow you to Ireland.'

'Eh?' Essex, all smiles, now frowned. 'Follow?'

'Yes, my lord. You spoke of an army worthy of your cause. So I will to my own county to raise a regiment for the fight.'

''Twill be good to have some Cornishmen in our ranks. Doughty fighters sure.' Essex's eyes narrowed. 'Yet can they not be sent for? I would want you warding my back as ever from the muster.'

A small confidence sometimes helped. 'There are some . . . troubles that I must settle first, my lord. A, um, private matter.'

'Oh, I have heard.' Essex instantly changed. He grinned. 'Tess has grown weary of your drunkenness, has she not? When will you heed the warning in Ecclesiastes: "For wine is a mocker, strong drink is raging." '

'Proverbs, I venture, my lord, chapter twenty, verse—'

'And she has settled instead on a certain fat knight to give her what you could not?'

John shook his head. This was not a conversation he wished to be having. 'My lord, she was gently born . . . as you know, your own lady's gentlewoman . . . and aspires to a title other than . . . than mistress of the tavern that your lady wife so kindly advanced sums for. Um . . .'

He trailed off. But the gleam had not left Essex's eye. 'I tell you this, my good servant. When I raise my standard, all my followers must rally straightway to it – and all private matters must be put aside. That same Sir Samuel D'Esparr wears my colours, while his estate is mortgaged . . . to me!' The grin widened. 'Thus he cannot marry without my permission. And I will not let any man marry when the coming chance may make his bride his widow. War and its hazards will perhaps leave Tess with . . . different choices, hmm?' He nodded, a touch of grimness to it. 'Many a man's fate awaits in Ireland. Mine. Tyrone's. Yours. Despair's.'

John could only nod, speech a faculty now lost to him. Essex had a way of surprising him – as now, proposing that Death choose between Tess's two suitors. He needed to think. By all the saints, he needed to drink! Surely one tot of aqua vitae, to aid in discovering a path through this thicket, would not go amiss?

And then he was spared the need for answer or argument.

Yells came from the stable yard. One of them he knew instantly, as a father goose always will recognise its young. 'Unhand me,' Ned Lawley cried. 'I will not go. Help, ho! Kidnap!'

Sketching the minimum of bows, John was already on his way to the stable door. 'My lord, my son calls. I must go to him.'

'Stay!'

John turned on the shouted command – to witness Essex draw his sword. 'As you to Ireland next week, so I with you now,' the earl cried, waving steel. 'Lead, comrade, and I will follow.'

'My lord, I do not think . . .' He broke off as more shouts came, the players involved now. Wondering briefly at the wisdom of appearing with a drawn Earl of Essex in the yard of Whitehall Palace, John rushed through the stable and out the other side.

VIII

Tug Before War

The scene had changed.

It was still lit by a brazier. Yet instead of this being surrounded by imbibing players celebrating a season's end, two armed gangs now faced each other across the flames. On one side stood the Chamberlain's Men, some with cudgels hefted. On the other stood Sir Samuel D'Esparr's three louts, rapiers drawn, with the knight himself in their midst holding a writhing Ned by the collar. A screen of the palace guard was between John and the confrontation, the men leaning on their pikes. No doubt they considered it like the recently performed play their betters had watched above.

John hesitated. To draw himself would lead almost inevitably to a fight and some stabbings. And then he realised that course was not open to him – he'd forgotten his sword in the garden. So how to extricate Ned, whose eyes beseeched him, without bloodshed?

However, there was another man with steel already out, one who rarely hesitated. 'What is this outrage?' cried the Earl of Essex, bursting through the guards. 'Men with blades bared – in the Queen's yard?' He turned to the corporal in charge of the guard and slapped his shoulder plate. 'This is treason! This is rebellion! Why did you not bar their way? Why do you not arrest them?'

The soldier winced, under further blows and furious words. 'They said they was with you, milord. Your men. They wear your colours.'

'My colours?' The shout would have raised the dead and certainly filled the busy yard. It probably carried to the palace above, which may have been the intent. Robert Devereux had the stage and he was going to fill it. 'You think that I – I! – would bring rebellion into her majesty's presence, broach'd on my sword? I, her most loyal slave?' He strode forward, swept his rapier against Tomkins's, ringing steel. 'Put up, ye dogs, put up!' Essex swivelled. 'And you, Despair? You dare to claim that you carry out this abduction in my name?'

The fat knight wilted, as his men hastily sheathed. Ned slipped away and ran to John's side, rubbing his neck. 'Not ab-abduction, my lord. And may I say it is . . . D'Esparr,' he bleated.

'You dare to correct me . . . twice!' The earl thrust his face close to the other's, spittle flying. 'I have a mind to disclaim your allegiance to me and exile you from my regard.'

'Oh please, my lord, do not do so!' D'Esparr was bending so low now he had resolved into a large tangerine-tinted footstool. 'I only came to fetch what is mine.'

'Yours?'

'My – my son, my lord.' A sausage finger was raised, pointed.

The earl turned. 'This boy? I know this boy. He stands before his father, my most loyal servant, John Lawley. I know his mother.' He turned back. 'You are not married to her.'

'We are plight-trothed, my lord, and—'

'It is not the same thing. It is a prior contract and not a contract itself.'

''Tis true, my lord,' a gentler voice intruded. 'Indeed the only contract that exists is the one between the youth and the Lord Chamberlain's Men. For Ned Lawley is apprenticed to us.'

All turned to look at the speaker, William Shakespeare. It was news to many there, for Ned was on trial and had not yet signed his articles. But John, as all the other players did, kept his face blank while Will continued. 'So if you would like to contest contracts, Sir Samuel, I am at your service. My family is one of the most litigious in the realm. It is why I draw lawyers so well.'

A laugh came. D'Esparr gaped like a gaffed codfish. Yet before he could rejoin, Essex spoke again. His tone had become more reasonable. 'Besides, Sir Knight, this is not the time to think of marital matters . . . but of martial.' He nodded at the playwright. 'An appropriate conjunction of words, Master Shakespeare, do you not think? You are at liberty to use it, if you wish.'

'I am . . . indebted to your lordship.'

Essex turned back. 'Yes, indeed, D'Esparr. Tomorrow I issue the call to arms. And I do not want men to answer it, to prove their martial virtues on Erin's fated green shores, who are forever casting lingering glances back to the marital bed.' Like a dog with a bone, Essex worried the phrase – and then he looked back at John and winked. 'No,' he resumed, 'leave off such soft thoughts till we have returned in triumph. And then' – his eyebrows raised, a new light in his eyes – 'let us have a wedding that befits a knight of my household.' He beamed. 'Which I and my countess shall, of course, attend.'

Given that his dealings with him were mainly amidst the chaos of war, John could forget that the man was also a politician and could not have survived so long at court if his only weapons were bluster and bravado. He had frightened Despair, then dangled delight before him. Having the foremost couple in the realm at your wedding removed any stain there might be from a baronet marrying a tavern mistress, howsoever gently born. Yet the wink had showed something else – John Lawley, as enmeshed as his rival, both men flies now in Robert Devereux's web.

D'Esparr was not so foolish as to provoke further. He'd been given an expeditious exit from where his arrogance had led him. 'My lord,' he said, sweeping off his bonnet, 'I shall in this, as in everything, obey you.'

It was the custom that when one man removed his headgear, all did. The few players who had them on took them off. John would have too if his was not now floating in the Thames. Essex inclined his head to acknowledge the salutes, quite transformed from the woebegone of before, content to be pissed upon. Give him action, John thought, the more furious the better, and he would charge into it and be uplifted. One of the things that made him a poor, if occasionally successful, soldier.

Fingering his brim, D'Esparr unbowed. 'May I beg, my lord, that I at least fulfil my fiancée's request and return her lamb to her?' he piped.

Essex flicked a glance at John – but it was Shakespeare who spoke. 'My lord, since young Lawley is newly apprenticed, he has tasks to perform at this, our close of season. Might we return him to his home later, when his duty is done?'

'Ah . . . duty! Every man's, every boy's calls him and must needs be answered.' Having glanced up again at the banqueting hall on these loud words, Essex turned back to D'Esparr. 'I think the tenant must retain the right for now, Sir Knight. You may tell your affianced that it is my will, not yours. Does that content you?'

'Good my lord.' Though the knight did not look content, he accepted it with another bow.

Yet John was. The marriage was delayed at least, its outcome placed on the altar of war. This was something he could live with. What concerned him, however – and something he might not outlive himself – was that he was beholden to Robert Devereux for the settlement.

The one man completely happy spoke again. 'So, friends,' declared Essex, waving once and then sheathing his sword, 'since we have mere hours before Lent begins, I intend to spend them with a tankard of good English ale in my hand. Away, all! Away . . . and prepare for war!' Then, with a last wink at John, the Earl of Essex strode off through a channel of bowing servants towards the palace doors.

The voice came softly from beside him. 'He's whistling, isn't he?' said Shakespeare. 'And I'd heard he was a melancholic, forever languishing.'

'You are a melancholic, Will, and you hardly ever languish.'

'Ah, but I am a melancholic of the blood, and so sanguine. Not choleric as he. I laugh against my sadness.' He stared after the earl. 'Why, man, I would like to follow him around for some days. He is a study, sure. What was that line about "rebellion broach'd on a sword"? Fine!'

'Marital and martial?'

'Well, perhaps not that.'

The two friends laughed, but were interrupted by a loud 'Ah-hem.' They turned to the throat-clearer – Sir Samuel, with his louts around him. 'Let me be clear,' the knight said, 'that though the earl has ruled us to a peace, it is a truce alone. Also that I will tolerate no further approach to my affianced. You have been warned.' Before John could counter, D'Esparr turned his gaze on Will. 'Player,' he said, then walked away, his hounds at his heels.

'I don't think I have heard such contempt laden on to "player" since we were whipped from Chipping Sodbury for performing

A Knack to Know without a licence.' Will shook his head. 'You would do well to avoid him, I think.'

'I am not frightened of Despair,' muttered John, then glanced towards the palace. 'But the Earl of Essex terrifies me.'

'Well, let us hope for England's sake that he does the same to the Irish.' Will smiled, looking back at the players once more gathered about the brazier, bottles passing. Ned was being jostled and teased and obviously enjoying it. 'We had thought to take your son with us upon the road. Do you think it possible now?'

'It is . . . difficult. His mother was never content with this course we embarked on. She let it pass when she saw Ned happy, but now she has ambitions of gentility again . . .' John sucked on his lower lip. 'I think I must at least return the lad to her tonight – and work on her perhaps tomorrow.'

'Despite Despair's prohibition?'

'Perhaps because of it.'

'Be careful, my friend. We should talk more on this.' He took John's arm, looking down. 'But if you seek to woo Tess anew, at least you can do so in good clothes.' He fingered the rich velvet sleeve. 'So you may keep Don Pedro's guise till Friday as long as you undertake to bring it – unsoiled, mind! – to the Blasted Bonnet in Brentford, whence we set out for Bath on Friday morn. With fortune you will bring Ned too. What say you?'

'I say I am grateful, William. For everything.'

'Ah, lad,' Shakespeare replied, 'you would do the same for me . . .' He broke off, then added, so softly John barely heard it, 'And for my son.'

'Will . . .' It was John's turn to take an arm, to squeeze gently. He had been in Spain when Hamnet Shakespeare had died of a fever three years past. Eleven years old, he'd be not much older than Ned's age now, had he lived. By the time John had been freed from his cells, and caught up with him, his old friend was past his tears. In the time since, he had not spoken of his dead son once . . . until this moment. Into the brown eyes something now came, or rather returned: the same sadness John had noticed there before. 'Will . . .' he began. But before he could speak further, someone called from before them.

'Od's life, if it ain't Caesar's ghost!' cried Augustine Phillips.

John turned. 'Gus,' he said, taking the hand extended. 'How fare you?'

'Well, man.' The rotund player pumped hard then stepped back to look John up and down. 'Better though if I knew why you was dressed as Don Pedro.' He clutched at his heart and staggered back. 'Lord tell me I am not to be replaced!'

'Our colleague decided that it was a fine night for a swim,' came another voice, and Dick Burbage stepped in. 'So your velvet was pressed into service to warm him after.'

London's premier player had placed his hand on the costume's shoulder. Now he dropped it to John's wrist, twisting hard. It was the first move for a wrestling bout. Burbage was skilled in the sport, had been a champion in his day. And he had ever tried to best John at it. The challenge between them was always on, with the stake of a gold crown that never changed hands. John, at last encounter, was three bouts to one up.

He dropped his shoulder, using his weight to sharply twist the other way, forcing the player to release, seizing in his turn. Yet he did not press his advantage, for he knew he did not have the stamina; simply turned the grip to grasp, each man's palm along the other's forearm. 'I am glad to see you, Dickon,' he said.

'And I you.' Burbage's bright blue eyes bored in. 'We needs must talk, you and I.'

'I received your summons, and here I am. Now?'

'Nay, lad. Come to the fire first for some warmth. Share a bottle.'

John looked at the group at the brazier. He did not see whom he sought, so glanced further around the yard. 'Might Kemp not object?'

Burbage shook his head. 'Kemp no longer keeps company with players except upon the stage. He prefers those who admire his skills more fulsomely – ostlers, scullions and such dainty folk. He has already departed with his admirers. So come. We will speak anon.' He winked. 'And wrestle too, if you've the balls for it.'

'Ah, Lawley!' Phillips smiled, clearing a space for him at the brazier. 'Ever the hero, eh. Were you, like Caesar, attempting to buffet the Tiber with your limbs?'

He took the players' and the fire's warmth, managed to pass the bottle of whisky on untouched, though it stuck to his hand and its scent in his nostrils all the while he was taking the tale of his son's rescue and the climactic swim to suitably dramatic heights. He was back where he most wanted to be – if not actually upon the stage, at least in the fellowship of actors – and hard drink would not keep him there.

Laughs swept him up and it took a while to realise that Will's was not one of them. Yet it was not surprising. For all he depicted them so well, he was not a carouser himself. And John knew that a last performance always sent his friend into the melancholy to which he was ever prone, as if he somehow feared this season would be his last.

Tale and bottle concluded simultaneously. 'Come,' cried Gus Phillips, 'let us load our properties and costumes on to the carts and hie us to Southwark. There's warmth and whisky – and some delightful ladies – to be found there.'

The company yelled assent as one, headed for the stables and their stores. Warmth, whisky and women, John thought. As long as actors played, it would ever be thus.

He felt his sleeve tugged. 'Father?' Ned was there, his face flushed from his little drink and his vast excitement. 'The company wishes to celebrate my triumph this night. May I accompany them to the tavern?'

John hesitated. The blooding was a rite that all boy players should experience after their first performance – and rue the next morning! Yet he also knew he must not be a part of it. He had not just clambered from a pit to slip into it again. In these dangerous times he needed to keep a firm hold on his five wits. 'You may go,' he said, 'but for a few hours only.' He cut off Ned's moan – the boy could extend one up and down the scales and for the space of near a minute. 'I will collect you there later. Now – to your duties!' As the boy shrugged, nodded, turned, John grabbed his arm, pulled him into an embrace. 'Well played tonight, my son,' he said, his fingers running through the boy's thick black curls.

He would have held him longer, but Ned wriggled free, smiled, and was gone, swallowed by a company loading carts, getting ever more boisterous. He saw Dick amongst them, organising. He would speak to him ere they departed. But first? There was a space at his side to be filled. He'd taken off his sword to piss. He was sure to need it. That was one certainty in an uncertain life.

The stable was empty, its straw unoccupied and a vision of paradise. John stepped through the doorway into the garden. Above, cutting through the music, he heard Essex's distinct bellow, calling for more wine.

The light spill was not enough to easily find his weapon. Touch brought him close when he pricked his finger on a rose thorn. He swept his hand to the left. Nothing. Odd. He moved it right, until another prick halted his progress. Surely no one had come and taken it? Perhaps it had fallen? He knelt, gravel digging into his knees, and felt amongst the winter-bare shrubs. He encountered nothing but dirt. Murmuring with exasperation, he reached further . . . and then someone spoke.

'Looking for this?'

For long seconds he was frozen in the darkness. Then the gate on a lantern was opened, its single candle still a dazzle in the dark. Blinking against it, he saw his sword. It was lying across a lap within the arbor. Yet John did not reach for it, for the lap it lay across was Sir Robert Cecil's – and from the way he caressed the leather, it did not look like the Secretary of State was keen to part with it.

IX

Spider and Web

He sat within the woven ash frame – what is it, thought John despairingly, with men of power tonight and this particular arbor? Though it was better proportioned to its newer occupant than its former. Where Essex had sprawled, Cecil sat comfortable on the little bench, being head and shoulders smaller than the earl – except, actually, in the shoulder, where Cecil exceeded on one side, sporting a hump near as big as the one Burbage had worn in the role of the 'bunch-backed toad', Richard the Third. Yet the small man was arachnid, not amphibian, sitting now as if in the centre of a web – with John feeling like a trapped fly. In the jungles of Darien, he had seen trencher-sized spiders, seen men die of their bites. Many shared colouring with the man before him now – reddish-tinged hair peeking from under his beaver fur bonnet, visible again in his trimmed, tapered beard. There was nothing ostentatious in his clothes, all from doublet to breeches was, like the hat, of soberest black, the uniform of the Puritan, if all well cut. The only distinguishing item was a mandillion, the half-cloak trying, and failing, to conceal the excess of shoulder.

He did not wish to approach – but he had to. 'I thank you for finding it, sir,' he said. 'May I . . . ?'

He gestured, and Cecil gave a tiny nod. 'Of course.' He did not reach the sword out, however, kept it on his lap. Swallowing, John took a step forward – and became aware of twin shapes the other side of the arbor, leaning closer. Candlelight reflected off metal, the breastplates of the Secretary's guards. Though he could not see them closely, he was aware of a certain dark immensity.

In range now he bent, keeping his movements slow and unalarming. When he had one hand upon the scabbard, between the other's two, he was close enough so that Cecil only had to whisper, 'Do you know me?'

'No, Sir Ro—' He bit his tongue. 'No, sir. If I may . . .' He pulled a little harder, to no avail.

'Strange. For I know you, John Lawley.'

Great turds, thought John clearly, even as the whisky headache that he had been holding off all day with ale and action descended with full force.

'Though we have not had the pleasure of meeting before, I warrant I know more about you than . . . almost anyone.' He smiled fractionally. 'Come now, sir, I believe you must indeed know me.'

John released the sword, unbent. His first strategy, of ignorance and speedy retreat, had been thwarted. 'I apologise I did not recognise you straightway, Sir Robert. It has been' – he sighed – 'a long day.'

'A string of them, or so I am told. But come.' Cecil rose, stood staring up from John's mid chest. 'Let us find somewhere more comfortable to continue our conversation.'

'Master Secretary, I am expected . . .'

'Oh yes, the players. Your son among them, is that not true? Nay, do not be surprised. I noticed the name of Lawley in the list of players that was presented to the Master of the Revels. We like to know who comes into the palace. So many threats against her majesty these days. I did not see your name, however.' He smiled again, as mirthlessly. 'Oh, on plenty of other papers to be sure. Not that one, though.' He stepped away. 'Do come. It is chill in this garden and I can offer you something within that will warm you.'

The Secretary was already proceeding down the path towards the palace itself. There was no question of not following, not when the two shadows stepped from the arbor's side and revealed themselves to be two very large guards, looming over him as he had over Cecil. 'Delighted,' he said, his mouth suddenly desert dry. He would even have drunk some of Tess's rainwater. Wondering if he'd ever be offered that chance again, he followed.

He had never been inside Whitehall before. But experience had taught him that nastier things happened on a palace's lower levels, so he was relieved to be climbing stairs, not descending them. The party passed close above the banqueting hall, from which the sound of a guitar could be heard playing some lament by William Byrd, an interlude while the dancers caught their breath. Plucked strings faded as they took yet more stairs, a half-dozen ill-lit corridors, a last, long one ending at a plain oaken door. It opened silently at their approach, the Secretary scuttling forward to lay the sword atop a vast walnut-wood table, awash with papers. The room was unornamented, save for an arras occupying one side wall, a hunting scene upon it, and a single portrait. John stared at that, while the two guards settled either side of the closed door, and Cecil into the chair behind the desk. 'Do you know who that is?' he asked, noting the direction of John's regard.

John considered. What was he there for? Sir Robert Cecil, as Secretary of State, was the most powerful man in the realm. He controlled the Privy Council; largely consisting of his appointees, he could sway them into doing nearly all that he desired – including dealing, in whatever way he chose, with a lowly soldier and sometime player. Yet what could he do now but play out the scene – and at least readily answer the easy questions. 'It is your father. Lord Burleigh.'

'My father, yes. Died only last year, may his soul rest in peace. Though of course it does, seeing as how he was such a devout Protestant. None of that Papist purgatory for him.' He nodded to the portrait. 'Did you ever know him?'

'I . . . I did have the honour of meeting him a couple of years ago.'

'Meeting?' Cecil gave his snort of a laugh. 'He interrogated you.'

John shrugged. 'Interrogate is such a . . . laden word, do you not think, sir? Your father and I *conversed*.'

'You did.' Cecil picked a roll of parchment from off his desk. 'For three weeks. In the Tower. Quite the . . . conversation. Ah!' A glass was placed on the desk and a larger pewter mug carried forward to John by the bald scribe who'd opened the door and who now swiftly retired to a small table in the shadows. There the man dipped a quill and waited. Cecil pledged John. 'To further . . . interesting conversations.'

As John raised the brimming pot to his lips, he inhaled. Sack, he thought. The sweet wine from Spain was not whisky; but it was far stronger than any ale John had used to gradually climb out of oblivion. It was the way of the martin drunkard, the method tested over many years, ending the debauch with a few days on ever weaker beer until he was himself again; sack, its strength, could upset the plan. Even a few sips would weaken him – and he could not be weak here, not with this man. So even though his mouth was as ash, and the drummer in his head urged him on, he did not sip, only pretended to, raising the mug to his lips, then lowering it to his side, tipping some liquid down his breeches. Apologies, Gus, he thought. I'll find a pregnant woman to give me her urine and clean Don Pedro's costume for you myself. If I am able.

Cecil sank back into his chair. 'On what shall we converse? No, it was not truly a question, Master Lawley. I know what we'll talk about. Or rather of whom.' He stared keenly. 'But first you will indulge me.' He found a pair of spectacles without really looking for them, slipped them on, lifted paper, read for a few moments in silence. 'A strange life you have had, sir. I wonder that your friend Shakespeare has not put you upon the stage.'

Here we go, thought John, as the Secretary continued. 'Strange from its very first moments, was it not? From conception. For Lawley is not your true surname, is it?'

'Thomas Lawley is the only father I have ever known.'

'Thomas Lawley the Jesuit.'

'The former Jesuit, sir. He gave up that allegiance for love.'

'For the love of your mother, who had already been *loved* by' – Cecil squinted – 'well, an unpronounceable name. A savage anyway, from a tribe of savages.' He looked up. 'Does that explain your extraordinary capacity for violence, I wonder?' He indicated the papers. 'For these are filled with tales of *your* savagery, sir.'

John took a breath, then exhaled slowly. 'I think you will discover, sir, should you be put to it, that in the heat of the fight, we are each one of us born savages.'

It was said with all politeness. Yet it was still a hit, for the dwarfish Cecil was not shaped for war or any of its training games – a fact that his rival, and champion jouster, Essex never failed to point out, loudly and in company. The Secretary scowled, looked down again, seeking . . . what next? John wondered. During that 'conversation' with this man's father, he had said many things he could now not remember. The elder Burleigh, for all his so-called Puritanism, had also been a convivial fellow and had succeeded in getting John drunk on several occasions. Anything could have spilled out and no doubt had. He would not otherwise have talked about his origins, the English not caring much for immigrants, as the regular riots against them showed. So he did not think about them, unless forced. Or as now, when a spymaster pored over his recorded words and he needed to defend himself against incrimination.

His father. His blood. Savage? Perhaps. But his mother, Anne, had spoken of a good man and extraordinary warrior who had given his life to save his tribe – the Tahontaenrat, People of the White-Tailed Deer, they were called – in that land across the Atlantic that the French were calling Canada. Anne had even taught him some of his father's tongue, which he could yet speak to startle companions in a tavern. The skill had landed him in trouble – most famously when he'd uttered a few phrases in a Falmouth alehouse that the pirate Drake had overheard. He had then promptly kidnapped John to be his interpreter to the tribes he hoped to encounter across the great water. In the near three years of that voyage, John had not used the skill once but he'd learned plenty of others – some of them no doubt recorded in ink on the papers before him.

'What a colourful life,' Cecil said, as if giving echo to John's thoughts. 'Part of Drake's voyage around the globe. Then you fought with him against the Great Armada.'

Because that Devonian cur kidnapped me for a second time, John thought but did not say.

Cecil turned a page. 'Indeed, wherever there is conflict, there may you be found. You have fought all of England's wars and a few others besides. You are reputed to be gifted with this' – he tapped the sword on his desk – 'as few men living. You studied the arts in Italy and in France, did you not?'

John nodded. A restless time after his return with Drake and the theatres closed by plague. He'd gone for a season – and stayed away three years. It was written down before the man and so undeniable.

'Well, sir. Most men reading this would come to one of two conclusions. Either you are a worse liar than Mandeville . . . or you are a spy.' Cecil looked up. 'I believe this story is too incredible to be untrue. Thus I must conclude that you are the latter.' He leaned forward. 'Are you?'

On occasion, John thought, but answered, 'Your father asked me the same question. I gave him the same answer. I am no spy.'

'Ah, yes. Your' – he smiled thinly as he pored among his papers – 'conversation with my father.' He lifted a sheet. 'You, ah, discussed your recent imprisonment in Spain. And how you were freed from it in order to return home . . . to kill the Queen.'

John lifted the mug, pretended another sip, breathed. This was dangerous ground, now as then. He lowered the mug, spilled a little more. 'No doubt you also can read there, sir, that I straightway reported the purpose for which the Spanish freed me, why I acceded to it to gain that freedom – and then spent three months in the Tower for my honesty. It is why your father wanted to interview me in person.'

'Yes. One of my father's last interviews in fact, alas,' he said, without a trace of sorrow. 'Well, I am sure it pleased him. In his dotage he was so easily amused.' He looked up. 'Are you a Catholic, then, that the Spanish could work on you?'

John hesitated. 'I was raised in the Catholic tradition, as many were. I am not a Catholic.'

'Raised but not. A little like your friend Shakespeare, hmm?' He squinted over the frames and, when John did not reply, lifted another paper. 'Indeed you do not seem much of anything. The last time we have a record of your parish – for you seem to come and go from records, sirrah, another tick in the tally of suspicion – you paid the recusant's fine and attended service, not every Sunday as is commanded, but merely twice a year.'

He could not deny it – and did not see the purpose if he could have. The Master Secretary was, like most in government, a lawyer. John presumed he was building up his case. But the pounding in his skull made him impatient. 'It is always salutary to hear one's imperfections tallied,' he said. 'Something to reflect upon when next I am a-praying. But I fain would know the purpose of their recounting.' He shook his head. 'What is it that you want with me, Master Secretary?'

Cecil took off his glasses. 'Want?' he snapped. 'Ask rather what I should do. For in these dangerous times, anyone looking at your record and your *associations'* – he gave the word a distinct twist – 'would think it safest to imprison you straightway.'

'On what charge, pray?'

'On any charge I choose, you dog!' He slapped the papers. 'These provide several. Spy. Assassin. Murderer. Any one of them could see you to the Tower for further, less convivial talk – and thence to a scaffold.' His voice dropped to a hiss. 'So I suggest you answer my questions rather than offer any of your own. Is that agreed?'

John felt his anger pulse – and quickly suppressed it. If he had drunk the sack, he might not have been able to. Instead he said, 'Master Secretary,' and lowered his gaze, as was required.

He heard a satisfied grunt, as Cecil bent to another scroll. 'And then there is your other extraordinary life as . . . a player, of all things. A *player*!' He gave it as unambiguous an inflection as Despair had done in the yard below.

'It is true, sir. The playhouse is my desired home.'

'Among the whores, thieves . . . and subversives? Of course!' He grunted. 'I do not like the players. Especially your dear friend Shakespeare. You would not either if people yelled "Richard the Turd" at you as you progressed through the streets.'

'A play written before your . . . ascendancy, sir.'

Cecil ignored him. 'While plays, the personation of people, are like likenesses of saints in a church. Sinful. We have purged our chapels of such devil's tools. We should do the same with our playhouses.' He shook his head. 'They not only encourage the baser appetites of man – and ungodly desires in women – they fail to give instruction as our divines' sermons do at St Paul's Cross. More, they ask people to think for themselves.' He shuddered. 'And what price the safety of the realm and of the Queen then?'

John coloured. 'Yet her majesty seems to enjoy their theatre.'

'Her majesty . . .' Cecil started angrily, then stopped and, for some strange reason, darted a glance at the left-hand wall, where the tapestry hunt hung. When he turned back, and continued, his voice was slightly different. 'Her majesty is a lady of taste and refinement in all things.'

John had glanced at the arras when Cecil did, faced him again when he turned back. Was there a hidden chamber behind it, with another scribe in it taking down Cecil's words as the scribe in the corner was taking down John's? Whitehall was a rattery of spies, each faction employing their own and everyone else's. It would not surprise him if Cecil's words were inked for the Queen to study. It reminded him again – be doubly wary! Yet he also knew this – as in a sword fight, you could only defend for so long before you were hit. You needed to counter – if only to deflect your opponent's assaults for a while, till his weakness could be found. 'I would not have thought from your applause this night, Master Secretary, that you hated a play so much.'

The counter surprised. 'You were there?'

'I watched from above. With the minstrels.'

'Did you? A prime spot for an assassin, I would say. I shall look into that.' Cecil barked his reply, then breathed deep and stared at him for a few moments, taking the corner of his moustache into his mouth and sucking upon it. 'And what is it you think you saw?' he asked.

John knew what he had seen. A play somewhat adapted for the very purpose Cecil had chastised the playhouses before – to make people think differently. The rise of one man. The fall of another. Yet why would he say any of that? 'Only the court enjoying themselves,' he replied. 'As I thought you did too, sir.'

Cecil stared for a few moments more. Then he smiled. 'At least this piece had some . . . salutary lessons to impart.' The smile left as he lifted another scrap of parchment, glancing at it. 'You say that the playhouse is your desired home, but it appears that you are an exile from it again as you have so often been from England.' He looked up, and his tone changed. 'Yet know this, Goodman Lawley – desires can sometimes be accommodated.'

John frowned. Had the conversation just switched from his potential as an assassin to . . . his return to the life of a player? He suddenly wished he had taken a swig of sack, not poured so much down his leg. Yet he withheld still, and asked, 'What . . . mean you, Master Secretary?'

'Only this.' Cecil leaned forward, his eyes bright. 'The Lord Chamberlain's Men are just one of the companies that are called to play at the palace. They could be less favoured. They could be cut out entirely. And their new works could have more . . . difficulty when presented to the Master of the Revels for scrutiny.'

John swallowed. What the Secretary was threatening might not make Will's life impossible, just very difficult. And this at the time when Burbage and he had mortgaged their all to build the new playhouse on Bankside. Yet an 'or' hung in the air, which Cecil got to before John could say it.

'*Or* they could be *more* favoured. More appearances at Whitehall. Fewer obstacles. For these favours, they would, of course, be expected to do some in return.' The smile came back, as mirthless as before. 'And they could begin by taking the exile back into their bosom.'

John wished that if he could not drink, at least he might sit. It had, after all, been a very long day from his waking in that tavern in Wapping. Yet he found himself longing for the company of his bedfellows. Their intentions had been clear – to filch his locket – while Cecil's . . . 'Master Secretary, are you suggesting that you might influence the players into taking me back?'

'I might.'

'While at the same time favouring them . . .'

'Rather than hindering? Again, it is possible.'

John tried to swallow, but his mouth was too dry for it. 'And in return . . . ?'

Cecil did not reply. But that false smile widened into a genuine one and he looked down to the papers before him, picked one up, read for near a minute, while John felt sweat pool in his armpits. When he laid the paper down and spoke, it was as if there had been no pause. 'In return, sirrah, many things. To the first of them – let us talk a little, you and I' – he removed his spectacles – 'about the Earl of Essex.'

At last, thought John. They were to it, the true reason he was there, as he'd suspected all along. Robert Devereux.

Cecil continued, gesturing to the paper he'd just laid down. 'You have been at his side for thirteen years. Engaged in every scheme he has concocted, every enterprise he has launched. You sired a bastard on his wife's lady-in-waiting. You are his man.'

John breathed deep before he spoke. 'The earl has done me the honour of trying to get me killed almost every one of those thirteen years. I do not think that makes me his man.'

'Indeed? When your career, as laid out upon these pages, fits so perfectly with his own?' Cecil jabbed a page for every word he spoke. 'Feckless. Debauched. Deluded. Grandiose.' He half rose from the table. 'You are both never so happy than with a sword in one hand – and a goblet in another. You make great gestures as if you were Tamburlaine setting out to conquer the world . . . and yet what do you achieve? Failure in almost everything you desire.' He leaned forward. 'Know this, knave. The day of the adventurer is past. We no longer need men who believe that being possessed of a comely figure and the ability to unseat another handsome idiot at a joust is qualification enough to rule the realm. This,' he said, snatching up a quill, 'is the weapon of the age. Not this!' He lifted and dropped John's sword upon the table. 'These are new times, sirrah. The age of empty chivalry is dead. This is the age of reason – and men of reason must rule it.'

A speech worthy of the theatre he so derides, John thought. And it has the quality of one aimed at an audience of more than one. Though if this conversation were a duel I was setting for the stage, this bludgeoning would be a moment for a small pause – followed by a swift counter to the heart. 'I agree absolutely with your worship,' he murmured softly. 'Though I do wonder how well reason has worked before, and will again, with the traitor Tyrone in Ireland?' He pointed to the quill. 'Will that suffice for him?'

Cecil, still half risen in his passion, settled slowly back. 'So. You trim the candle to the wick. Perhaps you are not quite the fool as these papers have you.' He nodded. 'Indeed. Ireland is at the nub of it. And my lord of Essex sent with the snuffer to snuff the candle out.' He shook his head, as if dissatisfied with extending the metaphor. 'It is a difficult task and Robert Devereux has shown little appetite for it, regarding it as some trick played upon him, some burden others will him to carry alone. That mood has lasted since he was appointed, yea, right up until this very night, and throughout the play. Yet shall I tell you when it vanished, sirrah?'

'I would be most obliged.'

'It vanished after his clandestine meeting with you in the garden!' Cecil nodded vigorously. 'Yes, sirrah. When he returned to the hall . . . he danced, which all know he hates! He caroused. He . . . charmed.' The eyes narrowed. 'So the first return for my goodwill, Master Lawley, is to hear precisely what you said to him this night.'

This last was spoken with another swift glance at the arras. Cecil was speaking on the record. So John would too. 'I know you have forbidden me questions, Master Secretary . . . yet may I be bold enough to ask but one?' He cleared his throat. 'Are you telling me I have been dragged here, confronted with my lowly origins, reminded of my sottishness, and my *playing*, been accused of treason, threatened with imprisonment or worse, and all because' – he paused – 'because I cheered the Earl of Essex *up*?'

Cecil's mouth opened – but it was from beyond the arras that sound came. A laugh, high-pitched enough to be a woman, but low from a stomach. A guffaw then, the words that followed equally deep and amused.

'In God's name, Master Secretary, enough! Help me from this hole.'

Cecil rose, and scurried over to the tapestry's edge. He lifted it and it bellied out as someone moved along its inside to emerge into the light – a woman who strode to the centre of the room, put her hands to her hips and spoke straight. 'Well, Master Lawley,' she said, 'you are a slippery eel and no mistake.'

And then that belly laugh came again, while the Queen of England leaned back and everyone else in the room dropped to their knees.

X

Vivat Vivat Regina

Oh, this day keeps getting better and better!

John considered it. From waking on a tavern's lousy mattress and the fumblings of larcenous scullions to kneeling before the Queen in Whitehall Palace. Why did I choose Shrove Tuesday to end my debauch? Would it have hurt to have extended a little into Lent?

He had seen her earlier from the gallery. Yet though he now kept his head dipped, his first startled glance had revealed much. Of a face beginning to break out of its layers of white lead paint, a high forehead from which the wig of red curls had risen to reveal the grey beneath. The breaks between acts in the play had been used for both refreshment *and* restoration. But the revels were ended, and disintegration begun.

'Rise, all,' she commanded, and they did, John to continue his study. If she was older than her disguise by a few decades, she was lively enough in her stance – hands still atop the wide-spread waist of her cream-white dress, the slit in it – he kept his eyes averted from the royal bosom – lined in river pearls. Her gaze too was lively, her eyes following the movements of men with impatience. These were mainly focused on him, a frown line between them as if she knew him from before and was trying to place the when and where.

A chair was produced – Cecil's, the only one in the room aside from the scribe's. The Secretary brought it himself, with some difficulty, from behind his desk, then stood behind it. Behind him, against the rear door, there was another newcomer, a maid who must have been with her mistress behind the arras. Yet John had no time to study her, for the Queen had sat, and was speaking again.

'A slippery eel,' she repeated, 'if eels can amuse. For you did indeed cheer my lord of Essex up – something that I and the Lord Chamberlain's Men had failed to do all night.' She tipped her head. 'I am also curious as to how.'

'Majesty, I—' John began.

'Wait!' Elizabeth threw up a hand. 'This is for me alone. Master Secretary, you may go.'

'Go?' Cecil's eyes bulged as he stepped around the chair. 'Your grace, I beseech you . . .'

'Go! Take your scrivener and guards with you. My maid only to remain.'

'Your grace, I cannot allow . . .'

'You cannot *allow*?'

The tone was so cold, John saw Cecil shiver. 'I only meant, ma'am . . .' He cleared his throat. 'You have heard how dangerous a man he is.'

'I have heard how dangerous he is to my enemies.' She looked at John. 'Are you going to kill me, Master Lawley?'

'No, your grace, I am not.'

'There you are. Go. And no re-entry behind the arras, sir.'

Dismissed, Cecil moved like a crab, reluctantly, to the door, turned at it. 'Ma'am, let my scribe stay at the least.'

'For what purpose?'

'To take down what is spoken.'

'To take down . . .' Elizabeth cried the words. 'You would take down the Queen's private conversation? Do you seek evidence against even me?' Forcing herself up on the chair arms, she continued in a yell, 'Out, saucy knave, out!' This last command came on a bellow and from the same place as the earlier laugh had done. Men scrambled to obey, and the door closed loudly behind them. 'Well, that was satisfying,' said the Queen, after a moment and in a tone of soft contrast. 'On occasion my little elf is oversolicitous. His father knew better than to try and manage my . . . everything. Or mayhap he was subtler in his ways.' She smiled, then focused on John again. 'It is important to keep a balance, sir, and of late I have been perhaps favouring the pygmy over the giant. God's teeth, when Raleigh was here it was all barking and snarling – three dogs and one bone 'tween them. Well, he is safely stowed building castles in Jersey. So only my two hounds need leashing now.' She waved at him. 'Do not stand there looking so uneasy, Master Lawley. For mercy's sake, fetch us both some sack.'

John bowed and moved past her to the desk upon whose edge the bottle, glass and tankard stood – alongside his sword. How many thousands of men, he wondered, both in the realm and beyond it, would trade places with him now? Papists and Spaniards in the main, who had practised for years to kill the woman behind him. Many had come close to succeeding. None had been nearer, with a weapon to hand and only a maid in the room to cry, too late, for help. The officers of the Inquisition who'd worked on him in that Seville dungeon could only have dreamed of such an opportunity as this.

He looked down. Beneath the papers on which his own name was clearly written, there was a large parchment. He saw an inked circle, several triangles bisecting it, calculations and Greek letters. Though he had little faith in such things, he knew others did. He thought it odd that part of their examination of him was to draw up his chart.

Then he was corrected. 'Are you gifted in the stars, Master Lawley?'

He turned. The Queen had swung partly around to study him. The Star and Anchor, he thought. The Indies Star and any other Star where whisky is sold. But he replied, 'I am not, your grace.'

'Then perusing my lord of Essex's horoscope should not delay your mission. Magister John Dee has drawn it up and it bodes well for his enterprise, that is all you need know. Now, sack, if you please.'

'Perhaps Magister Forman has reached similar conclusions, ma'am,' he said, reaching for the bottle. 'My lord of Essex told me earlier he was consulting him.'

'Forman?' the Queen snorted. 'A street mountebank. Magister Dee is a scholar.'

Why did I venture that? he thought. I must keep a bit on my tongue and only offer what is demanded.

He glanced at the maid – and his study was boldly returned. Her eyes were startling, near black or seeming so in contrast to skin whose tone owed nothing to paint and all to a natural beauty. She wore a coif from which one small tress had escaped, trailing golden and thick across the alabaster forehead. He inhaled, scented something spicy – was it cloves?

Yet before he could gauge her further, Elizabeth called. 'Come, sir, I thirst. You may ogle my maid later.' He finished pouring – a tot for her and, after a moment's hesitation, no more than a sip for himself – then returned. Bowing, he handed her the glass, lifted the mug. 'To what or whom shall we toast, Master Lawley?'

'May I toast your majesty's majestic eyes?'

She laughed. 'Oh, a courtier's response! When many take you for a mere ruffian. No, let us toast . . . someone. And that one embarked on an enterprise that needs our pledges far more than these tired orbs.' She raised her own glass. 'Let us wish success to Robert Devereux, my lord of Essex.'

He'd wished him in hell often enough. But he had pledged him too in their shared past. So it was easy enough to do so now. 'My lord of Essex. May he thrive.'

Both drank, he the tiny sip he allowed himself, immediately wishing he'd poured more. 'But can he thrive, think you? It is that I wish to discuss with you, Master Lawley.' She gestured to the arras. 'Sometimes it is necessary for me to hear and not be seen. I gleaned there that you have known my Robin a long time and have been his staunch friend. Would that he had many so faithful, but he does not. He has sycophants. He has enemies. Many of both and both do him almost equal harm.'

John was not going to dispute his designation of staunchness – nor the summation of the earl's position. But he was feeling the exertions of the day . . . and of the month that had preceded it. He had heard of those who, sleeping, had actions whispered in their ears which on waking they performed. He did not wish to find himself so entranced. So he said, clearly, almost what he had said to the Secretary, 'How can I serve your grace?'

There was a question in her study of him again, a different one he suddenly felt, especially when she swallowed it down, reverted to her previous thought, her pressing need. 'I wish you to do something – for me, for your lord, Essex, and for England, all of which you have served.' She hesitated.

'And that is?'

She looked above him now, her voice lowering. 'I know what is whispered of us. How all consider the earl to be my lover . . . in the sublimest sense,' she added. 'And I do love him. He is my sweet Robin, I his Bess, and when he is fond . . . ah!' She continued to stare above John's head, her eyes and thoughts lost to him. She was somewhere else, with someone else. Someone, he could clearly see, who made her both happy and sad in the same moment. Then she blinked as if startled he was there, and continued with strength again in her tone. 'Yet I tell you this – for years now the earl has been more son than . . . anything else. A loved son, but wayward, testing to the limits a mother's affections. I have scolded him, exiled him from my regard and person. I have forgiven him, put up with his tantrums and his neglect.' She sighed. 'It is what one does, I suppose, for love.' That look was there, of infinite sadness, there and gone again and she continued, more forcefully, 'People will do as much for hate, sometimes more. Witness my pygmy, my Secretary of State, who has always hated Essex from their time together in his father's house. I am sure my Robin treated him cruelly. He can be most cruel, as I well know. It is not something that has concerned me overly much. Hatred, like love, can be managed, at least in others. And there is something healthy in rivalry, is there not? Did not your friend the playwright thrive when Kit Marlowe, God rest his soul, was alive to goad him on?' A smile came fast, went as quickly. 'But it has gotten beyond the point of health now. Far beyond it. It blinds the rivals to the other's strengths. Their necessary strengths. And it is both their strengths that are required now.'

She swivelled, stretched back to the table, to the quill Cecil had thrown down, lifted it, turned back. 'Because my pygmy is not gifted with any other weapon, he considers this one to be superior. And indeed there are times when it is. War is not only cruel and barbarous, it is ruinous to the Exchequer and so most harmful to our nation's health. If I could use this and write away all wars, I would do so at a stroke.' She drew a great 'E' in the air, then turned and threw the quill back upon the table. 'But you and I both know that the Armada of '88 was not turned aside by words, no matter how many letters I sent Philip of Spain. It was defeated by the swords – aye, and the shot – of heroes like Drake, Howard, Raleigh. Those, and the prayers that brought God's providential storms, dispersing the fleet, ending the threat. England was spared invasion, the horrors that war

94

would have inflicted upon our land.' She closed her eyes for a moment, shuddered. 'But if Robert fails in Ireland, fails to subdue the Earl of Tyrone, that Irish traitor will be a threat equal to one any Armada could pose – for he will open his door to Spain, our most bitter enemy, letting him land a vast army there to be hurled again and again at our shores till at last we fall. And all I have lived for – Albion free, at peace, worshipping God in the truth of His word, not the idolatry of the Papist under the scourge of the Inquisition – will be set aside. We will be just another impoverished corner of their empire, subject to the barbarities they visit on all their conquered peoples.' She stared above him again. 'Something I will not live to see – for I will be burned as the heretic they have always called me, my stake one of thousands as my subjects burn beside me, lighting England's most sorrowful night.'

John had heard that the Queen was eloquent. She was also insightful. He did not claim to any great knowledge of strategy, but he had stood silently warding the doors of enough rooms while men of power discussed their options. Ireland in Spanish hands was a dagger at England's throat, already drawing blood. And he had experienced enough of those same horrors that Spain had perpetrated to wish his own country spared them.

However, before he could ask how much he could do for that cause – and how little, for he had ventured enough for England in the past and had his own life and his loves to consider now – Elizabeth rose, agitated by her speech and by her legs, which she bent to rub now, though her farthingale and the layers of her dress impeded her. 'Alack, I cannot rest still for long. I must be moving.'

'Shall I call someone?'

'No. Let me stand – and Sarah,' she called over her shoulder to the maid, who had stood too and drawn nearer, 'sit.' The Queen stepped towards the door and back again. 'Better,' she murmured, turning fully to him again and continuing. 'You know, more than most men, I suspect, my Robin's character. How he switches from the highest to the lowest spirits within a span of hours – well, we witnessed that tonight from his abasement at the play to his vaulting in the galliard! Yet when he is high, how he inspires!' Elizabeth's eyes gleamed. 'He can sweep any opponent from the lists – or any lady from her footing. In that mood he can do the same to Tyrone – if he has an army that will serve the purpose. That is my job and I will see it well done. The Secretary, whose genius such organisation is, will see it too. However much he hates my lord of Essex and desires him to fall, it is not at the cost of the realm – for he well knows who would be burning on my right hand.' She shook her head, began to pace again. 'Yet how to muster a sufficient army when the cause yields not treasure nor booty but only honour? And how, if they do rally, to inspire them? For an army alone is not enough. Both it and its commander must have the heart to triumph.' She halted directly before him, looked up, straight into his eyes. 'And that, Master Lawley, in a nutshell, is the matter between us. The reason you are here. The answer to your question: what it is that I require from you.'

John looked at her for a long moment. This nutshell seemed so crammed, he feared he had missed something. Between his head, his lack of sleep and a very long day concluding a month of them, it was entirely possible. So he licked his lips, said, 'Uh, majesty, I still do not quite see . . .'

'It is to do with the twin worlds you straddle,' she said briskly, as if impatient with his dullness. 'That of the sword . . . and that of the playhouse.'

'The . . . *playhouse*?' It was not anything he'd expected her to say. He thought she'd order him to be constantly at Essex's side, cheering him, as he had earlier that night. He was going to gently point out that with the earl's temperament, it would be easier to keep snowflakes whole upon a fire grate. He would then promise to attempt it – and seek a burrow to hide in till the army had marched. Now he swallowed, stuttered. 'H-how means your majesty?'

She smiled at his obvious confusion. 'It is not just worlds you straddle but men also . . . if you will excuse such inelegant phrasing.' She nodded. 'For you love two men, and have had an effect on both their lives.' She sat again. 'How long have you known Master Shakespeare?'

'For near as long as I have know the earl,' John admitted.

'And you have influence with him?'

'Some, aye.' John rubbed his beard, remembering how wild it was. If I'd known about a royal audience, he thought, but said, 'He listens to me – once in a while.'

'Then have him listen to this.' Elizabeth leaned forward, her eyes fixed hard upon him. 'What Englishmen need now is not a tragedy to sadden, nor a comedy to distract – they need a tale to inspire. I have preachers who can sway believers at St Paul's pulpit of a Sunday – yet far greater crowds than attend there attend the playhouse each and every day. So if the Lord Chamberlain's Men – my men, effectively, for they thrive by my whim – were to play something that inspires the apprentices, the burghers, the merchants, yea, even the very drabs of Bankside – for all know what influence they have on youth's ardour' – she let out another laugh before continuing – 'something to inspire them thus, I say, and send them forth from entertainment aflame with Albion's cause . . . why then, *that* is a fire that could reach Finsbury Fields! And one that, once my standard is raised there, will make those inflamed souls rally to it.' Her eyes gleamed. 'By the honour of my blood, if Master Shakespeare can so easily muster the tears and laughter that came tonight, he can as well muster the spirit of patriotism – and muster my Robin an army fit to crush the Irish snake!'

John considered. What was she asking for? A play to suit the times. Well, it was ever Will's delight to fix the spirit of the streets in ink upon paper and then release it upon the platform in speech. And as for himself – what was he being asked to do? Storm a breach? Spy? No. He was not even commanded to enlist, though that might yet come. All he was being asked to do was use his influence. 'I warrant your majesty that something . . . something may be done here.' He sucked at his lower lip. 'Yet surely your majesty has but to command him . . .'

Elizabeth shook her head impatiently. 'You misunderstand me – and, I think, underestimate the regard I have for the theatre. I do not want a proclamation, to be derided and ignored. I do not even want something obvious – such as the performance we witnessed tonight, with my pygmy Cecil influencing the players to goad his rival. Hotspur indeed!' She snorted. 'What I love in theatre, and especially in Master Shakespeare's plays, is how he makes his points *without* making them obvious. He fashions men who struggle with who they are and so, when they at last embark on a cause of honour, you believe that they will see it through because they have thought it through. It is not all bombast and rhetoric, that a crowd would mock. And because an audience sees someone like themselves –

flawed, contrary and thus true – they can believe in them and so follow them, perhaps even to the point of honour itself.' She nodded. 'I believe Master Shakespeare's best work is ahead of him, because he is beginning to understand that essence more and more. In writing a play to suit this great purpose, he will serve his art, and he will serve his country, in the hour of its great need.' She rose to pace again. 'Your friend knows his history. He has sketched some of England's sadder days when all was discord in our realm. He has written of civil strife, of usurpation . . .' She shuddered. 'Perhaps he now may seek a more triumphant time to suit the hour.'

Will could – and so could John. He bowed his head. 'Your grace, I will attempt it.'

'Do so, Master Lawley, and to your utmost. And let the playwright know this: that in helping England and his sovereign, he is also helping his friend.'

'Friend?'

She stopped before him, looked him square in the face. 'You, sir. Succeed in this and you will be the Queen's man. I will remember your services. And no one in this wide world can harm you then.' She glanced back to the desk. 'No one.'

John smiled. It was clear even to his befuddled brain. 'Do you know, majesty, I think we may have a deal.'

'A deal? You make a deal with your sovereign? Saucy knave! Ha!' She shrieked in delight. 'Now I see the spirit that has filled Cecil's papers with stories that eclipse Sir John Mandeville's.' She glanced back at the desk. 'But no contract can be written for this deal. My Secretary has words enough already – from both of us.' She studied him. 'If you were to conclude a bargain on the street, you would seal it with a handshake, would you not?' She held out a bejewelled hand. 'Let us seal this so.' He hesitated, then slowly raised his own hand, suddenly aware of how grimy it was. 'You may forgo the spit.'

He allowed her to take his – the opposite seemed presumptuous. Her hand was bony, heavily veined, blotched on the back as if an inkwell had spilled upon it. Yet there was a surprising strength in it. He shook once, made to withdraw, but she held on. He'd lowered his eyes out of deference but now he looked up . . . to find her gaze again fastened upon him.

'It is remarkable how familiar you seem to me,' she said softly, studying. 'Have I seen you before?'

He did not think he would mention that he was there, kneeling on the deck of the *Golden Hind*, when she knighted his kidnapper Drake. 'I . . . I played before your majesty in . . . '94, I believe. 'Twas not here but in—'

She shook her head, his hand. 'I do not mean as a player. I mean . . .' She turned his hand over. 'I have some gift in this,' she said. 'May I?'

He could hardly jerk his hand free and refuse her study. So he nodded and she bent to her perusal. 'Hmm,' she said, after a moment. 'I see a life lived in great violence. With more to come.'

He thought, what a surprise! Given all that Cecil had revealed, what else would she see? But he held his tongue and she his hand as she continued to pore – and speak. 'Yet I see something else too – that half your nature leads you to these deeds and half away from them.' She looked into his face. 'What is your lineage?'

'The Secretary summed up much of it before. My father was . . . of a tribe in—'

'Yes, yes. The savage. I know that. It accounts for much that is here. But your mother?'

He saw Anne now, as he sometimes did, especially in his dreams. Though dead these twenty-five years, she revisited him often in them. She would not want him to be speaking of her now, to this person. Yet how could he lie? His many admissions lay in ink on Cecil's desk. He could already have told all this to Lord Burghley. 'My mother was . . . a healer,' he said.

She nodded. 'I knew it. The balancing half. And her name?'

'She was married to my father. So . . . Lawley.'

'Stepfather,' she corrected. 'Before. Her maiden name.'

He swallowed. 'She was born near Siena, in Italy, majesty. But *her* father was French.'

'His name?'

He did not want to answer – for truly, the name he hesitated on now had been hovering on the edge of his consciousness since Elizabeth had first entered from behind the arras. He had a connection with the woman before him that he rarely thought of, partly because the story was so extraordinary that he scarcely knew whether to believe it. Partly because if it *was* true, then there was blood and death between them and neither was a good thing to lie between monarch and subject, as many a subject had found.

Yet this close, and held, how could he refuse his queen?

It came out boldly in the end, as bold as the man was said to have been, in the tales his mother had told him. 'His name was Rombaud. Jean Rombaud.'

He'd been wary – but he was still unprepared for the reaction. 'Rombaud!' Elizabeth shrieked, throwing his hand off as if it was a thing diseased, reeling back to stagger the few paces to her chair, fall on to it. 'Rombaud,' she moaned. 'I knew it. *I knew it.*' She raised her eyes to him, and they were no longer filled with interest, or humour, only with a desperate horror. 'And you know too, do you not? You *know*!'

He did. Something that he rarely thought of, as most will forget near all the fantastical tales told in childhood before the hearth. Except this tale was not a fantasy, though filled with things so extraordinary it could pass as one. For their two families, royal and common, had a shared past. It was not something he could say.

Not when his grandfather had killed this woman's mother.

It was not something he could say. But she could. 'God in his heaven,' she whispered. 'You are the grandson of the French executioner.'

His legs, weak for a long while, gave. He knelt. It had been such a long day, and this . . . this was too great an addition to his woes to keep him standing. Yet now not even deference could make him look down; he could only stare into eyes that stared back, bounden in horror.

No matter that Jean Rombaud had slain Anne Boleyn because it was his trade. No matter that when he had killed her, he also had saved her; by taking her six-fingered hand at the same time he took her head, by eventually burying this mark of her supposed witchcraft after a year of near impossible hardship and adventures. No matter also that Rombaud's quest had to be repeated by John's mother years later, when the hand's whereabouts was betrayed, ending in cataclysm across the Atlantic Ocean – and this time it was the threatened Princess Elizabeth who'd been saved, as her mother had been.

All that did matter now was between their eyes – and in hers, horror overwhelmed. The court rumours had it that never, not once, had Elizabeth uttered her tragic mother's name. He heard that horror in the voice now, expanding in the single word she hissed. 'Go!'

Their gazes held still – and in that one long moment before she wrenched her eyes away, John could feel that through him, through her, their ancestors looked too. Then he forced himself off his knees, on to his wobbly legs. Only at the door did he remember, and turn. 'Majesty, may I . . . my sword?'

Elizabeth did not look up, slumped now in her chair. 'Rombaud's sword,' she moaned, from behind her hands. 'Executioner's sword.'

She had left him. He hesitated, then moved past her to the desk. As he did, Elizabeth cried for her maid. He'd forgotten she was there, a silent witness to everything. As she passed him to attend the now weeping Queen, she stared at him, wonder on her face, and again he caught her scent, the headiness of cloves. Snatching up his sword, he moved swiftly to the door, wrenched it open and hastened down the corridors beyond. Yet though he descended them swiftly, it took a while to escape the sound of the Queen's sobbing, an oft-repeated word within it.

'Executioner!'

ACT TWO

For it is foolishness and endless trouble to cast a stone at every dog that barks at you.

George Silver

XI

Persuasion

No creature of Cecil's delayed him, no guards challenged him, as he retraced his route, via stair, garden, stable and out into the yard. Only there did he finally pause for breath. The night had turned chill again, yet he relished it now for he felt he'd been in a fever this last hour, and the cold air soothed. Closing his eyes, a vision of a soft bed, scullion free, came. He yawned, leaning against the wall.

And was startled off it in an instant by the voice. 'I hoped you would return, knave, so that I could give you the thrashing you deserve.'

It was spoken in the high-pitched tone of his rival for Tess, Sir Samuel D'Esparr. But his new-found wakefulness helped John realise the truth, and so he neither bared his blade nor took to his heels. Instead he turned and spat. 'Come then, man? Is it to be double or is it to be quits?'

'Quits,' replied Richard Burbage, one of the foremost mimics in the land, seizing John's left arm, twisting it up behind his back.

John grunted, pulled the other man off his toes, then dipped down. The grasp loosened enough for John to slip it . . . too easily. Burbage was not there to truly wrestle, it appeared – a fact confirmed by the man not pursuing but stepping back, arms raised, palms out. 'Nay, John lad,' he said, 'I would not take advantage of your weakened state. I'll find a fairer time to take my money back.'

'That's kind, Dick. And thus most unlike you.' John grinned. 'Why do you assume I am weak?'

'Because you have been drinking for a month,' the player replied, 'and quantities that would have daunted Bacchus, so I heard.'

'And how did you hear? I thought I had been discreet.' He sighed. 'Though it seems most of England knows.'

Burbage smiled. 'Not so discreet. You were in Southwark last week . . .'

'Though not to drink. I was there . . .' John pressed the skin between his eyes. Peg Leg had said he'd demanded his sword, but other than that . . . ? 'Truly, I do not recall.'

'Well, part of the purpose of your visit it appeared was to yell insults outside the Rose. I happened to be in the box office with Henslowe at the time. I have to say, John, that you abused the fellow in terms of anatomical entanglement that contrived to be both physically unlikely and bestially adventurous – even for Henslowe!' He laughed. 'Man, wherever did you learn to curse like that?'

John shrugged. 'Among soldiers.'

'Well, it gave me my chance. I had need of you, so when the watch chased you off, I dispatched a boy to follow you.'

'Ah. So that's how you found me.'

'Aye. Though I think it will take the boy a while to recover from some of the sights you led him through before your close in Wapping.' He stepped forward, put a hand on the other's shoulder. 'Come, let us talk. There's a tavern hard by . . .'

John resisted the tug. 'Dick, it has been the longest of days. I fear that one sip of ale and the warmth of a fire will send me straight into a snooze. Can we not speak here? I have my eye on a pile of straw nearby and my heart on a few hours' rest before I have to collect Ned and return him to his mother.'

'Then let us to the warmth anyway,' Burbage replied. 'I must to the players too. But I would have words with you first.'

John let the player lead him back to the brazier still crackling at the centre of the yard. They raised their hands to it, and John studied the player by flamelight. He was not an especially handsome man – a large nose centred in a long face, made longer by a beard close cropped to an arrow point. But his eyes were deep-set and of the most piercing green-blue; and when these went wide, lit within by some passion, they were accompanied by a voice so smooth it could clot cream – or raise the skirts of women across the realm. His conquests were as legendary as John's capacity for drink.

Now those skills are to be deployed for another use, John thought.

Dickon Burbage wants something. Which is good – because I also want something from him.

They had known each other a long time. So there was little need for casual talk. 'I am worried about him, John,' said the player. 'He is sad.'

There was no need to state who 'he' was. 'He was ever prone to melancholy, Dick.'

'Aye. But it usually comes and goes. This time it has lingered. He has not been writing much of late, which is always a bad sign with him. And for us, with our new Globe rising on Bankside. We want something new from him to launch it. Something special. And yet do you know what he talks about, the rare time he does talk?' He looked up. 'God's mercy on me, man. On us all, for' – that voice dropped to a whisper – 'he wants to rewrite Hamlet!'

John stared. '*The Tragedy of Hamlet*?'

'I know!' Burbage lifted his beaver cap to run a hand through oiled hair. 'Christ's bones, it was old when I was gumming my mother's teat. Shrieking ghosts, poisons and' – he shuddered – 'feigned madness. We lost money on it at Newington Butts, and that was three years back, remember? We don't want to open our new Globe with old dross.'

'Does he say why? Why this story? Why now?'

'You know he talks little till the work is complete. He hints that it can be brought into the present. That there are new ideas to explore in an old setting.' He shook his head. 'But that same gummed ma always warned me: you can't turn a sow's ear into a silk purse, for all your skill at sewing. We've all told him so. Me. Gus Phillips. Even Kemp.' He laid a hand on John's forearm, his voice mellowing yet further. 'You know how he loves you, John. You've known him longer than any of us. S'death, you discovered him. What would he be if you had not noted his spark? A glover in Stratford, with ten fat children and nowhere to put his dreams.' He leaned close so that the moisture in his eyes reflected the firelight. 'The world owes you an unpayable debt, my friend.'

John doubted it. That small Warwickshire town would not have held Will Shakespeare long, whether John had come along with the Admiral's Men or no, and been two actors short. Though the fact that Burbage was using all his skills to persuade him thus showed that the player was more than a little desperate. Already today the monarch of the realm and its most powerful citizen had sought a favour of him and had, after the threats, offered something in return. The thought emboldened him now.

'I am distressed whenever I hear of Will's sadness. I will endeavour to root out its cause and alleviate it if I can. For you are right, I've known him long and love him well. As to the other . . .' He laid his hand atop of Burbage's. 'What's in it for me?'

They were close enough for him to see the change in Burbage's eyes. The moisture was sucked back, stored for later, better use upon the stage. 'What do you want?' he replied, as bluntly.

'A place in the company.' He saw denial rise, intercepted it. 'Small roles only. Ostlers. Messengers. Work my way back up.'

'I'd . . . try. You have the stuff, we all know that. Could have reached high. Could still . . .' he added hastily. 'But not all like you as I.'

'Will Kemp.'

'Aye, him. That punch!' Burbage gave a small, admiring laugh. 'Yet it is not only that. There's your drinking.' He lifted his hand from beneath John's, cupped it again over the brazier. 'Now I like my ale as much as the next man. I will even indulge in the occasional bumper of aqua vitae. Yet I am moderate when I play.'

'As am I,' John retorted, 'but I am not playing now, am I? Kemp's seen to that. Even Henslowe won't hire me, and we know how desperate he is.'

Burbage smiled. 'He certainly won't now after you linked him carnally with donkeys and rams.' He shook his head. 'Let us bide for you, John. Your time will come again, sure. Yet what say you to this: if the father's light be dimmed – dimmed but not extinguished, I declare – what if the son doth rise?'

The son. My son, thought John, feeling his heart squeeze tight. My Ned. 'And how might he rise?' he asked. 'Have you something in mind?'

Burbage leaned back, sucking air between his teeth. 'Well, he has inherited the family talent, sure. But he is still an apple half grown.'

'He needs roles to ripen him.'

'Yet if plucked from the branch early, he'll be sour. Though if I was to take him on as my new apprentice . . .'

He let the tantalising offer hang. John studied it. 'Do you not already have two?'

'Aye. But Henslowe's trying to steal Jamie for the Rose. He might succeed too, for the lad's gone arrogant after his triumph as Mistress Ford.' His eyes glistened. 'Still, it means I may have a place.'

John went to speak, held back. Apprenticeship to England's foremost player was a route to success several had already taken. It was a much-coveted place. And yet . . . he could not help the feeling that came. Up to now, he had been all the tutor Ned had needed.

Burbage noted the conflict on his face, reached to probe it. 'Come, John. A Lawley treading the boards of our new Globe. Will he be carrying a spear, dancing a jig . . . or speaking some sublimity that your oldest friend will write for him?' He nodded. 'And in return, all you have to do is persuade him not to dabble with that poxed old punk Hamlet, and point him towards more suitable tales.'

More suitable tales? Had not the Queen, not half an hour since, urged him to just this course? She wanted something special from the playwright to enthuse a nation about to go again to war. Burbage wanted something to open and keep filled his new theatre. While Will? He would want to write – he moped when he was not – and to once more catch the spirit of the times.

An idea came. 'What if he were to tackle a different old theme, but in a new way?'

The player's eyes narrowed. 'Go on.'

'Did we not use to play *The Famous Victories of Henry the Fifth*?'

'We did. It packed them in at the theatre.' Burbage scratched his beard. 'But the Earl of Essex had just won his own famous victory at Cadiz – with you at his side, of course.'

'Well, Dickon,' John said, his own voice smoothing to near the tone of the master, 'the Earl of Essex is off to war again.'

'God's my life, man,' said Burbage, the fire in his eye more than reflected. 'God's my life, but you may have hit on it. With all this talk of war, it could catch the mob's mood, no?' He rubbed his hands vigorously. 'And listen to this, for here's an idea: wars, on stage and off, need weapons, do they not? The clash of steel? Yes!' He kicked the brazier's side, making sparks fly up. 'If we revived something patriotic, like Harry Five, we would need some lusty engagements. At Harfleur. At Agin Court, begod!' He leaned forward, all hunger and ardour again. 'No one knows weapons like you, Johnnie lad. Think on't! That could be your way back. We'd need someone to set the fights.' He beamed. 'And there's no one better. Even Kemp would have to agree.'

John nodded. It would be a toe upon the platform and a way back into his other life too. He would be in Southwark, near Ned. Near Tess – with her affianced away in Ireland and subject to all the hazards that war brought. For of one thing only was he certain – his new service to the Queen and to Cecil did not include further service to the Earl of Essex. He would find a way to avoid it. In that cause, he had given enough. It was time to look to his own – and it seemed that began with his friend, William Shakespeare.

John gave a large yawn, then shook his head to clear it. The vision of paradise that was the nearby straw faded. It appeared he had one last thing to do tonight. 'Where is he? Shall I come with you back to the tavern?'

'Nay. You know he is not much given to carousing, and even less so of late.'

'Is he in his rooms, then? Are they the same?'

'They are, but not for long. He moves to Bankside to be close to our new home. Nay' – an arm held John back as he was about to make for Will's house in East Cheap – 'he is not there now. He told me of an appointment he had this night.'

'Where?'

'Forman's'

John frowned. 'Forman the astrologer?'

'Nay, Forman the ropewright – he seeks a length to hang himself.' Burbage laughed, then crossed himself. 'I shouldn't make sport on that. Aye, he visits the magus. Indeed, he is often there.'

'Unusual in him. Unless he in love?'

'I do not think the consultations tend that way.' Burbage released his arm. 'So if you will find him now, seek him at the sign of Capricorn, in Blood Spit Alley, hard by Fleet ditch.'

'I do seek him. And I know it.' He yawned again, as the two men moved towards the stable yard gates. 'Once I have spoken to Will, I will come to the tavern to collect Ned. Where do you drink?'

'The Cardinal Cap Inn.'

'Ah.' John thought it might be one of the taverns from which he was banned. But he could always send in a boy. The two guards opened the wicket gate and they exited. 'Try to persuade Ned not to carouse too much.'

'I will attempt it. But now he will also need to celebrate the possibility of becoming Burbage's apprentice' – he gave an outsized wink – 'and he is his father's son.' The gate was bolted behind them. 'Fare thee well with our friend, John. For all our sakes.'

They went in opposite directions, Burbage for the Whitehall Stairs and a boat, John towards Charing Cross. From the relative peace around the palace, its wider avenues and larger houses, he soon plunged into the narrower Strand and the crowds that were about it. There were still a few hours of Shrove Tuesday feasting left before the Lenten fast began, and people were out celebrating, crowds were within and before every tavern, drinking; or within an ordinary, eating. Thinking that his yawns needed stifling and food might be the answer, he stopped at some carts. But he'd already cracked the coin Will had given him and was sparing with what remained. No meat then, and no white loaf either. Carter's bread for him, near all rye. He'd spit out the chaff still in it, and the remainder would lie in his gut for a while and give him the illusion of fullness.

He gave a farthing for a half-loaf of it, but the dryness sucked all moisture from the desert of his mouth, so he parted with a penny for a half-dozen oysters, their juices moistening the bread, making it palatable. Then he bought two onions. The stallholder, a large woman with cross-eyes, peeled and sliced one for him, cackling all the while about how sweet his breath would now be for his love. She won't let me close enough to sniff it, he thought, pocketing the unpeeled one.

Fortified, a little more awake, he moved along the Strand, straddling the filthy gutter in its middle where the crowds were less. And as he walked, he considered what lay ahead. Mostly his thoughts came back to a name.

Hamlet, Will? Truly? Whatever are you up to now?

XII

At the Sign of Capricorn

John could hear it as soon as he turned into Blood Spit Alley. Not unusual in the city, with walls thin and holes in the plaster and loam between the beams. Yet even the thickest walls could scarce have contained the sounds of such vigorous swiving.

He envied the couple their transcendence. It had been a while – almost a year since Tess had last weakened and allowed him into her bed. Sighing, he halted – for he realised that the lovemaking was within the house he sought. It was night dark but a gated lantern swung above a wooden board covered with pentangles, triangles and symbols. It showed the trade of the man within for those that could not read the single word: Astrologer. Beyond the door, Simon Forman, Magister Astrologae, was carnally entwined.

John hesitated. Had he missed Will? Or . . . or was he within, witnessing the generation of the sounds? It was possible. Will was a great observer of *all* aspects of life.

Then another noise came, a shifting in the doorway behind him. He turned, hand to the dagger haft between his shoulder blades. 'Who's there?' he cried.

Silence, for a moment. Then a voice, soft, familiar. ''Tis I. And that is John, if I am not mistaken?'

'It is.' He released his dagger's grip, along with a sigh. 'Ill met by lamplight, proud player.'

The playwright enjoyed being quoted to himself. And this was from a play they had performed together, *A Midsummer Night's Dream*. He chuckled as he stepped out into the faint light spill. 'Fairies hence,' he responded. 'And yet not so . . . it would be a

112

shame to forsake *his* bed and company just yet.' He gestured to the door before them. Within, matters were accelerating. 'They go to it, do they not?'

'They do.'

'You know,' Will said now, 'that what we are hearing is probably payment in kind.'

'A kind payment indeed. Yet who pays who? 'Tis hard to tell, for both seem to be getting as much from the transaction.'

Indeed, both man and woman were striving for the same height, in speed, in tone. 'The woman pays, I suspect. Forman is known for his lechery. And many a maid has saved herself silver by bending.' Will sucked air between his teeth. 'Though I'd wager she keeps her eyes shut. The astrologer is faced like the sign of Capricorn itself.'

Both men laughed. 'Are you en route to see him, or have you been?' John asked.

'En route. I did not come straight here from the palace and I was delayed by . . .' He waved his hand at the door, then turned. 'And you? Are you after his guidance too?'

'Nay, Will. You know I do not seek much amongst the stars. I am looking for you. Burbage told me where to find you.'

'Did he?' His friend stared at him. 'I wonder why. Though I think I know – he would have you work on me. Is it not so?' But before John could reply, he continued, 'Ah! And there we have it.'

If they did not, Forman certainly did, for one goatish grunt came in contrast to a single clear sigh – and one extended giggle. After a few moments' silence, John gestured to the door. 'Shall we knock and hasten them?'

'I knocked when I arrived, when the noises were less. They ignored me. Wait.' Reaching within his cloak, Will pulled from its pockets a tortoiseshell case. Opened, it revealed some wax tablets and a stylus. 'I would capture her tone,' he said, scratching. 'There was a false note to it, did you not think? And then there was . . . what did you say on hearing me first behind you? "Who's there?" was it not?'

'A challenge by any guard upon any battlement, William. Hardly original.'

'But the way you said it. "Who's there?"' He hissed it. Many forgot the skills of Will the player in the writer. And John heard the echo of two things in the voice – sudden, shrill fear and the slight slur that a month of spirituous liquors had given it. He was proud of neither.

'A good way to start a play, don't you think?' said Will, slipping the case back. 'Simple, immediate. The guard is frightened by his watch. The battlement is . . . haunted.' He breathed the word out. 'I have been thinking much of ghosts lately.' He stepped closer, took an arm. 'And you, John? You were not wont to startle so easily. Was it me or one of *your* ghosts you heard stir in the alley this night?'

They had known each other a long time. Many who'd shared wine with them were worm food. Many who were even closer. John swallowed. 'You know what they say now, Will. Ghosts are mere superstition. Papist superstition.'

'Is that what they say?' Shakespeare shook the arm he held. 'Well, you and I know better, do we not?'

It was an alley near the Fleet, no one close by. Yet walls thin enough to emit cries of love could take in whispers of heresy. The Church in England had declared that ghosts did not exist. Yet that did not mean that those raised in a different church would stop believing in them.

'Easy, friend,' Will said. 'When did you grow so cautious? Is this the warrior who sailed with Drake round the unknown world, then helped destroy the Great Armada? This he who stormed Cadiz beside our hero Essex? This the man who played the bearded Turk in Chipping Sodbury to three blind men and their dogs?'

He could do it in two sentences, the humour and the horror. 'I was drunk on two of those occasions.' John laughed.

His friend joined him, but stopped first. 'And are you drunk now, John?' he asked softly.

'You know I am not.'

'Do I? I thought perhaps with the excuse of young Ned's blooding this night . . .'

'I need no excuse. I have ended my debauch. That I had reason for it, you know.' Tess's face flashed before him, a tangerine-swathed shadow behind her, fat fingers reaching. He swallowed it down. 'But it is past now.'

'Is it? Oh good.'

His friend had known him a long time. Had seen him pledge, and abstain, and fall again. Yet the doubt behind the younger man's words rankled. 'Forgive me, Master Shakespeare, that like most lesser mortals I do not have your . . . forbearance,' John snapped. 'Not all can be as cool in the blood as the scrivener of Stratford.'

He awaited the return shot. Will could wither with words – John had seen him do it and been reduced more than once himself. Yet now he just shook his head. 'Cool,' he murmured. ''Tis what I am accused of – by several more than you. Which is why I find myself outside the house of a magus, seeking help in ways no church can understand.'

John's anger fled. 'Tell me,' he murmured.

Bolts were shot on the door they stood before. 'Later,' Will replied, raising his voice, brightening his tone. 'For behold, since the astrologer has exited, we can enter.'

Someone else had to exit first, however. Indeed, the door was scarcely ajar before a woman slipped past it, blending into the dark of the alley in a moment, vanishing before they could get more than a glimpse of bedraggled, unbound hair and a thin cloak. An odour lingered behind her, the faint whiff of the rut.

The two men stepped forward – and were instantly halted again. For a second woman appeared and they blocked her egress. This one was muffled against the night and recognition within a hooded cloak, a woven scarf around her face. Only her dark eyes were revealed, widening as she saw them. She gasped, drew back . . . while at her shoulder a face countered, thrusting forward. Perhaps the recent embracing had brought forth its beastly qualities, for nothing less than a satyr was snarling there. The face contrived to be both long and blunt at the same time, full of strange promontories, with eyebrows like bursts of gorse hanging over twin caves of green-ish eyes. Black hair was matted to the head except where it rose in two curving peaks atop the forehead. Teeth glimmered in light spilled from the candlelit room, canines prominent. 'Ehhhh?' came the rumble in the throat, an animal caught in an intimate act. The woman, trapped on the doorstep, turned, saw, cried out again.

John did not blame her. Simon Forman was never going to be handsome. But at least he could contrive to look human.

Yet this beast could speak. 'Master Shakespeare,' he said, thrusting out one hand, 'an honour as ever. And . . . Master Lawley, is it not? Twice honoured.'

In attempting to step aside, John had ended up going the same way as the maid. They both stepped the other way, and again he was blocking her. When it happened a third time, it must have appeared as if he were either teasing or attempting to dance. So he halted, she crashed into him, fluttered there like a bird trapped within leaded glass. She . . . crackled, something beneath her cloak. No traces of lovemaking rose, but another scent did. Cloves, a usual ingredient in perfumes. Popular, too; he had smelled it once already that night.

The maid slipped from arms he hadn't realised he'd raised and, with a little cry, ran into the gloom.

'Farewell, madam, dear . . . whatshisname,' Forman called, still grasping Will's hand and pulling him inside, 'and mark again, before month's end, the thrall of Venus.'

'The thrall of Venus, Master Forman?' Will had allowed himself to be dragged into the room, where a candelabra lit his face and the smile upon it. 'I would conclude that you are the one under its thrall.' He glanced around the small room. 'For were you not . . . *entertaining* two ladies at once?'

'It may appear so, sir,' replied Forman, 'but it was not so.' He attempted to smooth down the hair horns. 'The lady came for a consultation. Her maid . . .' He frowned, gave up his attempt at hairdressing. 'I am not certain what she came for, except to seduce me.'

'While her mistress . . . enjoyed watching?' Incredulous, John moved forward.

'It is unusual, sir, but not . . . unheard of. When people consult the stars and the whole magical world, different attitudes are displayed.' Forman shrugged. 'And yet I do not know if she took pleasure in the viewing, since I was . . . engaged. And I was unable to ask, as they were startled by your knock with me scarce able to conclude.' He clapped his hands together, went on in a very different tone as he stepped back, 'Can I offer you some ale? I can mull it, if you like. Or something stronger, perhaps, for the night is cold, is it not?'

Shaking his head – he considered himself worldly, but did not believe he would have displayed such disregard if he'd been caught in this situation – John followed his friend in. The phrase 'something stronger' paused him as well, as it always did. But he took a breath, then answered, 'A mulled ale would serve me well.'

'And I,' said Will, 'though sitting to enjoy it might prove a problem.' Indeed, every spare inch of the room appeared to be covered in paper. It filled the chair, covered the stools and the trestle, submerged the table, where sheaves appeared especially flattened.

'Ah yes. Apologies, gentlemen. I have been somewhat busy since the Queen's rapprochement with the earl, and his acceptance of her majesty's commission for war.' He lifted papers, put them aside. 'Soldiers, soldiers, demanding to know if death or glory awaits them. Or both. Ah!' Two joint stools had emerged from under mounds of paper that were swiftly perched atop other mounds, slag heaps formed and leaning precariously. 'Please.' He gestured, then moved to the fireplace. He shoved a brace of iron pokers into the coals, then pulled two pewter tankards from hooks on the ceiling, filling them from a stone jug.

'And the earl himself is one of your clients, I heard,' said John, sitting, balancing, as Will did.

Forman looked up. 'Ah, you have seen my noble lord? Indeed, he has so honoured me. Knows I am both excellent and discreet. For if he went to the court's supercilious Dr Dee, he would not only get a vague reading but the results would be broadcast to every ear in Whitehall.' He pulled one poker from the coals, ran a cloth over it to remove the ash then plunged it into a tankard. It sizzled and steam rose. He handed the mug to William. 'Good sir.'

It was true, John thought. Any horoscope, however confidential, would be shown near straight to the Secretary of State. Dog days or Mars ascendant, the crouch-backed spymaster, Robert Cecil, would want to know of it and use it for his purposes.

Shakespeare sipped. 'And as to the business, Master Forman? Have you had time to look into my minor matters, with so many weighty ones' – he glanced at the flattened papers upon the table – 'to occupy you?'

'I have indeed, sir. And nothing that concerns the welfare of the realm's foremost playwright can be considered minor.' He pulled the other poker out, wiped, plunged, then handed John the heated mug. 'You will excuse us, Master Lawley?' Forman pulled a stool close to the playwright on his other side.

As the two of them began to whisper, John swigged; wrinkled his nose. It was not overly hot, but the flavour was harsh. Another import from the Dutch wars, like the pox and . . . and the smell of cloves. The Hollanders brewed their beer with hops to make it last. This made it bitter. It also tasted strong. Double double, perhaps? Though it was not the same as whisky for him, there was danger in the stronger ales too. It was why he always eased off from a debauch with small beer. Drank himself sober, like any martin drunkard.

Still . . . he took a gulp. The effect was near instant . . . and pleasing. He suddenly felt more awake. His mind expanding again, he could focus on his plan. To help Burbage while helping his friend by dissuading him from revisiting a tired old play and focusing instead on something that suited the martial hour. To watch his son rise, while setting epic fights for Chamberlain's men. Perhaps to work himself back into a role. Woo Tess anew. And above all, to keep far, far, far from the reach of Robert Devereux!

He toasted the scheme with a larger gulp. The beer tasted better and he was awake again. Why had he even considered sleep? He looked at the whispering men. Perhaps when their business was concluded he could persuade his old friend Will to accompany him to the Cardinal Cap Inn in Southwark and cheer his boy. He could work upon him along the way. Besides, it wasn't every day that a Lawley made his debut before the Queen.

He raised his mug – empty, which was both strange and annoying. Then he saw something that pleased him even less. The magus was passing a bottle to the playwright. It was brown, squat, familiar. It was whisky. And though he had no intention of having even one small sip, it was hard that the rogues did not trust him enough to offer some for him to refuse. Or something. 'Let's share that then, if we be friends,' he found himself saying, as he rose from his stool and stepped in.

Will placed a palm on his shoulder, holding him off. 'Good soul,' he said gently, 'I know that this is probably your most difficult hour. Yet hold to your resolve. Besides' – he smiled – 'desperate though you are, I doubt that even you will enjoy the taste of Anne Hathaway's piss.'

John sat again. It took him a while to find the words. 'Forgive, William, the absurdity of the question. I fear I must have misheard you. Did you just say you were holding a bottle filled with your wife's urine?'

'I did.'

'Ah.' John had known Anne Hathaway, a little. A delightful lady, and pretty with it, though the last time he'd seen her, she'd thrown a stool at him. A fair gesture, considering he was waiting at her garden gate to kidnap her husband. The stool, of course, may well have been aimed at the willing abductee. Fortunately it had missed them both, so their brains remained unstoved, their jaws unbroken and they were able to tackle the roles they played for the Admiral's Men and other companies through that year and the ones that followed, that garden path leading through the byways of England, with some detours on the Continent, eventually to London.

Will's confirmation did not truly help him. All he could think was how queer it was that the last time he'd seen her the lady had been hurling furniture at him and now he was staring at a liquid that had once been inside her.

John shook his head, tried again. 'Another foolish question, Will, no doubt. But why are you holding a bottle of Mistress Hathaway's piss?'

It was Forman who replied. 'Your friend provided this so I could cast his beloved wife's horoscope.'

It was a final nonsense. 'Eh?' was all John managed.

'John, even a sceptic like yourself must know that astrologers are often referred to as – forgive me – "piss prophets".'

'No offence taken.' The magus bobbed his head. 'You see, Master Lawley, if I have something of the subject, I can cast their horoscope from it, even if I do not see them. And nothing is better than urine. As long as I know the hour and the place where it was voided, it does not even have to be fresh.'

'And since the roads are winter-poor and Greenaway's nags slow,' added Shakespeare, 'this took ten days to get here from Stratford. Fresh it is not. Sniff . . .' Laughing, he whipped the cork from the bottle and thrust it towards John, the sharp alkaline savour surging through his head like shot, clearing and nauseating at the same time. There was a collision, liquid slopped, its sour taint filling the room, at last dispelling the rich scent of love's conjoined juices that had ruled it to that point.

'And why . . . why, by cock and pie, William, are you casting her horoscope? Is it a gift for her?'

'No.' Will's laugh died. 'I will tell you, for our long friendship. But let it not go beyond this room.' He sighed. 'I would know this: if my wife can still bear me a child. A son to . . .' He paused. 'Another son.'

John tipped his head. 'She's not young, William. And yet . . . some do give birth older than she.'

'Some do,' Will replied, as quietly, 'but according to Forman's 'scope, my sweet Anne will not be numbered amongst them.'

'Alack, sir, Venus is retrograde in her chart,' added the astrologer, opening a sheet of parchment towards them. 'See how it wanes?'

John did not look there, but at his friend. This could not have been a surprise, her tale in the stars. Anne was older than her husband by some seven years. They'd had a son. He'd died. It was not something Will would ever talk about.

Nor would he now. He nodded once, then stood. 'Come then, John. I have my answer. And we must leave Master Forman to his work.' He turned at the door. 'Do you need to share my bed this night?'

'No, I must go collect Ned and return him to his.'

'Then we will walk a little way together.'

As John rose, a memory came. 'You spoke of soldiers' fortunes, did you not, sir?'

'I did.' Forman was restacking sheaves of paper. 'Men who go to war are most keen to know what the heavenly spheres foretell.'

He did not want to ask. He would never seek his own fate in the stars. And yet? 'And did you also say that you had been consulted by the Earl of Essex?'

'I did.' The goatish face was split by a satisfied smile.

Though avoiding him was John's plan, he could not help his question. 'Since I am also, in some ways, my lord of Essex's man, might I at least hear something of his . . . fortune?'

The goat face folded into its lines, closing itself off. 'I would not be as near to him as I am if I were to part with information only he should know,' Forman replied, his tone icy.

John nodded, turned to the door. But it was Will who spoke again. 'Of course we would not seek to violate the . . . seal of this confessional,' he said, nodding at the room. 'Yet Master Lawley has been . . . "enticed" might be the term . . . to war before by the noble earl. I think he would like to know that if this enticement were to reoccur, should he seek to avoid it?' As Forman still glared, Will stepped back, spoke softer. 'I would consider it a personal favour, Master Forman. With our new planet rising in Southwark, I am sure we will have need of many pronouncements upon our fortunes there. And I will have many opportunities to return any kindnesses.'

'You understand I cannot show you his horoscope?' Forman gestured behind him to a stack of papers.

'Indeed,' said Will. 'As I am sure we would not understand it if you did. That is your genius, sir.' As Forman's chest swelled, he added, 'A simple answer to a simple question would surely suffice.'

The magus inclined his head. 'What question?'

The playwright's lips moved before he spoke. 'Should the querent accompany the Earl of Essex to Ireland, to the glory of her majesty and the smiting of her foes?'

Forman stared at the two men before him for a long while. Both could see the candlelight playing in his eyes, and John, looking hard, could swear that their centres changed, from human orbs to goatish rectangles. At last the man turned, bent, began to search a stack of papers, slowly at first, then ever more swiftly.

'Strange,' he muttered, 'it was just here.' After a few further moments shuffling, he stood straight, turned back. 'It matters not. I will find it anon. While its import is burned upon my brain.' He tapped his head, closed his eyes. 'I see only this end for my lord of Essex's journey – hunger, sickness, failure. And on his return, treachery, harming him . . . and those near him.' He opened his strange eyes again. 'So, the answer to your question, querent, is plain: lie low and let the storm pass you by.'

It was ever his intent. So it was not the advice that made John gasp, but the doom that the astrologer had pronounced. 'Do you intend to tell the earl this?' he asked.

Forman shook his head. 'People do not pay well for the direst prognostications. And there is enough leeway in any aspects to leave . . . perhaps a little hope?' He shook his head. 'Yet even if certain death lay in my conjunctions – which it does not – the earl is bound to Ireland, and can do no other. So I will cheer him as I can, warn him as I must – and solicit God's mercy upon him whenever I am able.'

'Amen,' said both the other men.

They all looked at each other for a moment. Then Will said softly, 'I nearly forgot,' and returned to pick up the bottle. 'I bid you good night, Master Forman, and I thank you again for your advice. This, I believe, will settle our account.'

He handed across a small purse. Forman, all smiles now, took the money and immediately moved past him. 'I would delay you longer, sir, for I always take such delight in your company.' He opened the door. 'Alas, another appointment – two serving wenches have mislaid some of their mistress's fine crockery. They think it stolen. I will tell them where to seek it and of whom, the sweet young things.' He was again attempting to smooth down his hair horns as the two men paused beyond the threshold. 'I wish you joy for your rising planet, the Globe.' He smiled. 'I will straightway draw up a chart to show when its opening would be propitious.' He bowed to them. 'Good e'en, gentles both.'

XIII

Backswords with Silver

They waited till they were around three bends before they burst into laughter. 'Ah, I will put that fellow on the stage one day,' Shakespeare said. 'In fact, I have something in mind for him right now.'

'Why, Will?' John said casually. 'There is no soothsayer in Hamlet, as I recall.'

'Nay, but there is one in . . .' He broke off. 'Hamlet? Why do you raise his spectre now?' Yet before he could reply, the playwright stopped and closed his eyes. 'Ah, I see. Yes, you'd been talking to Burbage. So he sends you to work on me, does he? And what inducement did he offer for your persuasive services, I wonder?'

Before John could reply, loud shouts ahead drew their attention.

''Tis the apprentices,' John said. 'Shrove Tuesday, remember.'

'Aye, they will rampage before Lent chafes them.' Will smiled. 'Like you.'

'Perhaps.' He took his friend's arm. 'And Burbage sends me because he is concerned about you. As am I.' He squeezed. 'The matter for which you consulted Forman . . .'

'Ah.' Will looked up, to where stars could be glimpsed between the jutties. 'You remind me.' He reached again into the pocket of his cloak, drew out the bottle, unstoppered it. He studied it a moment, then bent to the ground over the reeking ditch that ran down the alley's centre. He did not dump it straight, but let it mingle slowly into the half-frozen mire.

John watched him for a moment before he spoke. 'You did not truly hope, did you? Anne is as old as I, and . . . and you visit her but once a year.'

The playwright, still slowly pouring, replied without looking up. 'You tax me with my stock role: the neglectful spouse.'

'I did not mean . . .'

Shaking the bottle for its last drops, Will rose slowly – then suddenly threw it hard against a wall. It did not smash, though the neck snapped off. Immediately a lean cat darted from a doorway, pounced, licked, hissed and took off in an arch-backed skitter in the direction of the swelling noises at the alley's end, where it gave on to the main thoroughfare of the Fleet. Shouts came again from there, louder, the words still slurred.

Both men watched Anne's urine mingling with many others, before Will spoke again. 'I knew the story of her age. The one of my infrequent visits. It seemed unlikely . . . and yet . . .' He shrugged. 'The idea of . . . of a son has been moving me of late.'

'Another Hamnet?'

'There will never be another such as he.'

John nodded, lost for a response. Till the obvious question came. 'Have you thought of . . . more fertile lands?'

'I have. Of course I have. God and you both know I have not always been . . . restrained in my affections. I am as weak as any of Adam's sons in that.' He sighed, finally looked at John. 'But to seek that . . . issue? A poor husband I am, but not that poor. There are bastards enough in the wide world without me adding to them, as well you know.'

'I?' snapped John. 'And what do I know? That my boy must hang his head under a title that I would remove in an instant if I could?'

Will shook his head. 'Nay, trust me. I spoke not of Ned, but to the general, and meant no offence. I know that you would legitimise him in an instant, if Tess would but have you.'

Anger went in a moment, replaced by something else. 'But she will not,' John replied mournfully. 'And yet . . . I have some hopes.' Half ones to be sure – but all connected to the man before him, the suit with which he'd been charged. So he drew himself up, lowered his voice, 'Now mark, young William, your elder's advice – think no more of the tragedy of Hamnet . . .'

The word froze him. His tongue had once again failed his mind. But his friend did not allow him to correct himself. He took John's arm. 'No more of him – nor of the play, neither! I will think on what you have said. After this' – he gestured at the broken bottle – 'perhaps 'tis not the time.' He released John with a squeeze, stepped forward. 'Let us on. I crave the balm of sleep.'

As they drew near the alley's end, shouts, jeers, drunken laughter grew ever louder. Someone shouted, 'Hold him again,' and the sound of a blow followed, along with a screech of pain, and a burst of high-pitched pleading. 'Come,' John said, 'let us double back and go around the brawl.'

'On Shrove Tuesday?' Shakespeare shrugged. 'Every route will have a gang of drunken apprentices athwart it. We cannot go round them all. Besides' – he tipped an ear – 'some child is the focus of their sport. They will not notice us.' With that he stepped from the gloom of the alley into a crossing of ways, a wider space made brighter by a lack of conjoined roofs.

It was Fleet Street, and just as the playwright stepped upon it, a body was flung against him.

The boy nearly knocked Shakespeare over twice. Once on the first collision, once again when he realised that the doublet he clutched was velvet and so belonged to a gentleman. 'Please, sir,' he yelped, scrambling up into the other's arms like a cat fleeing a dog, 'I ain't done nothin'. 'Elp me, yer worship. Save us!'

John, who'd steadied his friend as he stumbled backwards, looked beyond him. A crowd had spilled from the alehouse on to the cobbles, peering over the shoulders of seven youths, each of whom sported the blue aprons of apprentices. Flaring torches in sconces on the tavern's walls showed they were of different trades, judging by the stains – red smears upon the butchers' boys, a rainbow of paint upon the dyers', black ink upon the printers'. They were uniform in two respects alone: every one of them was big; and each had the same expression upon faces reddened by ale, of a beast tormenting its prey. It was the one seen on the faces of those at the dog or cock fights, the bear or bull baits: a bloody conclusion was sought, the crueller the better.

John recognised the look – and the danger. Leaning in, he spoke low. 'Do not interfere, William. These bullies will have blood and they will make him bleed who tries to deprive them of its taste. Release the boy and let's be gone.'

The fugitive flung his arms round the playwright's neck. 'No! They 'ave me wrong, sir. I ain't no thief.' Blood fell from his nose. He sniffed it back, wailed louder, 'I ain't no thief!'

John could see his friend's eyes narrow. He was ever kind-hearted, and it was a rare beggar or stray dog that left him with nothing. But before he could speak again, with more urgency, someone else did.

'He *is* a thief,' the largest of the large apprentices declared, stepping forward, 'for by Jesu, I found his hand in my pocket. So now' – he hefted a large, jagged-edged cleaver – 'I am going to cut it off.' He turned to the crowd and waved it. 'And since Donnelly is my master, the little piss-rat won't feel a thing.' The crowd cheered at that, while the boy wailed and buried his face in Shakespeare's neck. 'So you'll release him to me straightway, sir, and let justice' – he lifted his blade high – 'be done.'

Will waited for the cheers to die a little – not entirely, for he had a voice to command a playhouse, and so this little stage. 'Gentles all,' he cried, 'he is but a child. If he is a thief also, let the law have him. One of you, call the watchman!'

'The watchman?' The big apprentice hooted derisively. 'He's lying under a table in the tavern behind me, his fist up some trull's skirt.' Laughter came at this. 'No,' he bellowed above it, 'we are the Ludgate Boys, and we will have our own justice.'

'Ludgate Boys! Ludgate Boys! We are the Ludgate Boys.' The chant began behind him. He grinned, stepped closer. 'So give him over, sir.' He pointed with the hatchet. 'Or protect him at your cost.'

'Leave him, Will,' Lawley hissed. He had been in enough street skirmishes to know his odds. These were poor at best; while his friend, for all his courage, handled words and a quill better than blows and a blade. 'Leave him.'

Shakespeare, however, had another idea. 'By your patience.' He turned, called, 'What say you, fellows, if I were to buy you some flagons of sack? Upon my word, I will see this youth into the hands of a magistrate, where all may come and swear to his crime.'

John sucked in breath. It was a fair offer to apprentices who could afford only ale or beer this day; sweet sack would be a rare treat. Indeed, several of the seven looked as if they would readily accept the offer.

Yet it was the crowd who swayed it, for most of them would not be partakers. These jeered, and the butcher's lad was with them. 'I think not, sir,' he declared. 'For we are Ludgate Boys, true Englishmen, and so cannot be bribed from justice.' Jeers turned to cheers at this, and acknowledging them, he stepped forward. 'So you'll release him to us – or take the consequences.'

If John knew the odds of a street fight, he also knew its mindset. There were always those uncommitted to its extremity. These could be swayed. Bribery had just failed to do so – yet swift ferocity might work. So he stepped away from his friend and the still bawling boy, to give himself the room required.

It was good plan, to take out the biggest threat, and transform the rest into nervous bystanders. May have worked too – if John had not been betrayed by the unevenness of the stones underfoot, a misjudgement of distance and the lingering effects of the heated double double ale he'd just drunk.

He drew, screamed, 'Heya!' and leapt. Tripped. Fell, his sword clattering on to the stones. Somehow he kept a grip upon it, which aided him not a jot, what with the apprentice's boot upon it.

'Oh John,' he heard his friend say. He squinted up at the butcher's boy looking down.

'Now that,' the youth said, 'was not very friendly, old man.'

He might have taken more offence if he were not lying with his ear pressed to shit-rimmed cobbles and if the youth had not continued, to the crowd, 'You all witnessed who drew first. So I'm going to let him rise – and then give him a little lesson in swordplay.'

The boot withdrew. John rolled clumsily away, got on to knees, thence on to shaky legs. The butcher's boy stepped back, handed his cleaver to a friend, then reached to his side and began to draw, very slowly, a rapier from its scabbard. The weapon's speed was partly dictated by its length – at least a foot longer than the limit decreed by her majesty. Once clear, he also withdrew a long dagger, raised both weapons into the air, to another huge cheer, the onlookers so thrilled by this escalation that not one yelled out when the accused thief, cause of the quarrel, slipped from Shakespeare's neck and sprinted off down the alley.

Escalation . . . escalated. Where two swords were bared, suddenly there were nine, for the six other apprentices also now had their rapiers out. As Will drew his, John stared. 'Is there not an ordinance, Will,' he mumbled, 'that decrees only gentlemen may carry rapiers?'

The butcher's boy overheard – and smiled. ''Tis true indeed, sir, which is why we carries 'em.' He turned and grinned at his companions. ''Cos we is all fucking gentlemen.'

More cheers at that. They were spreading into a half-circle when, from behind them, flagons appeared, borne by drudges from the tavern, the landlord following, a large man who shouted as he came, 'A sixpence says it is over in less than a minute. I offer odds of three to one!'

'I'll take sixes,' a man cried out. 'These *are* real gentlemen, after all.'

'Done,' replied the landlord. 'Fetch the minute glass!' Men scrambled for coin, others for ale as odds were given, taken and liquid dispensed. For the moment, enjoying the cheers and excitement, the Ludgate Boys made no move.

'What now, John?' Will whispered. 'This is your arena, I think.'

'And you saw how well I did with my first assay,' muttered John back. 'I'd run, but they'd catch us easy.' He sighed. 'Let me to the fore and ward my side. If I can yet take out the big lout, take him hard, the others may crumble. They are lads, and I warrant they have seen little true combat.'

The butcher's boy, having received sufficient acclaim, turned, swished his huge rapier through the air, then settled into his stance. John swirled his own weapon – not for show, but to get some movement in his wrist, arm, shoulder. Yet it had no effect on the fog still swathing his brain. Only one thought pierced it – that he must attack first, and end the fight before it began.

He was just preparing to attempt it when a voice, unheard till then, cried out, 'What, John Lawley? Art thou drawn among these heartless hinds?'

The voice was deep and strong enough to silence the buzz for beer and betting. Each man, spectator or combatant, turned to see who had spoken. It was John who first recognised the man who stepped into what had become an impromptu arena.

'Silver,' he said. 'Well met.' He turned to his drawn friend. 'I don't believe you two know each other.' He gestured between them. 'Master William Shakespeare. Master George Silver.'

Each man bent slightly from the waist. They were of a height, and so their heads near met somewhere close to John's mid chest. He looked down upon them, noting the contrast under the caps – his friend's receding yet still brown locks, his former Cadiz comrade's now as grizzled as his name, though still thick. The latter lifted first, extended a hand which Will met with his left, keeping a grip on his hilt. 'I knew you on the instant, sir, from your wonderful playing at the Curtain,' said Silver, pumping enthusiastically. 'And even more from your wondrous words.' He smiled shyly. 'You may have noted that I quoted you, sir, your play of Romeo and his Juliet.'

'Indeed,' replied Will, 'I thought they sounded familiar, though I couldn't quite place them . . .'

''Twas Tybalt, sir, happening upon Benvolio drawn in the street. It seemed appropriate, given your situation.' He glanced at the drawn apprentices, then more specifically at their swords, then sniffed. 'Lads,' he continued, 'I understand why Italians in Master Shakespeare's play wielded rapiers. But true Englishmen like you . . . ?'

The apprentices gaped, still stupefied by the man's appearance and his words. 'Master Silver is a great proponent of the vantages of English techniques of swords and swordplay over the foreign,' said John. 'He has published a book on the subject.'

'Principles, sir, not techniques,' admonished Silver. 'Techniques will fail when principles always apply. And the book is not published yet. I amended it, after your kind comments. It is at the printer's now.' He turned again to Shakespeare. 'I would be honoured to send you a copy, sir.'

'As I would be to receive it. Perhaps you would care to . . .'

'OY!'

It was surprising, John supposed, that the Ludgate Boys had restrained themselves to that point. Perhaps they'd been well trained not to interrupt their betters. But ale and ardour and blades still bared now overtook their manners. 'Leave off all this talk!' the butcher's boy bellowed. 'Are we going to fight, or what?'

'Or what indeed!' Silver now turned back to the mob, stepped forward, ignoring the sword points. 'Surely, however my friends have offended, it can be forgiven over some foaming English ale?'

'I already tried that approach,' said Will, 'but they prefer to drink hot blood.'

'Never a harm in establishing cause, sir.' Silver spoke softly from the side of his mouth. 'The law will so interfere in an Englishman's right to quarrel these days. 'Twould be well, if this came to court, that there be witnesses who recalled we offered a truce.'

'Enough!' The butcher's apprentice stepped forward, swishing his sword through the air. 'We will fight. So get out of the way, short arse!'

Silver turned back. 'Did I hear aright? Did this red-tinged piece of offal presume to comment upon my stature.' He smiled. 'Joy!' he cried, drawing his sword with a flourish, scything the air with a sound twice as loud as the rapier had made. As the crowd gasped and commented, he spoke aside again. 'A wonderful opportunity, John, to demonstrate the principles I have expounded in my treatise. To whit' – he raised his voice – 'the innate superiority of our short English backswords and bucklers over the foreign fancies of the bird-spit rapier and dagger.'

John replied quietly, 'George, there are but two of us.'

'Three,' said Will, taking his stance. 'I know you doubt me, John, but I have of late been almost continually in practice.'

'Three! A band of brothers indeed!' cried Silver. 'Would that the odds were greater!'

'I think these will suffice.' While John spoke, Silver slipped a small round steel shield from his belt. 'Also I have no buckler. Neither does Master Shakespeare.'

'I have one spare,' Silver said brightly, turning the other hip. 'Always carry one in case an opponent lacks. Take it.'

With a sigh, John tucked his sword under his arm, then fumbled with the ties until he could slide the shield off. As he did, he muttered, 'Though I do not doubt your new skills, Will, let the soldiers handle it if at all possible, eh? We need a few plays out of you yet.'

'Indeed!' cried Silver, hearing. 'Lads, do you not know whom you threaten here?'

'Enough!' With another bellow, the apprentices' leader waved his cohort wide.

They obeyed, looking to him for the start. Yet Silver pointed the tip of his sword skywards and cried, 'Indeed, sirs! I think I should warn you who it is you face here. I leave aside my own modest talents. But my friend' – he clapped John on the back – 'is a hero of more wars than you have hairs under your codpieces.'

John sighed. 'May we not merely proceed, please?'

'Nay, John, they should know with whom they contend – and take warning!' He turned back to the crowd, which had quadrupled in the interim, the ruckus drawing customers from other taverns and ordinaries nearby; while someone had pulled up an eel cart and was doing a brisk trade. 'For this is John Lawley – master of defence to the Earl of Essex.'

'I am not . . .' John began.

But he was immediately drowned out by the roar. 'Essex! Essex!' cried the crowd. The drawn apprentices all looked at each, their choler cooling in this wash of patriotism. Silver, seeing it, spoke loudly again.

'And surely some must recognise the other standing here. That prince of players, that master of poetry, the bard of the age . . .'

'Enough!' The huge butcher's apprentice had had the impetus taken away from him by Silver's appearance and talk. He had to restore it. 'We don't care if they is Sir Lancelot and Geoffrey Bloody Chaucer! They've let the bloody thief escape. Bollocks to the bard, I says!' He spread his arms wide in appeal. 'Bollocks to the bard!'

This crowd, as most, was easily shifted by a slogan. 'Bollocks to the bard!' The cry was taken up by all his fellows and a good portion of the rest, and with that cry, all the apprentices, with a whistle of steel in air, once more took their guards.

Silver had drifted to John's right, drawing three men to face him. To his left, William stepped tentatively towards the smallest apprentice, who, to John's swift glance, looked as apprehensive as the playwright. Finally, movement forced him to focus fully on the three ranged against him.

Their guards told him much. Two were sloppy, their legs too far back as if to remove their bodies from their weapons, their points wide. Only their leader looked as if he'd had lessons. That would make him either more or less dangerous according to how many. Too few and he'd be thinking style and fail to fight. Many, and he could be good. His guard was, the rapier stretched out in his right hand but with that leg full back, so that the dagger's point was near level with the other, warding it, like an attendant upon his lord. It was a closed door of pointed steel that John would not try to enter directly. But there were always other ways in.

The three began to advance slowly, yelling taunts. It gave John a moment to remind himself: he must not kill here. It was near as important as not getting killed himself. For he already had the Tyburn brand, M for murderer, upon his thumb. He had escaped the noose by using the scholar's excuse: he could read the 'neck verse' from the Psalms. The brand showed that he had done so and could not do so again. And even if he was able to plead self-defence and enough witnesses testified on his cause, the least this riot could mean was months in the Clink – and what of his hopes for rehabilitation then? What of Tess, Ned and the Globe?

With this in mind, and striving to ignore Silver, who seemed to be conducting a seminar – 'Remember, Lawley, the superiority of the blow over the thrust!' – John recalled suddenly the first rule of any duel, beaten into him by the master he'd trained with in Italy, Viggiani of Bologna, to whom he'd been apprenticed in his youth. 'Before you even come to the blows, Gianni, make of yourself a great devil,' the old Italian had said, 'and make your opponent believe that you are there for the express purpose of whisking his soul straight to hell!'

Recalled and straight acted upon. 'Buffoon!' John bellowed. 'Whoreson dog! Do you think I have time to play with fools and children? I am going to pluck out your liver and eat it raw before your fading eyes.' Accompanying this with a great swish down through the air with his cutting edge, he leapt forward, seeming to cover a lot of ground while only taking a pace, then bringing his back edge fast up, steel whistling through the air. Next, he put himself into guard – but not in a quiet way, for as he yelled again, he took the step back he needed for room, at the same time sweeping his sword up in a great stroke against the edge of his buckler, making the small shield clang. At shout and strike, the men before him again slowed, so once more he brought his sword hard down from the height, ringing metal on metal again, taking another step back. Then, with a final retire and his guard low, he jerked the sword tip hard up in an unmistakable severing of man's most precious part. All winced as he then aligned his sword's tip with his buckler, thrusting both forward, peering over the twin steel even as he stepped back once more.

It was a true swashbuckle. He had executed it well, perhaps lessening the memory of his previous slide to the cobbles. A cheer came from the crowd, drowning Silver's 'Oh, sir!' at this breach of

English restraint. Yet both men knew also that the noise had caused a distraction. Both used it now.

John heard that swish of steel beside him, a first yelp of pain, the last things he heard. It was ever thus with him in a fight, the near silent place he went to, entering it even as he launched himself. Thought and action, one.

The main threat was in the middle, so he avoided it directly, slamming the blades on his right with both his own weapons, collecting his foe's with a slight circle of his own sword, before knocking aside the first thrust at his side with a downward sweep of his buckler. The boy who'd delivered it recovered with a step back, taking guard again, giving John the moment to close right, keeping the rapier and dagger he'd gathered with his sword while sweeping his elbow up, driving it into the apprentice's cheek.

His weight was behind the blow. The youth went down, falling into the butcher's boy, blocking another advance – which gave John the second moment he needed. As the apprentice on the other side lunged at his face, from the crouch where his elbow strike had taken him John swept his blade across and hard, knocking the weapon away, exposing the man's face to the buckler, driven in like a fist, a metalled fist, straight to the nose. The youth cartwheeled backwards, dropping both his blades as he went, and smashed into the eel cart.

'Oy!' the stallholder screamed, steadying his stall, though not enough to prevent some of his produce from flopping on to the cobbles.

The butcher's boy, clear at last of his fallen comrades, thrust now at John's side, exposed by the blow he'd just delivered with his buckler. It came close, only a leap backwards and a hard strike diagonally downwards with the shield deflecting it, and that only by a finger's width. But the leap made him stumble, stumble turning to slide as his sole connected with an eel. He did not go down, knew he mustn't – not when the butcher's boy, with a whoop, was driving his dagger . . . straight towards John's left eye.

Knee and sword-grip knuckles on the ground, he pushed off them, shooting his arm up, blade reversed and square before his face, diverting the thrust. Rising, lifting the dagger as he came, John twisted his wrist, flicking the sword tip back and over his shoulder. The parry and the force of his own thrusts had caused the apprentice to step too close, his over-long rapier now flapping uselessly above. So John pulled back fractionally . . . then popped the pommel of his sword straight between the man's eyes.

He dropped, so hard and fast that his weapons landed a second afterwards. He was undoubtedly unconscious; in a day his eyes would be blacker than Satan's arse. But in the swift glance he allowed himself before he checked for more enemies, John could tell, and thank heaven for the fact, that at least the youth was not dead.

He breathed deep, shook his head to clear it, which allowed a thought to enter. 'Will?' he said, turning on it.

But his friend was safe. Indeed, he and his opponent were standing side by side, swords under their arms. Both were looking at John with mouths open.

'What?' said John, crossing to him. 'Are you well?'

'I am. After one pass, we came to an immediate truce, this lad and I. But John, I stand humbled. You are a fine player, sure . . .' Shakespeare shook his head. 'But you are an extraordinary fighter.'

John shrugged – but it was Silver who spoke. 'You are indeed. Bravo, Master Lawley.' The swordsman was himself standing in the centre of a pile of three groaning young men. 'A touch unorthodox, kneeling to receive a thrust. I would not on the whole recommend it. But the pommel to the face? Pure backsword. Could you do that with a rapier, I ask you?' He turned the question to the crowd, not even looking down to kick away the dagger the butcher's boy, one eye already shut and swelling, was groping for. 'I ask again, could you?'

'Nay!' came a great shout, amidst more toasting and the slurping of eels.

'And this is the weapon that accomplished it,' he said, swishing his backsword through the air. 'No foreign fancy of rapier for John Lawley. A yard of true English steel! And, I venture, it will be one such that brings the Irish traitor Tyrone to bay, and forces him to kneel before his conqueror, whose men we are.' He thrust his point towards the sky. 'The Earl of Essex!'

The name provoked the same cry, the repetition. 'Essex! England! Essex!'

'Speak for yourself, Silver,' John muttered, looking past him, over the heads of the crowd . . . where he could see, approaching from the

134

direction of the Strand, the halberds of the watch. Murderer he might not be this day, but he could still spend Clink time as a street brawler. 'Come!' Seizing his friend's arm, he called back, 'Master Silver, we must away.'

Their comrade was in the midst of a pressing throng which included some of the risen Ludgate Boys, clutching heads and bellies. 'I think I'll stay awhile. These are stout English lads, with high spirits, that is all. It is not their fault that they have been corrupted by devil-ish foreign customs. Now that they have learned their error, I would explain more of it – and inform them when and where they can get a copy of my book, for their further education!' He winked, smiled as someone handed him a pot of ale. 'To a good contest between Englishmen, and no hard feelings,' he cried, lifting it. 'God save the Queen.'

Another universal cheer broke out at this. Cries of 'The Queen!' 'Essex!' 'England!'

'Come, sir,' John said.

Once more he was resisted. 'Do you know, John,' said Will, staring around him, his eyes wide, 'I think I have been too long in my closet. There is a mood abroad, is there not?'

'There's drunkenness, certain. Come . . .'

'Nay, something beyond the courage that sack, ale and whisky give.' He looked at John. 'Do you not think it?'

'Perhaps.' As he looked more closely into his friend's eyes, he noted that the melancholy he'd seen in them before had been displaced. There was a fire now – and he knew the fuel that everyone he'd encountered that day would have him feed it. Cecil. The Queen. Burbage. Even Essex, though he had not asked it of him. Each one wishing the man before him to write a different play than the one he'd been brooding on. So he said, gently, so as not to startle, 'Then, William, is it not time to address that mood? Something engaging?' He started to hum. 'Methinks I hear the Te Deums sung at Agin Court.'

His friend stared, then turned away with a softly spoken, 'Perhaps I hear them too.'

And in that moment, with those quiet words, John knew he had lost his friend. They walked together, up to the Ludgate, through it into the City. But they did not speak, and parted with scarce a murmur, John to Southwark to retrieve his son, Shakespeare to his lodgings to . . .

Well. As he crossed the bridge, John smiled. He could sense that Will would sleep little now, for he was again about it. While he himself would happily lay claim to influencing his friend, if ever he was asked. Perhaps he had.

When he passed through the archway of the gatehouse and into Southwark proper, he paused. It was past midnight, but taverns were still full, revellers moving between them and Bankside's other attractions. All would be crammed till dawn, when Ash Wednesday ushered in Lent and a month of sobriety for most. But, John realised, he was ahead of them – for he was sober now. Threats of death – the first in a tavern in Wapping that morning; the last, he hoped, in the recent clash between rapiers and backswords on Fleet Street – had finally cleared his head. He needed sleep, certain. But now he knew he could achieve it without the necessary oblivion that whisky brought. Knew it because, at last, he had a little hope.

To reach the Cardinal Cap Inn and his son, he had to pass the building site of the Globe. They had only just broken ground, yet already the timber frames for walls were rising, scaffolding shrouding the whole. The game's afoot, he said to himself, smiling as he passed it. The game is afoot.

XIV

'Cry Harry'

29 August 1599

As the hum of sackbuts and tabors faded, the drums beat out one last martial rhythm before yielding to a single bugle. Two notes, high and low, alternated. It was a call to hunt. Indeed later Burbage would cry 'the game's afoot' and compare his comrades to greyhounds in the slips. Well, if there was some grey around his muzzle and he had waited behind curtains like this uncountable times, John could still feel his heart quicken.

'Here I go,' he thought, and licked dry lips.

Gus Phillips strode out to some applause. 'O for a muse of fire,' he declared, 'that would ascend the brightest heaven of invention.'

Leashes were slipped. They were off. He took a deep breath. It had been a while. Two years . . . almost to the day, he reckoned, since the punch that felled Will Kemp. But the clown was gone now, quitting the Chamberlain's Men even as they moved into their new premises, his antics both off stage and on finally too much for his fellow players.

Before the curtain, the Chorus was speaking of planting proud hooves; behind it, John considered the roles he'd inherited from flux-stricken Sam Gisburne, after his sobriety and modest behaviour had impressed all. Not too taxing for a return after a fair absence – one bishop, one traitor and one French lord – together with his body in the fights on both sides. Since he had set these, he was confident he could remember them. His lines, though . . .

He licked his lips again – God's teeth, it was becoming a habit!

– and looked to see one coming towards him who must have sensed his concern and swooped, like a red kite falling on offal. 'Do not worry, Father,' said Ned Lawley, all mock solemn. 'The groundlings may forgive the memory of so old a man.' He grinned. 'Just try not to trip over your skirts as you enter.'

John gripped the fingers held out to him and twisted them, eliciting a yelp. 'Respect for the aged, boy,' he growled, then pulled his son into a brief clasp before moving past and joining the Archbishop before the curtained entrance.

'Ready, John?' enquired the appropriately named Master Pope.

'As I'll ever be, Thom.'

'Then let us to it.'

To pipes wheezing the approximation of a Te Deum, John Lawley walked out for the first time on to the platform of the Globe. Once upon it, fears were dispelled by the familiarity of the situation. In truth, he had little enough to do and did it fine; free, for the most part, to stand at the back in an attitude of attention, and study the house as he had not before. As an actor.

What a playhouse! The first that ever was built, under the players' strict supervision, for themselves. Tiers of galleries rose before and around the platform, with noblemen or the richer of the gentry in boxes closest to the stage. Their inferiors, those who could or would not pay the extra penny for a seat, stood in the yard, their eyes level with the players' feet. Yet these groundlings had as good a view as their betters, could as well take in the gorgeous surroundings. John had stood out there with them, been as dazzled, smiling as he thought of his friend Will, who was thought to possess the first penny he'd ever earned, parting with many to create this wonder. The pillars that supported the roof over the stage were beautifully faux-marbled, Corinthian-crowned in glittering gilt, while every gallery was fronted in polished wood and, on their lowest levels, had bronzed statues supporting the ones above. The purpose was to create wonder, to open the spectator's mind to the possibilities of magic, then to focus his imagination on the plain wooden scaffold which, except for the odd statue, stool or chest, rarely had anything upon it but men and boys, sumptuously clad, their clothes all the brighter for the simplicity of the setting. Everything was shaped to these ends: to transport the audience to higher realms and foreign lands, to send them out at play's end entranced and, especially, to make them eager to return and part with more coin on the morrow.

Yet all is mere gilding, John thought. For at bottom, what are they truly here for? Words. Ink once on the playwright's pen, transformed to energy and thence delight through skilled men's mouths. John had little doubt that the audience was being so transported, just as he had been from the first time he'd watched the players in an inn yard in Much Wenlock; finding himself not in Shropshire, but in Athens as both blind Oedipus and himself did weep.

He looked out – and frowned. Not so much because the house was scarce a third full. The Globe was built to hold three thousand, so even such a proportion meant takings of seven pounds, not too bad for a hot August day. No, it was more the faces. These did not accord with his thoughts. They did not look transported. They looked . . . sullen.

He glanced at his fellows. Burbage was talking balls – the Dauphin's tennis ones, transformed to gun stones. Yet he was not speaking with his customary subtlety, was trying to force a passion he appeared not to feel.

The scene ended. The court swept off, with Thom Pope muttering as he passed, 'I told them this one was played out. But would they heed me?'

Swiftly exchanging the robes of priesthood for the livery of the traitor, Scroop, John kept an ear on the stage. For Ned was upon it, in his largest role so far, and the first one not in a dress. He was playing the Boy, apprentice to the rogues, a cherubic contrast to the cauliflower-nosed Bardolph. And from the laughter, it appeared he was playing the opposite well. John was happy – and, he admitted, a little envious. The boy inherited his comic skills from him, after all. He wished any of his roles contained even one laugh. Perhaps there was something he could do with Scroop. 'Scroop . . . stoop,' he muttered. Strapping on his sword, he entered with his fellow conspirators.

Treason and dispatch! This was better, for Londoners were attuned to whispers of conspiracy, especially that summer; all knew the Queen was under constant threat of assassination. So when their plot was uncovered and they were condemned by the King, John got some hisses for his craven pleading and one laugh as he was bundled into the trapdoor after his fellows – and his stiff leg got stuck. Pleased, he descended into Hell, as the understage was known, and scuttled between the columns that supported the stage above. He had a little while before his next incarnation as Lord Rambures, and only a fleur-de-lis surplice to throw over his armour in exchange for the cross of St George. Meantime, Ned's largest speech was coming and John wished to hear if his advice for its delivery had been heeded.

Emerging from Hell into the storage space behind it, John wove between a cornucopia of costumes and props from other plays. All that was necessary to the day was above at the level of the stage, so here he saw Roman shields and swords, Bottom's ass head, clothes on hook and hanger. Pausing at a rack to finger a maroon velvet doublet he recognised, he chuckled. His friend had once lent him Don Pedro's guise when he was wet. Perhaps he would let him wear it correctly one day if they revived *Much Ado* – and he continued both in sobriety and in the company's good graces, of course.

'I was unaware, Master Lawley, that I had written the character of the conspirator Scroop with a limp.' The voice came sternly from right behind the doublet. 'While I am also certain that Gisburne does not avail himself of one.'

John parted the costumes, revealing a cramped alcove, a lantern lighting papers a-muddle on a table. Behind it sat William Shakespeare. His quill was poised above parchment and in alignment with his nose, making the shaft of a T that his raised eyebrows completed across the high dome of his forehead.

'Limp?' repeated John innocently, stepping between the dangling clothes. 'Oh, you mean the wound I took at Zutphen?' He bent, rubbed at one knee. 'It plagues me sometimes, Will.'

'Strange.' The playwright scratched between his brows with the feathery end. 'For I have never noted it upon the street, and yet there, upon the stage, it was . . . pronounced. Clump, clump, clump. It echoed back here. I thought my new theatre was ready to fall about my ears.' He sighed. 'How goes it out there?'

'With me?'

'I know how it goes with you, John. Clump, clump, clump. The words "duck" and "water" come to mind.' He shook his head. 'I was referring to the whole piece, not your expanded part within it.'

'Ah.' John found a small unoccupied corner of desk to set a buttock on. ''Tis barely a third full and the crowd . . . restless, I would say.'

'Restless? Aye, the citizens of London have not had much rest of late. And this play that once so distracted them from their woes now worries them, like a burr under a saddle cloth. They take . . . *different* things from it now.'

John studied his friend. He had not seen that much of him, despite his daily attendance at the theatre. Will was in a fever of writing, squirrelled away at his new lodgings near the Clink gaol. He played only rarely and if he must, hiding between scenes, quill in hand, scratching. His fingers were as ever ink-stained, his brow ploughed with new furrows. Careworn, thought John, and regretted briefly any lines he might have added. Though in truth, when he had suggested a theme that would please the Queen – a play to suit the martial times and help inspire an army for Essex – the playwright had needed little persuasion. Such a piece was already half in his mind, he'd said, and the famous story of Henry the Fifth had brought crowds to the old Curtain playhouse in April and, even more importantly, to the new Globe when it opened in July. The crowds had cheered it, just as they had cheered the noble earl when he set out from London for the Irish wars.

It was as if Will read his thoughts. 'I've excised it, you know. That speech. You will not hear it played this day.'

John nodded. Her majesty was known for her meddling across the affairs of the realm. When it was seen that her wish was being acted upon, a further note came from the palace requesting that Master Shakespeare set down some few words in his play that spoke directly to the situation. Reluctantly Will had inserted the lines, some of which he'd taken from the earl's own lips that night at Whitehall in the palace yard:

Were now the General of our gracious Empress
As in good time he may – from Ireland coming
Bringing rebellion broach'd on his sword . . .

It had gotten cheers in April. In August it got jeers – and flung fruit. 'Wise, I think,' John murmured.

'Tell me,' Will continued, in a lower voice, 'for I have been distracted. What news from Ireland?'

'There is never news from Ireland.' John's voice lowered to match his friend's. 'Cecil has forbidden news on pain of imprisonment, unless he issues it. But there is always its companion, rumour. Whispers on the street.'

'Then tell me those. For you know 'tis my delight to give those whispers echo on my stage.'

Both men glanced around, then John leaned nearer. 'Tess has had a letter from her –' he shuddered – 'affianced. Combined with what I have heard in taverns from some returning soldiers . . . it does not go well for my lord in Ireland.'

'Then your whispers agree with mine. Gus Phillips has a brother there – and a letter arrived only yesterday saying that the earl has at last acceded to the Queen's commandment and marched north from Dublin to confront the rebel Tyrone.'

John nodded – and once more gave silent thanks to God or the Devil for sending astray every messenger that Essex had sent in search of him. He had made himself most hard to find in the dank boltholes of Southwark; waiting it out till the earl's butterfly attention alighted elsewhere. He had also sent one note, telling Essex that as soon as his recurrent fever passed – a fever, he gently reminded, that he had contracted during his time in a Spanish gaol, after saving his lordship's life in Cadiz – he would hasten to join him, bringing men and weapons. No reply had found him; and he had stayed indoors when Essex rode to such acclaim from London that late March day, so avoiding the chill he would undoubtedly have contracted when the skies opened over Islington and soaked the bravely marching men and their plumed leader. From what little had been heard from Ireland, his subterfuge appeared a better choice each day.

'It seems a hopeless task,' Will continued, once more voicing John's thoughts, 'for rumour also whispers that his own are less than half the Irish forces, with half of those diseased.'

'He should be happy then,' John grunted. 'With those odds he will have to win as famous a victory as Harry did at Agin Court.'

As he spoke, a great shout came, and the clumping of many boots. A deep voice boomed. He listened to Burbage's exhortations breachward. Teeth were being set, nostrils stretched wide. He stood. 'I should go. Ned's speech comes.'

'He grows by the hour, your Ned. I think his bent is more for comedy. As we shall see tomorrow.' Will smiled. 'Does he like the role I have created for him?'

'The wanton country lass? I think he relishes it. Though being raised entirely in Southwark, he needed to be informed both of their accent and of their . . . somewhat different ways.'

'And from your vast experience of these, you duly informed him? Good.' Will nodded. 'Well, I hope that *As You Like It* delights as Harry Five no longer does.'

'Nothing for me in it, though?'

Will smiled. 'Small steps, John. You have shown restraint of late and served us well. The fights continue to thrill, at least . . .'

'Thank ye.'

'. . . but certain of the sharers remain to be convinced of your conversion. Let *As You* pass.' He gestured to the papers before him. 'There may be something here for you, though. We will need strong men.'

'Another tragedy?'

'Tragedy and history both. I attempt a life . . . and attempt the life . . . of Caesar. Though truly it is more a portrait of his assassins.'

John had taken a step away. Now he stepped back. 'Caesar? Conspiracy and murder? Coup and counter? Is that wise with what is happening out there?'

'I write it *because* of what is happening out there.' Shakespeare's eyes gleamed. 'You know what we do, John. Our company is different because we do not give the people only food for their stomachs. We feed their minds too. Since they cannot talk of news upon the streets for fear of spies and inquisitors, they can hear it talked of here, within this wooden O. They see Caesar's fall, Rome's state shaken, while outside they witness each day soldiers in arms upon the streets of London, the unceasing threats to our sovereign and *her* state. Their unrelieved thoughts swell into a boil' – he jabbed with his quill – 'and I lance it. I do not suggest a cure. But at least I attend to the symptoms.'

Above, Burbage was building to a shout. 'So, Physician,' John said, 'who is the hero of the piece, as Henry is of this? Caesar or Brutus? Monarch or rebel?'

'Neither.' Shakespeare shrugged. 'For the whispers on the street also tell me this: these days people are believing less and less . . . in heroes.' He rose. 'Come. I must into the garb of the King of France. What follows for you? 'Tis Rambures, yes?' He clapped a hand on John's shoulder. 'Does the French lord also have a limp?'

'I thought perhaps a st . . . st . . . stammer,' John replied, his face sober.

'God a mercy! You dragged one of those out for hours in Melton Mowbray! Consider, John. We have a new play to present on the morrow. We would not hear the chimes at midnight.' His smile faded, his voice lowered again. 'I heard another rumour. Or was it speculation? That all those soldiers on the street are not to repulse the Spanish. No one truly believes their Armada will come now. Few believe any more that it was ever intended.'

'Then why has a nation been in arms these long hot months?' John asked. 'Why have yeomen been held from their fields and merchants from their trade?'

'Can you not guess?' Will pulled his friend closer, his voice descending again to a whisper. 'Master Secretary Cecil keeps an army in the field in case his rival Essex should bring his back with him from Ireland. It is not Tyrone's rebellion he truly fears . . . but Robert Devereux's.'

Will released him, moved to the stair, but John remained for a moment, considering. London had indeed been abuzz with the Spanish threat and the forces raised to counter it, citizens mustered by ward or guild to defend the realm. Almost daily reports had the enemy landing, repulsed, marching on the capital, sailing up the Thames. Parchments found on dunghills had Papist assassins lurking in every long shadow, graffiti had Elizabeth dead or fled. But this was not 1588, with a nation rallied. Eleven years later, the Queen did not appear in armour at Tilbury. The populace had grown tired of false war, only to be roused again by another threat that also was not delivered. So while the players above him now told a tale of patriotism, the playwright added stronger spice for a hungry people to feed upon. If the French were thrashed again at Agin Court and a nation cheered, men and boys died horrible deaths while cowards plundered for themselves. Not all was glory, within the wooden O or beyond it.

Shaking his head, John followed Will up the stair and into the tiring house. While his friend donned the robes of the French monarch, he doffed St George's cross and pulled on the fleur-de-lis. While he did, he heard Ned speak his lines – boldly, cheekily, in the accent of the streets he was raised in. He got his laughs. Will was right: the lad's bent was to humour, and he looked forward to seeing him on the morrow once more in a dress, in the new comedy. He would watch from the galleries, pay the extra pennies for the place, two cushions and a bag of cob nuts – to share. For he would have a companion, one he had been as carefully, soberly, wooing over the summer as he had the players. Perhaps he would take her hand as they watched their son. He might even venture so much.

Tess! The thought of her, and how she had agreed to accompany him to the play, focused him. He spoke his remaining few lines stammer-less.

And then he had a sword in his hand.

The man he'd replaced, Sam Gisburne, was a good fighter, one of the more skilled in the company, having served some time in the army. So John had placed him in combat against Burbage, who, though nimble and swift, tended to remember his many lines better than he did his cuts, thrusts and parries.

Now it was John's turn to manage him. And this day the player was also angry – at the poor house, at their inattention. The King came scything in, a great overhead swoosh fit to cleave a skull when he should have gently lunged. Taking the blow on his shield and high to lessen the force, John let the other's blade slide across the wood, before slashing hard at Burbage's face. The player was up the stage and John down, so most of the audience was behind John's back and the blow looked a lot closer than it was. A section gasped . . . and it startled Burbage, no matter that it never truly threatened to mar his beauty. With half a dozen others clattering together and trying to represent the combined might of France and England, the noise was enough for John to hiss, 'My eyes!' and not be heard by any but the man he fought. Burbage did hear, looked, nodded. He was back, John's partner again, each man in each other's eyes as they alternated attack and defence.

He had quickly learned that since the audience was near all round them, below in the pit that lapped the platform and in the boxes above it, it was not possible to disguise all blows. Better to give lustily, to hold back little . . . and to kill with a hard slap of the side of the blunted broadsword straight into the gut. No matter that it was armoured there – a blow, a step in, a sawing blade and his own screaming as he folded over it created the illusion that a chink in the armour had been found. It was always the victim who made the strike look good. And John gave Burbage's victorious final blow its due reverence. The audience gasped as he hit the platform hard, blood spilling from the sheep's bladder he wore beneath. The French fled, dragging dead Rambures with them by his ankles, a red trail left behind. Trumpets announced the triumph of England.

Speeches followed the action. John waited in the tiring house while Henry wooed the French princess, a scene of charm that the audience enjoyed as much as he. So the applause at the end was warmer than had been expected from the play's early reception.

He took his bows, his salute reaching from the topmost gallery to the toe of the lowest groundling, content. He was back among the players. Even if it was only as fight master and substitute, a chink had opened, one he could surely widen. Not only this one, for if this theatre day did not proceed quite as those of old – with pots of ale in carousing company – he had hopes it would end in an inn nonetheless. In the Spoon and Alderman, with his feet just a little further under Tess's oaken table.

XV

As You Like It?

The press was thick when John and Ned exited the Globe, for their own lingering audience was immediately swelled by that of the nearby Rose. Excited chatter filled the air as the two crowds met and compared experiences. John, taller by a head than most there, was able to see to the doors of the other playhouse, noting that a larger audience than their own was spilling forth. 'What played there, sir?' he asked of a prosperous-looking gentleman in an emerald velvet doublet, an equally well-clad lady on his arm.

'*The Shoemaker's Holiday*,' came the reply, accompanied by a loud guffaw. 'Man, Alleyn had the crowd in a roar from his very first words. Have you come from the Globe?' On John's nod, the man continued, 'What piece?'

'*Henry the Fifth*.'

The man grimaced. 'Ach, I've seen it. 'Tis tired, sir, tired. I'm for a comedy, and the Admiral's Men play them superbly.'

'We play a new comedy tomorrow, sir. The ink scarce dry from Master Shakespeare's quill.' Ned produced a playbill from the stack in his satchel. All the players had them, for distribution that night and on the morrow.

The man took it, his wife studying over his shoulder. '*As You Like It*,' she read. 'Is it amusing?' she asked.

'Oh aye, ma'am,' replied Ned. 'A hilarious tale of a country girl who spurns her clod suitor because she is in love with a court-trained clown.'

John smiled. Ned's role in the piece was minor. But he

remembered how he'd once described *Medea* from the point of view of his personation of the second sentry.

'And you play, do you, boy?' the lady asked.

'Aye, mum,' said Ned, dropping into a courtesy, speaking on in a rural voice, eyelids fluttering. 'Oy be the maid, see.'

'Oh, Geoffrey, let us to it. It sounds charming.'

Man and wife melded into the crowd. 'I wonder if Master Shakespeare knows how his whole plot revolves around Audrey the milkmaid,' John said.

Ned grinned. 'Oh, I am sure he'll realise when he sees me perform it.'

They moved on, seeking. Both were hungry, and they were assailed on all sides by higglers, some behind carts, others with trays. They could choose from a great variety of beasts – finned, furred, feathered – prepared in dozens of ways. It being September, there was an abundance from the fields and little of it would be salted – they would have enough of that in the winter to come. Ned was keen on poultry, but that was richer than John's purse. So he sought out a familiar stall where the humble pie was made from only the freshest deer entrails, and the seasonings rich in nutmeg. One apiece, followed by a hunk of crumbly cheese and an Orange Pippin, sent down with a mug of cider, did the trick.

'Well, Father,' said Ned, licking his fingers clean, 'shall we to the birds?'

John shook his head. He was as fond of cock fighting as his son. But his purse would certainly not stand any wagers, and besides, he had his responsibilities – and his instructions. 'Nay, lad,' he said, 'for you know the conditions your mother imposed on your continuing at the theatre. They include your early return home and no dalliance.' He laughed at his son's frown, pulled him from the ground by his collar. 'Besides, do you not still need to study your role for the morrow?'

'I learned that in less than half an hour,' Ned snorted. 'I would they gave me something more to prove my mettle.'

'From what Master Shakespeare has told me, he has such an advance in mind.' John pushed his son back into the crowd. 'They are pleased with you, lad.'

'Aye. I only hope . . .' He broke off, chewed his lip.

'Hope?'

'You talked of my mother's conditions. She still sees my time with the players as short-lived. As soon as Sir Samuel returns from war . . .'

He again left his sentence unfinished. Both knew what that return could mean. 'Would it be so bad then, to be a squire's stepson?'

John asked the question softly. He had long ago learned with Ned that if he tried to persuade him to one course he would straightway choose the other. Obstinate as an ass, his son, and he had an idea where he got that from – his mother! So he had not spoken out against Despair once during the summer. He had simply let his son fall fully in love with playing.

As he had. 'What? To get all my excitements from chasing dumb creatures across a field? To live in' – he shuddered – 'Finchley!' Ned looked around at the thronging, raucous street. 'Southwark is the only home I've ever known. And my future is with the Chamberlain's Men.' He turned and gripped John's arm. 'I cannot leave that, Father. You must see to it.'

He placed his hand over his son's. 'I shall try,' he replied. 'There is still time. Irish wars drag on. And war itself brings dangers – even to fat knights who hide their bulk behind others and try to avoid them.'

His grin was not matched by Ned's. 'I do not know, Father. The time may be closing. My mother had another letter.'

John slowed his stride. The Spoon and Alderman was in sight, the spire of St Mary Overies rising behind and as if from it. 'What news?'

Ned halted, looked around. No one stood near. He had learned, as everyone on London's streets had that summer, to keep his voice low. Men had disappeared who voiced rumour as news too loudly. Boys too. 'Sir Samuel says little . . . save that he may soon be home. For it appears that the Vice-Regent has brought the rebel to a reckoning.'

John frowned. Whispers of a battle would have been on the streets, and all Cecil's spies would not have been able to contain them. 'What sort of reckoning?' he asked, his voice as low as his son's.

'A meeting. Tyrone has submitted, kissed the royal ring. A truce has been negotiated.'

'Truce?' John frowned. A truce was not submission. A truce was a

149

parley between equals who both had reasons not to fight for a while. It did not sort with the rumours that had come – of an English army chasing through bog and forest an enemy who would not stand and fight but just kept building its own strength while its opponent's wasted. And it did not sort with Essex, who would hurl himself unarmoured into a hundred foes if he could win glory that way. He had been sent there not to negotiate with traitors but to bring back 'rebellion broached on his sword' – words Will had been wise to cut from the play they performed that day.

Something was amiss in Ireland. John did not truly care what. Others' kingdoms could go hang. He had already sacrificed enough for them. All that concerned him now were his own – his son before him and the woman he loved. If truce meant Essex's return, it was bad enough news, for he would be held to some sort of account for his absence. But Sir Samuel returning to claim his bride was far, far worse. He had not endured the thirstiest summer in a dozen years only to lose the prize.

'Come, lad,' he said, 'I must talk with your mother.'

But then he did not move. There was a low tavern immediately to his left, the Larkspur, as filthy as the Spoon was clean. He'd frequented it often in the past. The thought came sudden, and hard: he could send Ned ahead, go in and have one whisky. Only weak ale and small beer had washed out his mouth since Shrove Tuesday. He licked his lips. One, then. One would sharpen his wits for the interview that lay before him.

'Father?'

He looked down. Why was his son looking at him that way?

'To Mother's?' Ned asked.

'Yes. Yes, come on,' he muttered, stepping forward again. The first steps though were strangely hard, as if his ankles were held in shackles.

They took the alley down to the rear of the inn, the tumult of the street reduced to a hum. Before them to the south lay fields, stretching away to distant hills whose ridges were dotted with windmills. Every yard of the land was cultivated, and in this late summertime, fecund with crops. Women moved along the rows, gleaning leaves for the sallets that most, save for the very rich, would eat. Others collected cabbages, beetroot and cucumbers – it was the pickling time, the strong savour of vinegar or verjus in each man's nostrils. The sight was calm contrast to the streets they'd left. John sighed. He had grown up in fields like this. It was . . . unexciting. Was that what he needed?

'Father?' Ned had extracted the key from its hidden place in the crevice between bricks. 'Shall I?' he said, pointing the metal at the door.

John took a breath. It was all the bracing he would get. He nodded.

Ned turned the key, opened the door. John saw into the garden, the ordered contrast to the sprawling exuberance behind him. Standing in the middle was Tess, a basket of vegetables before her. She was wearing her pickling frock.

She smiled. 'Welcome,' she said.

They entered. Ned replaced the key outside, locked the door again with another within. 'How went the play?' she asked.

'Well enough,' the two Lawleys answered as one. Ned ran to her, gave her a hug, which seemed to surprise her. 'Greengage?' she said. She pulled two from the basket, threw one across to John. Ned took his, ran for the inn's back door. 'Off so quickly?' she called.

'I have my role to work on,' he replied, taking the stairs two at a time. 'Father,' he called back, 'I'll see you at the play tomorrow?'

'That you will. 'Tis a promise,' John replied.

A nod, and their son was gone. 'He is in a hurry.' Tess raised a hand to pull a curl of tawny hair off her forehead. 'To get somewhere – or to leave us alone, would you say?'

John did not reply. Instead, he looked at the greengage, a bloom like fairy dust upon it. He wiped it on his doublet, bit into the soft flesh. It was as sweet as its promise. It wasn't whisky, but it would have to do. 'He cons other roles as well as his own,' John said, separating flesh from stone with his teeth. 'He hopes, like many do, that the actor above him will break something so he can step in. He would be Juliet, ready to encounter her Romeo.'

Tess stooped, picked up one of several baskets that lay at her feet, each crammed with produce from her garden. 'The players will not revive that, surely?'

'Why not?

'It is hardly in keeping with the times.'

'Surely a tale of such love, begun with a single look, is timeless?' She had reached for another basket. 'Here. Let me.' He gathered the three there, threading his arms through the wicker handles. 'The brewhouse?'

'Aye.' She nodded, headed towards the huts behind the inn.

He followed. 'You did not answer me.'

'On a tale of timeless love? No, I did not.'

'Why?'

'You know why.' She glanced back at him, one thin eyebrow arched. 'Really, John, you were not wont to be so brazen.'

'I know not what you mean.'

She snorted. It was almost the exact sound Ned would make, rich in scorn. 'Nor such a poor dissembler.'

At least his look of hurt made her laugh. She turned away, pushed the brewhouse door open. Damp warmth filled his face as she led him past the tuns where new brews fermented beside the casks of the near ready. Ducking through hanging wreaths of drying hops, they came to other barrels. The sharp tang of vinegar cut through the malty fug.

He put down his load, resumed his quest. 'Why do you suspect my words?'

'Because there is design in them.'

'Design?' he queried, eyes wide. 'What design?'

She looked straight at him. 'You try to woo me anew, with memories of that first wooing, of a more innocent time. As if it could erase the memories of all the years that followed.'

Those years were not when he wanted to dwell. It was time for a new tactic, one that had worked, on a few glorious occasions, before. 'Innocence is hardly what I remember of those times,' he said softly.

'Nor I.' She smiled. 'Though before I first saw you, I considered myself innocent enough.'

Her tone of voice! The laugh had returned to it. A better course, sure – though there were rocks here he could easily still founder on. Gently, he thought, then said, 'Is it only in my memory that the first look wrought such devastation?'

'You know it is not.' She shook her head. 'Love at first sight only becomes a problem when it is reciprocal.'

'As ours was.'

152

She hesitated before replying. 'As ours was.'

She sighed, then bent to the baskets, removing cucumbers, laying them on the table. Carefully, he thought. There's hope in that sigh. 'What did you say the French called it, Tess? It was not a phrase I'd heard before. Nor felt, certain.'

'*Coup de foudre*,' she said, still bent, not looking up. But she had stopped sorting.

'That was it. A strike of lightning,' he murmured. 'We were scorched by it, were we not?'

'Scorched. Yes.' She unstooped now, looked at him, then above him. 'I had not known desire till then. Had not been armed to deal with it, beyond precepts and counsels, just so many cold words.'

'I remember few words, for I was struck dumb. I remember following you to the river bank. I remember . . . taking your hand there.'

'Another lightning blast. Have not the alchemists dreamed of harnessing the bolt's power to transform one metal to another?' She laughed. 'It changed me, certainly.'

Her voice had lowered still further. He wanted to reach out to her again, see if his touch still possessed that lightning. But he had worked slowly all summer to get her here, to slip past the strictures, slide beyond the ring she wore. He must not rush it now. 'I did not know I had such an effect. I never had before. There had been women . . .'

An eyebrow raised. 'Many women.'

'Not so many.' He rushed to cover his error. 'None that transformed me as you did.' He stepped a little closer to her. 'And I knew I'd discovered in a moment what those alchemists had searched for through centuries.'

She did not move away. 'And what was that?'

'The philosopher's stone. The quintessence of life itself. Not in what each made. In what we made together.'

Their faces were close enough now for him to take in all that he had not, in an age – the meadow green of her eyes, an exact shade, streaked through with swirls of copper; the scent of her, cutting through the fug in the hut, reminding him of riverbanks, of clean flowing water. The grass he'd laid her on, the bulrushes that had hidden them.

'Well, sir,' she said, not withdrawing, only that one eyebrow lifted a little higher, the husk fully restored to her voice. 'I thought your friend Will held the patent on such poetry. Now I see that he borrows all from you.'

'Nay, I am blunt for all that. Sharp only in this one thing – my love for you.'

It was the time. Leaning closer, he kissed her.

She did not resist him. Yielded as she'd always done, once she decided – completely as she had that first time, as she had perhaps half a dozen times since over the years between. She was dressed for the tavern, not the court, and no farthingales pressed against him, preventing his body reaching hers. They were locked from lips to toes, and in the middle he felt the instant surge he always did with her, that had been diminished not a jot by time.

She felt it too, gave back, till she could no more. 'No, John, no,' she whispered. But she did not push him away with more than words.

'And you claim that *Romeo and Juliet* will not still play,' he said, his voice as low as hers. He'd pulled back a fraction to say it – and realised his mistake. He'd brought in the outside world again – especially the playhouse – and it was between them in an instant.

'No, John, no,' she said again, differently, as firm as the hand that was suddenly in his chest, pushing him back. 'We must not.'

He reached, as a drowning man will reach. 'Tess, why . . . ?'

'Why?' She slipped from between his arms, stepped away, smoothing down her dress, reaching up to that tress of hair come astray, returning it to its prison. 'You have heard, haven't you? 'Tis why you are so bold now. Desperate, rather. For the wars are over.'

He felt anger replace his forestalled lust, tried to damp it down. 'The wars are not over, Tess. Paused. That's all a truce is.'

'Truce?' Her eyes narrowed. 'Ned told you of my letter, did he not?'

'He did not,' he lied. He did not want his spy exposed. 'The rumour is upon the street.' He went on, overriding her interruption, 'And soldiers do not leave at a truce. They hammer out their armour, sharpen their blades and wait for combat to recommence.'

'Nevertheless.' She had stepped closer again, not with desire, but to search his eyes. 'You fear that a truce might send some home, do you not? My fiancé, for instance. That is why you are so bold.'

'I thought my boldness was my charm.' His smile did not move her, and he continued in a different, humbler tone, 'If I am bold, it is only that I believe I have some hope. I am back with the players' – a half-truth, but one he could build on – 'and I have been moderate the summer long. I have . . .'

He trailed off under her gaze. It had changed, from accusation to something else. He was terrified that he saw pity there – his observation immediately confirmed. 'Oh John,' she said, 'I have been delighted in your . . . rehabilitation. It has lasted longer . . .' She paused, continued, '. . . lasted a long time. And Ned has so enjoyed your company all summer. I am sorry, though, if my delight has been misinterpreted as anything more . . .' She shook her head. 'No. My troth is plighted to Sir Samuel. And whether he comes home soon, or afterwards, I will await him. For I gave him my word.'

He stared at her, sought some giving in the firmness he'd always known in her. He could see none. That anger pulsed again. 'And what was this?' He gestured to the table. 'I know what I feel. I know you feel the same.'

'Oh John,' she said again, then laughed. 'You will always have an alchemist's power over me. It is not something I can defend against . . . except in this' – she raised her hand, and Despair's ring gleamed faintly – 'and in the knowledge that the life your lightning ripped me from, I may have again.' She glanced around. 'Yet I must take care and not let myself be alone with you. For it seems my flesh is still . . . transmutable.'

She said this last as she crossed to the door. Swinging it wide, she gestured him outside. He went slowly to her, past her. He thought of all the things he could have said, and had not said. Of all the weapons he had not yet unsheathed. But he, the master of so many, had none to reach for under her firm stare.

He crossed to the garden's gate. 'You will still accompany me tomorrow to see our son perform?' he said, over his shoulder.

She smiled. 'Of course. We promised Ned, did we not? His parents together, cheering him on. He has been disappointed in so much in his life; he will not be in . . . in that.' She faltered at the reproof in her words, continued more gently. 'Come for me at eleven.'

'I will.'

He turned the key. 'Can I not offer you an ale within?' she called.

He did not answer her, just waved, opened the door, exited. He could not sit in her tavern and drink her beer, however good it was. He needed another place. He craved a different drink.

XVI

Lost

The Larkspur was nearest and of a dark dinginess to match his mood. It was in part a brothel, stairs leading to upper rooms with cots; even on the ground floor there were alcoves that curtains could be pulled across to conceal acts that did not warrant a tedious climb nor many minutes. Several of these were drawn, but fortunately the tavern was crowded enough that its noise dulled all others. He did not need to hear lust being slaked, however tawdry the transaction.

At the trestle before the casks, he hesitated. He knew what he wanted, and the urge to purchase a bottle of aqua vitae, and drink it all himself, near overpowered him. He wrestled with that for a full minute as the landlord served others. When the man returned, John slapped down a mill sixpence for a tankard of the double double – a compromise; it was the strongest ale they served. Praising himself for his restraint, he turned, spied a stool in a corner being vacated. The apprentice who had just lowered himself on to it relinquished it without a murmur. Perhaps it was on seeing John's eyes.

He drank off half the tankard at a clip, felt its effects almost immediately. It was the most potent thing he'd had all summer. He would have to be careful. Double double ale was not whisky. Yet it could weaken him enough to put him on the path to his true desire.

His true desire? What had small beer and sobriety achieved for him since Shrove Tuesday? A limping lord upon the platform, a few fights arranged, both of which had given him enough coin for ale, humble pie and little else. It had not given him what he truly sought – a troth plight sundered, another joined, with him again and forever in his sweet Tess's bed.

He took another swig. Plague on the bed, he thought. I'd have had her against the table and that's a fact. He could still feel her body pressed to his at every point that mattered. He could feel her heat responding to his. And then it had been dampened, suddenly, cruelly, by her scruples. Dampened, but not extinguished he had felt, seen, known.

He eyed the whores moving between the tables, saw the late rival for his stool, the apprentice, stumbling upstairs in pursuit of one. They were a mangy lot, the Larkspur a mangy dive. Yet strong ale tended to beautify even the most staled of punks. He would have to be twice careful.

The bottom of the tankard had mysteriously been reached. He knew what he wanted next; knew also that his purse, short a sixpence now, would no longer bear the cost. Well, there were other ways to obtain his desire. He could entertain with a yarn. He could recite a string of soliloquies; he could threaten. He was practised in these ways and others. What I should do, he thought, is retire to my straw. Perhaps accompanied by the tawny-haired drab across the tavern who was giving him the eye and who reminded him of someone he couldn't quite recall. She would be cheaper than whisky.

He became aware of a pot boy standing before his table. John thought he must want the vessel and shoved it across towards him. But the boy did not take it. Instead, he put something down.

It was a glass, unusual in the Larkspur, where glass was more likely to be thrown than drunk from. More unusual still, it was filled with a liquid that sparkled in the rush torchlight and whose scent wafted to his nostrils.

Sweeter than any perfume of Araby. Sweeter even than a woman who smells of bulrushes on a summer riverbank. For there was nothing sweeter than the water of life.

'The lady sent it ya,' the boy said.

'Lady?' John looked around the room. 'What lady?'

'In the alcove there. Proper one she is. Smells somethin' lovely.' The boy sniffed, wiped a flowing nose. 'Asks if you'd care to join her.'

John followed the boy's finger. The alcove he pointed to had lately been occupied by three raucous seamen and two whores. But its curtain was now drawn and only silence came from it.

John rose, picked up the glass and carefully threaded through the mob across the tavern floor, spilling not a drop. When he stood before the curtain, he bent close and said, 'I am here. What do you want of me?'

The voice came low, but strong. 'Enter, sir, and we shall see.'

He pulled the curtain back. At the table sat a lady, alone. And the pot boy was right – she did smell something lovely. Smelled just as she had before when he'd seen her in the Queen's company and, he now shockingly realised, leaving the astrologer's. She smelled of cloves.

He remembered the scent. But he had not appreciated how pretty she was. 'Your health, ma'am,' he said and, draining the glass, let the curtain fall behind him.

It was cruel, the awakening, as they often were. On a sustained debauch, like the month's he'd undertaken before Shrove Tuesday, the pain felt at each dawn – or noon, or evening, whenever he'd happen to awaken – would be less and could be lessened further with immediate reapplication of what had caused it. It was John's first thought on waking; and, trying to keep his movements to a minimum, he groped around him for glass or leather, any vessel that might contain relief. His hand found none, but something else. Something that moaned when probed further.

He sat up swiftly, almost crying out for the jab that sent through his head. Whoever was beside him gave another whimper, then fell silent. Carefully he reached for the blanket that covered them both, lifted a corner . . .

He knew her before he saw her. Knew by the scent that rose, muddled though it was with others now. The realisation came with his first clear thought – that like many things that appeal at night, the scent of cloves was distinctly less pleasant in the morning.

He pulled the cover off her. Eyes so brown they were almost black – and all the blacker for the contrast with the unbound golden hair that fell to her shoulders – were fixed upon him. 'Good morning, my lover,' the Queen's maid said.

'Is it morning?' he muttered, then realised it had to be. No candlelight flickered over them. He was studying her by what passed the shutters, stripes of light over them, falling only on skin, for both of them were naked.

As his eyes took her in, she stretched, arms back, head up, the long hair falling behind, her breasts thrust forward. Her nipples were large and hard and he could not help noticing that the skin around them was chafed, with what appeared to be scratch marks running towards each. She noticed his gaze, cupped her breasts, pressed them together. 'Do you see what you did to me last night? You were cruel, sir, most cruel.'

He swallowed. 'I am sorry, I . . .'

'Did I say I minded?' She laughed, almost a musical sound, like someone running up and down a scale on a viola. 'In fact, I think the reverse is true. I think, indeed, I recall encouraging you in your cruelty.' She let fall her breasts and, putting a hand between her legs, gave a groan. 'You were most animal-like, sir. Had it been a while?'

It had, but it was not something he would discuss. 'Again, I apologise.'

'Again . . . do you hear me complain?' She laughed, as musically, then dropped down upon the bed. Propping her head on one hand, she smiled up at him. 'Forsooth, I was most pleasantly surprised in you. Most Englishmen, especially sots, are swift in action – if indeed they can be roused to it – and soon spent. Here' – she snapped her finger – 'gone! But you' – she reached up and ran a painted nail down his bicep – 'though as drunk as any man I have seen, you still contrived to take your time. I wonder how you managed it?'

A flash came – of another country, another scent. Another woman. La Contessa Lucrezia. Sable hair to this one's fair, blue eyes to her black. 'I lived awhile in Bologna,' he mumbled. 'They . . . manage things differently there.'

'Ah, an Italian education. It explains much.'

Fingers came together and pinched. He withdrew his arm, stared at her a long moment, then shook his head – which he instantly regretted. Carefully, he looked around. The room was small, barely furnished, undecorated. He had no idea where he was. He had vague memories of walking, and water; of leaning upon a woman he soon lay upon and beneath.

He spotted bottles on the floor, reached for them. The first smelled temptingly of what it had contained, yet yielded but a drop.

160

The second was near full, but further disappointment came when he found it contained only water. He rarely drank it. Yet with his mouth a desert and his brain an anvil in use, he did not restrain himself.

'Heya,' came her call, 'save a little for me.'

He passed her the bottle. When she took it, he fell back on to the bed beside her. 'Christ's bones,' he moaned, wrist over his eyes.

'Amen,' she said, laying the bottle aside, descending to rest her arms upon his chest.

He squinted up. 'Why . . . why am I here?'

'Why?' She smiled. 'You are taking pleasure here, are you not?'

'And you? Are you here for the same reason?'

'Undoubtedly. You are a lusty lover for one so old. And I like it when men take such joy in what I offer them. However,' she sighed, 'I am here for business, too.'

'Business?' His soggy mind would not let him quite take this in. 'I fear I have little to pay you with.'

'Not that sort of business, you fool. Do I talk or act like a drab?' Her voice had sharpened, her eyes narrowing. Then both relaxed. 'No, my business is different, even if perhaps it shares some . . . superficial similarities.' She smiled. 'My business is information.'

'I see.' His mind, though still wrapped in fire, was at least allowing him to think again. 'And you are paid for this information by . . . Sir Robert Cecil.'

'He is my principal employer. Not my sole one.'

'And did you' – he glanced around the room – 'earn your wages last night?'

'Perhaps. You were very talkative. About oh so many things. A few of interest to my employer. Most not. Talkative . . . and then just active. Oh so active.' She laughed again, stretched.

He could not help his smile. 'I am glad to have been of service, lady.'

'Well, you were, in some areas.' She looked down at her breasts, hovering a hand's breadth from his face. 'And you weren't in others. I tried to get you to address my concerns, but you would keep harping back to your own.' She shook her head. 'I now know much about the coldness and cruelty of one Tess. And I know far more than I care to of the lack of abilities and the deep well of envy of certain players.' She mimed a yawn. 'Yet I know little of what I

161

truly want to learn.' She reached down, and grabbed him firmly enough around his cods to make him gasp. 'Would you care to tell me those secrets now?'

His privates, he discovered, were tender and no doubt as chafed as her breasts. 'Since you have my complete attention, lady, ask.'

'What communication have you had with my lord of Essex?'

It was not a surprise. She was Cecil's creature, and had also been present in his interview with the Queen. Most of that discussion had concerned Robert Devereux. She must also, he realised with a clarity that startled him, have stolen the earl's horoscope from Simon Forman, while another maid, or a drab hired from the street perhaps, distracted the magus. 'I suppose it would not appease you to learn that I have had none?'

'It might me. But it would not my master, and then I will not get paid.' Her hold upon him changed. Where she had gripped, now she stroked. 'May I not prevail upon you to satisfy us both?'

He was surprised to find, after a night such as the one he had just spent, and with the blacksmith in his head still pounding his strokes, that his flesh responded to her touch. Still, there was little he cared to say. 'I am afraid I can help you in one way only. Not the other.'

'And I was afraid you would say that. Pity.' She sighed – then struck him on his cock with enough force to make him gasp. She stood, reaching for clothes which flowed on in a series of swift movements. She changes costume as swiftly as a player, he thought. Which, of course, she is.

He found he could not move, only watch her. She ignored him till she was fully clothed. Then she glanced at him once, put two fingers in her lips and blew a startlingly loud whistle. Thumps came almost immediately upon the stairs.

John was up in a moment, seeking among the pile of clothing for his sword – which was not there, for the simple reason that it was in the hands of the large man who came through the door. He was followed by two more even larger. For just a moment John considered forcing the shutters. But he did not for several reasons. His nakedness, which would produce a hue and cry in moments; the three men, who looked fast enough to catch him and capable enough to have colleagues outside; most of all, his stomach. Running at speed while puking was a trick he'd never mastered.

So he just stood there, holding his hose and doublet before him.

'Get dressed,' said his lady of cloves, the gentleness gone from her voice. 'For I do not think the Master Secretary would care to see you as I have.'

XVII

Lollards' Tower

The sun pierced him cruelly. Judging by its height, it was about mid morning – the only thing he was able to tell before a hard shove in his back propelled him from the doorway on to the street. It told him little – except he was no longer in Southwark. He'd have recognised the dwellings, smaller in the main, and usually beside some place of business, be it shop, brothel or tavern. This street's houses were larger and well made, the common silvery grey of untreated oak beams here painted over with black, the beiges and umbers of loam, usually unpainted, here daubed a pristine white. A prosperous street then, and such inhabitants as he saw well dressed. Merchants or . . . clerics, he thought, the idea confirmed when they rounded the first corner and he took in three sights: the river before him, Westminster Abbey upon its far shore and, immediately before him, the thrusting stone and stained glass of Lambeth Palace.

His party halted on a word from the lady. She studied him for a moment, then turned to the others. 'Guard him well,' she said, 'for he is full' – a little smile came – 'of tricks.' She turned and made for the river. There was a wherry dock at Lambeth Stair, John knew. She was bound, no doubt, for Whitehall. His feelings were jumbled as he watched her walk away and he resisted a further shove to look after her.

'I do not know your name,' he shouted.

She did not even break stride, nor turn back. 'No,' she called, 'you do not.'

Since the push had had no effect, strong hands took him on either arm and he was propelled forward. Away from the river. Towards

Lambeth Palace. When he realised it was their destination, if he could have run the opposite way, he would.

London was full of prisons – and he had seen the inside of most of them over the years: the Fleet when his debtors caught up with him; the Clink for drunkenness. Newgate, where murderers were held, was the filthiest, fever and fellow inmates offering a variety of ways to die swiftly, long before the tumbril fetched one to Tyburn. Yet there were only two that he truly feared – the Tower of London, where suspected traitors went for examination, as he had on his return from Spain. And the one to which he was now being marched, the only one he had never visited.

Lollards' Tower.

If it was far smaller than that royal palace where monarchs and nobility had died, it had near as sinister a reputation. The men who had perished within it, and who gave it their name, were now honoured as martyrs, forerunners of the Protestant faith. They had died horrible deaths there, tortured and eventually burned. Half the structure they were rapidly approaching was the Archbishop of Canterbury's London residence, a palace of beautifully carved stone and sublime coloured glass. But it was the blunt thrust of granite blocks that John focused on. In the dog days of this summer, with the Spanish enemy over the horizon and armed Papists on every corner stalking the sovereign majesty, he was sure many people had disappeared into the darkness ahead. He was equally sure that few, if any, came out – on their feet at least.

His own must have dragged. 'Come on, you,' the leader of his captors said, seizing an arm. A gaoler emerged from a wooden shack beside the stone. 'Any others up there?'

The man shook his head. 'Last one was taken out this morning.' He jangled keys, selected one, went to the stone wall. 'If you stand downwind, you'll smell the Jesuit dog roasting in about an hour.'

His guard turned to John. 'Just think – a whole tower to yourself. Last one who had that was a duke of the realm. Funny thing – his noble blood was just as red as the next man's.' He laughed, then shoved his prisoner forward. 'In you go.'

The door into Lollards' Tower was a tiny contrast to the edifice, a wooden wicket barely the size of the granite slabs it was placed between. John had to stoop, and then stopped when he found that the stair beyond was not much wider than his shoulders. 'Up,' came the command, accompanied by another firm push. John stumbled, for the first few steps were narrow and, he saw by such light as came from the occasional reed torch, much worn. The stair circled upwards, his elbows grazing the stone pressing in on either side. Eventually it splayed and ended at a wooden door, far wider than the one below, studded and braced with iron. It was ajar, and with nowhere else to go, John pushed it open and went in.

The room reeked of fear, as such places usually did, a compound of piss and shit and the rancid sweat constant terror produces. It was a scent that John knew well; and he suddenly yearned for a touch of clove, even though he had found it sickly on waking. There was also always a feeling in such places as if the stones themselves had absorbed the prayers and pleas of all who'd been there. Stones . . . or in this case, wood, as John confirmed when his eyes became accustomed to the dim light entering from two arrow slits. The four walls were covered in oak wainscot. Not just at their base, as was the custom; everything was panelled here, even the ceiling. There was nothing else in the room, of wood or stone, not a chair, table, cot. All he could see were eight metal hoops, about two hands in diameter and bored into the oak in regular intervals around the walls.

He shivered at the sight of them. 'Cold, are you?' the leader of the captors said. He'd followed John in, along with two of his fellows. 'Well, there's a fireplace there. Some prisoners get wood, depending on their rank, or how . . . cooperative they are.' He eyed John's much-patched and simple clothes. 'I suspect you'll get none.'

He turned to go. 'A moment, friend,' John said, and, when the man stopped, continued, 'Might I ask your name?'

'What's it to you?' When John did not reply, he shrugged and said, 'Well, since I doubt you'll have much time to dwell upon it, my name is Waller.'

'Could you bring me some ale, Master Waller? Or water, if you must,' he added, seeing instant refusal in the man's eyes.

'Why should I do that for you?' Waller replied. 'I have not been given orders to withhold it. Neither have I been told to make you comfortable. What's in it for me?' He thrust his chin forward. 'Have you money?'

John had not checked his hidden purse, but it felt light against his spine. He studied the man before him. He was about his own age, and had a certain bearing. 'Would you do it as a kindness to a fellow soldier?'

The eyes appraised. 'You served? Where?'

'With the Earl of Leicester in Holland. With Drake against the Armada.' He thought it best not to mention Essex, given the circumstances.

Waller looked at him for a moment. 'I'll see,' he said, turning again, following his men down the stairs.

The door slammed shut, bolts were shot and John did not even bother to go examine it. He did go to the chimney, bend to look up the flue. It was narrow, as ever, but more of an impediment were the iron spikes that would allow smoke egress but not flesh.

He stood, too quickly. The blood in his head surged. And then he was charging across the room, his vomit preceding him by a foot. Most he managed to direct into the bucket. Not all.

'By the beard,' he said, wiping his mouth, then sinking with his back to the wainscot and within range of the receptacle. When the quivering in his guts abated enough, he rose to slowly make a tour of the walls. Little to see, except those iron rings whose function he did not wish to contemplate too closely; also some scratching. Someone had attempted a rough calendar. However, it was mainly words – the names 'Edwin' and 'George', and some others less legible; prayers. 'God preserve us.' 'To thy mercy . . .' All the phrases were in English. The little he knew of Lollards was that they were the first to read the Bible in their own tongue, disdaining the Latin that restricted the Lord's words to an educated few. Now all did so, and rejoiced in it. Then, they had burned for doing so, waiting in this room for their conflagration, just as Jesuits waited now.

The little he could explore, he had. All that was left was to sink down near the bucket, and put his head on to his knees.

It had not rested there long before the sound of bolts raised it. He stood as the door swung open. A guard came in – not one of the ones he'd had before – while another, also new, stood at the door, a cudgel in his hands. The first one stepped two paces into the room, put down another bucket, then, as wordlessly, left.

John waited for the bolts to be shot again before he rose and crossed. He lifted the pail's lid . . . and smiled at its contents. Two

167

leather bottles with cork stoppers. A hunk of maslin bread. And a rag.

'Bless you, Master Waller,' he murmured as he unstoppered. One bottle contained ale, and he drank some swiftly. It was weak stuff, which was just as well. The other contained water, which he put to its only proper use – first he washed his beard and doublet front clear of vomit, then watered and wiped the approach to the bucket. Finally he sat against the wall opposite the bucket and gnawed at the bread. He did not relish it, but, like the ale, he would need it for his mangled guts and wits.

Long after he'd scraped the crumbs from his beard, and washed the bread down with the last of the ale, with the arrow slits causing sunbeams to lengthen across the floor, he heard feet upon the stair, and then the bolts repeating their refrain. The door opened and Waller came in. John began to rise, to thank him for his kindness. But the officer shook his head in a clear gesture of silencing, then stepped aside to admit another.

Sir Robert Cecil did not need to unstoop. He scuttled in, and stared down at John, who'd fallen back. 'What, sirrah? Do you not rise to kneel before your betters?' the Secretary of State declared.

In his considerable experience, John had found that defiance was a tactic that sometimes worked with interrogators while cringing only encouraged them. So he was about to respond defiantly when someone else entered the room. One of his betters, sure, and one who brought John instantly to his knees.

'Well, John Lawley,' said the Queen of England. 'We have a situation here and no mistake.'

XVIII

Queen's Messenger

If she was not dressed as he had last seen her, in the finery required for the Shrove Tuesday revels, she was dressed well enough for all that, as if fresh from an especially fashionable hunt, with a brown velvet riding habit trimmed with ermine that flowed over a large russet-red skirt. This was swelled by a farthingale, a miniature version of the whalebone edifice that supported a court gown, supporting her now as she leaned upon it, bending from the waist as far as she was able.

'God's breath!' she puffed. 'Those stairs! I warrant they are torment enough for any prisoner – without need for your other devices, Master Secretary.'

Sir Robert looked past the Queen to the doorway. 'Ho! A chair here for her majesty!'

'I do not want a chair. Did I command one? You know my legs cannot abide much sitting, and those torments grow worse. I need to lean . . .' She raised a hand. 'You, girl, attend me.'

If John was surprised by his royal visitor, he was as much by who came in now – his lady of cloves, though he could detect none of that scent now. And she was also much changed from when he'd last seen her. Those golden locks were held under a lady's bonnet, not a hair astray to betray her wantonness. Her dress, cut in the fashion, would have exposed her bosom, but hers was discreetly veiled in lace. No doubt it would be hard to explain the marks his passion had wrought.

'Come, Sarah,' the Queen said. 'Your arm.'

That's it. Sarah, John thought. Yet her name was all he got of her for now. The black eyes were demurely lowered, as they had been at that first interrogation at Whitehall. She placed herself and braced the Queen.

'Better. Up, sir!' Elizabeth muttered, though her nose wrinkled in disgust. 'The air in here wants sweetness,' she continued, then looked at him. 'I know it is the pickling time, Master Lawley, but it is meant for cucumbers, not men. Phew!'

If that is all she smells on me, I shall be much relieved, he thought, rising, glancing at the maid again.

Sir Robert moved crabwise to the door. 'In,' he said, and the same bald clerk who'd attended him before entered. He was laden, a folding table under one arm, a satchel under the other. He set up the one and tipped the contents of the other out upon it, a sheaf of papers. Cecil waved him out, bending to spread and sort.

Strange, thought John, eyeing the preparations. He had been examined in many ways before. This did not resemble any of them. The presence of the sovereign would seem to preclude torture – for the moment; she could always leave.

He wished his brain did not hurt so much. He wished he had not drunk all the ale nor used the water for washing. Most of all he wished to know what the devil was going on.

Then Elizabeth told him. In a way. 'Master Lawley, are you the Queen's loyal servant?'

'I . . . am, your majesty.'

'And are you also a friend to the Earl of Essex?'

Careful, he thought. 'I saved his life once,' he replied. 'Perhaps more than once. Certain Indian cultures I encountered when on the voyage with Sir Francis Drake have it that I am therefore obliged to him, not the other way around, as civilised men think.' He took a breath, aware that his tongue could run loose after such a night. 'So I do not know if I am his friend. But I am . . . obliged to him, your grace.'

'An intriguing answer. You are an intriguing man.' She studied him for a moment. 'Well, perhaps that will be enough. And perhaps he will feel a . . . civilised man's obligation too, and heed your advice. Advice taken direct from me, sir, and from the wise heads of my Privy Council, as represented here by my Secretary of State.'

The scribe had withdrawn. No one was setting down words. But John had no doubt everything was being noted in the book of minds, to be recalled later in ink. And Sarah had more than one employer, she'd said. Who else would she be reporting this conversation to? Yet what most pierced the miasma in his brain was the word 'taken'. Until he heard more on that, he could only stutter, 'I . . . I am at your command, ma'am.'

'Then hear this.' The Queen took another deep breath, pinched the top of her nose for a moment with her eyes closed, then opened them straight into a glare. 'My lord of Essex has displeased me mightily. He has displeased the realm. More, there are rumours that his actions may have so exceeded his mandate as my vice-regent in Ireland that they could be construed as treason. As treason, sir!' She frowned at him as if he were Essex himself, standing before her, accused. 'And if he has not yet gone so far in his pride, he has gone further in his stupidity.' The glare doubled in intensity. 'For he has concluded a truce with the rebel Tyrone.'

John raised eyebrows. 'He has, majesty?'

'He has? He has! I tell you that he has. And do not tell me you do not know what half of London does.'

John knew that to be exaggeration – though there would be several who received letters as his Tess had done. He also knew that Essex would not have sent his reports only to the Queen and her council, for such news would be immediately manipulated. Essex would know that his enemies would be doing so straightway. Thus he must do so too, and swiftly.

'Come, sir, I have it on authority that you do know.' It was the Secretary's turn to frown at him. 'Do not attempt to juggle with us here. It will go ill with you if you do.'

John took a moment to look at Cecil's 'authority'. The maid kept her black eyes down. Yet even through his fug he detected something interesting here. The Secretary was threatening him, as was dictated by his role and its setting, this infamous prison of traitors. But it did not seem quite real. It *was* a role, and he was playing it. Having some experience of players, both good and ill ones, John also saw that behind Sir Robert's blustering performance lurked a certain desperation.

He looked again at the Queen – and also noted something beyond her glare. These people are frightened, he thought. And they think I can ease their fears.

His mind cleared on the thought. Fear was power – over queens as well as swordsmen. His pain remained – indeed he knew that only time or more of what had caused it would reduce it entirely – but he was master of it now. 'I admit I have heard a little of this. But, your grace, sir, if you require something of me, then perhaps you would be good enough to tell me what it is?'

Both Cecil and Elizabeth exhaled loudly at the same time. They probably had not meant to do so, for it was a sound that confirmed his sobering thoughts: that they needed him far more than Cecil's desire to harm him. For now, anyway. And if now would see him out of Lollards' Tower – especially as the palace bell had just tolled eleven, reminding him that Tess would be watching for him in Southwark – he had first to listen to what they had to say.

The silence lasted a moment before the Queen spoke. 'Tell him, Master Secretary. Tell him everything.'

Cecil looked appalled. 'I will tell him, majesty, as much as he needs to hear.'

If Elizabeth noticed the rebuke, she did not react to it. 'Perhaps I *will* take a chair,' she said, her voice weaker. She leaned more heavily on her maid, who braced herself to support her.

'A chair for her majesty,' Cecil called.

'And a pomander for the stench. Also some cordial,' she added.

Orders were relayed, a line of servants curving round the tower's stair no doubt, each bearing whatever might be required for the Queen's comfort. A chair was brought, sweet herbs in their metal ball placed in one hand, a glass in the other. When the last servant left, Elizabeth sat, sipped then waved. 'On, Sir Robert.'

The Secretary donned spectacles, then raised a parchment. Dangling from it was a tangerine ribbon at the base of which was an oval of sealing wax. ' "Most beauteous . . . " ' he began.

'Dispense with the tributes, Master Secretary,' Elizabeth snapped. 'One can only hear so many odes to one's eyes before they nauseate near as much as the air in this room. Since I have been pulled prematurely from the chase for this' – she gestured to her habit – 'you will to it, sir. The hart has been bayed. To the kill!' She settled back with a slight smile for her metaphor.

Cecil gave a half-bow, then scanned down the tightly inked lines. It would be hard to discover the hart in those thickets, John knew.

He had received letters from the earl himself and knew them to be full of rhetorical flourishes and devices obscuring the matter. Eventually, somewhere near the end of the second page, the Secretary flushed his prey. ' "Majesty," ' he announced, ' "as your viceroy in this land, we have used your power as deputed to us to force the Earl of Tyrone if not to his knees, then to his horse's withers in water. For he paid to us, and through us, to you, due servility. With Lagan's stream lapping at his mount's belly, all hatless, did he most humbly accept terms. To wit: not to violate the peace of the realm for six weeks. Such terms to be renewed at six-week intervals, until either side gives a fortnight's notice. To such peace the rebel swore binding oaths, while your vice-regent merely signed an assurance as befitted our status. Moreover . . . " '

Elizabeth's legs had been writhing during Cecil's recitation. Now they propelled her up. 'The dastard!' she cried. 'He tries to make this out to be our victory. Ours! When it is clearly *his* defeat. Terms with a traitor! Not his head on a pike. Terms, by Jesu!'

John frowned. There were several things he did not understand. 'Lagan's waters, sir?' he asked, addressing Cecil.

'We have a letter here from a witness to this . . . treason.' He glanced at the Queen as if seeking approval for the word, as she moved back and forth behind her chair. Unrebuked, he picked up another paper. 'It appears that the earl, having failed to bring the rebels to battle, agreed to meet their leader between the armies . . . in a stream! It matters not that Tyrone was bonnetless in the waters and Devereux wore his helmet on the bank. For they were alone. Alone!'

Alone. Very little surprised John when it came to Robert Devereux – but this did. He would have thought that the title of vice-regent would have put some sense into even that muddled head, but obviously it had not. To converse with an avowed rebel *unwitnessed*? Anything could have been said and agreed. Anything. And the earl was not only a general at the head of the Queen's army, he was also a dog snapping around the only . . . the only bitch in the pack, John thought, glancing at the wandering Queen. Her Robin was the leader of a faction. To consort with traitors in this extraordinary way . . . it was as if a mastiff in a bear bait suddenly made compact with the bear. It could well be construed as treason – and he knew that the earl's great rival, the Secretary, was construing it exactly that way.

Except now, cunning man that he was, he did the opposite. 'Yet certainly the earl is valiant. His army has been much reduced by the bloody flux, which has struck officer and man and wasted even himself.' He tutted, shook his head. 'Perhaps this truce is for the best.'

'The best?' Elizabeth halted her pacing to screech. 'The only thing he has wasted is the power I have bequeathed to him. The only thing he has wasted is my goodwill. My love . . .' She broke off, choking on the word. She turned away for a moment, turned back. 'This contemptible truce must be immediately repudiated. The Vice-Regent must resume the war and destroy Tyrone with the forces he now has. If he does not, before the winter makes the land impassable – though when is it truly not in a country where the rain it raineth every day? – then he is to take to winter quarters and await the spring and such reinforcements as we can send. Heed me!' She stamped her foot, her voice rose, and she stooped till her face was a hand's breadth from John's. 'And above all, this. You are not to return here, sir. At no instance are you to return to England, to my court. I forbid it! Forbid it, do you hear?'

Her voice had risen to a yell. She was staring hard into his eyes. And John could see in hers several things at once. The first, fury; then, close behind it, barely veiled by it, her desperation. Yet what made him lower his was that both were directed not to the man whose eyes she gazed into. She was looking at her sweet Robin himself.

'Your Grace . . .'

It was the Secretary's hesitant voice that pulled her fast upright. She flopped on to her chair, turned away, her forehead on one hand. A silence came, tense and awkward. Then Cecil spoke again. 'You have heard Her Majesty's commandments. They will be conveyed again in her own unmistakable hand and tone. Yet if he fails in all, disobeys all, dares to return . . .'

'He must not. Will not.' The Queen looked sharply up, all confusion gone from her eyes. 'Not when I have ordered it so.'

Cecil turned, rubbing his hands before him. 'Aye, majesty, but the earl is rash. Why, only last year Lord Grey prevented him drawing on you . . .'

John winced. The scandal had swept London, from court to

abattoir. Rebuked, the earl had rudely turned his back on her. Furious, Elizabeth had boxed his ear. The earl had then shown an inch of steel and was narrowly constrained from showing more. They sang ballads about it from Brentford to Shadwell and no doubt the length of the realm. But he warranted the Queen was not often reminded of it.

Her reaction confirmed his thought. 'You d-dare to . . .' Elizabeth stuttered, half rising.

'Only to recall to your majesty,' Cecil continued, hastily, 'his lordship's extreme rashness. He may defy you again. He *may* return. Yet if, against commandments, he does' – he took a breath, and directed the remainder as much to John as to his queen – 'he must do so without his army.'

And there it was, at last, John knew: the heart of it, as Cecil now confirmed. 'We do not want the people shouting "Bolingbroke", as they do in this man's playhouse,' he concluded.

The name hung in the air, almost visible, like one of the tower's martyred ghosts. John could have pointed out that the playhouse was hardly his; while the play that the character of Bolingbroke was from, *The Tragedy of Richard the Second*, was an old one, upwards of five years, and thus most unlikely to be played again because it would not draw an audience. In addition, the tale was based on the true one of a mighty subject, Henry Bolingbroke, usurping the throne and causing a monarch – God's appointed – to be murdered. However much Will liked to lance the boil of people's emotions, as he had put it, he would not be foolish enough to revive that. Not now, in these dangerous times, when an aged queen sat on the throne and people ceaselessly – and at their peril – voiced opinions about her successor. And especially not when, as the Secretary had just observed, the names Essex and Bolingbroke were already being linked, in pamphlets and in whispers on the street.

Even the maid finally flashed her black eyes at the spectre hovering between them. But it was the Queen who dismissed it. 'He is not to return . . . in any way.' She rose once more, shakily now, and faced John, looking at *him* again, not his sometime lord, her sometime lover. 'That, Master Lawley, is the message you will take to him.'

So all his fears were realised. They wished to send him to Essex

– the one man in the wide world, save only for the executioner, that he would most avoid. '*I* will, majesty?'

She took it as a statement, not a question. 'Indeed you will. You will also bear other commandments – and our written displeasure too. But since you have always had some influence over him, and he is . . . obliged to you, perhaps you will also convey some sense behind the orders.'

He had to try. 'Your grace, I have pressing matters of my own . . .'

'More pressing than the realm's and my own safety? Naughty knave, there are no matters beyond that.'

He thought of Tess, and of Ned. The palace bell recently striking the eleven. He could still make the play, as he had promised. 'I could set out tomorrow . . .'

'Tomorrow?' Cecil stepped up to him now. 'You would do the Queen's and the realm's most urgent business at your leisure?' He shook his head. 'No. You will depart as soon as the letters are sealed. With fair weather, a calm sea and little sleep, you will be in Dublin in five days.'

Dublin! The name was a curse. He had another place he needed to be, now. 'Then perhaps while the letters are being drawn, I can go to Southwark. My business—'

'Southwark!' Cecil snorted. 'To let you slip back into the slough you've just risen from? No, sirrah. You will be thrown in a cow trough to bathe and issued with clean clothes so that you do not reek, as befits the Queen's messenger. You will be given a good horse, a purse of silver to hire more, our commissions and a party to accompany you the first fifty miles.' He glared. 'And you will ride for Ireland at two o'clock.'

At two o'clock, Ned would be glancing out wondering if his father might still make it. Yet perhaps he had heard of John's most recent fall – Southwark was that small, and the Larkspur near its centre; would be thinking, even as he spoke the country girl's lines, that his father had failed him once again. Will would clap a hand on his shoulder, sigh – and think about a different player for his upcoming Caesar. And Tess? Would Tess have heard of the siren who had lured him to his fall, of her blonde tresses and her sweet, sickly scent?

He looked up at her now. The black eyes were raised to him. There was a smile in them . . . and the hussy even gave a small wink! He turned from her eyes, to others' – the Queen's, her minister's. There was no pity in any of them. He knew they would not even allow him to send his excuses – for a royal messenger's departure needs must be secret.

He looked above them all to the wainscoted walls, those hooks set in them. Only fanatics denied their captors in Lollards' Tower, and he was not prepared to burn.

He knelt again. 'Your servant ever, majesty.'

Though they expected nothing less than complete obedience, still the Queen and her Secretary of State allowed a moment of brief relief to show. This business accomplished, they set out for the next.

Cecil went to the door. 'In,' he called. 'Clear away.'

The servants came. The scribe collected the papers, folded the table, departed. A guard took away the Queen's chair. Sarah took the pomander and glass from Elizabeth, curtseying as she did, staying down. 'Majesty,' said Cecil, also bending his knee in the doorway, gesturing that she should precede.

But the Queen did not move. She was still staring at John. Now she spoke, softly. 'I wish a moment alone with my messenger.'

John, glancing away from the monarch's piercing regard, saw the Secretary and the maid pass a look. He also recalled Cecil's shock on his dismissal at their previous meeting, when Elizabeth also wanted to speak to him alone, her anger when he baulked.

It appeared that Cecil recalled it too. He took a breath, let it out, murmured, 'Your grace,' and left.

'Sarah,' said the Queen, 'follow.'

Darting him a look, the maid left too.

And they were alone. When last they'd been, she had prised from him the history of his blood, and of hers, how the two of them were linked through his grandfather, Jean Rombaud, killing her mother, Anne Boleyn. Killing . . . and saving. He hoped it was not that of which she wanted to speak. He was not sure what he could say.

It was not. It was something of more . . . immediate concern. 'There is one last message that I ask you to deliver to your lord,' she said, 'and only after my anger, my commandments have been fully understood – and obeyed, mark you, sir, obeyed. Then, Master Lawley, you will find the right moment to give him . . . this.' She reached within her sleeve and drew out a handkerchief. Raising it to her face, she kissed it, then held it out. John rose to take it . . . but she did not release it straightway and they were joined by it.

Something passed between them along the spun silken threads. He felt as if he had been there before, doing this same thing before, receiving . . . something from a queen's hand, in a place much like this one.

Elizabeth swayed, as if feeling the same force, till the cloth was stretched between them, then spoke again. 'Tell him to bring this back to me in person. Tell my champion to wear it as my favour on his lance and' – a glint came into her eye – 'and if he stains it with a traitor's blood, so much the better.' She took a deep breath. 'And tell him, finally, this.' She sighed. 'That when he comes to me, bringing this silk woven through the laurel wreath of victory, he shall find me . . . most forgiving.'

Her gaze held his. He found he could not speak, only nod and lower his eyes. The moment he did, she released the handkerchief and turned swiftly to the door. She opened it wide – to Sarah, on the other side, turned away. 'Are you spying there, girl?' the Queen snapped.

'No, no, your grace. I' – she swallowed – 'I . . . I waited to help you down the stairs.'

Elizabeth did not reply, simply seized the arm that was held out. Together the two women descended, the spiral taking them swiftly from view.

John listened to their descent; knew that before long he would hear boots coming up, men arriving to bathe him, clothe him, supply him with what he needed and hasten him on his way. For the moment's peace he had, he looked at what he held – a square of richest silk, unblemished . . . except in the corner where there were two initials, monogrammed in orange. No, he corrected himself. In tangerine.

E and E were entwined, the first E's lowest bar forming the second's middle.

He looked at each one in turn; and though he knew it was not there, yet he thought he could see another letter. An L. L for Lawley. Caught, like him, between the two of them.

Between Elizabeth and Essex.

ACT THREE

The Trouble with Ireland

They have produced no other effect there than a ship doth in a wide sea, who leaves no longer print or impression in the water than for the very instant, the waves immediately filling the way she makes, so as the same cannot be found . . . It is strange that Deputies are not restrained from running still this wild goose chase.

Anonymous minute writer to the Privy Council, on Ireland, 1599

XIX

What Country, Friend, Is This?

'Put about! I am the Queen's messenger and I command it. Put about, damn ye!'

He screamed to be heard above the storm. He would not have been able to understand the reply, for the master of the sloop spoke little English, and Welsh was not one of the languages John had. The mutter and accompanying shrug were easy to translate though: a turd for the Queen and another for her messenger!

The man bellowed at his three sailors. John doubted that any of the words were to turn the vessel back to Dublin, whose wharves they'd glimpsed just before the surprise storm drove them past its port. Chewing his lips, he squinted into the rain. The shore could still be glimpsed despite the deluge. Yet John was sailor enough, after his time with Drake, to acknowledge that to try and turn about was a risk only a desperate man would take. He was that man. The master, for obvious reasons, was not.

Pox on him! John thought, his shoulders slumping. To be held up here, at the last, an arrow's shot from his goal, when the whole journey had hitherto been so easy. The best horses from every stable led out on production of the Queen's warrant, a hot late summer keeping the roads dry. He'd slept little, and made Bangor in five days, the warrant and a dose of silver securing passage on a fishing boat just about to set out. The sea was calm, the wind set fair, and Dublin in sight within hours. And then this storm from nowhere, and driven before the wind, which could blow him anywhere. What then of his hopes? All of them were centred on reaching the earl, executing his office and returning with as much dispatch as he had come, to Southwark.

He raised his head into the rain, sniffed. Was there a lessening? A little light in the grey? He strode after the captain, took him by the shoulder, turned him. The Welshman shrugged his hand off, and growled like a dog. 'Hear me,' John said, and it seemed to him he could shout a little less, 'the wind slackens. Put about for Dublin.'

The master shook his head. 'Wind bad. Sea bad. Wait.'

He turned away. John seized his sodden jerkin at the shoulder with a grip that could not be shrugged off, turned him with one hand, drawing his dagger with the other. This he raised into the other man's sight. It was a language all understood. 'I can't wait, you sheep-puddler,' he said, his face thrust close to the other's. 'Now put about or—' He glanced to larboard. The land was closer again. It was not a long walk to Dublin, surely. 'Or put me ashore here. Here!'

The man dragged his gaze from the dagger to look. 'Here? No port.'

'Then . . .' John looked around. Lashed to the aft deck was a small skiff. 'Get me close. I'll take that.'

'Boat?' The man's face eased slightly, and John was close enough to see the thoughts in his eyes. These narrowed. 'Boat. Money. No get back.'

John nodded. He didn't care. He had spent almost nothing on his ride, sleeping in stables, snatched meals in taverns. The Queen's coin could be used for her service and his own. 'Money,' he agreed, sheathing his dagger.

It did not take long. A foresheet raised and two men leaning on the tiller pushed them shorewards. The skiff was unlashed, oars put in it. It was lowered, tethered to the side in the bucking sea. His purse lighter for the loss of too much silver, his satchel of letters strapped firmly across his chest, John was handed over the side. He nearly lost his balance, for the skiff lurched with waves that were much taller closer to. He sat heavily, suddenly reconsidered, looked up . . . to be slapped in the face with the flung tethers. The two vessels swiftly parted, the last sound John heard, before the wind took all, some raucous Welsh laughter.

The rain and wind *were* slackening a little perhaps, but they still drenched and buffeted. The heron's feather in his cap drooped soaked before his eyes and he plucked it, chucked it, peered. The wind was onshore and the waves were pushing him thither, but along it too. He lifted the oars, wishing he had a paddle and was in something called a canoe, which he'd used with Drake on the western coast of America. The natives there had been skilled in their use and had passed on some of their knowledge – such knowledge useless in this vessel, a swimming cow to the other's otter. He dipped the oars, lost them from the rowlocks, strove again. He was not making much headway, and that as much sideways as forward – until he suddenly was, for the waves picked up closer in. One large one caught him, moving him fast towards the shore.

Too fast! He leaned on one oar, put weight behind it . . . it was snatched away, its twin emulating it next moment, gone. Now he had nothing to stop or even slow the boat's sudden forward speed, could only scrunch down and stare in horror at the fast-approaching land as one wave took the skiff, shoved it, dropped it, another picked it up, bigger, much bigger. Somehow it kept straight, did not go side on and flip. He glimpsed a break in the rock face ahead, some lighter colour. Sand, he thought, he prayed, he willed. It was the only control he had.

'Oh. Oh-oh-oh-oh-OH!'

The boat rode the wave easily. Not so the land, which it struck prow first, and stuck. He was at the back of the boat, which shot up, hurtling him forward.

He was flying, and he knew he was no bird. But within his body, some tumbler's instinct – from his early days as a wandering player, when he'd flipped and vaulted to draw a crowd – made him curl. He hit the ground hard but took some of the impact in a roll, which continued through three more before he smacked down, face planted into coarse sand.

He lay there for a while, only turning his head to spit out beach and take in air. As if it was done with him, the storm slackened, rain diminishing then halting altogether. The sand yellowed with sunlight. He heard seagulls.

And a voice. Human, though it shouted something incomprehensible, yet akin to the Welsh he'd lately not understood. The words were followed by a sharp jab in his back. He flipped over.

Standing above him was a scraggle-bearded man in a plaid cloak. He hefted a pike and he was bringing it hard down again.

John did not think, just moved; rolled aside, let the pike's butt drive into the sand, gathered his legs and swung them hard into the man's, who was not braced and went over fast. In a moment, John was atop him, dagger drawn, point placed close to the man's eyes. 'Easy, lad. Do not move.'

He didn't know if he was understood, but steel conveyed what words might not. The man froze, his terror clear. John stared at him, considering his own ignorance. Why had he not listened more closely to tales of the Irish wars? How much land did the English hold? Was he in enemy territory, paper truce or not? And just how far was Dublin?

Yet before he could find ways of asking this of a man who probably would not understand it, another voice came, this time in a tongue he knew. He even knew the accent, which, if it was not from Southwark, was within a Roman mile of it.

'Oy! Let go of 'im, you spyin' bastard.'

John did not let go, nor lower his knife, but he did look up. Standing a dozen paces away was a soldier, in breastplate and helm, with a musket in his hands. Pointed at John. He nodded at it. 'Powder's probably wet. You might misfire.'

'I might,' the soldier replied, 'but we all won't.' As he spoke, another six men came from the rock face, some dressed as John's captive, some as soldiers. They all had muskets levelled.

'Ah.' John shifted slightly. 'Yet just before I do, Corporal, let me say this. I am not a spy, I am the Queen's messenger. And I come on urgent business from her majesty.'

'We'll see about that,' the soldier replied, then jerked his gun. 'Now, let 'im go.'

John did so immediately, standing up and sheathing his dagger, stepping back with arms raised. The prone man rose and joined his companions. The Englishman took a pace forward, musket still pointed. 'You 'ave some way of provin' what you say?'

'I do, if you'll allow me.' John reached under his cloak to his satchel, opened its clasp, extracted the Queen's warrant. His recent captive came and snatched it. Took it back to the corporal, who

184

studied it while the others crowded around. So intent was their scrutiny that John could have walked silently away, but didn't.

'Well, that looks real enough,' the soldier said with the confident air of a man who obviously could not read, 'but I'll 'ave to show it to me officer. Could be a fake. You could still be a whoreson spy. You look like a bloody Spaniard.'

'Then will you take me to him straightway?' John replied. 'For as I said, my business is most urgent.'

The man chuckled. 'Is that why you arrived with such speed? I've never seen the like. When you flew from that boat and tumbled! My poor sides!' Chuckle had become guffaw. 'And unless you aimed for it, you was lucky, for this is the only strand in three miles, rest is rock. 'Swy we're 'ere, keepin' watch for smugglers . . . and spies.' On the word, he turned to the others. 'Both sides of 'im. Leave him his weapons for now, but watch close. And I'll keep this.' He waved the warrant.

He was obeyed; the guard formed up around John. The corporal placed himself at the head of them, and they set off along the beach, veering soon towards a cleft on the rock face.

'What is your name, Corporal?'

'Russell. Sebastian Russell.'

'Of Southwark?'

'Near enough. I was raised in East Cheap. But me pa's a higgler on Bankside. Sells puddin's.'

'I may have eaten some of his wares not five days since.'

'Woz you there?' The soldier's eyes shone. 'Place still the same?'

John had been a soldier. 'As full of sin as any man could wish.'

'Wunnerful. And I will take my fill of it, soon as I am shot of this God-cursed 'ole.' He turned, spat into the wall of the rocky defile that led away from the beach.

It was never too soon to glean information. 'Perhaps you will get that chance soon, man. With this truce . . .'

The soldier assembled another impressive amount of phlegm, expelled it. 'Truce? 'Ow long will that last? This war's only over when we've starved or thrashed these bloody peasants into submission.' He'd looked at the Irishmen as he spoke.

'Our allies?'

'Allies? They'd sell their mother for a pot of ale – once they'd

185

swived 'er enough.' He looked to spit again, then swallowed it down. 'These take our coin for now. Tomorrow it will be their own chieftains' again.'

They'd climbed to a clifftop. Ahead, John saw a small white-walled house, a barn beside it. Both had turf roofs and rough musket holes knocked in their walls. Stunted trees bent to the wind beside them. 'This close to Dublin, though, surely they are loyal?'

'Dublin's six mile off, sir,' came the reply. 'And every one of them miles filled with these bog-trotters, all aquiver for loot. When we travel, we travel in armed bands. They are cowardly shitters, the lot of 'em. Won't fight us proper, no matter how the earl tries to provoke 'em.' He laughed. ''E even challenged Tyrone to single combat. Not a chance.'

They approached the house. Last opportunity for a little fore-warning. 'How is the earl, have you heard?'

A shadow came into the soldier's eyes. 'Not well, sir, so it's said. Not well.' He looked up, the shadow left and he grinned. 'But you may discover that soon enough for yourself. He likes to examine spies personal, so it is said. In the dungeons of Dublin Castle. You can 'ear the screams all the way to the docks.'

This was new. Essex had ordered some examinations and executions in their times together, as any general must. John had not noticed him revelling in them.

They'd arrived before the hut. The corporal halted his party with a raised hand. 'My captain's within. He'll consider your papers, decide if you're bound for Dublin's dungeons or not. If he's awake this close to noon, which is unlikely,' he said, stepping to the door, adding in a mutter, 'and if he's sober, which is less likely still.'

He knocked, hard. There was silence for a few moments, then a garbled shout. John didn't understand it but the corporal did. 'Yes, Captain. Quite right. But I 'ave a prisoner 'ere. Might be a spy. Though 'e 'as papers.'

Silence again, even longer, then a loud sigh, finally a slurred voice. 'Come then, damn ye.'

The corporal raised his eyebrows at John, pushed the door open, went in. More muttering came from within, querulous, un-intelligible . . . then one loud cry. There followed the sound of staggering, and the door was flung wide.

'Well, well, John Lawley,' came an instantly familiar high-pitched voice. 'Can you give me one good reason why I do not hang you as a spy?'

Looking up, John gazed for one long moment into the bloodshot eyes of Despair. Then he closed his own.

XX

Ambuscado

It was a shock. And yet a part of him immediately acknowledged a kind of inevitability. It was simply the way his fortune had been going lately.

'Samuel,' he said, shaking his head.

'*Sir* Samuel, insolent dog. I am a knight of the realm and a captain of my lord of Essex's army. What are you?'

John was about to respond in similar vein. Yet he held himself back. He could see it in the man's fat face, hear it in that strange piping voice – D'Esparr was both suffering from the debauchery of the night before and a little ways into remedying it with its repetition. What purpose would be served by provoking him? The man could at the least order him beaten before he truly studied the warrant clutched in his hand. 'I am the Queen's messenger, Sir Samuel,' he replied. 'If you would take the time to study the commission . . .'

He pointed, and the knight looked down and jerked, as if startled by what he held. He raised the paper close to his face, so close he looked as if he were sniffing it. 'How do I know this is not a forgery?' he muttered. 'You always were a spy, Lawley. Who are you working for this time?'

John sighed. 'I have other papers in my satchel, personal letters from the Queen to her vice-regent. Her signature would be hard to fake, as would the Master Secretary's.'

'Let's see them, then.'

A chubby hand was held out. John looked at it – then around at the men gathering from stable and barns. A mixed crew of English and Irish. 'Perhaps, sir, we should discuss this inside. In private.'

Sir Samuel looked as if he were about to refuse – until he too noted the forming crowd. 'Very well,' he said, 'I will admit you. But Tomkins.' D'Esparr's man had appeared behind him in the doorway, rubbing eyes as bleared as his commander's. 'Take his weapons and keep a hold.'

He turned back into the room. With a grin, Tomkins called two others over and, with eager roughness, stripped John of his sword, dagger and buckler, jabbing hands within his clothes to seek out more, discovering the blade he always kept between his shoulder blades. Finally they took the satchel from him and, satisfied, pushed him up the stairs, Tomkins keeping one hand under John's arm and retaining his knife in the other.

The room was a mess, bottles lying atop most areas of floor and straw palliasse. A small table, equally laden, had a chair behind it into which Sir Samuel dropped, producing a volley of creaks. He proceeded to sweep the table clear, leaving room only for the satchel and a single bottle, from which he now swigged. John was simultaneously relieved and disappointed to not be offered a chance to test his latest vow of abstinence. Thirsty, he watched as the man tipped the contents of the satchel on to the table and rifled through them. It did not take long; all were royally sealed and he did not dare tamper. The only one that wasn't was John's commission, so this Sir Samuel returned to, holding it close to his face again, squinting.

'Well,' said the knight at last, 'what am I to make of this? You could have landed in Dublin and gone straight to my noble lord. Instead you arrive like a sneaking spy on the beach I am deputed to watch against that very design.'

'There was a sudden storm,' John answered, breathing to control his temper, 'and my vessel was driven before it. Rather than delay delivery of these urgent tidings, I chose to attempt the shore.'

'Storm? I noticed no storm. Did you, Tomkins?' On the man's head shake, Sir Samuel continued, 'Weather's balmy, man. Your story don't hold up.'

Taking an even larger breath, John stepped closer, Tomkins's grip slipping and re-establishing. 'You may ask your corporal outside, D'Esparr. The storm came and went and I took a chance. The urgency, sir.' He pointed at the paper in the knight's hand. 'Her majesty has vital communication and commandments for her vice-regent. I do not think she will appreciate any delay in their delivery. Nor any delayer.'

The threat was made softly, but still penetrated the blur. Anger and nervousness warred briefly in the man's wet eyes. But John knew which would triumph. Though he had had little to do with D'Esparr, they had both been involved in Essex's raid on Cadiz in '96. John had been constantly at the earl's elbow; Sir Samuel had been crouched over a bucket – long, it was said, after the symptoms of the flux had passed, but the hot action certainly had. 'So give me a horse and I will ride for Dublin,' he continued, as gently, 'and you will be free of me.'

'Alone? You will ride alone?' D'Esparr stared at him a moment and then broke into harsh laughter. 'Tell him, Tomkins. Tell him.'

'No one rides alone in Ireland,' the man said. 'No Englishman anyway. Even this close to Dublin. You'd be stripped, robbed and sodomised before you got a mile. And then they'd eat your horse.'

'Sodomised!' guffawed Sir Samuel. 'Though being a player, he'd hardly notice, I'd wager.'

John sighed. 'Then give me half a dozen men and I'll take my chances. That corporal, Russell, looks steady. Give me him.'

'What, and split my command? I have orders, sirrah, given personally by my noble lord. How can I let him down?'

For all his faults, Essex knew the worth of a soldier. Sir Samuel's meagre office on this beach showed his. But John did not get to voice this, or anything else, as D'Esparr now slapped the table and lurched to his feet. A certain craftiness had displaced the whisky in his eyes. 'No, begod! There is only one thing to do. I will take the risk. Your worthy corporal can stay in charge here. I will deliver you to the viceroy personally. And he can deal with you, as spy or messenger, accordingly.' He looked at his man. 'Tomkins, select five men. All English, not that peasant scum. We leave immediately.'

'Sir!' Tomkins shook John's arm roughly. 'And him?'

'Him?' D'Esparr was staggering about the room, seeking under detritus for what he needed. He paused, looked up. 'Until it is proved otherwise, he is a spy. While you muster the troop – tie him to a wheel!'

John again bit down on his anger. There was no point quarrelling with drunkards. This treatment would be repaid, given the opportunity. D'Esparr obviously wanted to return to the centre of the action in the land. As long as he took John to it as well, vengeance could wait.

He was tied, ineptly, to a fence, not a wheel. He could easily have loosed his bonds, but didn't. The men assembling would lead him most directly to his desire, and the one beyond it, the true one – to deliver the Queen's messages and return by the next boat to England, there to try – try! – to salvage the life he'd been so close to regaining.

Sir Samuel strutted and fretted. Five soldiers, all English, in breastplate and helm, were mustered. Under Tomkins's direction, they gathered their horses and two more besides. The fat knight with some difficulty mounted one. John was untied and led to the other. It was spirited and danced beneath him, but crooned words and firm reins soon settled it. A horse could tell a good rider – as Sir Samuel's still prancing mount could tell the opposite.

'My weapons,' John said, pointing at Tomkins, who had them slung in their belt and scabbard across his back.

'Not yet, Lawley,' came the high-pitched voice. 'You might stab me in the rear. Forward!'

Thinking that Sir Samuel's rear was a target a blind man could not miss, John watched him lead the troop forward, though he soon allowed Tomkins and another trooper to ride just ahead and set the pace, the knight's own horse settling in behind them. John rode in the middle of the troop, as befitted his uncertain status. The lane they followed was muddier than its English or Welsh counterparts, but his mount picked nimbly between the wheel ruts and puddles.

Yet he was not alone for long. 'And do you not bring letters for me, Lawley?'

Sir Samuel had let his horse ease in beside John's mount, which proceeded to nip at it. Moving its head away, John smiled. An opportunity for revenge had come swifter than he imagined. 'From whom, sir?'

'You know from whom, sir,' the other man growled. 'My love.'

John reached up to scratch his head. 'I was not aware that any of the whores at Holland's Leaguer could write, Sir Samuel.'

Watery eyes blinked at him. 'Whores, sirrah? I refer to my love, to whom my troth is plighted.' On John's uncomprehending stare, the high-pitched voice squeaked higher. 'I refer, damn ye, to Teresa.'

'Who? Oh, Tess! Landlady of the Spoon and Alderman. Soft-hearted, all-forgiving Tess.' John sighed. 'I have spent many happy hours in her fair company of late.'

'You have?' The pig eyes narrowed even further.

'Well, for all her steadfastness, she runs a tavern, as you know, in a dangerous part of the city. She gets frightened. She would have someone around who can take care of things. And since her hero is away on his country's service . . .'

'What kind of things?'

'Oh, the usual. Drunken customers, knife fights, money owed.' John clicked his tongue. 'And she does complain of the cold. You know her bed . . . no, you have not seen it, just troth-plighted, aren't you? Well, it's a four-poster had from her mother, but the curtains are frayed and do not keep out the draughts. And since Old Ralph her mastiff died, she's lacked a body to warm her at night. So she asked if I would . . .'

He broke off to duck under an oak's low branch. They had entered an especially wooded stretch, and leaves that showed the coming of the new season were pressed in upon them. The knight's mouth had been opening and closing like a carp hauled suddenly from the water. Now he bellowed, 'So? So what, ye dog?'

'Well,' John said, leaning a little closer, placing his arm atop Sir Samuel's as if they were side by side at a tavern's fire and not a-saddle, 'it is like this. Tess and I . . .'

He had no opportunity either to satisfy or further torment the knight, because the leading trooper was suddenly ripped from his saddle, shrieking as he fell. As he struggled to control his spooked horse, John glimpsed what had unseated him – a rope, tied across the path.

'Ambuscado!' he yelled, a little unnecessarily considering the gun-shots that coincided with the word. Four rather than a fusillade, and only one of those finding its mark, a soldier to John's left, who clasped a hand to his neck, failing to staunch the blood that sprayed between his fingers. But his wet scream was topped by different yells – men fighting their bucking horses for control, others running screaming through the trees. Impossible to tell how many in his instant look. More certainly than the three troopers left wheeling their mounts, and the triumvirate of him, Tomkins and Sir Samuel. The latter was squealing and attempting to stop his horse from throwing him; the rest at least had their swords drawn by the time the first ambusher ran from the trees.

A pair ran at John, one leading with a spear, the other diving for his reins. He jerked these hard back and his horse responded, coming up on its rear legs, front ones flailing; threw himself forward again, partly to counter the horse's movement backwards, mainly to dodge the spear thrust where his side had just been. The man was obviously surprised to miss him, and his chest slapped into the horse's rump, close enough for John to smash a fist into his assailant's temple. Knuckles connected, the spearman fell, while the other, dodging hooves, tumbled back. When John let the reins ease and the horse plunged down, he was able to glance around.

One horse was on the ground, thrashing, its rider pinned, surrounded by yelling Irishmen stabbing down with a variety of weapons – mauls, axes, sickles. Tomkins was a-saddle, his sword scything air, keeping men back. Two of the other troopers were emulating him while another, still mounted, burst into the tree line, dragging three attackers, who clung to him. Sir Samuel's horse had gone into a frenzy of kicks and bucks, keeping all attackers at bay. The knight, his face white with terror, was safe as long as he held firm, though his reins were lost, his feet unstirruped and his hands gripping the mane.

John had endured ambushes by Spaniards, and by Indians, and survived them all. But survival required a lot of fight to gain the opportune moment for flight. And it required a sword – his sword, which was in his scabbard over the shoulder of the man ahead.

The big Irish spearman had only been briefly dissuaded by the blow to his head. He came again now, yelling, point levelled. Kicking his heels in, John drove his horse on, away from the thrust, dragging the reins from the other man's snatching hands. He was next to Tomkins in a trice. 'Sword!' he bellowed, leaning back to avoid the swishing cuts that were keeping the attackers at bay. The man heard, saw. He may have been a cur serving a dog, but he obviously had been a soldier and he recognised bad odds and some aid. Catching the nearest attacker with a cut that took half his ear gained him the moment to bend at the waist towards John, and it took but that moment to snatch out his backsword. As soon as he had it, he was whirling it without aim; just as well as it rang off the steel of two thrusts, knocking both aside.

The trees pressed close, narrowing the path. The ambushers swarmed, to John's eye a score at least to their five survivors, but their farmyard weapons revealed they were probably not soldiers and his escort were; and they were mounted. Even if only four of them were actually fighting, Sir Samuel's spinning horse was keeping several of the assailants occupied. John, taking advantage of height, struck down, the folded weight of his backsword dropping as sudden as a thunderbolt. He drove forward into Tomkins's assailants, forcing men to duck, plunge, weave, more concerned now with dodging steel than striking with it. One man ran at him, wielding a sickle, leaning back to swipe. But he had a balancing hand forward, so John cut it off.

A terrible shriek, more sprayed blood, a slight drop in ferocity . . . and then a cry louder than all the rest. The huge Irishman who had first attacked John was running at him again now, spear levelled – and by the way he held it, he, at least, had held one before. Placing his head alongside his horse's neck, John kicked hard with his heels, and the horse leapt forward. The running giant had not allowed for it, nor the backsword thrust ahead, which John used to deflect the spear tip along his mount's flank, flicking his point back in time to let the man impale his neck upon it. As he fell, John twisted then withdrew his blade.

It was the moment. The attackers were suddenly aware of their diminished numbers, with their leader, John presumed, felled in their midst. Tomkins felt it too. 'Ride!' he screamed, and John joined the others in heeling their mounts into a gallop, ducking under the rope, riding clear, only screams pursuing them. There was a hill; the horses climbed it easily, their eyes wide, foam on their chests. At the top, the tree avenue ended and they were looking down at a plain, the track ahead of them leading to a walled city about a mile away.

Exultation! The four men who reined in and sheathed their swords were all laughing, at the thrill of survival. Yet John's laugh ended abruptly when he looked around, looked again, and realised. 'Where's Despair?'

Tomkins swivelled, then gazed back down the avenue. They could not see the place of ambush. But they could hear a variety of cries from the trees: agony, fury . . . and one high-pitched squeal. 'There,' he replied.

It would not be the first time John had wished his rival dead. The feeling that came was instant: joy, for the main obstacle on his path back to Tess was e'en then being removed, separated into parts by Irish farm tools. Then, immediately, that feeling left. For all his hate of him, Sir Samuel was, for the nonce, a comrade. You left no one to your enemies' mercy, especially when they would have none. That was as ingrained in him as a hard parry to quarto. Also he knew himself, knew he would not haply reclaim Tess with her fiancé's mutilated corpse a spectre at any feast.

'We have to go back for him,' he said. 'Are you game?'

Tomkins spat, nodded. 'Fat bastard owes me six months' wages. I'll get none if he dies.' He turned to the two surviving troopers. 'Draw swords, boys.'

Each man blinked at him. 'Corporal, we can't . . .'

'What?' Tompkins roared. 'Are you refusing an order? That's a hanging offence.' Then frown changed to grin. 'Come, lads, this is what you were trained for.' He drew his own sword again. 'Charge!'

John drew, as, with less enthusiasm, did the other two. 'For England!' he cried, bringing his horse up on its rear legs.

On his cry, the four set spurs to flanks and galloped back down the hill. A further thought came, as they built up speed: Sir Samuel had strapped the satchel with the Queen's papers around his chest. John needed them back. He did not relish explaining Elizabeth's messages, and her wrath, to the Earl of Essex.

The ambushers were obviously not expecting them. They had gathered around the fallen men and were engaged in stripping them of all they possessed. The horses had already been led away, so the avenue was clear. The Irishmen squealed, leapt up, tried to scatter, a group of five rising from the large, tangerine-swathed bulk of Sir Samuel – four who had held a limb each, the fifth who must have been prodding at him with a sickle. John directed his horse straight into them, relying on his mount to avoid the prone body, not caring too much if the knight took the odd hoof strike. He slashed down, slicing one man on the shoulder who screamed and fell. Jabbed after another who must have felt the steel thrust at his back, threw himself forward, tumbled, rolled and next moment was running into the tree line. John looked around – Tomkins had knocked one man down and his horse was trampling a second underhoof. The troopers were cutting at the backs of men fleeing fast into the woods. In moments, only Englishmen held the field.

John looked down. Sir Samuel was sobbing, his hands pressed to his face, his body twitching in anticipation of blows. The sickle had already made slashes in the velvet of his doublet, pink flesh wobbling beneath the rents. 'Samuel,' John called, 'they are gone. But they may return. Mount and swiftly!'

The knight made no reply, just carried on weeping into his palms. 'Mount, sir,' John called again, again to no effect. Sighing, he called to Tomkins, 'I'll hold your reins. Get him up and over.'

The other man threw his reins across, one trooper did likewise to his fellow, and both men, after a struggle, got the quivering knight to his feet. But he still would not cease his blubbering nor use his hands to mount up behind John – who lost patience, for he was scanning the woods and shapes were again gathering there. 'Throw him up, a God's mercy, and let us away!' he cried.

With some difficulty, the two men obeyed. When the bulk of the knight lay across his horse's rump, John leaned down and whispered, 'Hold tight, for if you fall off, I swear I will abandon you. We'll see who's sodomised then.'

It had its effect. Sir Samuel grabbed the rear of John's saddle, held hard. Another of the wounded troopers was atop another haunch. With a jab of heels, the men cantered out of the forest, stopping only at the same hilltop when his burden looked certain to slip off. John dismounted, prised D'Esparr's fingers from their grip and lowered him to his feet.

'They were going to . . . they were about to . . .' the knight babbled, gesturing vaguely towards his groin. 'If you hadn't come they would have . . .' He sobbed, then grabbed John by the neck, daubing his collar in snot. 'Thank you, my friend. Thank you for saving me.'

'I saved these,' replied John, already regretting his heroics, unstrapping the satchel, slipping it over his own shoulder. 'You were the bearer. Now up, sir, and let's away.'

A riderless horse had followed them on their last gallop from the forest. Sir Samuel was hoisted into the saddle. The wounded trooper had one broken arm but could cling on to a comrade with his other.

'To Dublin,' John said.

Descending the reverse slope of the hill, his heart calming till it no longer threatened to burst from his chest, he took stock. It appeared that though he had not been at war for three years, he'd forgotten little. Yet the thought that prevailed shocked him.

Was it possible? Was he actually looking forward to seeing Robert Devereux? For all his faults, the earl would provide a happier time than he had experienced so far on Erin's shore, surely?

XXI

Sodom and Gomorrah

He was wrong. So wrong.

He knew something was amiss from the moment they arrived at the city's gates. The guards were drunk, alternately officious and venal. A silver shilling from the Queen's purse, with the pledge to drink the health of the majesty depicted upon it, saw them inside the walls. Thereafter, through every narrow street they threaded, aiming for the rise of Dublin's castle, there was more of the same. Soldiers sprawled before taverns in late summer heat, red faces raised to the sun, tankards and bottles to lips. Whores with their flounced skirts and naked shoulders moved among the mob, hard-eyed and seeking custom, and not having to seek far. Men who'd gone to war and returned wished to celebrate both, in liquor and in loins.

It was a city given over to celebration. Yet John, who'd enjoyed any number of victory feasts, recognised that this one was different. For no major battles had been fought, no enemy conquered and only excess could transform the word 'truce' into anything close to 'triumph'. He could see too that the strain of pretending anything else was telling on the participants. It was near a fortnight since the rebel and the general had agreed terms in Lagan's waters. Two weeks in which all the drinking and the drabbing were no longer having their same lulling effects. In almost every inn they passed, John noted men staring angrily ahead, watched fights flare into sudden viciousness, swords drawn, daggers wielded, cudgels plied. Heat and ale and disappointment had taken their toll, and if the Queen's soldier could not make an Irishman fight him, he could at least turn the Englishman before him into a good substitute.

The three remaining troopers accompanied them as far as the castle. There D'Esparr, who had used the slow progress through the choked streets to calm his breathing, clean his clothes and gather himself, dismissed them to the town's pleasures. Only the three of them asked for entrance, and the guards, only marginally less drunk than the gatekeepers before, demanded twice their fee.

Sir Samuel knew the way and they followed him up the circular stair. On each curve the tumult ahead grew, and by the time they stood before a huge oaken door, the roar of carousing beyond it was unmistakable. Two guards sat there, leather bottles in hand, pikes leaning against the wall behind them. They did not bother to rise, just glanced at the warrant Sir Samuel now produced – that John had failed to reclaim from him – and nodded them to the door.

'Tomkins,' D'Esparr declared, straightening his empty sword belt, tucking his shirt into his collar.

His man stepped around him and opened the door . . .

. . . on to Sodom and Gomorrah.

John knew the story well enough. When a lad, it was one of the few that interested him in the Bible, and all those in the Old Testament where battle and copulation could be had. The inhabitants of those towns had been punished for their sins. Yet what those Israelites of old had managed to bring God's wrath upon them, their counterparts of England had equalled if not outdone.

Where is a smiting angel of the Lord when you need one? John thought, gazing upon the scene.

The hall was as large as the one at Whitehall where John had seen the Shrovetide play. But that one was dressed in the latest fancies, with new tapestries and stained glass, its flames neatly contained in lanterns and candelabra. It was modern, of its time. This hall looked as if John had stepped back two hundred years, with a vast fireplace at its centre over which the carcass of an ox still dripped fat, while reed torches on vast fluted columns lit the assembly in further flame.

Or perhaps the angel has passed over and smitten, John thought, as D'Esparr began to thread through the sprawled, raucous crowd. For these indeed looked like denizens of some circle in hell, their faces smeared with animal grease, their shirt collars rubied with wine. Gluttons perhaps, forced to overfeed for eternity.

To his left, in the centre of a rough circle of men, something was moving up and down. Someone. He glanced, looked away. Gluttony was not the only sin on display, gentility had collapsed, these so-called noblemen turning as base as any common soldier, for they were not even bothering to remove themselves to slake their lusts. If the whores were a trifle cleaner, a little prettier than street drabs, they were paid a little more. Yet another glance told him that women were not the only traders here this night. Noblemen usually kept such things discreet, often in the country, away from the court – sodomy was a capital crime. Discretion did not apply here, that was certain, for comely boys lolled on laps, feeding, being fed.

They were making for a raised dais at the room's end, a table upon it, as medieval as the hall. Behind it sat the leaders, setting an example as leaders should, for whores and boys were all about. It looked like the corruption of a painting he recalled seeing in Italy – a last supper of apostles and fallen saints. He recognised the lords Mounteagle, Cromwell and Sandys, heads close at one end as if singing a catch. At the other sat a clutch of earls – Rutland, Sussex and Bedford, each with a woman on his lap, each laughing to his fellow around his trull's exposed bosoms.

Continuing the line of earldoms, linking end to middle, John saw one he knew better – Henry Wriothesley, Earl of Southampton. He knew him because he had been, for some time, his friend Shakespeare's patron. Some said he was more than that, though if true, Will was as discreet as these noblemen weren't. He had dedicated glorious love poems to the earl, whose beauty, almost female in its nature, astonished. Once Southampton was sucked into Essex's orbit, patron and poet had seen less of each other, though John knew Will was still fond of the younger man.

I do not know whether he will inspire such poetry again, he thought, frankly studying. That youth who had dazzled London for near a decade was fading. The beauty was still there, but it was like a rose out of season, curling and brown at the edges. He was leering now, fending off the questing hands of the woman to his right, all his attention focused left and somewhat downwards. And John, who had been seeking just one man, found him now where he expected him, slap in the centre. He'd only missed him because he was face down on the table.

D'Esparr called, 'My lord! My lord of Essex!'

And there he was. 'What?' bellowed Robert Devereux, jerking upright, staring wildly about. 'Who is't who dares disturb me?'

'Uh, uh, I, my lord? Sir Samuel D'Esparr?' The knight swallowed, continued, 'I . . . I . . . have left my post to bring you urgent—'

'Silence!' roared the earl, glaring not just at the knight before him but all around. Lutes that were being untunefully plucked ceased. The chorus of lords at table's end halted their unharmonious drone. There were giggles and moans still from those too engaged to be distracted. But Southampton rose to add his bellow, commanding a bugler to sound. The man did, though the off and distressed notes showed him to be as drunk as any there.

While tumult subsided, over D'Esparr's shoulder John stared only at the earl, trying to reckon him, gauging how hard his mission and thus his swift escape might be. First glance was not inspiring. The eyes were milky, the near bleached whiteness of his skin emphasised by fever-red spots upon his cheeks. Worse though was his gauntness, for he looked as if he had dropped a third of his weight since their last encounter. John had seen him thus before, in the Netherlands. A man glowed in this manner when gripped by the bloody flux. It did not tend to leave him in possession of all his wits, and his lordship rarely had the full arsenal to begin with.

John closed his eyes. Let me be done with this and soon, he prayed. Let me deliver the Queen's message and depart. Let me not get sucked again into the madness of Essex.

Another bellow forced them open. 'What is it, Despair?' yelled the earl. 'Why are you not upon the coast? Why have you deserted your post? Desertion, by Christ's bones!' he roared.

'No, my . . . my lord . . . I . . .' His little eyes swivelled around. 'I bring you the Queen's messenger. I thought it my . . . my . . . my duty to accompany him.' He swallowed. 'We were ambushed, fought our way out.' His voice piped still higher under Essex's continuing glare. 'This man saved my life, came back for me when I was down.'

John shook his head. He suspected Sir Samuel had not planned to babble like this; was sure, indeed, that he would try to claim all glory from the ambuscado, while forgetting altogether the rolling and squealing and soiling. But the Earl of Essex had rattled him. He had that effect on most men.

'Man? What man?' his lordship cried.

'Er, this one, my lord.'

Sir Samuel reached back, grabbed John's arm, tried to shove him forward. Shrugging off the grip, John took a step towards the table.

The earl peered, rubbed his eyes, peered closer. Then, it was as if his face transformed into another's, or he contrived to briefly shed twenty years of hard living in a moment. 'Od's heartlings!' he cried. 'Od's breath! My old friend.'

People were standing now in the hall, the better to see. At the table, all the nobility half rose to peer down at him. John winced. His plans to deliver his messages quietly and disappear were at naught. 'My noble lord,' he said softly, bowing from the waist.

Essex stood too, arms opened wide as if to embrace. 'Do you know who this man is?' he shouted. 'This is he who rode cheek by jowl with me into the Spanish ranks at Zutphen. This he who warded my back there and at Cadiz! S'blood, I owe him my life thrice over.' Those reddened eyes, always watery, flooded their banks now. 'And see how he comes, once more in my hour of need, risen from his own fever-racked bed, and with reinforcements from his native Cornwall, stout hearts like himself, no doubt. Ah, if only you had come a week since, my friend, to share our glory.' He sniffed, bent, picked up his tankard. 'A pledge to him, to this gallant sir, the peerless . . . John Lawley!'

The hall resounded with his name. Suffering Christ, thought John, and tried to smile, to think of something to say. But it was Sir Samuel, a gleam in his eye, who spoke next. 'I owe him my life too, my lord,' he piped. 'Coming to bring him to you, we were beset by fifty ruffians. I went down under a dozen swords. All alone John Lawley came to my rescue and snatched me from my certain doom.'

'John Lawley! John Lawley!' came the cry from the hall. Jesu on the cross, John thought, I will be a ballad in Dublin's taverns by nightfall. 'My lord,' he called, as the shouts died away, 'I have news for you. Missives . . .'

Robert Devereux was having none of it. 'Witness that,' he shouted, waving to the hall as if it was a playhouse and his dais the platform. 'Here not a day and once again a hero. Beating of a hundred villains, saving a knight's life.' He gazed down at the two men before him, a new fire in his eyes. 'A knight he has little reason to love, now I remember me. And yet' – he swayed, gripped the table, steadied, continued – 'and yet he risked his life to save him. Jesu risen, but is that not nobility? Is that not a display of true knightly courtesy?' He swivelled. 'My lord of Southampton, what is the number of the knights we have dubbed on this campaign?'

Henry Wriothesley rose shakily. 'A mere eighty, your lordship. And' – he smiled down – 'I can think of few who are so worthy of the honour.'

'Yet is not this fellow, gallant though he may be . . . a player?' Lord Sandys it was who spoke, accompanying the derisive term with a sneer.

'Aye, a prince of players,' the earl retorted, 'and if we cannot make him a prince, we can at least make something else of him.' He swept his arm around the hall. 'Clear away there! Bring me my sword of state.'

John gaped. 'My lord, do not do this. I am unworthy . . .' but words were lost in a rush of drunken fumbling, of tables being pushed aside, chairs thrown back. John stood, a still centre to the swirl of preparation, shaking his head. This could not be happening, surely? And yet it was known that on three campaigns Essex had created as many knights as Elizabeth had in her whole reign; it was also said that little made her rage more. Though it was his prerogative, as viceroy, it was one honoured more in the breach than the observance. And John had never sought it, though the opportunity had arisen before. Indeed, he'd avoided it. For one, he knew he was no gentleman; but far more than that, to be one of Essex's knight bannerets would forever yoke him to the earl and his cause; while such love from Essex would attract an equal and opposite hate not only from the Secretary of State but probably from her majesty herself.

He looked around – to the windows, the door, even the rafters. No escape anywhere. Besides, what would he do? Hurl himself from the battlements? All he did see was Tomkins, who had proved himself a better sort in the skirmish, grinning large at him . . . and then the look of purest horror on the porcine face of Sir Samuel D'Esparr. And in the look he realised something.

Despair would now have a knightly rival for Tess Morton's hand.

Dazed by that thought, by everything, John shook his head, surrendered. Marched to the hall's entrance, he was surrounded there by belted earls, hedged in by nobility. To a trumpet's wobbly peal, and the drunken cheers of whores, nobles and scullions, he was marched back in. He knelt before his lord, wincing as the viceroy's sword swatted his shoulder and clanged upon his skull. He rose when commanded – whereupon Robert Devereux clasped him tight, dropping tears on to his shoulder. 'Sir John! Noble brother in arms. Ah, Sir John!' he wept, hugging hard.

John looked beyond him. The hall was re-forming around fresh pots of liquor; whores were again circling, pretty youths gathering. Another spiral of debauched celebration was about to begin – with him as its cause and focus. Though this was as meet an occasion as ever whisky called for, he knew he could not; or rather he knew he could, it was all his desire, yet he must not. New knight he might be, but he could not get stuck there serving his ennobler. To avoid that, to discharge his duties and return to salvage his life, the Queen's messenger had to speak to the Earl of Essex immediately, and alone.

'My lord,' he whispered, hugging back, 'I bear messages from England.'

The earl released enough to fix him with a watery eye. 'From whom?'

'From the Queen.'

The eye widened, the voice dropped. 'Has she heard . . . heard of the truce I have concluded?'

'My lord, she has.'

'And is she . . . is she pleased with her Robin?'

The words were spoken as if by a small child. It seemed cruel to reply as he had to – but crueller to delay the truth. 'My lord . . . she is not.'

At this, the earl suddenly released John, pushing him back, clutching at his guts. 'Ah, my torment comes! With me, man. Your arm, I beseech you.'

They began to push through the exultant mob to the arras behind the high table. Southampton, armed with a flagon, all smiles, tried to delay them, but with a groan Essex shoved past him, almost running now to the arras's end. 'Lift it,' he moaned, fumbling at the buttons on his doublet. 'Jesu mercy, be swift!'

John lifted the arras, opened the door it concealed. There was a corridor beyond that Essex ran down, opening buttons as he went. It ended in a semicircular turret, arrow slits in its walls, which contained Robert Devereux's greatest desire – a hole the size of a platter set into a stone ledge.

The earl had no time to undo the points that attached doublet to trunk hose. No time even to fiddle open the last of the ivory-faced buttons. Ripping them, they pinged off stone as he cried, 'Jesu! Aid me!' and it was not to his saviour he appealed but to his newest knight, now acting the role of body servant. John knew what to do, had indeed done this before and more than once. Seizing the other's padded shoulders from behind, crushing the gilt and lace, he pulled hard and down, peeling doublet and hose from the earl's body as if they were one piece – which in a way they were, since all was tied together. The heavy folds of fabric hit the ground, the man's bare arse poked from under his lawn shirt. Swivelling on the spot, for his ankles were wrapped still in hose, Essex plunged straight down over the stone hole . . . and only just in the nick.

A sound like grape shot came, together with a stench that would have maddened horses. 'Yes! Oh yes,' the Earl of Essex cried, his face filled with more ecstasy than wine or whore could ever conjure, head raised, eyes closed, lips moving, undoubtedly in mumbled prayer, to which he was much given. It took a long while for the other noises to subside, and only when they had did he open his eyes, look at John and say, in a voice almost normal, 'Tell me then, what words my sovereign sends me.'

John swallowed. 'Shall we not wait, my lord, till you are . . . finished in the jakes?'

The laugh that came was bitter. 'Finished? I could be here all the night and there would never be an end. I have conducted whole campaigns from this position, as you well know. Perhaps your friend the playwright could frame that irony into verse.' He groaned, farted wetly, shifted. 'So tell me swiftly what lies my sweet Bess now believes of me.'

'My lord, I think it would be best if you read them yourself.'

On his words, John delved into his satchel and finally executed his mission – he delivered the dispatches from Elizabeth, Queen of England, to Robert, Earl of Essex.

From one throne to another.

XXII

Wise Counsel

The earl received the satchel as if it contained what he had but lately
voided. He reached in, drew out two packets. Laying aside the one
sealed in the arms of the Duchy of Lancaster, he ripped off the royal
seal and unfolded the parchment. ' "My Lord",' he read, then looked
at John. 'So cold,' he sighed. 'She does not even greet me as her
Robin.' He looked down, read, muttered, stray phrases emitted and
echoed by a splattering beneath. 'Perilous and contemptible,' John
heard. 'A hollow peace.' The earl read the parchment through,
muttering the while, then held it to the side while he stared at
something far beyond the castle's stones. John glimpsed tightly
scrawled writing. Barely a page, but if it consisted of such words as
Essex had let slip, it would be more than enough. Her majesty was
known for both her concision and her corrosive wit. John watched as
the man before him burned.

Essex read the page again more slowly, but now it was as if he were
in angry conversation with his accuser, rebutting each point. John
was no longer there; the argument was between the Queen and her
vice-regent. 'Face the issue?' he spat. 'What know you of the issue
sitting safe in your palace? Come here, come command the sick and
weary dregs you have given me to the heights you demand.' He read
on, muttered on, eructed on. 'God's teeth!' he suddenly shouted.
'She makes Tyrone's private submission to me an incitement to
treason. Treason! Me! Who has ever been the most loyal of . . .' He
trailed off, seeking something else amidst the spider's scrawl. Gradually the muttered indignation faded. He read more carefully, his

stares above John's head lasting longer. Finally his gaze lowered and settled on the face of the man before him.

'Her majesty did not write this letter.'

John hesitated. What good would it do to contradict him? Yet over the years he had always tried to steady the volatile man before him. On occasion, he had succeeded. 'My lord, she gave it to me from her own hand.'

'And she may have used that hand in its creation – but not her heart.' He narrowed his eyes. 'Who was standing over her when she wrote? Hmm? Did you see her alone?'

'No.'

'Who was with her?'

John hesitated. Yet there was no point in lying. 'The Master Secretary.'

'Ha ha!' Essex threw himself back. 'Cecil! That bottle-backed spider, that malevolent toad, that . . . of course he was there.' He nodded vigorously. 'He needed to witness that the poison he dripped into her ear had its foul effect.' He reached out, gripped John by the front of his doublet, pulled him down till their faces were close, though he still bellowed. 'My most bitter enemy dictated this letter and forced the Queen to sign it.'

This close, John could see in the earl's eyes that he would accept no contrary argument. But he could perhaps be distracted into a better vein of thought – by a silken square John had, not in the satchel, but in a pouch within his doublet. 'Good my lord . . .' he began as he reached.

'What letter, Robert?'

The interrupting voice came from down the corridor. Released, John turned to see the Earl of Southampton hurrying towards them. On his heels were Mounteagle, Rutland, Sussex and Lord Sandys.

'This!' As the men drew close, Essex shook the paper he held. 'It purports to come from her majesty. But I declare she was coerced into signing it. It is not her sentiments. My sweet Bess was ne'er so cruel. Humpbacked Cecil wrote it.' His gaze shifted. 'Is that not so, Sir John?'

For a moment, John wondered whom the earl was addressing. He even looked behind him. When he realised, he started, then considered. He had to be careful here. The men in the corridor were all, in name, Essex's. But any one of them could also be reporting to Cecil. Such was the nature of faction. 'I think you will find, my lord, that the Secretary has sent his own missive.'

'Hmm?' Essex reached for the parchment he had thrown aside before. He held the seal of the Duchy of Lancaster for a moment – another title he had craved and been passed over for – then crushed the red wax, tossed it, ripped open the pages – there were several here – and read. As he did, the fever spots on his cheek deepened and it took but a moment for the oaths to come, a string of them accompanied by a whine from his guts that was almost feral. 'As I thought,' he cried, 'the turd repeats coolly what he forced my Queen to sign in heat: that the peace is contemptible, that the truce must be repudiated on the nonce, that I must bring Tyrone to a pass of arms immediately – and that the forces I have already been given are ample to the task. Ample!' he bellowed. 'He sits on his inflamed arse in London and tells me how to conduct a campaign, this cripple who has lifted nothing more deadly than a fork. He plots against me in Council. But worse! He turns my sweet Bess's regard against me with his lies. Lies!' He half rose from his stone seat, waving the paper in the air. 'I will countenance them no longer. This is what I think of Sir Robert Cecil and his words,' he declared, and reaching behind him, he took the Master Secretary's letter and wiped his arse with it.

The lords cheered. John closed his eyes. This, he thought, does not bode well.

On the instant, his thought was confirmed. 'In the devil's name, Robert,' cried Southampton, 'there's treason in the court. The toad has corrupted her majesty. He must be confronted. He must be . . . dealt with.'

'We must go at once. To the court. To the Queen,' yelled Mounteagle.

'To the court. To the Queen,' echoed the others.

Essex was trying to dislodge the paper stuck to his fingers. Finally it fell into the jakes. He sat again, heavily, doubt displacing fury on his face. 'Elizabeth expressly forbids my return,' he said. 'She orders that I stay and confront Tyrone.'

'With what, sir?' demanded Southampton. 'A sick army against twice their number? A sick general too, for you are not well.'

''Tis true,' Essex sighed, and farted, 'I am not.'

'And as you yourself said, my lord,' added Lord Sandys, the eldest man there, with a face twisted into lines of bitterness, 'such impossible orders do not come from her majesty anyway. They come from your greatest enemy. He commands the impossible, knowing your gallantry will make you assay it. Yet even Achilles and all his Myrmidons could not triumph here. Cecil wishes to see you destroyed for one reason alone: so he can rule the Queen unchallenged. Make his damnable peace with Spain. Secure the succession for James of Scotland!' He looked around for support. 'It is not action he commands here. It is treason!'

'By God, sir, you are right, sir.' Essex rose again, lifting off the hole as he spoke. 'To return now is not only the necessary choice for myself. It is right for the Queen. It is right for England.' His eyes misted. 'By all the saints, it is my duty and I will not shirk it.'

The noble sound of the declaration was lessened by the sight – his lordship with his clothes snagged about his ankles, his shirt hanging to his naked thighs. John went and stood behind him, bent and lifted doublet and hose together. As Essex shrugged into them, Southampton spoke again. 'Then let us gather the army, or the vanguard of it. A thousand brave knights riding under your banner? England would flock to it as it once did to Bolingbroke's standard. We will march on the capital . . . and spike the traitor Cecil's head on London Bridge.'

All there cheered – save John. He had stepped around to help Essex with such buttons as had survived, and was alarmed to see a familiar gleam in his eyes. He had seen it before – at Zutphen, at Cadiz – and it always heralded some mad act, some charge against the odds. Also, this was the very thing Cecil had feared the most, warned him against. He was already tainted with the title: Essex's man. Now he was his newest knight banneret, a title that could readily see him hung, drawn and quartered. For this was treason being spoken here, no question, and labelled with a usurper's name. 'My lord,' he said softly, holding him by his lapels, his own eyes seeking to secure a gaze already fixed on future glory, 'do not do this. If you return to England thus, they will cry you traitor. Word will precede you that you come to make war upon the realm.'

'No! Only upon Cecil and his cabal.'

'But Cecil controls what people think,' John continued urgently, more loudly, to top the murmurs of protest building behind him. 'You say that he turns the Queen against you. What will he say to her when you march through the land at the head of an army?'

'He will not be able to say anything with a spike through his skull.' As he spoke, Southampton stepped close, reaching to John's hands where they grasped near the earl's neck, trying to pull them away. 'Unhand, sirrah!'

But John would not be budged by a mayfly – and he was thinking fast. He knew the rash man he held, and that gleam, well enough to know he would not now be dissuaded. Yet he was ever malleable – perhaps he could be moulded into a more pleasing shape. 'Think, Robbie,' he whispered, at last trapping the earl's shifting eyes with this rare personal address. 'If you go with an army, you needs must go slowly. Your enemy will be forewarned and make preparations. Perhaps it will come to a pass of arms with all its hazards. At the least, London will be turned into an armed camp against your coming. And then the venomous toad will have all the time he needs to drip that poison into the ear of your sweet Bess. But if you were to arrive before he even knows you have left' – he let a smile come – 'well, good my lord, you will be there swiftly enough, and in your beloved person, to provide the antidote.'

The earl's watery gaze finally settled upon him. 'What is it you suggest, Johnnie?'

Ignoring Southampton's continuing tugs and protests, John replied, 'This. I have just made the journey from London in five days, and you are twice the horseman I will ever be. So ride, with only your closest companions. Ride for Whitehall, make straight for the Queen. Your words, your presence. She will listen to you, heed your grievances, see your truth.' He leaned nearer. 'And then she will dispatch your enemies.'

He had no idea if what he said was true. Having spoken to the Queen twice now, and knowing the cunning of Cecil, he suspected not. Yet he had been in enough of his friend's plays to understand a little of the horrors of the civil war Essex's armed return would bring. This alternative was better – for England, for Essex . . . and for himself. A proclaimed traitor would never win Tess back. Ned would never rise as a traitor's son; while the players would never let such a one share a platform with them. They will have enough problem with a knight, he thought, flushing cold, something he had not yet considered.

He released Essex's lapels, stepped away. Southampton and the other lords swarmed in, countering his arguments. But though his ears were full of other earls' words, Essex's eyes were still on John Lawley. 'Let be!' he bellowed, loud enough to command a silence. He took a step towards his new knight, nodded once, then turned back. 'Sir John is right. I will to the Queen, by the swiftest of routes and with only you, my choicest brothers in arms.' He raised a hand against the clamour that came. 'Should it be necessary, do you not believe that we alone will be swords enough for Cecil's paltry crew? But I do not think such extremity will be necessary – for I will neither sleep nor rest till I am once again all alone with my sweet Bess. Then I will provide' – he glanced at John, and smiled – 'an antidote to poison.' He turned back, raised his arms high. 'Gentlemen,' he cried, 'we ride for London!'

XXIII

Nonsuch Palace

It was the cobbles that woke him, the sudden clatter of them under his mount's shod hooves. He jerked upright in his saddle, looked around him, bleary eyes confirming what his ears had already told him – they had at long last left the unending countryside behind. They had reached the City.

Or at least Westminster. The abbey's unmistakable spire was directly ahead of them. They were riding towards it.

The thought made him swivel. If they were heading towards the abbey, they were heading away from the palace. Away from the goal that had sustained them through the four days and nights of hard riding. Away from the Queen. Had they already failed? While he nodded on his horse's neck, had Essex lost his gamble? And were they now making for Westminster to seek sanctuary in its cloisters from her majesty's wrath?

'She's not there,' came a voice from beside him. It had an Irish lilt to it, and John glanced sharp right. Captain Christopher St Lawrence, six foot six of Hibernian braggadocio, was riding stirrup to stirrup with him. He'd known him a little in the Netherlands. A good and loyal soldier, one of the few he'd at least been happy to see in Dublin. The man smiled. 'I thought you might slip off. So I was here to catch you.'

'Much obliged.' Sleeping men *had* slipped off their horses in the hurly-burly dash across the realm. Most had survived with bruises. One knight had broken his arm and been abandoned on the roadside. There was to be barely a pause in their journey, only the briefest of halts to commandeer fresh horses at country inns, plunder their

212

larders, sleep for a scant few hours in their barns and ride on. John thought he had made the journey to Dublin in a record time of five days. Essex's return had taken only four.

He yawned widely, stared at the man beside him. Even the big Irishman, with all the vigour of youth on his side, was looking exhausted. What had he just said? Why were they making for Westminster?

His confused looks must have been question enough. An answer came. 'She's at Nonsuch Palace,' the captain said. 'We enquired for her at Whitehall and were told so.'

Nonsuch. John's sigh melded into another vast yawn. It was ten miles south of the city, nothing when compared to all the miles they'd cantered – from the valleys of north Wales, through the vales of Evesham and the White Horse, over the hills of the Cotswolds and the Chilterns. However, like most journeys, the last part seemed endless. He remembered how interminable the Channel had appeared after two and a half years away with Drake.

For mercy's sake, could he not just sleep?

The party clattered on to the dock at the Lambeth ferry. On the opposite bank, Lollards' Tower thrust up from the Archbishop's Palace. It had been but two weeks since he had been a prisoner within its black stones, had that audience with the Queen and her secretary. Now, perhaps, he was to see them both again.

Men were dismounting, and he did the same. There was an ordinary near the dock and its proprietors were being kicked awake and commanded to produce a meal of last night's stew, stale bread and ale. The ferry was across on the Surrey shore but was even now under way, moving towards them. John leaned against his mount's warm flank, and glanced downriver, east. It was lightening there, and though he could not see around the river's bend, he knew that the rising sun would already be gilding the tower of St Mary Overies, Southwark. Close by beneath it, Tess and Ned would still be sleeping, ignoring the toll that came, as Lambeth's now did, to summon them to another day's endeavours. The thought of curling around either of them, feeling that horsehair mattress beneath him, inhaling the warm night sweetness of their forms? Ah! It was a vision of heaven and he found himself seeking a wherry at the dock. There were several fellows asleep in their craft, any one of whom would happily awaken at the jangle of the coins in John Lawley's purse. He still had several that the Master Secretary had given him for his mission. He would have traded every one of them for a swift conveyance to his Bankside paradise.

A shout followed by laughter drew his eyes back. The Earl of Essex stood close to the water's edge, in the forefront as ever. Someone had brought him a tankard and he held it aloft, beer foam frothing over its lip, pledging. John heard the familiar words: 'A health to her majesty and damnation to the toad!' It, and other such oaths, had sustained them in their journey. And when any flagged, they'd find Robert Devereux at their elbow, cheering them on, inspiring them with his fervour, the damn-near-holiness of their mission. No longer were they chasing Irish wraiths through the rain-sodden bogs, trying to close with an enemy who would not fight in any honourable manner. No longer were their shoulders hunched against the sudden ball and flung spear of ambuscado. They were riding unthreatened through England's fair lanes, and on a mission they could under-stand: to free the Queen from her treasonous counsellors. To save the realm from disaster.

And they were riding for him. John shook his head, as Essex bellowed again and quaffed and men cheered. For all his mad arrogance, he was again a leader to inspire. The sorry fellow voiding his bowels in Dublin Castle's jakes had gone. He was once more a commander of men, leading them to glory. No matter that what awaited could be a Queen's cold fury, and a traitor's cell for all of them. Each man there, as most did in the land, played at dice; each this day sought the hazard in the earl's rash roll.

Essex, a head taller than all save for the hulking St Lawrence, espied him above the crowd. 'Sir Knight,' he shouted, 'join us.' As John came near, he continued, 'Marry, Johnnie, I have never known a fellow could sleep so soundly on a horse's back. You scarce woke up from Carnarvon to Slough. How do you do it?'

''Tis the purity of my life, good my lord. It gives me nothing but sweet dreams and easy rest.'

Hoots greeted this, the loudest coming from Essex. 'It must have been your pure life that helped your bare arse pump up and down so vigorously in that Cadiz señora's house,' the earl countered, then thrust his leather tankard out. 'Here, let's drink to the ladies of Spain.'

'The ladies of Spain!' came the cry, and John pledged, drank, looking over the rim at the men around him. Each had sagged over their mount's neck in the previous few days – Southampton, Wooton, Danvers and the rest – but all looked now as if they had been revived by their leader's fire, eyes and cheeks glowing with it. They could see the destination ahead, believed certainly in their triumph. With such a captain, how could they fail? And even John, who knew him better than most, began to doubt his own doubt. After all, no one in recent years had had more sway over the ageing Queen than handsome young Essex. And if he was no longer quite the gilded youth of yore, if dissipation, the flux and Irish compromise had all taken a toll of him, he was still the Queen's champion, Earl Marshal of England – and perhaps yet her sweet Robin?

John thought again of the handkerchief she'd entrusted to him, still folded within his doublet. In the four-day pell-mell ride, he'd found few solitary moments to pass it over. And when one brief one came . . . he'd hesitated, and the chance passed. He had not sought another. The Queen, after all, had forbidden Essex's return unless he came wearing the laurel wreath of victory, this token woven into it. Besides, John knew the earl well. He could carry a day with his blood hot – as he had at Zutphen, at Cadiz. Righteous anger might keep it so – but not, John suspected, the uncertainties of a queen's love.

John looked again downriver . . . and visions of a soft bed passed. He would see this through. For better or worse he was Essex's man – at least on this day. And if the earl triumphed – well, Sir John Lawley might not be such a bad title to be taking back to Southwark. Especially with a certain fat knight still guarding a lonely beach in Erin.

The ferry bumped into the dock. The ferryman was calling something and the Irish captain went to talk with him. He returned, his black-browed face further darkened with a frown. 'The Toad may be forewarned,' he rasped. 'The ferryman tells me he only just dropped a fellow on the south bank. 'Twas that scoundrel Grey.'

A collective hiss. All knew that Lord Grey was the earl's enemy, all the more bitter because he had once been his friend. Essex had knighted him on the Cadiz expedition. Grey had repaid him by siding with Cecil.

'Traitorous dog! Would he pre-empt me with her majesty? God's wounds!'

Amidst the hubbub, one voice rose. 'Let me ride and overtake him,' said one Sir Thomas Gerard. 'We are related, through my wife, and he was wont to call me cousin. Let me persuade him to a pause at least.'

It was agreed. The Essex party crowded the gunnels of the ferry, all the more tight-packed for the one horse – Gerard's. The rest of the mounts would be brought across on the next trip.

The ferryman heaved on the rope, aided no doubt by the leaning of the whole group, yearning for the Surrey side. As soon as the ferry ground into the dock there, Gerard mounted and took off at a gallop. The rest disembarked . . . and a shout came immediately. 'Whose mounts are these?' yelled Essex.

John looked to a copse of oak. Beneath their branches, fifteen horses stood. Two grooms attended them, staring open-mouthed at the new arrivals. When Essex strode forward, the lads fell to their knees. He repeated the question and one of the grooms stammered the reply. 'They . . . they . . . they belongs to my ma-master, your worship. Squire Martyn of Cheam, come last night to do business in the t-town.'

Essex stared down. 'Is he a true Englishman, lad, and loyal to the crown?'

The boy gaped. 'I . . . I . . . I believes so, aye.'

The earl nodded. 'Good. Then he will not mind us commandeering them, for our mission is entirely for her majesty's safety. Saddle them.' Without waiting to see if he was obeyed – he was, on the instant – Essex turned to his men. 'Here's a gift from the Almighty himself. He blesses us in our endeavour. Praise him and mount!'

One of the few things that Essex had taken time to do in his hurry was pray, to which he was much given. Amens and hallelujahs now echoed around the trunks as the party rushed forward to aid the overwhelmed grooms in their labours. Even the earl helped and, driven by desperation, the horses were saddled and bridled in moments. The men mounted. 'To the Queen!' yelled Essex, rising high in his stirrups.

The party took off at a gallop. Mud clods flew up, for this major route to London had been much chopped by hoof and wheel. Ducking his head, John felt the strikes of earth on hat brim and chest. He kicked his new mount and, finding it sprightly, moved through the ranks to ride beside his lord in the van, where less earth flew.

Yet they had travelled barely a mile when a horseman came the other way, halting them with his cries. 'My lord,' yelled Sir Thomas Gerard, and all reined in around him. 'News, my lord,' continued the knight breathlessly. 'I caught up with Lord Grey and asked that he slow and await your coming. "I have business at court," he declared and rode on. I followed, asking that he at least let you precede and announce yourself to her majesty.'

'And what did he reply?' asked Southampton.

'He looked along his nose at me and wondered if the plea came from his cousin or his lordship himself. Either way, he would not be delayed,' Sir Thomas growled.

'Plea? The cur!' Essex slapped the saddle before him, making his mount skitter. 'He means to warn the Secretary whose creature he is.'

'By the Devil and all his imps!' yelled St Lawrence, drawing his sword. 'I will ride now and skewer this traitorous dog. And then, begod, I'll ride ahead and do the same to the Toad.' He waved his sword above him, yelling, 'Who is with me?'

Several. John was not one of them, and was trying to think of some way to halt an act which was both murder and treason – when he did not have to, for another did. 'No, friends. No!' The earl was once more up in his stirrups, despite Irish steel whirling close to his head. 'We will deal with Grey and all traitors when we arrive. Once we have secured the Queen's person and, again, her love. Many false friends will then learn the cost of their betrayals.' He turned to St Lawrence. 'Put up, good fellow. Your blade will find its just mark soon enough.'

'By God,' yelled the Irish knight, 'and isn't it my family motto: "Never put up a clean sword"? So . . . there!' he continued, impaling his thumb on the tip, drawing blood. 'There's a drop for your thirst – and my lord's promise that you will soon have a draught!'

A loud cheer came. Spurs were dug into flanks and the gallop resumed. Eight miles left to Nonsuch, and despite the mudded track, they were taken at speed.

It was yet early, and the sun, as they crested the last rise, glittered brightly in the scores of windows, plain leaded or stained, that covered the palace. It was shaped like a castle, with towers at four corners, but it was never designed to be defended. And indeed, no guards manned its false battlements nor even stood with halberds raised at the gatehouse. As they slowed to ride in pairs over the bridge that crossed the waterless moat, all were aware of the silence. Only their mounts' metal shoes echoed around the cobbled court-yard beyond, no alarms. Glancing up, John saw a shape move away from a thick-glassed window. They were noted, but not challenged.

A lone horse stood, loosely hitched to a post. 'Grey's,' declared Sir Thomas, but of the rider there was no sign.

Everyone dismounted – save for Robert Devereux himself, who was looking up at the windows as if he expected Bess herself to open one and call to him. John watched apprehension war with hope on his broad, mud-smirched face. In the dash across the realm, his dreams could be sustained by frantic momentum. Here, in pause and the unnerving silence of the palace, John could see him falter. He was like a dice thrower with a huge stake before him. The next roll led to fortune or the fall.

It was the moment, he realised, for the earl looked like a man who needed a sign from Fortune herself. So, handing his reins to St Lawrence, John crossed to the earl's stirrup. 'My lord?' he said, raising his hand. Essex took it, descended . . . and opened his to find the Queen's handkerchief in it.

'What's this?' Essex murmured.

'The Queen's favour. You are her champion still, and your sweet Bess awaits.'

'Bess,' replied Essex as softly, fingering the entwined tangerine Es. His eyes misted, as if he looked not at his newest knight, but at the Queen herself. When they cleared, bravado was in them again. 'We go to her majesty!' he called, tucking the silk into his doublet. 'But let no man draw his sword – unless I do! Yet if he do' – his eyes found the tall Irishman – 'let him not put it up clean.'

The acclaiming shout propelled him to the steps and through the main doors of the palace. There were servants in the entrance hall beyond them, including a steward who bowed and wrung his hands and tried to interpose his body before the headlong rush. He was brushed aside as Essex led his party, taking the stairs two by two. At the top he did not hesitate, for he had obviously been there before, sweeping down a corridor that had portraits between doors on one side and tall windows on the other. John glanced through them, noted the garden below, the patterned parterres surrounded by hedges of box, the paths between made of different-coloured gravels. At one end stood a stone fountain. At the other a raised mound with a table and chairs. The table was covered in bottles and candelabra. Perhaps the Queen had dined there late last night and so was still sleeping, unaware of what was striding to waken her in mud-caked boots.

The thought made him slow. Momentum and excitement had carried them to the Queen's threshold; but did they truly mean to cross it? To surprise the Queen in her sanctum where, it was said, no man had ever passed?

The answer lay ahead, down a second corridor at right angles to the first. At the end of it were large oak doors, the approach to them lined with chairs on either side. Rising from these now, hastily snatching up their halberds, were two guards. Putting their backs to the doors, they held their weapons at port and nervously watched the approach of so many armed men.

'Halt here!' Essex flung up his arm.

This allowed the steward who had first tried to stop them in the entrance to catch up, slide through the group and place himself between the guards before the door. 'My lord!' he cried, his hands raised before him as if in prayer, though he rubbed them as if he had some itch. 'Please do not proceed further. Her Majesty is wont to lie abed of a morning and not receive before noon. If it please you, return for an audience then.'

'It does not please me.' Robert Devereux drew himself up to his full height and glared down. 'Tell me, sirrah, do you know me?'

'In . . . indeed,' quavered the man. 'You are my lord of Essex.'

'I am!' came the bellowed reply. 'More, I am Earl Marshal of England. And I come with tidings of treason. I come to save her majesty.' He bent closer, as if examining a small insect. 'Has a certain Lord Grey passed this way?'

'Lord Grey? Why . . . n-no . . .'

Essex snapped upright. 'Good. Then we are in the nick.' He switched his glance to the two guards. 'Stand aside, fellows. Your commander commands.'

The two guards looked at each other, did not move. But their gazes snapped back at a growl from Captain St Lawrence, who stepped forward now, hand on hilt. As the huge Irishman loomed, both men scrambled aside. 'Doors,' Essex commanded the steward.

Despite his obvious terror, the man did not jump to them. He looked first at the menacing captain, then at the crowd behind, finally again at Robert Devereux. 'My lord,' he gasped. 'So many men in the Queen's bedroom. It would be' – he closed his eyes, as if awaiting a sword stroke – 'sacrilege!'

The word paused the ever-religious earl. John knew – all there knew – that the Queen was appointed by God to her throne. What they were about to do could be considered treason – or at the least a violation of holy sanctuary. Essex turned back, raised a hand, pinched the bridge of his nose between closed eyes. When he opened them again, John saw the same uncertainty that had gripped him in the courtyard below. He spoke, hesitantly. 'I . . . I will proceed alone.' At the chorus of protest that arose, he looked around the faces before him. 'I must. I am the Queen's champion and perhaps have some right to surprise her thus, but . . .' He studied them again, his hesitation plain. 'But . . . I am loath to go entirely unattended.'

His voice had risen in plea, a small boy suddenly afraid. Stronger voices rose in reply, all seeking to be selected. 'Take me,' cried the Earl of Southampton.

'Me,' shouted Sir Thomas Gerard.

'Nay, me!' yelled St Lawrence, his bellow rising above all others, as each fell to quarrelling over right and precedent. Only one man there said nothing. No, no, thought John Lawley, sliding behind the Irishman's broad back. But the fellow stepped away, to argue with another. And, of course, Robert Devereux was looking straight at him.

'Will you accompany me, Sir John?' His voice halted the rest as the men turned to regard the man several paces to their rear. Essex continued. 'You are the Queen's messenger and brought me the news of this conspiracy. It is fitting you are beside me to bear me witness.' He nodded. 'And you have ever warded me in the darkest of days. Will you ward me now?'

A cockerel crowed somewhere in the garden beyond the windows. Like the apostle Peter, John thought, I have recently denied *my* lord at least twice. Yet here, under such scrutiny, he could not. Keeping his sigh to himself, he bowed. 'Yours in the ranks of death, my lord.'

'Well.' Essex nodded. 'Let us pray it does not come to that.' As John moved to him, the earl turned to loom again above the cringing steward. 'And now, fellow. Open!' The man bowed even lower, turned to the two guards, shrugged. One handed his halberd to the other, then reached to the door handle. He twisted it, pushed . . .

And the Earl of Essex marched into the Queen's apartments. While at his heels, like a forlorn hound, trailed John Lawley.

The first room was a large antechamber with a single chair at one end, facing the door. No doubt this was where the Queen would greet her first visitors of the day. There were two truckle beds and a maid lately risen from each, who clutched each other now, their faces as white as the shifts they wore. Behind them, a door was open and they did not try to stop the men striding towards it, only averted their eyes as if from some horror.

Noises came from beyond, urgent whisperings, a rustling of cloth, the sound of chests being slammed. The earl paused in the doorway, looked back. 'Wish me fortune, Johnnie,' he whispered; then, breathing deep, he stepped into the Queen's bedchamber.

John followed . . . and bumped into Essex's mud-spattered cloak, which had halted suddenly before him. Stepping slightly to the side so he could see, he did – and froze. There were six women in the room; not one was moving, each as still as if they posed for an artist – though no artist in the kingdom would have dared to depict ladies thus. Only in Italy perhaps could one be found to capture, in marble or in paint, the slight rise and fall of breasts against linen, the only sign that any there lived. Three were at the rear door, their hands raised as if beckoning, while two more were at centre and jointly held a dressing gown above the shoulders of the last woman, who stood between them.

It was only the attention that everyone else in the room was paying her that made John know this thin old lady at its centre. He had always known her age, though no one in England dared mention it. Perhaps he knew it better than most, he thought, given that his grandfather had killed this woman's mother.

Elizabeth was sixty-three years old. The woman standing before them looked older.

Scant hair hung in grey tendrils across a wrinkled forehead. The whole trend to the face was downwards, sagging from brow to the wattles of her neck, all of it sallow. Her lips, about whose fullness scores of sonnets had been written, were thin and flaking. It was her eyes, though, that showed the years most, for the orbs which the poets had so praised were dull, glazed, dragged down by pouches of flesh. Yet it was what was in them that made John finally cease an appraisal that must have taken mere seconds; the many things within them. There was fear, certainly, at armed men violating her chamber; rage too, for she was still Gloriana. Though what turned him away finally was not his fear.

It was pity. Pity for the aloneness of someone whose being had been suddenly, violently exposed as a lie; the mask ripped aside, to display the saddest of truths: that Time had transformed even the Faerie Queene into a crone. Yet the worst of it John only realised after he'd looked down, and closed his eyes: the woman had been so brutally exposed to the man who had been her last, perhaps her greatest, love. Artifice had allowed her to pretend that handsome Robert Devereux loved her, desired her. In the horror that must have shown in his eyes, this fantasy shattered. And the ache that came to his stomach now was part for her and also part for Essex. There would be no forgiveness here, no redemption – for him. For his lord. For a love so suddenly betrayed could only turn, as suddenly, to hate. The handkerchief was so much ash.

Whatever his eyes betrayed, the courtier could not falter. Did not. 'Majesty!' Essex cried, breaking the binding spell that held everyone, transforming all stillness to sudden movement. As he strode across the room, sword slapping his thigh as he marched, the maids who held her gown dropped it on to her shoulders, having time to tie only one swift bow before Essex was upon them, his big body scattering them as he flung himself down before Elizabeth, seizing one hand, kissing it again and again.

'My lady! My sovereign! My queen! Oh, my sweet, sweet Bess!'

The devastation in her eyes did not halt her words. 'What means this outrage? Why have you burst so rudely upon our—'

But her words *were* halted by Essex's sudden rising – and his equally sudden descent upon her neck. 'Oh my soul's delight!' he blurted into it, covering it with kisses. 'Do not chastise your sweet Robin. Forgive my intemperance, my rashness. You *will* forgive all when you hear why I have come. When you learn the threat I am here to deliver you from.'

He bent, seized both her hands, began kissing each finger separately. John could not help but look up again – and then wished he had not. For over the earl's mud-flecked hair his eyes met Elizabeth's. And he could see in their sudden narrowing both recognition and the fury of having these private intimacies revealed to others. Terrified she may have been. But she was still Queen.

'Out!' she roared, directly at him, and then turned it on all the others in the room. 'Leave us alone!'

An elderly lady-in-waiting stepped forward. 'Majesty, I should not leave you unattended. I will—'

A slap ceased her words. The Queen had freed one of her hands from Essex's attentions to deliver it. 'Out, I say. Everyone! Only my servant, the earl, will remain.' Her gaze returned to John, who flinched under it. 'That includes you, you . . . saucy knave. Out!'

Never had he been happier to obey a sovereign's command. While the maidservants fled through the rear door, he retreated the way he'd come. He did not wait for his commander's dismissal. Essex could not have given one, lost as he was to his caresses and the tears now flowing freely over the Queen's mottled hand.

XXIV

The Upshot

As soon as he stepped into the corridor, he was surrounded.

'What news, fellow, what news?' cried the Earl of Southampton.

'Is my lord kindly received?' asked Sir Thomas Gerard.

'How did her majesty take his sudden coming?' urged the Irishman, St Lawrence.

'Lords, gentlemen, cry you mercy, please.' The crowd gave back slightly from the door against which they pressed him. He passed through them, led them a little way down the corridor, spoke softly. 'The earl has been received most graciously. Her majesty was startled, 'tis true, for she had only just arisen . . .' He paused, knew he could not, must not dwell on his glimpse behind Elizabeth's masks. 'She has dismissed all save the earl himself. She will hear his plea in private.'

'In private? Sure, that is when Robert is at his very best.' Southampton's smile was lascivious, and several other gentlemen giggled. 'His victory is assured.' He turned back to John. 'Is that all, sir?'

'All, my lord, for now. Like you, I will await developments in prayer and contemplation.'

Southampton stared at him, trying to sense if he was being mocked. But John had discovered in his short time back in the Essex camp that all followed their leader's example and took their religion most seriously. Indeed, several captains now dropped to their knees while others opened their hands at their sides and stared to the heavens through the panelled ceiling. John used the chance the murmured prayers gave him to step away and lower himself on to a chair. His legs, jellied enough from four straight days in the saddle, had been further undone by the Queen's hate-filled stare.

In the event, he could neither rest long, nor were many prayers uttered before the doors were flung open and Robert Devereux strode out. On his face was the same ecstasy that infused his words. 'Her majesty has been most gracious, most royally loving!' he cried. 'She has greeted me with all kindnesses. And though I have suffered much trouble and storms abroad, I have found such a sweet calm at home.'

'Does she dismiss the Toad?' Southampton asked, stepping close. 'All her kindnesses are naught compared to that.'

'In good time. In good time,' Essex replied cheerily, waving his hands. 'She has asked for a postponement to our talk, that she may dress and I repair some of the ravages of our swift coming.' He looked down at his road-smirched clothes, then sniffed. 'Indeed, she says I have turned centaur, for I smell more of horse than of man.'

He laughed uproariously, all the party joining in, as if suddenly released by the Queen's humour, eminent lords transformed to schoolboys, leaning on each other, knees weak with laughter. 'Come, gentlemen,' cried Essex, mastering himself, setting off down the corridor. 'While her majesty dresses, I am to seek water, borrow a soldier's cloak and return promptly. Help me all.'

Wearily John rose to follow . . . to be halted by a hiss. He turned – to see Sarah, his lover from just two weeks before, step from the Queen's apartments. Her blonde tresses were caught up in a ribbon, and she had a gown over her shift. He had not noticed her among the ladies-in-waiting. Had not noticed much, truly, beyond the Queen's fury.

Closing the door behind her, she came to him rapidly. 'A word, sir,' she said curtly.

'And delightful to see you again too, my sweet.'

She pierced him with a look from eyes he now recalled, startlingly black in her fairness, then looked to the two guards at the door, their halberds at port, as if they now would hold it against all comers. 'Here,' she said, taking his arm, leading him a short way down the corridor to another door, which she opened, passing through ahead of him. He followed; she reached behind him, pulled the door to. Their bodies were close and he inhaled her. Not cloves this time, but something of the night and the morning too.

'Maid,' he said, smiling, 'I am flattered that you wish to greet a returning warrior thus, but alas . . .'

She grunted, crossed to the far wall, where shutters were etched in light. She flung these open and he squinted against sudden sunshine. She turned back. 'In sooth, keep your foolery to yourself, sir, and tell me what you are about here,' she said, her voice harsh and low.

'Foolery? Unless you can raise the dead, you'll get no fooling with me.' He stepped towards her. 'Sarah, is it not?'

She held up a halting hand. 'I say again – we have no time for games, John Lawley. Why you are here?'

'Here?' John glanced about the room, a small one for dressing, by the racks of clothes and table of face potions.

'You know what I mean.'

'I am not sure I do.' He moved past her, fell heavily into a chair before a tall mirror. He looked at himself, his ragged beard, his heavy-lidded eyes, the dabs of mud. He sighed, pressed the palm of a hand into a socket. 'Sarah, I have been four days in a saddle with almost no sleep. So all I am certain of is that I am not armed for a duel of wits with you. You wish no fooling, so let us be plain: when you ask what I do here, you ask about my lord of Essex, and his intentions, do you not?'

She stepped nearer. 'I do.'

'Good. And when you ask, you ask not for yourself but for the Queen?' When she didn't respond, he added, 'Or perhaps for your other employer, the Master Secretary?'

She tipped her head to the side, considering. 'In this case, I would say both.'

'So he is here, is he?' On her slow nod, he continued, 'Forewarned by my lord Grey who preceded us?'

'I know nothing of that.'

'No, you were with her majesty.' He sucked his lip. 'Keeping out of the way, is he?'

'Would you not? You know the hatred the earl bears for him.'

'Indeed. A hatred evenly returned.' He smiled up at her. 'Well then. How can I be of service to you . . . all, ma'am?'

She studied him a moment. 'You mentioned the earl's intentions. Do you know them?'

'Some of them.'

'And they are?'

He smiled. 'Sweet, surely that is a matter for the two of them? Intentions he will make plain when he is admitted again into her presence.' He frowned. 'He will be, will he not? Be readmitted?'

'He . . . will. Despite her rage.' Her voice dropped a little. 'You must have noticed, sir, how distraught she was. Only her closest ladies ever see her in . . . in that state. No man has for . . .' She hesitated, continued, 'For a very long time, it is said. If ever.' She bent, to look into the mirror behind him, smoothed the skin of her face, went on in the same low voice. 'And of all men to do so, how could it be he whom all her pretence was for? She will never forgive him. Never.'

Her body was close again, the shift and gown pushed away as she bent, her breasts free beneath. Od's faith, he thought, exhausted though I am, I could have her now. Yet she was right – for all sorts of pressing reasons, in Southwark, closer to, the time for foolery was past. So he raised his eyes, asked, 'Will she not?'

'Not unless she is forced to.'

'And what could force her?'

She whispered the words. 'My lord of Essex's army camped over the brow of yonder hill.'

So they are scared, all of them, John thought. They need to know if their worst fears are realised, if Essex comes in armed insurrection. Still, they would know soon enough. Skulking though he might be, Cecil would be active. Messengers and spies would be streaming from his quarters. It was a little enough thing to give to his interrogator. 'So you wish to know if he returns with an army?'

'If you please.'

'Well then, lady . . . he does not.' He continued over her sigh, 'Yet I do not think he needs one.'

'No?' She turned back to the rack of clothes behind her. 'I must return to my duties. Will you help me dress?'

'It would be my delight.'

Sarah moved to the rack. 'So you do not believe he needs an army to coerce her?'

Dropping the gown from her shoulders, she stood in a shift that ill concealed her voluptuous body. Giving a little sigh, she placed a finger in her mouth as she considered the clothes. The obviousness

227

of the action made him smile. 'No. If force was his choice, he'd be standing over her e'en now, sword drawn. The grey, I think. More in keeping with the solemnity of the day and, of course, it would suit with your eyes.'

She flashed them. 'Oh sir,' she said, before slipping a farthingale over her head, settling it on her hips, then unhooking the grey kirtle. It was of a piece, bodice already joined to skirt. She handed it to John, raised her hands over her head, looked up at him from under her thick lashes. She'd moistened her lips, preparing them. He bent . . . then dropped the heavy material over her, muffling the surprised gasp that came. While she was engulfed, he spun her fast, and by the time she emerged, his hands were already busy. John had helped many a boy player into woman's wear in the tiring house, and his fingers were quick on the laces.

'Then how will he persuade her, do you think?' she asked.

John pulled the laces though the eyelets. 'With love?'

Sarah snorted. 'Love? After this morning, I do not think . . .' She broke off, then pulled him over, still tying, towards the mirror. Before it, she began to brush and put up her hair, her reflected eyes finding his. 'And yet? She may be Queen but she is also . . . a complicated woman. Capricious. She has forgiven him his behaviours time after time, and even this outrage . . .' She laughed, addressing the mirror and her tangles. 'Well, one of the ballads she so loves could be fashioned around this – his riding pell-mell from Ireland to fling himself, mud-caked and weeping, at her feet. Though she would be radiantly dressed to receive him, of course. Set to the lute by Cowper, who knows? It could work wonders. Hmm!' She put down the brush, began to set tortoiseshell combs into her locks. 'This needs considering. For if my lord of Essex's gallantry were to triumph and he to rise again . . .'

'. . . then the Master Secretary would fall.' John leaned in over her shoulder. 'And you would have lost your patron.'

She looked at him in the mirror. 'Not my only one, as you know. I am a lady-in-waiting to the Queen. Yet she is not overgenerous – except in cast-off dresses.' She turned from side to side, regarding herself – and him. 'While I . . . I have greater ambitions.' Putting the last comb in place, she bent to the table, to some pots there, dipped her finger into one, began to daub her lips in carmine. Her gaze found his again. 'Perhaps, Master Lawley, we can aid each other,' she turned, reaching to run a wet finger down the line of buttons on his doublet, 'in diverse ways.'

Interesting, he thought. She was still seductive, and yet . . . the artifice of it was so plain, now that he had taken no whisky to obscure it. Yet he would not show her that realisation – for she was right. They could be useful, each to the other.

He bent a little closer. 'As you said, lady – this needs must be considered.'

Their look held, their faces a palm apart; neither moved. And then through the door noise came – boots on a wooden floor, men's voices raised. She ducked under him, crossed to the door. 'That sounds like your freshly scrubbed lord returning for his second interview. The Queen will have been able to do little more than I to repair the ravages of night. Enough to receive her lover, perhaps. I must to her side.'

John felt the vibration of men marching, heard familiar voices raised. 'Before you go, let me tell you this. I agree to your offer, lady.'

A plucked eyebrow raised. 'Which one, sir?'

He stepped close enough now to whisper over the noises beyond. 'That we each aid the other. Who knows who will hit the hazard this day? Romantic Essex or practical Cecil? Eagle or toad? Whoever does, you and I, mere hired players in this scene, will thrive or fail.'

'Your suggestion, then, sirrah? Swiftly, for truly, I must to the Queen.'

John spoke as he thought it – for if Essex did fall, he must fast flee the crash or be brought low by it. 'This next meeting will decide all. Is he to be the subject of sonnets . . . or a disobedient traitor? If she forgives him, if she succumbs to his charms, if Essex's star is again to rise at the court . . . let me know it with a nod when he emerges from her chamber, like so.' He moved his head slowly up and down. 'Yet if that star is to fall, well, then inform me thus.' He shook his head, slowly, clearly. 'Then will I be forewarned and plan accordingly.'

She studied him for a moment. 'And will you promise that if he does rise, that my lord of Essex will be as generous as the Secretary ever was?'

'More generous. He is far more – for he loves a lovely woman.'

'Oh sir,' she said coyly, lowering her eyes. Then she lifted her head and gave an imitation of his slow nod. 'A deal, then. On your honour?'

He remembered the deal he'd made with the Queen over Essex, the delight she'd taken in the word and the handshake. Something else was required here. 'A deal made,' he said, 'and sealed.' And saying it, he kissed her.

She let him, for a moment; even responded. Then she pushed him away, turned and was gone. He stared at the door she'd left ajar, listened to the voices raised beyond it, tasted the lead in the paint she'd left on his lips. He heard his lord cry out, in that accent with the trace of the Welsh borders he'd never quite lost at court, 'Your majesty, I have returned!' John stepped out into the corridor and into the hubbub.

There was a crowd there now. Not only Essex's fifteen, but many from the house, gathered to behold the marvel of his return. These pressed in, asking their wonder. The nobles ignored them, talking amongst themselves. The unknighted, precious few, held forth. The tall Irishman, St Lawrence, had gathered a gaggle of maidservants, all staring up his mud-spattered frontage in awe.

At the head of them all, directly before the door, stood the earl. And before him was Sarah, standing between the two guards. John heard her say, 'I will discover if her majesty is ready for you, my lord,' before she slipped inside, closing the door behind her.

Essex turned. He had cleaned up, a little. The mud was largely gone from his face, though John noticed a darkening still in one ear. He'd borrowed a cloak – and a doublet, too small for him, and short of the lace with which he covered everything of his own. But it was clean, unlike the breeches beneath to which it was barely laced, whilst his riding boots were still thick with road dust. Wedged into one of them, John glimpsed white – a corner of the handkerchief.

In the end, John thought, it isn't a poor combination. The worst of the dirt removed so as not to grossly offend; some remaining to remind of the effort he had made to reach his sweet Bess's side.

Which he did not do immediately. Despite his pacing, the muttered oaths becoming increasingly audible, the door remained closed. There was time enough for three flagons of Rhenish to be brought and consumed by the party, some bread and sausage to be chewed and swallowed. John consumed his share sitting down. It took him out of the eyesight of his lordship and gave much relief to his legs.

After a while – John reckoned a good half-hour – there were noises from the front, a general shifting. He rose, and being taller than most there saw above the heads to the door opening, another lady-in-waiting – not Sarah – standing there. 'Will my lord – and only my lord – care to enter?' she asked, curtseying.

Essex looked back at his silent followers, swelled by gawkers. He took a deep breath, reached down and unbuckled his sword belt. Handing it to the Earl of Southampton at his side he said, 'Wish me fortune, friends.' To their cries of 'Fortune' and 'God's love', Robert Devereux marched into the Queen's chamber and to his fate.

For a while, men moved before the door, as if their yearning could open it again to the earl and triumph. But minutes passed, many of them, the bell in the courtyard beyond tolling the quarter, the half, and then the ten strokes of ten. One by one, the men of Essex's party joined John upon the chairs in an order of precedence stretching from the door, the earls Southampton and Rutland closest to it, the noble lords Mountjoy and Rich next, down through the knights like Gerard to mere captains like Danvers . . . and St Lawrence, who dropped heavily on to the chair next to John's, making it creak.

'What think you?' he said. 'Will our lord thrive in there?'

John shrugged. 'With God's help. I am sure you know as well as I.'

'Ah, but there was I thinking you might know a little more,' replied St Lawrence. 'After your private consultation with her majesty's maid, that is.'

John looked up. 'For an Irishman, you don't miss much.'

The man ran his tongue over his lips. 'Now there's the mistake you English always make about us. You think us stupid, when we are far from it. As the Earl of Tyrone has recently proved.'

'You speak of him with pride?'

'I may despise his loyalties and his Roman faith, but I do not underestimate his intelligence – unlike most of you.' He smiled. 'Though I suspect, John, that you are one Englishman who does not. Just as I suspect that you know a little more than most after your tryst in yon dressing room.'

'Tryst?' It was John's turn to smile. 'Hardly that. The maid and I have some . . . former acquaintance.'

'Sure, I wouldn't mind some such acquaintance with her. A saucy minx indeed, you can see it in her hell-black eyes. Look now, I'll swap those two for your one in a heartbeat – for I am sure these come as a pair.' He winked at two housemaids, hovering on the edge of the crowd of servants, who giggled and blushed. 'Did she tell you aught?'

John thought, then spoke softly, carefully. 'Only that the earl still throws for the hazard – and that he may or may not yet achieve it.'

'In the balance, then? Good enough for me.' St Lawrence slapped John's thigh, then rose. 'I think I'll just be over to those two plump partridges there. I'll make certain they are snared – in case you are mindful of that swap.'

He winked, then crossed to the two maids. John took another small sip of wine. He did not want too much, for he was sleepy enough. He had to stay awake to see the result of Essex's roll. He had to . . .

He jerked up . . . on bells tolling the half-hour – which one he could not know – and the louder, nearer sound of a door being flung wide. 'Her Majesty has been most kind!' bellowed Essex, his hand upon the wood. 'She has listened to our plaints, acknowledged their validity, asked that she be given some time now for prayer and contemplation. Praise God! Praise the sovereign! *His* vice-regent on earth!' Amens and shouts of praise echoed him. As they faded, he continued, 'And the Queen takes such care for us, she asks that we rest a little, eat and drink well and return in two hours. Then we shall further discuss' – he beamed – 'everything. Come!' he cried, striding off. 'Let us pledge this happy reunion. God save the Queen!'

A cheering crowd echoed him, then followed him down the corridor. Only John did not. Standing before his seat, he watched them go, before swivelling back to the door of the Queen's apartments, yet ajar. His heart was beating fast. Essex appeared so sure. Perhaps he *had* thrown his hazard. Perhaps all his daring and his gallantry *had* won the greatest pot of all. And thus, perhaps, to be Sir John Lawley, his newest knight, would not be too bad a thing.

He stared at the empty doorway, waiting, hoping; even – rare for him – praying. It was a habit from his youth and only used now when the need was great, usually before battle. Yet he could remember no fight when the result had been more important than this one.

His lady of cloves appeared in the entrance. Her eyes found his, held for a moment. And then she moved her head, slowly, clearly.

Side to side.

His prayer, the prayers and all the hopes of his lord of Essex were ungranted. The earl had not hit the hazard, had rolled some failing number, leaving the dice to Cecil to roll and hit and snatch up the stake. John did not see the door close behind him, for he was already moving swiftly along the corridor, down the stairs. From the dining hall came sounds of joyful carousing. He ignored them, despite thirst and hunger, continued out to the courtyard and the stables beyond.

While he waited for his horse to be saddled, he leaned against a railing, forcing himself to stay on his feet despite the alluring proximity of heaped straw. If he lay down, he would be lost.

There was no question – he must flee before Robert Devereux's fall pulled him under. If the earl's actions were proven to be treasonous – something the lawyer Cecil would, even now, be working hard to do – then those nearest him would be labelled traitors too. That path led only to one place: the scaffold. And he doubted his recent knighthood would guarantee him the noble's swifter death of an axe – he would be hung, drawn and quartered. Yet even if Essex's course was deemed merely foolish, and his enemies were contented with his fall from all power, his financial ruin, John was certain that he himself would not be allowed to just slink away. For he had been the Queen's messenger, charged with a duty to her. And he had reappeared with the man whose return he'd been sent to prevent – and then burst into her bedroom to see her naked!

John shook his head, as if shaking could dispel the hatred in the look she'd given him. But even if she could hate and not act upon it, what then? Cecil would never leave him be. Not when he already had him marked as a spy, a Papist and even – God's teeth! – one of that breed he most despised, a player! Men had vanished from London's streets with far, far gentler reputations.

No. The rest of those who'd ridden with Essex from Ireland would be arrested right there at Nonsuch, while he . . . ? He would flee. South for Southampton and a fast packet to the Continent, beating the Master Secretary's instructions to detain him on sight. He still had friends in France, in Italy. What he should not, must not do was go to Southwark. It would be one more foolish act in a lifetime of them.

Which he would do. He could not help it. He had to see Tess and Ned. He knew he had no hope of making amends, nor of getting them to believe the truth of what had happened to him. But he had to try. His exile might be long, and he could not live it with them thinking the very worst of him.

He yawned widely, as the groom made the final cinches, and mounted. Yes, he thought, for finally all I know is this: that things always become clearer in Tess's green eyes.

Swinging out of the palace gates, he turned the mare's head towards London.

XXV

Southward Regained

He was trying to get into the theatre. The trumpet had sounded, the last of the spectators admitted. Yet every door was closed to him. He went to the rear, to the players' entrance, forced it. He could hear voices declaiming above. What play was this? *The Spanish Tragedy*? He had played it, but long ago. They were approaching his entrance. What lines must he speak? He grabbed a roll from a table. It was his part . . . but someone had spilled whisky upon the ink, blurring all. Throwing it aside, he stumbled towards the stage, trying to remember anything. But the stairs led down, not up. He tripped. Someone shouted at him . . .

Any one of three things could have awoken him. The first was the terror of the actor's nightmare, which they all got. The second were the voices nearby. But what probably did was the third thing – the sudden thrust of sharp metal an inch from his face.

He dreamed like a player . . . but he woke like a soldier, one hand on the attacker's weapon, the other reaching for his own dagger, rolling on to his knees even as he twisted the pole he held and shoved hard back. A yelp came, and he followed the sound as his eyes cleared, followed the jerk as whoever held the weapon fell backwards but clung on. In a moment John was on to him, pressing his assailant down with the pole across his chest, his knife out, point poised above the startled eyes . . .

. . . of a farmer! A wide sunburned face, a hedge of sun-bleached hair, terror babbled from thick lips. 'Zur! Zur! I did not know. I would not have . . . Pleaze, don't hurt us!'

John kept his knife where it was, looked about. There were others there, all clutching the same type of implements John saw he was pressing against the farmer's chest – a hay fork. All were dressed similarly, men in aprons, women in bibs above kirtles. 'What make you here?' he growled, his voice indistinct with sleep.

Someone understood him. A large man stepped forward. 'Zur. We come for the hay, see. No one knowz you was sleeping under it.'

John rose, sheathing the dagger in one hand, pulling his victim to his feet by the pole both still clutched. 'I apologise. I was . . . surprised.' He looked at the hay pile. Vague memories came – of tying his horse to a tree, lying down for the briefest of rests. He looked up, squinting over the peasants' heads at the sun. It seemed lower in the sky than it should be. And in the wrong place. 'What hour is it?' he mumbled.

The man he'd lately put down replied, ''Tis an hour after dawn, zur.'

'An hour after . . .' He lurched forward and everyone gave back a pace. 'You jest with me!'

'No indeed, zur,' replied the large man who'd first spoken. 'No jest.'

John looked behind them, to what passed for the road. He saw the one tree nearby, to which he must have tied his mount. No mount was there. 'My horse,' he exclaimed. 'Where is it?'

'We ain't seen no horse, zur,' the same man replied. 'Jus' you.'

It was impossible to tell if the man was lying. And no point in trying to find out. After their initial shock, the peasants seemed have remembered that there were many of them and all clutched weapons of a kind. While his situation was clear, even in his befuddlement: he had slept a day and a night through. His horse was gone. And a long walk lay ahead of him. 'Tell me, friends. Is there an inn nearby? On the London road?' he asked in his pleasantest voice.

'Nearest north would be the White Hart, close to Wimbledon.' The man pointed. 'About two hour thataway.' His eyes narrowed. 'But if it's a thirst you have, Oi've some zider here can slake that.'

John indeed had a thirst and paid too much for some swigs from one of their stone jars. Before drinking it, he made room for it beneath the ash where he'd tied his missing horse and voided while he cussed. The reverberations of Essex's tumble would certainly have already reached London. If he had been proclaimed a traitor, there would be a round-up of all his followers. Even if he had been detained for future decision, Cecil's men would still especially be seeking the recent Queen's messenger, who had failed so spectacularly in his mission. That it was hardly his fault Cecil would not care a jot. He would want to interview him personally and probably with various methods. And his officers would seek him first in Bankside.

John considered. A sensible man would turn south now, make for a port. But he'd never been called that.

Draining cider so sharp it could have stripped rust from ancient armour, he set out.

In the near distance, the bell of St Mary Overies tolled noon. He had made good time, Shanks's pony being succeeded by a real one, after the walk to Wimbledon. He was not sure that it wasn't the same mare stolen from him that he'd hired again at the White Hart.

He rarely arrived from the south. For him, Southwark was the banks of the Thames, the sum of its delights within bowshot of the water. Now he could see how the borough had spread, new shacks, taverns, ordinaries and warehouses lining the Queen's highway of Long Southwark and encroaching upon the fields and market gardens.

As at the ending of his debauch in February, he made again for Peg Leg's tavern. He needed a bath after five days a-horse and a night in a haystack, for if he was to have any hope of persuading Tess – to what, his poor mind had still not been able to decide – that hope would be nil while he stank thus. He also knew that if Cecil sought him, his men would be at Paris Garden Stairs and at the foot of the bridge, staked out around Tess's tavern and perhaps the playhouse. A disguise was needed.

Peg Leg, wary at first, was happy enough to see him since he was sober, and happier to take a few coins in exchange for services – a bath that had not been too much occupied; a sponging-off of the worst road excesses from his clothes, with the loan of an old cloak and wide-brimmed hat to conceal them; a jug of small beer, a plate of pottage . . . and the dispatch of a pot boy to the Spoon and Alderman to enquire after its proprietress, with the instruction to note if anyone was watching the doors.

John was just trimming his beard when the boy returned. 'Barman says she's gone to the Globe,' the lad reported, adding helpfully, 'Gone to see the play.'

John reached for his still damp, somewhat cleaner clothes. 'Any watchers?'

'None that I could see,' the boy replied.

As John dressed, he considered. The boy might have missed Cecil's men, or they may have followed Tess to the playhouse. Or – he paused in his dressing to consider – or was it possible that they were not there at all? A sleep had cleared his muddled head somewhat. Surely the Secretary of State would have many things on his mind, not least organising the complete fall of his rival. He might have missed the disappearance of her majesty's messenger. Indeed, he may not even have been informed of John's return from Ireland, with so many earls and knights and what not. The interim was his – and the playhouse the very place he most wanted to be. He would find his woman there, his son. Shakespeare.

Will! The cleverest man John knew. If he could not cudgel his own brains and solve the dilemma of what the devil to do, his friend the playwright could. And lend him some more money too, for the Queen's purse was now much diminished.

It was amazing what some sleep, some ale, a bite of food, cleaner clothes and not stinking like a five-day corpse could do for a fellow! He was home; he had survived the latest madness that Essex had thrust upon him. He was, after all, a tiny cog in that mighty engine. Scarce worth anyone's notice.

John was whistling when he set out into warm autumnal sunshine. He was going to the theatre, where, at the worst, he had three thousand people to hide amongst. And, of course, there was a play to see. He wondered if it would be a good one. What was playing this day? He just hoped it wasn't *The Spanish Tragedy*. There was a part of him that had never shaken the nightmare he'd woken from, and he had no desire to return to it.

XXVI

Play Within A Play Within A Play

John discovered what not five paces on to Rose Street, when he stopped at a milk stall.

'Why, 'tis the tragical tale of the emperor Julian Chaser,' the apple-cheeked proprietress answered his enquiry as she handed over a leathern mug, brimming white. 'Played it for four days now and the town's agog. They'll play it again all this week if the crowds come like this.' She beamed at the hordes around. 'I'd like to get to it myself if'n I can sell me wares.' She smiled prettily, if gap-toothedly, as John handed back his mug. 'All the quicker if you drain another, handsome sir.'

John laughed, but shook his head. The penny he'd handed over for the drink now had few companions. He'd need one of those to gain admittance to the theatre, another to mount to the gallery where Tess was sure to be.

He swam into the swelling crowd and a gusty wind. On it scraps of paper were borne. He snatched one from the sky. Read. 'Julian Chaser, indeed,' he murmured.

The playbill proclaimed the newest offering from the Chamberlain's Men. 'The sad and profound history of that greatest of men, Julius Caesar; his tragic fall to murderous conspiracy; and the bloody civil strife that followed.'

So he had finished it.

John shook his head. Like any who had attended grammar school, he knew his Tacitus, the Roman's sonorous declensions rapped into knuckles by a teacher's corrective ruler. It was a bloody tale indeed, of assassination, political turmoil, troubled succession, the

239

dire consequence of noble men taking what they considered honourable necessity. What was Will doing writing it now, when a
monarch tottered, two men had a royal arm each and tugged, while
armed men mobbed the streets and no one knew what would come?

John shrugged . . . exactly what Will always did. Slaking the thirst
of people not allowed to drink freely. To a populace who received the
government dole of vinegar, a play like this was sweet sack indeed.
No wonder they were playing it an almost unprecedented five times
straight. No wonder the crowd that bore him along hummed. He
was excited himself – and he had other purposes in the theatre than
to see a play. He would pursue them – but he could cock an ear while
he did.

The crowd surged against the playhouse's main doors. John
stopped short of the entrance, exchanged a ha'penny for a handful
of Kentish cob nuts, shucked, munched and observed. Gatherers
took the audience's pennies, dropping them into the slots of clay
boxes which would all be taken to their office for breaking and
counting. John noted one fellow who either had a bad case of nits or
was stealing a quarter of the take. His hand reaching up to scratch
his bare head every fourth coin probably meant he was dropping
the penny down his ample collar. Noting his pockmarked face to
report it to Will later, John shifted his gaze to those not clamouring
to enter. Several stood by, singly and in pairs, watching the crowd;
most, no doubt, were seeking to rendezvous with companions.
Others could be watching for him. Two had an especially steady
gaze and a soldierly lean.

There were many reasons why some men sought others. The
theatre drew rogues, and so was a place for the watch to apprehend
notorious cutpurses. However, he was not going to risk being taken
himself, not this close to his goal. Not when there was another way
in, and one, besides, that he was more used to using.

The players' entrance was not mobbed; but there was still enough
of a crowd for John to remain concealed. Boys had gathered to watch
for the main performers, and two hung from scaffolding that rose
from the back of the playhouse to its roof, repairs being effected on
the thatch, though the boys were being ungently prodded off by a
doorman with a long pole. Some well-dressed merchants' wives
lurked too, hoping perhaps to draw Burbage's eye – he was notorious

for his dalliances. Servants attended them, for no gentlewoman went to the theatre alone, whatever her intentions. Again, two men stood out for John for their watchfulness, their bearing.

He might be mistaken. However, trying to enter as one of the company was a risk, especially when he paused to explain himself to the doorkeeper. What to do?

Howling turned him. Along Maiden Lane, past the edge of the Rose Theatre, which stood directly behind the Globe and before whose main entrance a far smaller crowd moved – its manager, Henslowe, would be gnashing his few remaining teeth, he thought – John could see to the baiting ring beyond. Mastiffs were being taken from their kennels, dragging their grooms as they tried to maul their rivals, the men jerking hard on chains and plying their whips. Near them, coming down the westerly road, was a coach.

It was a rare enough sight on London's roads to make John stare longer. It was plush, with highly polished wood, its driver in maroon livery. He kept an easy control with a touch of his lash when mastiffs lunged near his horses, coming on to rein in right by the players' entrance. A boy, also in maroon, hopped from where he'd been clinging, lowered steps, opened the door . . . and a man descended, reaching his hand back to a lady.

The man was Lord Grey, who'd preceded Essex to Nonsuch and who bore the earl such enmity. The lady he handed down was Sarah.

John moved under the scaffolding to observe. Noblemen as high-ranking as Grey expected the best treatment at the playhouse, and paid accordingly. Part of that money bought this quieter entrance backstage, seats in the minstrels' gallery – and, this time, a reception from none other than the playwright himself. Will came out of the doorway and bowed. All in the crowd stared.

It was not distraction enough to go to the door and have that conversation with the doorman. But it gave him his opportunity – for like any stage conjuror, John knew that there was a single moment when an audience looked elsewhere. With the leap and twist of the tumbler he'd once been, he grabbed the cross scaffolding above. It groaned under his sudden weight, but held as he swung himself up to the lowest platform, pressed himself flat upon it, peered over its edge. Shakespeare was reciting some rehearsed speech of welcome, and even the watchers had stepped closer to listen. Close enough for their eyes to be hidden by their hat brims. Silent and swift as a monkey, he climbed the remaining two levels. Only as he swung himself over the last one did his scabbard clatter against wood and he felt, rather than saw, someone's attention turn upwards. By then, he was lying flat again.

Applause came. It seemed a good time to make his last move, and he slid over to the hole in the thatch that was under repair, wide enough just to admit his body. He peered into the gap – the thatch gave directly on to the theatre's upper gallery. He could see heads, the men in caps, women with their hair dressed high. He was poised above the space at the very back, a narrow gap between the last bench and the lath wall. The thatch gave as he placed hands either side of the hole, reaching his foot to the beam directly below him. He was tall, but there was still a small drop. For a moment he balanced upon it, until, with a grunt, he swung over, dropped and entered a playhouse in a way he never had done before – through its roof.

There was a couple just settling to his right. They turned, the woman yelping at his sudden closeness, the man grabbing for his dagger hilt. John raised empty hands. 'My apologies,' he said, shifting away, 'for I see this place is taken.' He turned, moved against the flow of the crowd entering, to the usual complaints. The stairs were blocked by incomers, but when he saw a slight gap, he pushed into it and descended to the middle gallery.

Pressing himself to a pillar, he scanned the crowd. What now? Or rather, who first? There were several that he sought here this day. Ned and Will would be almost below him, in the tiring house beneath the minstrels' gallery. Tess would be . . . out there! The theatre was already near full, and with the hour approaching, yet more were cramming in. The yard was a blur of movement as the groundlings settled, the galleries only less so as the spectators who had paid a penny more fought for diminishing space just as their inferiors did in the pit. Until movement ceased, John would have little hope of spotting Tess in the three thousand – and not much even then.

That decided him. Ned would be better able to spot her from the stage with that uncanny player's ability to know where someone special was in a packed house. Besides, John also needed to see Will as soon as possible. For his counsel – and for the loan to fund whatever course the playwright suggested.

To further curses, John moved towards the minstrels' gallery. The railing in front of the last bench was just below and to the side of it, so close he could hear a viola being tuned. To a woman's loudly voiced annoyance, he forced himself on to the bench between her and the wall, then watched the pit below, awaiting the distraction that would inevitably come.

It came fast – a woman's loud scream, and the hue and cry beginning immediately with roars of 'Thief! Stop, thief!' and a rustle through the whole crowd as everyone felt for their purses. More than one cutpurse had been struck guilty by the yells, for three youths were surging for the doors. Everyone on the galleries leaned over to better view the chase, including the disgruntled lady to his left. As she did so, John stepped up on to the balustrade, swayed, balanced, then pushed through the gap between curtain and pillar.

'What mean you, sir?' came the immediate yell as he narrowly missed puncturing the skin of a tabor, and a fife was snatched from his way. He got his balance. 'Afternoon, Giles,' he said.

'Lawley,' replied Giles Tremlett, master of the consort, slowly lowering a viola. 'What make you here, man?'

'Your pardon. I will not disturb you longer.' As he spoke, the trumpeter above their heads sounded the beginning of the play. 'If I may . . .' He began to pass in the direction to which he'd motioned, the stairs to the tiring house below. But his progress was immediately blocked by the people he barged into coming up.

'Zounds, sir, what do you think you are about?'

John recognised the nasal voice. He had heard it whine and complain on a few quarterdecks off Cadiz. 'Your pardon, zur,' he replied in what he hoped would pass him off as one of the peasants he'd met only that morning. Might have done too, if he hadn't stepped sideways with his head down and so failed to see his passage was blocked by another.

A softer landfall. Better scented, too. 'Well,' said Sarah, 'if it isn't the fellow we were just speaking of, Lord Thomas.'

'What's that?' Grey stooped to peer under John's brim, then gave a grunt of astonishment. 'S'death! Whip me if it's not.' He turned and peered behind him. 'Master Shakespeare, this is the very rogue you were just enquiring after. And here he appears like one of your damnable *deus ex machina*, what?'

One deferential step below his lordship, Will gazed up. 'I see him, my lord,' he replied drily. 'He was always wont to make . . . unusual entrances.'

'And exits.' Lord Grey smiled humourlessly. 'For he was the only one of Essex's party of ruffians not accounted for at Nonsuch.'

'Was he, my lord?' Shakespeare turned from noble to sometime player. 'His lordship has been most graciously informing me of the recent extraordinary events. Seemed to think I might fashion a drama out of them.'

'Well, master scrivener, knowing your taste in both high and low, I think you would find both in Robert Devereux's recent exploits,' Lord Grey drawled. 'Though whether the climax is to be comic or tragic, end in a jig or an execution, we have yet to discover.'

Since this last was directed menacingly at John, he had to respond. 'My lord of Essex was well received when last I heard.'

'Then you stayed but for the fourth act, not the last.' Lord Grey was like a dog with a lump of gristle, for being in a playhouse, his allusions were all theatrical. 'The finale contained as much drama as before, but less romance. I was just about to tell Master Shakespeare of it – the last cold interview with her majesty . . . though more warmly dressed, what?' He gave a little guffaw, continued, 'Then her dismissal of the earl to be judged by the council of his peers. They were fleet in their condemnation and she as swift to act upon it.'

He paused. Beside them, Giles Tremlett hissed, 'Will!' and gestured with his bow to the stage. The trumpet had sounded, the crowd was hushed, all anticipating the music that would announce the players' entrance. Will held his hand high, commanding a moment, then asked the question that caused John's heart to beat all the faster. 'And the denouement, milord? Is my lord of Essex condemned for treason?'

Lord Grey waited, his large nostrils distended, as if he was aware that he held not only his small group of listeners but the whole Globe in pause. Then a smile came to his thin lips and he said, 'Not . . . yet. As a peer of the realm he is entitled to a hearing before his peers at Westminster Hall. Whether his acts are treasonous will be decided then, along with the punishment. For now he is confined to the Lord Keeper at York House. Egerton will have the watching of him, and just two servants there.' The smile, lips and nostrils, stretched. 'Won't that teach him to see the Queen naked?'

And what will it teach me, who saw the same? wondered John. Still, it was not treason, not yet. It might still give him a chance to distance himself from Essex's further fall. But the fact that Lord Grey knew that he had been at Nonsuch, and not taken, confirmed what he suspected. Cecil would be looking for him, and the men outside were almost certainly his seekers.

He saw Tremlett raise his viola again, appeal clear on his face. Will saw too. 'I thank your lordship for his courtesy in telling me this,' the playwright said. 'And now if he will sit and observe the play . . .' He gestured with one hand to the two chairs set there and with the other to his musician, who, relieved, counted four. The consort struck up.

Lord Grey, with another sneer, passed John by. Sarah followed with nothing for him but the slightest of winks. Then she was sitting, as his lordship acknowledged the cheer his appearance produced, while behind him, his friend was pulling John none too gently down the stairs.

They descended all the way to Hell, no words spoken, except upon the stage, where shouts followed hard upon the music. As they passed by the tiring room directly behind the platform, John sought his son among the players readying themselves there, nearly missed him when his eyes passed over a comely Roman noblewoman with long brown curls under a headdress. 'Ned,' he muttered, taking a step. But a firm hand restrained him, tugging him on and down.

The grip was not released until John had been shoved into the alcove. The cramped space looked the same as before, scattered papers of whatever play Will was working on, ink pots and quills, the one chair behind the table. A window had been added, cut into the lath and filled with leaded glass, admitting light. It gleamed on Will's high forehead as he turned from drawing the drape, closing them in. 'By Christ's foot, man!' he hissed. 'What mischief are you about now?'

'I . . .' John opened his mouth, could not speak. How did he begin to explain?

Fortunately the playwright prompted him. 'The last I saw of you, you'd achieved your heart's desire, had your foot back upon the platform . . .' He gestured beyond the drapes, where players' voices rang. 'That foot even had a limp, so I knew you were back. And then' – he clicked his fingers – 'gone again. There are rumours of a debauch that shocked even Southwark, you vanish, then reappear three weeks later like a street mountebank in my minstrels' gallery while I am being told that you are part of a damned conspiracy – and that you have burst into her bedroom and seen the Queen naked!' He gaped. 'What are you thinking of, you damned fool?'

John winced. The tirade was all the more forceful because it was conducted in a whisper. 'I could not help myself, Will. I . . .'

'Oh no, John Lawley never can. It is never his fault but always some devil in a pleasing shape beguiling him. Sometimes that devil is contained in glass. Sometimes she wears silk. Sometimes *he* wears ermine. In this case, if I understand both rumour and Lord Grey, it is both. And you, poor helpless fellow, peep out, like John O'Dreams, unable to take action for yourself. God's mercy on me!' He waved at the papers on his desk. 'You sound like the fellow I conjure now, Prince Hamlet.'

'I thought I'd persuaded you not to write that, Will,' John said weakly.

'Never mind what I write. My conspiracies are upon the stage, sirrah, not in the Queen's bedchamber. God's wounds, man, even by your low standards this was a lunatic act.'

John sighed. What could he say? The facts condemned him, utterly.

Will studied him for a moment, then, sitting back upon his table, rubbed a hand over his crown, and pressed a palm into his eye. In a gentler tone he continued, 'How deep are you enmeshed in this debacle, Johnnie?'

Upon the stage, voices rose, rendering 'Julian Chaser'. He remembered some of his Tacitus. 'As deep as Casca perhaps. Not a mover but . . . drawn in. And it gets worse.' He shook his head. 'Essex knighted me in Dublin.'

Shakespeare's eyebrows shot up. He stared, open-mouthed. And then he began to softly laugh. 'Christ a mercy! The first player ever to be knighted. And the last I warrant, for we will ever be rogues and vagabonds.' The smile vanished. 'But that draws you even closer, John. You stand now with your hand upon the very trunk – and when a mighty oak like Essex falls, it brings down many lesser trees around it.' He sucked his lip. 'Yet to break from him is to make a slew of new enemies without gaining friends who will trust you.'

'It is a dilemma indeed.' John lowered himself on to the table to sit beside his friend. 'Have you a solution to it?'

Will stared again, while above them on the platform a scene ended in a burst of applause. As it tailed off, as trumpets sounded and other voices spoke, he began again. 'I know your great desire, John. To return here and be one of us. But that cannot be.' He forestalled the protest that came with a raised hand. 'I do not exile you for ever. But until the tragedy of Robert Devereux is played out, the Chamberlain's Men must keep a distance from it. I must even shun the Earl of Southampton, and you know how that will grieve me.' He shook his head. 'No. If we are seen to pick sides, we are doomed. I may depict conspiracy upon my stage, but I do not become a part of it. I show the world a fire but I do not feed it wood.' He paused, reached back to a quill and ink pot, dipped, wrote three words across a page; and John, despite the certain ending of one faint hope, could not help his smile – for his friend, come catastrophe or flood, always had one part of his mind on his creations. He would wager the playwright had a wax plate and stencil beside any bed he made love in and would not hesitate to pause, mid thrust, if an idea took him. Will looked up, continued. 'Besides, can you truly see Dick Burbage playing the King beside a real knight?'

He laughed, and after a moment John joined him. 'I suspect, like much else, my dubbing will be forgotten if Essex is arraigned for treason.'

'Indeed. Well, we shall await th'event. I here. You . . . somewhere else.' He reached down beneath his doublet and uncinched the purse that dangled there. 'I can help you in this, at least. For I suspect you are, as ever, short of funds?' On John's nod, he passed the leather pouch. It clinked reassuringly. 'What will you do?'

'Lie low until it is seen how many are brought down in the oak's fall . . . This will help' – he raised the purse – 'and I thank you for it.' He tied it swiftly to his belt.

'Where will you lie?'

'I do not know.' He shrugged. 'Not here. As you say, rumour runs Bankside. I may take ship for the Continent. I may go back to Shropshire for a while. My stepfather still lives there.'

'Does he? Then he must be older than Methuselah.' Will rose, placed a hand on John's shoulder. 'Go well, my friend. Yet howsoever you go, go swiftly.'

'I will. There are two who I must see first. Try to . . . explain.'

Shakespeare frowned. 'I would not go to the Spoon and Alderman. If you are sought, as Grey maintained, it is there they will begin.'

'I do not have to. Both whom I seek are within this wooden O.'

'Tess watches your boy? Good.' He smiled. 'He does well, your Ned. Try to note his Calpurnia today. So far, his bent has only been for comedy. If he can carry this off I . . . I have something bigger in mind.' He gestured back to his table. 'But it is not ready yet.' He looked from John to some point above him and his voice, when it came again, was distant. 'A son is a fine thing to have, John Lawley. Never forget that, nor neglect your love to him.'

John reached up, laid his own hand over his friend's. He knew Will was speaking of his own dead son; knew the regrets Will had, for making a career in London had meant he rarely visited Stratford while the boy lived. For once there were no words needed. 'Go now,' said Shakespeare, opening the drapes for his friend, standing aside, pushing him through. 'Send word if you can. And if you need more funds, well . . .' He shrugged. 'By God's good grace this will all blow over soon.'

'Aye.' John halted. 'Where do you think I might discover Ned?'

The playwright, the drape still in his hand, cocked an ear to the stage above them. It sounded like a crowd upon it, many voices raised. 'This scene is soon to end and he has a time after that before his next. His biggest one. Speak to him, then watch him play if you can. I'll pray for you,' he added, then drew the drapes upon himself.

John stared at them for a moment. 'I thank you for it, Will. For many things,' he said softly. Then he turned, and climbed the stair to the tiring house.

His emergence from Hell was unnoticed, as so many were sweeping in from the stage. Caesar and his train, for he had noted

248

Augustine Phillips's strong tones as the aspiring tyrant, and the man came in now, a wreath in his hand. Behind him came Ned.

As actors changed swiftly for different parts, gathered props, checked rolls, John stepped further back beyond the light spill, pulled his hat low over his head, shrugged his cloak around him and watched his son. He'd noted how he bore himself as a Roman noblewoman, feminine but strong. Saw too that he had observed at least one of the precepts John had taught him: he did not leave the part until he had completed his exit and the curtain was fallen behind him, hiding him from the audience's view. Indeed, it was clear the role absorbed him, for long after others were speaking upon the platform, he held the posture, staring ahead, seeing his next scene – even while the rest were fretting or joking quietly around him, Ned remained still, contained. It made John remember his own recent return to the stage, the limp he'd imposed, and he flushed at the memory. Once, he had been more than a bag of actor's tricks. Once, he had been in love with theatre, as his son so clearly was now.

At last the boy broke, rolled his shoulders, came forward. John was just to the rear side of a table full of artefacts for the stage. Ned paused before it, seeking one. 'Son,' John whispered.

There was enough light, or he had become accustomed to what there was, to clearly see the boy's face. See the changes that came over it, in succession: the start of surprise, of recognition; a brief flash of relieved joy; then, hard upon that, an anger that moved up in red and settled in fire within the eyes. Painted as these were, so that those in the uppermost galleries could see him, they lit up the gloom in fury. He turned away on the instant.

'Ned,' John hissed, catching the boy's arm. It was thrown off immediately, but at least the motion was halted, and he stood there, his back to his father, a wall against him and his words. 'Lad, I am sorry. I had to go. I could not help—'

'No!' The whisper came hard. 'I do not want to hear any excuse. You promised to come to see me as the country maid. You broke your promise. Nothing to you, whose word can never be taken. Something to me, who'd thought . . . who'd hoped . . .'

He broke off. John swallowed, stepped a little closer. 'I know. But I was powerless. The Earl of Essex—'

'Did I not tell you: no more excuses!' Ned whipped around, and the heat in his eyes scorched. 'As soon as you speak, a lie comes. A lie! Because I know, however it ended, whoever ended it, a bottle began it. Is it not so?'

'It is . . .' John hesitated. What reply could he give? There was no forgiveness in the stare, none to be had. Any explanation would not be heard. And he did not begrudge that. He was not sure he'd have believed anything he could have told either. So all he could say, he did. 'I have to . . . to go away for a little while. A short time, I hope. I will return. Your country maid will be in the repertory. I will see it and many more. I will . . .'

Yet it was his son's voice, not his closeness that held John, the iced venom of it. 'Do you not understand? Let me be clear then.' Ned leaned in, some shaft of light gilding those painted eyes. 'I do not care. It is better for me not to have a father. Leave me alone. Leave my mother alone too. She has made a new life apart from you. She has a new husband and I . . . I, a new father in my tutor, Master Burbage. We are content. Leave. Us. Be.'

At that, he walked away. John wanted to follow, grab, persuade, somehow. But he did not move. Men stared. If they did not hear the whispered words, they sensed the feeling, as good players will.

He took a moment to master himself. There were so many cuts, he did not know which to staunch first. The deepest he discovered when he probed was that Burbage was Ned's new father. Yet his son was right in this. Choices had been made. Consequences must now be lived with.

When he was ready, he shook himself, straightened. As he made for the stairs, what he forced himself to dwell upon was not his sentence of banishment, but the first thing that Ned had shown him, albeit in a flash: his relief. Buried deep within his justified resentment, he was glad his father lived. That would have to be enough for him, for now.

During *Henry the Fifth*, John had explored the new theatre top to bottom, and had discovered a viewing hole in the uppermost level of the playhouse. He made for it now. The winch that was up there to lower characters from heaven was obviously not required for this piece. No workers awaited their cue in the cramped space. So he was able to tread carefully to the front wall to peer, to seek. Yet how, in that vast horde, would he ever be able to pick out Tess?

He sought. Faces blurred as he scanned them. He knew she'd be dressed simply, demurely – but so was most of the audience that sat in the galleries. She would have her natural hair, not a tower that testified to the tirer's art. Again, that only ruled out a few. He looked where he had sat with her before, and did not find her.

He lowered his eyes, rubbed them – and then admitted another sense. He began to listen. To Burbage. At first he tried to pick fault, as if the player's rendition could make him unworthy to be Ned's tutor; yet soon admitted that there was scarce a fault to be found. The deep voice rolled like smoothest moleskin over the house, enfolding all in warmth, heating John where he sat, directly above. And then he was taken beyond the sound, to the words themselves. John had known his friend's words from the beginning, had spoken not a few himself. The playwright had always had a way with him. But these? There was something different to them, to the way the verse moved. It was . . . simpler, swifter somehow, direct and all the deeper for it. The way the character talked . . . Burbage was Brutus, the noblest Roman, that John knew. But Brutus was not telling others who he was, as was usually the way. He was telling the audience, of course – but he was also telling himself. More – and this made John's heart beat a little faster – he was using the audience to decide his course of action.

Words floated up.

Between the acting of a dreadful thing
And the first motion, all the interim is
Like a phantasm or a hideous dream.

It was thrilling. Uncanny. Will had written soliloquies before. None like this. And because he was lost in it, staring out into the play-house, transported, no longer seeking, he found – and looked straight into Tess's face.

XXVII

The Battle of the Bridge

She was sitting right in the centre of the second gallery. She was as enraptured as he had just been. As they all were, either side of her and all around. Even the fidgety groundlings, silenced and still, held in the alchemy of playwright and his player.

John had to break free of them, could not lose himself to rapture. Especially when, in seeing her and studying a path to her, he also saw possibly the only two men in the playhouse who were not caught in Burbage's spell. They were not looking at him upon the stage. They were looking all around the house. One was the man who'd lately stood sentinel at the players' entrance. The other was the officer who had arrested John and taken him to Lollards' Tower – Waller, was it? Who'd been kind enough to give him some ale. Cecil's man.

It did not matter. He had to be gone. But first he had to see Tess.

He moved to the stair, as soft as any mouse. If he had escaped Burbage's entrapment, he would not distract any other from it.

As he descended the ladder, he wondered how he could approach her. He assumed that Cecil's officers were wise enough to have followed Tess from the tavern. They would know where she sat, and another man, one he had not spotted, might be watching her. No answer came as he passed quietly through the tiring house, and no player noted him, all their attention forward to the platform. He descended again to the players' entrance. A keeper he did not know eyed him as he bent to the grille. There was no one watching there. Cecil's men had obviously decided he was in the house.

He gestured to the bolts, was let out. He merged swiftly into the crowd that still moved towards other Bankside entertainments, inns, cockpits, brothels. Left them at the Globe's main door. Hesitated there. It was foolish to go in. He had a purse to see him out of London. He could send Tess a note, explaining all.

It was foolish – and he did it. I have my reputation to consider after all, he thought. Fool. The one title I truly own. May as well own it, and let Tess make up the triumvirate of those who so justly condemn me this day.

Latecomers were always admitted, if they had their penny. John opened the purse, saw his friend had treated him well – there was gold, five angels' worth in various coins, some shillings and sixpences, some brass . . . and just two pennies, which were what he needed now. He handed the first to the doorkeeper for entrance, the second to the gallery man, who admitted him though muttered there was little room to spare. At the top of the stair he peered down, marked Tess in the front row. A servant was beside her, her chaperone.

John gnawed at his bottom lip. He glanced at the stage, where conspirators had given way to Brutus and his lady. They began to speak . . . and John was jostled by a boy trying to pass him into the gallery, a tray of oranges held before him. John moved aside . . . then reached, grabbing the boy by the arm, pulling him close. 'Listen, lad, do you want to earn a tuppence?'

He whispered instructions. The boy nodded, disappeared the coin under his rags, then went about his business, whispering his wares. When he reached the row behind Tess, he bent and said something softly into the serving man's ear. He jerked his head around . . . and John ducked from view down the stairwell.

People rose and moved around the galleries all the time – to piss, to buy nuts or oranges or beer, to liaise and flirt. They could be cursed, especially during an intimate scene like this one. John heard some angry mutters; and then the serving man appeared. He halted at the top of the stairs on seeing John, who reached up, caught him by the sleeve and pulled him down a couple of steps and out of sight. 'Do you know me?' he said, low and urgent.

The man, one of Tess's brewers with a gut his trade had given him, nodded, his eyes wide.

'Then I ask a favour of you: I wish to hire your seat for a time.'

'My seat?' The man scratched his beard. 'I don't think the mistress would like . . .'

'I assure you, the mistress is expecting me. Besides' – he raised a silver shilling – 'you look thirsty.'

The brewer licked his lips. 'I was enjoying the play, though. That Burbage . . .'

'Yes, yes, I know,' said John testily, 'the prince of players. Well, you will return to him soon enough.' He shoved the coin into the man's hand. 'Oh,' he added, 'and I will need to borrow your bonnet and cloak.'

The exchange was swiftly made. Fortunately the brewer had a head to match his stomach, and John was able to pull the brim well over his eyes. As the man descended for refreshment, John climbed and, to more curses, made his way to the vacant place. It had been expanded into, but with a forceful insertion, he was down.

'Really, Matthew, can your bladder not hold till a noisier time?' whispered Tess.

John peered under his brim at the two of Cecil's men he'd spotted before. The officer who'd brought him beer in Lollards' Tower was staring at them. John froze until the man's stare went elsewhere. 'Gently, love,' he said softly, 'do not startle.'

He was watching her from the side of his eyes. Hers narrowed, moved towards him, for an instant showing that same relief that had briefly lit Ned's. As swiftly it passed, and if their son's anger did not come into them, what did perhaps hurt John even more – a sad resignation.

'So. You live.'

'I do. No thanks to the Irish, nor my lord of Essex.'

'But some, surely, to the whisky and the lady with blonde tresses?'

She'd heard. What could he say? 'Tess . . .'

Her head shook, short, sharp. 'No. No excuses, John. Remember, I have heard them all before.'

John sighed. 'I see now whence our son derives his lack of charity.'

'You've seen him?'

'Aye. Though he has made it clear it is for the last time.'

Behind them, someone hissed, 'For shame, sir. Burbage speaks!' Tess leaned a little closer. John inhaled her, some potion of lavender and comfrey about her. He closed his eyes for a moment, enjoying a far sweeter scent than cloves.

'Can you blame him?' Tess whispered, even lower. 'He has not the experience of your broken promises that I have. This time he had hopes . . .'

'Stop,' he whispered back. 'You cannot whip me more for it than I have whipped myself.' He could not think what next to say. So instead of trying, he reached within his doublet and drew out the letter that he had kept there in all the miles from Dublin. Wordlessly, he handed it to her.

She took it, stared at the familiar seal, broke it, began to read the words of Samuel D'Esparr. John turned again to the stage, where a thunder roll ended one scene and heralded another – one that brought Ned back on, following Gus Phillips. They took their positions, began to speak. And somehow John was able to mostly forget what the woman beside him was reading, and listen. Ned was clear . . . yet he seemed to John a little stiff. Perhaps our recent encounter has unsettled him, he thought, to his regret. Yet when Ned said:

When beggars die, there are no comets seen;
The heavens themselves blaze forth the death of princes

a sigh ran through the Globe. There had been many signs and portents in the summer skies over London. And England had an aged queen.

His attention was drawn back by the folding of paper. He glanced sideways. Tess was staring forward, but not at the stage. At something beyond.

'My . . . Samuel says that you fought together. More – that during an ambuscade, you saved his life.'

'I did.'

'Why?'

'Why what?'

'Why did you save him? Would it not have suited you better to see him dead?'

John frowned. 'Undoubtedly it would,' he said, 'and I admit there are still times when I hope the Irish succeed where last they failed, and pierce his fat guts through.' He shook his head. 'But even if you condemn me in so much, Tess, you must allow me this: I am not

255

a dastard. I would never seek to win you through Despair's death if I had the power to prevent it.'

He had whispered with some heat, provoking more hisses from behind them. Tess reached over and laid a hand on one of his, squeezed briefly, withdrew it. 'I know you are not, John. You are, despite it all, a noble man.' Before he could venture that he was, in more ways than she could yet know, she continued. 'Though I wonder much at this,' she said, lifting the letter. 'My fiancé speaks more . . . feelingly than he was wont.'

Or I'll not trust whisky, thought John. He'd made sure that Sir Samuel had taken a skinful, was suitably maudlin and still full grateful when he wrote. A sober morning and Despair might have produced a very different letter, glossing over John's rescue, emphasising his own courage. Still, his missive had achieved this much at least: his love was no longer looking at him with that terrible mixture of pity and disdain. A small victory that perhaps could be followed up. 'Tess, hear me. I have to g—'

'Will you cease your prattling, varlet?' The bellow came from right behind him, accompanied by a hard shove, and continued, 'We are trying to listen to the play.'

The noise would perhaps not have drawn so much attention. It was the custom in the playhouse for people to converse, to comment, to voice their displeasure. Not even Burbage could hold them silent for ever. Unfortunately, the matronly shover had a bass bellow that would not have disgraced the platform, produced from a chest that would have disgraced no mastiff. Beside her, a terrier of a man equally glared, and when John said, 'Lady, I seek only to . . .' he got no further, for the terrier snarled, reached up and threw John's hat from his head.

The stage was shaken by more thunder. Most people were drawn back to it. But John, as he bent to retrieve his hat, noticed that a few weren't – most especially Cecil's officer, who was staring straight at him.

He turned to Tess. 'I have to leave now. But know this first: I will return and I will try to make amends. For ever this time.'

He was half up when her hand delayed him. 'John, what is wrong?'

He glanced around. More than one man was converging. 'I have made a powerful enemy. Adieu.'

With that, he headed for the stairs to accompanying snarls from the mastiff and her terrier. He gained the stairwell – and met a man hastening up who straightway betrayed his allegiance by reaching both hands to grab John by the throat. Sweeping his forearm round in a pugilist's block, the clash hard enough to draw forth a yelp, he silenced the man with a straight left palm to the mouth, knocking him down the stairs. He followed fast, but though the man tumbled, he still managed to grab John's legs as he tried to jump him. He fell, hard, caught himself on his hands, got a leg free and kicked back, encountering he knew not what; but the result was a cry, and a slackening of grip. John was free of it and through the door.

He headed straight down Maiden Lane, aware of shapes following him fast from each side of the playhouse. These did not hue-and-cry him. They had their own reasons for taking him silently and without the interference of citizens or the watch – which thought added speed to his legs. He wove, ducked, threading through the people. Yet the crowd was not thick, for so many were within the places of entertainment.

London, he thought, running fast. Southwark was but a suburb, half country, too open to lose himself in. The city was a badger's sett, looping streets like tunnels so closely did the house's jutties conjoin. With lanes and alleys that twisted into darkness, thronged with crowds that lurched from taverns for drink to ordinaries for vittles, and between them every sort of business. Perfect cover. And he was decided – he would not go abroad. A night hidden and he'd creep with the dawn to the Bell Inn near the cathedral, where Stratford's carrier and Shakespeare's friend, William Greenaway, kept horses for hire. Three days to Will's birthplace, two more to Much Wenlock, if he did not take it at an Essex-like pace. His family home. It still had a priest hole from when his stepfather was a Jesuit. Sanctuary.

Yet first he had to cross the Thames. He nearly swerved to Paris Garden Stairs, thought better of it. He could hear the pursuit, in boot heels upon the cobbles, close behind. He was ever fast – like his father had been, his mother had once told him – and fancied himself in a foot race. But to pause and discuss a fare with a boatman? No. He kept going straight . . . towards London Bridge.

It would be crowded, as always. A narrow street and a hundred shops, each with their customers before it. A thicket within which any fox could lose the hounds.

He slipped between the stone columns of the churchyard of St Mary Overies. There were bookstalls there, but few buyers – Southwark catered more to loins than brains. He crossed the yard swiftly, and as he exited, turning on to the bridge's approach, the church bell tolled three. Back at the Globe, Caesar would be falling to conspirators' daggers – while ahead and above him the reward for conspiracy could be clearly seen.

John did not pause to study the traitors' heads affixed to spikes on the gate tower, just pushed through the gawkers, under the arch and on to the bridge itself. He did cross himself, as his stepfather the lapsed Jesuit had taught him – a warding gesture against the fate of traitors impaled above him. It had never seemed to press him so closely.

He could not run, the crowd prevented it. But neither could his pursuit, and he risked a glance back while moving forward. Hard to tell at first in that impelling crowd. Then he saw Waller, a head taller than most, as John was. Thirty paces back only. Maybe less. Close enough for their eyes to lock. Turning forward again, John sought avenues through the press, little shifts of flesh to glide through. The crowd thickened, both man and beast, for horses were being ridden or pulled wagons, dogs ran free or were attached to carts, sheep were loose and harried forward by collies. John moved through them all, content with his steady progress. Unless his pursuers drew swords and began hacking, they could not clear a path any faster than he. Thirty paces clear on the city side and he'd have three alleys to choose from, each as twisting as the next. One led to an especially low tavern that John would sometimes frequent – the Flounder's Head, hard by the Billingsgate market. He'd slip inside, order an ale and be sipping it as Cecil's men passed by.

There was a house about a third of the way across, more ornate than any other, a confection in wood, with domes and curlicued gables, spires that would have suited a miniature cathedral, its frontage decorated with balconies and alcoves, these occupied by Greek gods and heroes, gilded statues shining in the sun. Its pieces had been brought whole from Holland and assembled in place with naught but wooden pegs. It was renowned, he had brought Ned to stare at it many a time . . . yet for the life of him he could not remember its name! Such forgetfulness was happening to him often of late.

He'd been looking up. He should have been looking ahead, for he slapped into a back, strove to slide around it, was blocked by another and yet a third. Progress was halted and voices now surpassed the cries of pedlar and hawker. Human, demanding the way be cleared; and animal, a sudden loud braying, its 'Eee-aw! Eee-aw!' an ascending note of frustration and pain. John managed to slip past a few more bodies before he was halted entirely. Close enough to see over heads to the obstruction.

An ass cart was stopped right under the house's narrow archway. The ass was rearing up in its traces and the driver was standing before it, tugging on its reins with one hand and punching it in the muzzle with the other. 'Move, you damnable wretch,' he cried, landing blow after blow. His accent was distinct – and Irish. An unfortunate one to have in the summer of 1599, with another English army failing across the water.

'Clear the way, you bog-trotter,' came a London voice, immediately joined by a dozen more, all heaping various insults upon the man's person and country. He realised his error, gaped at the crowd around him and, in a panic, began redoubling his punches upon the beast's nose. It produced no effect but a shying and a bucking, and the cart shifting a little backwards into packed people, who cried out. John knew it wouldn't. About the only thing that would was to shove a sword point into the ass's arse.

Punches, insults, brays continued. John looked about him, seeking a way; looked back to the crowd packed as tightly behind him. Saw again the officer, who saw him and, seeing, started to shout. His voice, battlefield trained, rose above even that babel.

'By the command of her majesty – clear the way for her officers! Clear the way!'

It had an effect. People turned to look back. Seeing a sword raised, and determined men driving forward, the crowd shifted again, squeezing whatever way it could, which was little enough. John looked about, seeking any avenue. Ahead, men were climbing up on to the cart, the Irishman leaving his blows to remonstrate with them. There was a slight giving, and he found himself picked up by the surge, carried to the side, and finally flung against a fantastically carved door. Surprisingly it gave – and he tumbled over its threshold. Stairs were before him, shouts of 'Clear the way' closer behind. He had no choice. Thrusting up from the floor, shrugging off the men who'd pushed him in, he took the stairs two at a time.

Shouts doubled behind – and one came before. 'What make you here?' yelled a man on the landing above, spectacles on his nose, a quill in his hand. The house belonged to some trading company, that much John remembered; the young fellow, with brown hair falling on to his wide white collar, would be a merchant or his secretary. John climbed towards him. 'I would be obliged, sir,' he panted, 'if you would show me a way out.'

'A way out? It is the same as the way in. Take it, varlet.' He shook his quill in John's face. 'Take it now!'

In the street, the officer's voice rose above brays and blows. 'Your pardon, sir,' said John, 'but I cannot.' Brushing aside both quill and its angry wielder, he discovered that the landing led to another stair, then a corridor, which had to pass over the arch below, with doors either side and one ajar at its end. He rushed through that, into a room with desks, thick leather-bound tomes on shelves, windows on three sides. Another door, open, revealed a descending stair. But before John took it, and despite the continuing rebukes of the clerk who'd pursued him, he came back into the room and went to the window that faced the Southwark shore. The glass was leaded but not too thick; he could see down to where figures milled. Indistinct, but he could make out that several wielded swords.

Both exits blocked. He went to the only other – the window that gave on to the river. He could smash it, he supposed. But he'd swum in the Thames in February and did not fancy another dip. Moreover, he could see by the foam that the tide was turning, gushing between the narrow stone arches of the bridge. Experienced boatmen would not attempt it now. Wild youths would dare the race in skiffs, and many had died doing so. He was a good swimmer – but drowning was the best chance that way.

John turned to the door and the only option left. As feet pounded on the stair opposite, he undid his buckler's straps. Grasping its leather grip, he slipped his sword from its sheath.

The clerk was still in the room, shouting at him. He chose not to listen, to focus instead on the man about to come through the door. When he did, John attacked him.

There was no room for anything indirect. Simple usually worked best anyway, especially allied to surprise. The guard – it was not the officer John had encountered before – yelped as John ran at him, brought his own weapon to guard . . . too late. With a sharp flick of his right wrist, John knocked the blade aside even as he continued his run forward, following through with his left, his buckler hand, driving the small shield into the man's face, knocking him down and, John suspected, out. He did not pause to check, leapt the falling body, was in the corridor beyond the next instant.

Two men were there, both drawn. Rapiers, each with the balancing dagger in their other hand. The briefest flash of a man came into John's mind – George Silver, the master swordsman and advocate of the superiority of English weapons over Italian. Had he written in his treatise of a fight in the confined space of a corridor? If not, John knew he had at least written what he practised now. 'Aaargh!' he yelled, charging forward, sword whipped over his head to make the steel sing. The first guard gave back immediately, trying to find room for his longer blade – a mistake, as John was already running and closed the distance fast, stepping inside the man's guard. The dagger came up, John deflected it on his buckler, flicked his blade tip to the ceiling and smacked his sword guard straight into the man's nose. He fell, poleaxed but alive, John hoped. He knew he mustn't kill anyone here. He was in trouble enough. And the Tyburn brand on his thumb urged restraint.

The second man had stepped away from his friend's fall, taken guard. John now saw it was Waller, the officer who had sent him ale in Lollards' Tower. Cecil's man, with no kindness in his eyes now. 'Surrender, Lawley,' he shouted. 'There is no fleeing from here. I have many men below.'

'Then summon them all, for I will pass!' John used the moment of shouting to take hanging guard and assess his opponent's stance. Waller knew his trade, sure; there was a lot of sharp steel between John and his man and thus between him and escape. Considering that if he triumphed he would have to tell Silver just how, he attacked.

His downward chop with his sword was avoided, the points of

261

steel opening and admitting them like gates, closing behind, an immediate thrust forward that had John ducking to save an eye. He was still too far out and so at the advantage of the rapier's reach. Since he was low already, he stayed so as he gathered forward fast, buckler raised above his head like a legionary in a testudo, feeling the rapier sliding along it as he advanced. But the officer was retiring as swiftly, his dagger low and pointed at John's face, seeking to hold him off till he could withdraw his rapier and thrust again. The narrowness of the corridor forced John to pull his sword back, not swing wide into a cut as he would have liked. Swords paralleled each other's movements, neither man sure who would gain position first.

Yet John had one other advantage – the rapidly approached stair. His opponent, aware too, paused, then, in his hesitation, slapped his rapier atop the still raised buckler. Ah ha, John thought, flicking his wrist the fraction he needed. He was falsing, looked like he was preparing for a belly lunge when, already low, the knee could be struck on a lunge. A cut only, some pain and blood, no more, move past . . . and have the advantage of height on any other man as he charged down the stairs.

Yet in that tiniest moment between thought and action, it was over. Something thumped, and hard, into the back of his head; a voice came clearly. 'There, whoreson dog! That will teach you to invade my home!'

John fell. As he did, Waller stamped on his blade, close to the hilt, driving him faster down, since he refused to let it go, before it snapped from his grasp and his head bounced into the wood-tiled floor.

The blows did not drive him straight into oblivion; the descent into darkness was slower and he was able to note a couple of things: the book that had felled him, thick as a butcher's forearm, landing beside his fading eyes – an irony which perhaps his friend the playwright could make something of, that John Lawley was, in the end, laid low by words; the conversation of men walking away backwards, debating between gaols. Yet a different thought accompanied him into the final darkness; a word. For he finally remembered the name of the house in which he was lying, the one with such fantastical carvings.

'Nonsuch,' he mumbled, or perhaps he didn't. Same as the palace where he'd seen a queen naked. The one he'd fled only the morning before to avoid being taken was where he *was* taken.

Will could doubtless make something of that irony, too.

XXVIII

Consequences

The waking was as hard and cold as the stones he lay upon. Darkness held him, unrelieved no matter how wide he opened his eyes. He was in a cell but did not bother to explore its extremities beyond the wooden door. There was nothing he could do in a windowless vault except wait and hope that this was not the end of his journey but a pause along the way. Not that shortest of pauses either, the one before the gibbet walk.

In the event, he did not wait long after wakening, a few hours at most. Light showed the door frame, there were footsteps, the slam of bolts. John rose, to at least meet murderer or interrogator on his feet. Of only one thing was he certain – he would not die quietly. He had no weapon, save his hands. But he'd killed with them before.

A man entered, cautiously, flaring torch in one hand, cudgel in the other. It was the officer who'd apprehended him, who'd once brought him ale in another cell. He was flanked by two guards of near equal size. These held manacles.

'Easy or hard, Lawley?' enquired Thomas Waller.

'That depends. Are you going to murder me?'

'No. Some questions only.'

The man was not lying. John smiled faintly. 'Easy or hard?'

'Easy. Someone wants to talk with you alone. Thinks that you are dangerous.'

'Why does everyone always think that?' Sighing, John held out his hands.

The guards came, fastened chains to his wrists and to his ankles, attaching these to a hook affixed to a flagstone on the floor. Task

264

completed, Waller leaned out of the door and called. 'Master Secretary?'

In walked Sir Robert Cecil. 'Is he secure?' he asked.

'He is.'

'Then leave us. But wait close by.'

Placing his reed torch into a sconce, Waller bowed and left with his guards. Cecil closed the door partway then turned back. He regarded John for a long moment before he spoke. 'Well, knave, do you know why you are here?'

'I do not even know where here is.'

'The Tower. It is the customary place for traitors.'

'Then I am mishoused. For I am none such.'

'No?' Cecil stepped a little nearer, though still beyond the tether's reach. 'Your recent actions speak against that claim. For you have conspired most treacherously with the Earl of Essex, and accompanied him, all armed, even to the heart of the Queen's sanctuary.'

'As I was ordered to do by the Queen's vice-regent. It would have been treason to disobey.'

'You were the Queen's messenger, sirrah, and should not have obeyed a traitor.'

'Is my lord of Essex condemned as such?'

Cecil shrugged. 'Not yet. He is given over to the Lord Keeper and will be held to await a trial of his peers. As a nobleman of England it is his right under Magna Carta.'

John raised his manacles. 'Now I am no lawyer, sir, as I know you are. Yet I have acted a few in my time and know this much: under Magna Carta the right of habeas corpus was also created. It states that any free-born Englishman, lord or commoner, cannot be imprisoned without cause, and a warrant sworn before a justice.' He nodded. 'Have you brought such an indictment?'

Cecil laughed. 'You are not so naïve, sir, not to know that laws can be suspended in times such as these?'

'What times?'

'Times of treason. Of faction. Of conspiracy.'

John raised arms that clanked to scratch his head. 'I have been gone from the realm a short while, and back but a day. Yet I am sure I would have heard of a suspension of such a fundamental right. And perhaps joined the riot against it.'

Again Cecil smiled. Again there was no humour in it. 'You *are* naïve, sirrah. For when conspiracy threatens the very person of the sovereign . . .' He halted John's interruption with a gesture. 'Oh yes, I know you were simply obeying orders. But these orders took you far beyond the limits of any viceroy's power. Took you, indeed, into her majesty's bedchamber. You violated the temple. You beheld the core of the mystery.' He glared. 'Villain, you saw the Queen naked!'

'She was not completely nak—'

'The earl her general,' Cecil interrupted. 'You her messenger. Servants. Betrayers. There will be no forgiveness . . . for either of you.'

John thought then of that look Elizabeth had given him, the hate in it. But that was in a terrible moment. Surely . . . 'Her majesty will eventually realise that I was simply being loyal. She may also recall, as she so generously has before, my former service in her wars and—'

'The only thing her majesty recalls,' Cecil cut in, 'beyond your seeing what no man should see, is this.' He lowered his voice to a whisper. 'The evil that your family has wrought upon hers.'

'Evil? What do you m . . .' And then he remembered another look she had given him, at their first meeting at Whitehall on that interminable Shrove Tuesday. Not hate then. Just horror, as she looked at the grandson of the man who'd killed her mother. 'She cannot hold my birth to account . . .'

Cecil's laugh was harsh. 'Sirrah, do you not know that in England that is almost all that *is* held to account?' Then, for the first time, he looked away. When he spoke again, his voice was softer. 'The Queen . . .' He considered. 'Her majesty is not always focused entirely on the day. She lives partly in the past. Her . . . horrible past. You are somehow a part of that, in a way I do not understand. Her heart is hardened against you. Indeed, if I brought her your head on a platter, I think she would be right pleased.'

John shook his head, while it was still on his neck. The conversation had entered a different world. It was connected to the place where they were; but it went far beyond the Tower too. And it would not help him to get beyond it himself. He didn't know what would, and he needed to; needed some hope in whatever lay ahead. 'I am curious then, Master Secretary,' he said softly, 'as to why you are here. Your orders would be enough to have me incarcerated, where and in whatever manner you chose. You are not a man who would risk the race under London Bridge simply to gloat.' He shook his head. 'Why do you concern yourself so closely with me? Surely I am but a pawn in the great game you play against the Earl of Essex? And if a pawn can be reluctant, I am so. Because I am sure, since you know so much about me, that you also know this – I have ever sought to avoid his service. My sole desire is to return to my life in Southwark.' He raised the chains. 'Why do you bother with me? Why, in God's good name, do you all bother with me?' He shrugged. 'Is it only because I am good with swords?'

Cecil listened, then stared down for a moment, before looking back at John. 'I will tell you why. Part of the reason why, anyway.' He inhaled deeply through his nose. 'My father and I disagreed . . . on many subjects. Especially during the last few years of his life. Yet something I never doubted was the keenness of his eye.' He looked around the walls. 'When he interrogated you in this very place, he noted certain things about you. Your weaknesses, of course, of which sottishness is the main. Your foolishness, shown most in your absurd aspiration to be naught but a player. Yet.' He took another breath, exhaling it slowly. 'He also noted this: that you have been close to the centre of most of the important acts in our recent history. I think of Drake. Of war in the Netherlands. The Armada. Cadiz. And some-times, sometimes your foolishness has been overta'en by . . . dare I say this, a certain *patriotism*. And when it is, it is coupled with an ability to act decisively, rare in most men.' He shook his head. 'You are right. You are a mere pawn in the game, John Lawley. But you are an intriguing piece for all that. One does not sacrifice a pawn unless one needs to. I will decide when that time is right. Until then, you will await my move.'

He moved to the door. John's voice caught him there. 'Could you at least give me some idea of the duration, Master Secretary?'

'How, when I do not know it myself?' Cecil's dark gaze was on him again. 'We shall both await th'event. If my lord of Essex is judged to be a traitor by his peers, well then, many around him will also be so condemned . . . and punished. If he is merely repri-manded, he will be exiled to the country, never again allowed to see the Queen, clothed or otherwise.' A gleam came to the hooded eyes. 'Yet I think we both know that Robert Devereux is not one to lay down the dice while he has breath in his body. He will forever seek to hit the hazard.' He nodded. 'So I will give you time to brood on loyalties. To consider where they might best be placed. Eventually you will, I am certain, come to realise which shade of pawn you should be.'

With that, Cecil turned and left the cell. John wanted to call, to delay, to bargain, but found he could not speak, his voice taken away by the truth in the man's words. For he had always been a slave – to other men's ambitions, and to his own appetites, equally. He *was* a conspirator in one way, for he had conspired to bring himself here, to this cell, to this fate. His son; Tess; Will: all had been right. He had chosen his own way. Now he must live with the consequences.

Those began now, with guards re-entering the cell. John raised his manacled hands . . .

ACT FOUR

They are the faction. O Conspiracy!

The Tragedy of Julius Caesar

The Gaoler's Man

Fifteen months later. 6 February 1601. Morning

When he was ready, John spoke.

> *I have been studying how to compare*
> *The prison where I live unto the world.*
> *And for because the world is populous*
> *And here is not a creature but myself*
> *I cannot do it. Yet I'll hammer't out.*

He regarded his audience – one man, his face near all beard now his eyes were closed. Matthew Wingate, turnkey and John's sole bene-factor.

Well, he thought even as he declaimed, the company at the Globe are the Lord Chamberlain's Men. At the Rose play the Admiral's Men.

So in the Tower, I must be the Gaoler's Man.

As patrons went, he was more generous than most lords. They gave little more than their name. Matthew supplied additional food and ale, the opportunity for air and movement in the courtyard, two extra blankets, candles, and a far more regular change of floor reeds than his dull and rule-abiding predecessor. And all because he'd discovered that his prisoner was the very thing that was his soul's delight and that he spent most of his spare hours watching: to whit, a player. In return for his favours he only asked for John to exercise his talents, which he was more than happy to do – as now – even beyond the benefits they brought. Near a year of brooding had been ended these last three months by his appointment as the Gaoler's Man. Better food had strengthened him. A warmer cell had kept sickness away. And the last benefit, perhaps the best, was that he had finally gained news of the world.

Yes, thought John. Sending Matthew to Shakespeare, with the note to treat him well, had worked extra wonders. The gaoler had returned ever more fired by his tour of the playhouse and a seat near the stage he could never have afforded; and he had brought back with him some quartos – play scripts for John to speak from, a delight in themselves, but even more for what lay concealed in their leaves, his friend Will having read his mind: letters.

A joy indeed, to hear word of the world he was exiled from . . . until last week's script, the very one from which he was reciting. The play had speeches worth learning – but placed within a split sheet was the news he had long feared he would get. It was the first he'd received from Tess, and the last he wanted. Short in letters. Long in their implication.

Sir Samuel is returned from Ireland and our plans may now proceed.

Tess would have known how the brief words would scorch him. She did not try to cool them, or explain. It was clear what actions would follow. They were already troth-plighted. The banns could now be read. In three Sundays they would be married. Ned would be a squire's son, Tess a squire's wife.

He flushed hot on the thought and, even as he built to the conclusion of his speech, studied the man before him. He was grateful to Matthew – but he was still the first barrier between him and escape. Since receiving the note, he had thought of little else, of what he would do in the short time he would have. Many thoughts revolved around blood, the letting of it. But when his own cooled, he realised: he had nowhere to go, not as a fugitive, forever hunted. He might lie in some Southwark stews hidden awhile, but not for ever. Someone would betray him. Or, more likely, he would betray himself, as was ever his way. He needed freedom. And for that he depended, curse them, on others.

His one hope lay in what letters did not bring, but rumour did.

Though February's chill gripped, the streets of London burned with it. Conspiracy was at the centre of the flames – with one man, whom John knew well, feeding it ever more fuel. And if London exploded, as was being whispered, it would blast open many a cell door.

Then, as if in echo to his thoughts, his own door was flung wide and the gaoler's boy came running in, cutting off speech and schemes. 'There's one coming,' he screeched.

They had planned for this. Matthew had to conceal his liberality. So while John dragged the chest from beneath the table, sweeping all the quartos into it, stowing the cheese and sausage more carefully before shoving it back, Matthew swiftly emptied tankards on to the rush floor. The boy grabbed the one stool and two blankets and was gone, the turnkey following with spare candles and the horsehair mattress, slamming and locking behind him.

John looked about. In the pallid morning light that came through the one grille set high up, the cell looked as bare as it was meant to. He sat upon the straw pile. Suddenly chilled, he wrapped the remaining and most threadbare of the blankets around his shoulders.

Who is the one who comes? he wondered. Executioner? Torturer? Murderer? Deliverer?

Footsteps sounded in the corridor, flame light moved in the grille. The key was thrust in again, the squeal came, the door opened. Three men walked in. One he recognised.

'Easy or hard?' said Thomas Waller, holding up manacles, just as he had done before. Yet this time John could not muster the spit for defiance. He simply held out his wrists. Waller secured them but did not yoke his ankles again. Instead, the two guards came either side of him, took an arm each and held him, while their officer peered, then walked deeper into the cell.

'What's this, Lawley?'

John craned around. Waller was holding up a play script. John recognised it at a glance. The one he'd lately been reciting from. The one he'd least like discovered. 'Oh, just something I am reading.'

'Indeed. I did not know you were allowed such pleasures.' Waller shoved it into his cloak. Then, on his nod, the guards followed him from the cell, a firm grip on each of John's arms.

When they emerged from the depths on to a stone walkway, freezing wind drove snowflakes into his face. He bent against it. Is this it? he thought. The moment every prisoner tried not to think on and ever did? Trussed, taken to Tower Hill, handed over to the executioner? Hung, dragged, disembowelled to the cheers of the mob? No. Since he had never had a trial, it was either a sham version of that first . . . or more likely he would be murdered in a cell with easy access to the river gate.

He closed his eyes to the driven snow. He'd always believed he would fight, no matter the odds, the futility. In his day, it would have taken more than even these three large men to stop him. Now he tripped, was hauled upright and back on to his feet. Over a year in prison had sapped his strength, despite the recent better treatment. His will too. Though it had been nothing compared with the cruelties he'd endured in Spain, after Cadiz, yet it had still diminished him. Every day had begun with the little hope that today he might be freed. Every day had ended with the dread that tomorrow might be his last. And now that end had perhaps come, could he only meekly accompany his killers to murder cell or gibbet?

Yes, it seemed. He felt his guts churn, his legs weaken.

They left the Martin Tower, his prison within the prison. Yet they did not make along the ramparts in the direction of the Hill, its scaffold shrouded in the swirling snow. Instead they swivelled towards the looming shape that stood as the still centre of the whole fortress. And when he realised it was there that they were bound, John finally pushed his arms out against his guards, dragged his feet, a weak rebellion, swiftly suppressed.

The White Tower, he thought. Jesu save me.

All knew what occurred within its grey and ivy-clad walls. Even though they were reputed six feet thick, and the dungeons far below ground, some days he had still believed he heard, like the faintest bat's squeak, the shrieks of a prisoner undergoing torment. Like every other unwilling resident, he had ignored them. Like every other resident would now ignore his.

Yet when they'd manoeuvred him up the slick steps and through the main doors, they did not descend the dank, dark stairwell. Instead they went up, into an area for administration. Through half-open doors he glimpsed clerks plying quills at desks. Then he was before a door at a corridor's end. A sharp knock brought a cry from within. 'Come!'

Waller opened the door. Behind a desk overflowing with parchment stood Sir Robert Cecil. 'So, knave,' he said, waving them into the room, 'have you a bow for your better?'

The Master Secretary had only just arrived, by the snow clumps encrusted upon his cloak. He also had bags beneath his eyes that had not been there before, and a face thinned by care, John suspected, rather than winter's leanness. His appraisal was returned. When the guards stepped back an arm's length, he made the bow required, as far as his chained state allowed.

When he rose, the other man was still staring. 'You look . . . well, Lawley,' he said, as if this peeved him. 'Fifteen months in a cell is meant to diminish a man.' As John shrugged, the officer, Waller, came past the group and placed the play script on the desk. 'What's this?'

'I found it in his cell, sir.'

The Master Secretary picked up spectacles from the desk, held them up to his eyes – which widened beneath the thick lenses. ' "*The Tragedy of King Richard the Second*",' he read aloud, then looked up. 'What are you doing with this?'

'I . . . found it. The former occupant of my cell must have . . .' John shrugged. 'You know.'

'I know a fable when I hear one. And I know that this' – he raised the quarto – 'is a treasonous text.'

'It is merely a play, sir.'

'Merely? Oh indeed! One that *merely* speaks on the overthrow of God's anointed king. On mere regicide. On a paltry insurrection. In times such as these, dangerous times, this' – he waved the paper in the air – 'is incitement. Performed by your old friends, of course, the Chamberlain's Men.'

'Not for many years, sir. 'Tis an old work.'

'It matters not. The mob has a long memory. And a text like this reminds them.' He waved the paper in the air, threw it down, then picked up a leather-bound volume. 'As does this, the recently published *History of Henry the Fourth*. By one Dr John Hayward.' He peered over his glasses. 'Do you know him?'

'I do not.'

'No. I do not suppose that prisoners mix much within the Tower.' Cecil's smile was as mirthless as ever. 'For he is also here, some three floors below where you are now. Under *examination.*' He let the word stand a moment before continuing. 'And can you guess why? No, it is not really a question, Master Lawley. I will tell you.' He leaned forward. 'As if it is not effrontery enough to write about this subject at this time, he has the gall to dedicate the book to none other than the Earl of Essex.' He nodded. 'Oh yes. Dr Hayward not only tells the story of Bolingbroke's armed rebellion and his seizing of the throne; he offers it to the man being hailed as his reincarnation. For that is what the people that daily pass Essex House call out. "Bolingbroke!"' Cecil shouted the name. 'And the earl must hear them, since he is again in residence.' Cecil glared. 'Yes, sirrah, the mob calls upon the usurper.'

John thought of speaking what he, the unfortunate Dr Hayward and many in England knew: that the said Bolingbroke may have been a usurper but he became King Henry the Fourth, father of the victor at Agin Court and one of the Queen's illustrious forebears in the House of Lancaster. But he doubted the other man required such a history lesson, nor was it for him to speak it if he did. The snow on the man's cloak showed that he had come hastily, through nasty weather, for this meeting. That he had not even taken it off before summoning him showed that John was there to listen . . . and then perhaps be required, in some way, to act.

As he considered, Cecil continued. 'Only last week the Queen declared: "Know you not I am Richard the Second?"' He nodded. 'Yes. She has ever feared rebellion, and with good reason. Some of these so called noble men still live as if it were one hundred and fifty years ago, and it is their prerogative, nay, more, their chivalrous duty to muster their retainers and march.' He rubbed his forehead. 'I, and my father before me, have spent too much of our energies defeating plot after plot. And yet I will tell you this, sirrah – never have we faced such a perilous time as now. For never was there such a threat.' He nodded. 'Never. And we both know who that threat comes from: your particular friend, the Earl of Essex.'

John thought of denying all allegiance. But he knew he must not . . . yet. Not until he knew more. For rumour had reached inside the Tower and spoken of an earl who had survived his violation of the Queen's sanctuary and the desertion of his command with a reprimand; but he had been stripped of his offices and thus the income by which he fended off his myriad creditors. It spoke also of his followers, back from the Irish debacle, an impoverished and reckless crew gathering in low taverns around Essex's house on the Strand. And of his noble friends, a faction whose wagons were hitched securely to the falling earl's star, failing with him. But rumour, as ever, was short on details.

Carefully, John thought. 'What threat is it you speak of, sir? I do not know much of what happens beyond these walls.'

Cecil, who had left his desk to pace behind it, stopped to consider him. 'I suspect you know near as much as I. Which is not enough. For until most recently I was receiving regular, alarming reports. Of plots, and schemes, and secret meetings. If these did not actually take place within Essex House, they were decided upon there. With my lord of Essex's approval.'

'Then, good sir,' John asked softly, 'if all this is certain, why do you not move against him?'

'Do you think I would be standing here, talking with you, if I could?' Cecil snapped, glaring. 'For as you pointed out before, in this very fortress, even a court of his peers would, tiresomely, require actual proof of treason. It would be different, of course, if the Queen willed it . . .'

He broke off, looking at the other three men, silent as statuary. John finished for him. 'I take it that the Queen does not?'

Cecil stepped closer. 'The Queen, sirrah . . . the Queen . . .' He hesitated, then turned abruptly to those other men. 'Leave us,' he commanded. 'Wait close at hand.'

'Master Secretary.' If Waller was concerned for his master's safety, he did not show it, just bowed and, with a flick of his head, ordered his guards from the room.

Cecil waited till the men had pulled the door to before continuing as if he'd not interrupted himself. 'The Queen is not well. She has not been entirely well for a while now. In her body she is still horse-strong. But in her mind . . .' He glared again. 'You understand I will have your tongue cut out if you repeat a word of what I tell you now.' At John's acquiescent nod, he continued, 'In her mind she conjures a different Robert Devereux. Her "sweet Robin".' He snorted. 'She sends him broths and poultices for his never-ending illnesses. She receives his execrable verse as if newly plucked from the reopened grave of Philip Sidney. She has even been convinced that his act of bursting into her bedroom was the most romantic gesture imaginable. God defend me!' he shouted at the ceiling. 'She will not see him . . . but neither will she condemn him. Not without proof.'

He came from behind his desk now, stopped before John, stared up at him hard, as if seeking within his eyes. After a long pause he said, 'You had the gall to once ask me in this place what my desire was. Well, Master Lawley, now I ask you yours.'

John took a breath to calm his accelerating heart. Only when he was quite ready did he speak. 'My whole desire? It is only this – to have my life back again.'

'Is it?' Cecil studied him, sucking on his lower lip. 'And do you understand that the fulfilment of that is entirely in my gift?'

'I do so understand.'

It was obviously said humbly enough to satisfy both the man's need to subject . . . and another need John saw in his eyes, their faces being so close. 'Well then, Master Lawley,' Cecil continued, as quietly, 'in order for you to receive that gift, you must earn it.' He nodded. 'And the first thing you must do is rejoin the household of the Earl of Essex.'

Ah ha, thought John, but said, 'May I ask, sir . . . why me? Surely you have men within it already?'

'I did. Several.' He paused, to rub at his eyes, 'One by one my sources have fallen silent. The last of them only last week. The silence is permanent.' He looked up. 'For men who swim in the Thames in February lose the ability to speak.'

Not always, thought John, but said, 'You wish me to spy upon my lord of Essex.'

For once there was no equivocation, no threat or bluster. 'Yes,' was the simple reply. Again it came with that flash of desperation in the dark eyes.

Though his heart was beating fast once more, John had spent a lifetime giving people what they wanted, to gain what he wanted. Matthew, the gaoler, was only the most recent. So now he breathed, shrugged, and spoke softly. 'Then I will do so.'

Cecil's eyes narrowed. 'You forsake a lifetime's loyalty in a breath? I warn you, sir, I will not be juggled with.'

John raised his hands. 'Good sir, you asked me before we last parted to *brood* on loyalty. I obeyed – and I began with a tally. Not the usual calendar that prisoners carve on walls. Here.' He tapped his head, his chains jangling. 'This, then, is what Robert Devereux has done for me.' He looked above Cecil's head. 'He has caused me, an innocent man, to spend time in gaols such as this – and worse – for long periods of my life. He has contrived to have me killed by various of his enemies – Englishmen, Irishmen, and too many Spaniards to count. He has stolen my life more often than any other man, with the exception, possibly, of Sir Francis Drake. But at least with him, no matter how much I hated him, I always knew I was fighting for my Queen and for my country.' He paused. 'But if the name of Lawley has ever been linked to treason, it is only because it was yoked to the name of Essex first.'

'You sound as if you . . . as if you almost hate him now?'

They were so close John could see it there again in the other man's eyes, hear it in his halting voice. Hope allied with need. If he had just expressed his whole wish, he now knew Cecil's too. His heart slowed – because he knew that he could grant it. 'Almost?' He shook his head. 'Nay, Master Secretary. Do not qualify my hate with such a word.'

Cecil stared for a long moment. 'I have always wondered about you, John Lawley,' he finally said. 'That *savagery* in the blood we talked about, the night we first met at Whitehall.' His lips scarcely shaped the words. 'How far could you go in it? What are you capable of doing?'

'Capable?' The man had leaned so close that John could have bitten off his ear. Or wrapped the manacles around his neck and snapped it before the guards had got the door open. Both things he was *capable* of. Neither would satisfy either man's desire. So instead he whispered, 'If I could 'scape all consequence? On earth at least?'

The slightest of nods led him on.

'Well then,' he breathed, 'I would cut his throat in the church.'

The stare held for another extended moment of scrutiny before Cecil turned and moved back to his desk. When he reached it, he spoke again, without looking up. 'And what would be your price, John Lawley, for such an act? I am not so foolish to think you will switch allegiances for love of me, Queen or country. Men act, at the last, for themselves.'

'They do.' John raised his chained hands. 'You spoke before of your power to end my life entirely. You also have the same power to set me entirely free.'

'Agree to serve only me, you will be free this hour.'

'Leaving here would only be the first freedom. "Entirely" was the word. To never again have my life placed at someone else's command.' He swallowed. 'Master Secretary, for what I must do in your service . . . which may require something in the end that you can guess at . . . I will need something in return.'

Cecil still did not raise his eyes. 'Name it.'

'Absolution.' The man looked up at that, startled by the term. 'I know it is a word from the old faith. It is not a concept your Puritan one admits. And I will not seek it from God, or any of his intermediaries, at least not yet. But I seek it from you, here, now.'

'What . . . absolution could I grant?'

John paused. In all the nights of dreaming for a moment when he could again take action for himself, this was one course he had considered. But the other man need not know that. 'I . . . I would require a document. A pass. One that will relieve me of the consequence of any crime that I commit on your behalf. It will free me also on the instant from arrest. Any crime,' he added more forcefully, in case the point had been missed.

The look in Cecil's eyes showed that it had not. 'What you ask of me is nearly impossible.'

John kept his voice steady. 'Then that makes two of us.'

The other man's head jerked up. The two of them stared at each other. At last Cecil moved behind his desk. 'How do I know you would not use such a document against me? I could sign this . . . carte blanche here, you could stab me the next moment and then walk free.'

'I think you know that is not what I would do. Nor what would happen. My freedom, whatever the paper stated, would be short after such an action. Along with my life. Besides ' – he stretched the chains around his wrists to their limit – 'you have heard where my hatred lies.'

Again Cecil stared. Then he forsook his desk, moved away again, and with his face to the wall spoke softly. 'What you speak of, only one man in England has ever had before. It will give you impunity in the realm to do . . . anything.'

'Anything,' John repeated, as quietly. 'As it will give me freedom from all of you. From the Queen. From the earl. Even from you, Master Secretary.'

Cecil nodded. 'Then I will draw up the document you require. I will write it myself. Here, now, and have it seen and witnessed only by the Constable of the Tower – though I will not fill in your name.' He turned. 'Such actions as you contemplate should remain un-assigned. It will also be stated that it is . . . redeemable just once. Otherwise . . . what a career a man such as you could have, Master Lawley!' That thin smile came again. 'You shall have it, a handsome purse for your expenses, and your freedom – within the hour. Waller!' he shouted. The man was through the door within a moment, hand on sword grip. 'Master Lawley is to be freed. Find him fresh clothes. Give him his choice of weapons. Return him here when he is ready.'

'Sir.' Waller gestured to the door. John, suddenly aware that these were the first steps to the freedom he craved, not quite believing, took them slowly.

Cecil's voice halted him. 'Yet know this, Lawley. You do not make such an agreement with me and break it. If you betray me, I will find you out. I will see you disembowelled on Tower Hill if I can. Yet even if this paper protects you once from the law, you would never sleep easy again. For it will not save you from a dagger in the night. Your only precedent discovered that.'

John clasped the door edge – and though he wanted to be gone now, he could not help the question. 'And who was that man?'

The Secretary smiled. 'It was my father who gave it to him. You may have known him, since he moved in similar, overlapping circles to you. For he was a man of the theatre. And he was a spy. His name was Christopher Marlowe.'

A wave of hand dismissed him finally. In the corridor, Waller unlocked the chains, but John barely acknowledged him, just stared at the door. 'Poor Kit,' he murmured. He had indeed known the man. Thoughts of him, of the near past, the immediate future, kept him motionless, even when Waller bade him walk. For once he moved, the path could lead to many fates as unpleasant as the dagger in the head that had taken the life of Will's great rival.

He'd been speaking his friend's words not an hour since. But it was Marlowe's that came to him now. ' "Our swords shall play the orators for us",' he mouthed.

'What mumble you, man?' said Waller. 'Come now.'

He came. The Master Secretary had mentioned weapons. Waller was leading him to them. But more than a sword, what he truly required was a dagger – small, well balanced, where he always carried one, in a sheath between his shoulder blades. He knew he would need it there, and soon, for his very first reunion, the one he walked towards now.

He would need it when he next saw Robert Devereux, Earl of Essex.

XXX

Conspiracy

The wherryman threaded his vessel between frozen clumps, the winter having recently loosed its grip only enough to thaw the ice that had bound the Thames for a month. Mist rose, a chill exhalation that easily penetrated through the layers of clothes John had been given. Shrugging deeper into his cloak, so that his ears were covered, he peered between hat and scarf, envying the boatman the warmth of his exercise. The man was even sweating. John had offered him double the shilling he would normally receive to row him, solo, all the way from St Katherine's Stair at the Tower to his destination.

As they cleared the race under the bridge, the temptation to land at Southwark near overwhelmed. Yet John kept silent, ordered no detour. For there was no life there, only delay. Until he had achieved what he had resolved to do before Sir Robert Cecil, there was no life for him anywhere.

He looked as they went by, of course. At the spire of St Mary Overies, close by which Tess would be planning her nuptials in the inn she would shortly be selling. At the Globe, where Ned, at three in the afternoon, was perhaps essaying one of his last roles for the Lord Chamberlain's Men. The thatched O itself brought memories, of John's last time there, the day of his capture and imprisonment. They had been playing *Julius Caesar*, and he had heard Burbage declaim words that he had read since, again and again, in quarto, in the Tower.

Between the acting of a dreadful thing
And the first motion, all the interim is
Like a phantasm or a hideous dream.

He was caught in that interim – the river's mist, the snow-choked sky, the chill that gripped his bones, the plash of oars, the boatman's sweat all seeming to hold the boat where it was, caught between his decision in the Tower and the acting of it that lay ahead. Shivering, not just with cold, John took his gaze from the playhouse and tried to bring his mind with it.

And then they were there. As the bow scraped the dock, he stayed for a moment longer on the bench. Up ahead, across some gardens, the fifty chimneys of Essex House thrust up against the snow clouds. Perhaps five emitted smoke. Though the day was as cold as a nun's teats, he knew his noble lordship had little money to spend on firewood. Little to spend on anything. Yet desperation so loves company, boats like his were moving like water beetles across the Thames, filled with men clutching weapons to their chests – and threads where their purses should hang. Most would not even bother to whisper their treasonous aims. If the drum did not beat, and no piper skirled, the summons to rally was still loud to men as desperate as their lord, loudly answering his call.

At last John rose, stepped on to the dock, paused again, jostled by customers who sought his vacated place. Pulling his cloak tight, he felt about him all that the Master Secretary had given him: the carte blanche, sewn into the edge of his new doublet; his restored sword and buckler; his silver-filled purse; a slim vial that smelled of apothecary's tincture and was a cure only for life itself; finally what he suspected he would rely on most in the end, as he always had: the dagger sheathed between his shoulder blades.

Before he took the first step, he glanced downriver one last time, his gaze resting again on the thatched roof of the Globe. What had Will chastised him with there, the last time he'd seen him? How he could never help his actions, could never take action for himself? 'You sound like the man I conjure now, Prince Hamlet!' he'd declared. Well, old friend, John thought, if I never see you again, perhaps you will hear of this, at least. And know that in the end, I did act.

Shaking his head, he turned from what lay behind to what was ahead.

A crowd prevented him going in the river gate. Men stood there, cloaked and booted, with wide-brimmed hats pulled low over brows, scabbards clattering together as each sought a way through the press, and snarled like dogs at each other when they were prevented. Thwarted, John took the alley beside the easterly wall, discovered the postern there equally besieged. One of its guards, however, was as tall as the gatepost, and John knew him.

'Captain St Lawrence!' he cried, his player's voice piercing the hubbub.

The huge Irishman peered through drifting snowflakes. 'Who calls me?' he bellowed.

''Tis I, Captain. John Lawley.'

'Master Lawley!' The dark face split in a smile. 'Come forward, man. Make way there, all of you.' He was grudgingly obeyed, and John pushed through to the gate. 'I'fecks, but it is good to see you, man. The leader will be delighted. I am delighted.' Surprising John with a rib-squeezing clasp, he released him, and added, 'Sure, I'll bring you to him myself.'

He led John through the gate. To its right, a long table was set up. It was awash with weapons, and men stood before it carefully searching those who had just entered. 'I am sorry, Master Lawley, but all must give up their blades, without exception,' St Lawrence said. 'There's whispers that men are being sent to assassinate the leader. All weapons are to be left here.' He pointed to racks behind the table. 'You may want to wrap your scarf around yours so you know it again.'

As he removed his scarf, sword and buckler, John looked at other men being thoroughly searched. Hands were being passed over breeches, shoved into boot cuffs, thrust down doublets. He stiffened as a man approached him . . . but the captain stepped forward with hand raised. 'There'll be no need for that, man. Do you not see who this is? Master Lawley, his lordship's most loyal follower. May as well search the Earl of Southampton.' He laughed, and clapped a hand upon John's back, low enough down not to feel the hardness there. The man nodded, took the sword and shield, placed them in a rack.

St Lawrence led John forward along an arched pergola, its vine winter-bare. A tunnel of sorts, down which noise swelled and which gave out on to the garden. Tess had vouched for it as one of the finest in the land – for the way to gain the Queen's favour was ever to captivate her passions, and in gardens, as in everything, Essex had sought to outdo his rivals. From previous visits, John recalled paths of coloured gravel that swirled around a fountain before sweeping up to a mount crowned with a banqueting house. A pump at one end had sprayed water upon the parterres to dapple the plants with a simulation of dew. A bowling green had occupied the other end, its grass clipped as precisely as his lordship's Cadiz-cut beard.

That garden had gone. It had been submerged beneath another place, one with which John was far more familiar – an armed camp. Rainbow gravel had melded into multicoloured mud; the bowling lawn was torn by poles that hoisted canvas; and there were men everywhere, lying on camp beds, astride chairs, circling fires fed by beams from the destroyed banqueting house.

The noise, the crowds, both were a shock after the solitary quiet of a cell. He halted, and with him St Lawrence, who mistook his expression for something else. 'Grand, is it not?' He grinned. 'You'll recognise plenty of the lads from Dublin – and many others too. Welshmen, Scots, Irishmen – why, there may even be a few Englishmen about!' He laughed, but as he gazed around, his expression changed. 'Sure, but it is a combustible crew, and so pressed together. And then there's the drinking, which goes on day and night. Though some of us prefer the consolation of God to that sought in a bottle.' The frown was again displaced by a grin. 'Still, the time for action fast approaches. So you have arrived in the nick again, Master Lawley. In the nick! Where have you been all this time? About some secret work for the earl, no doubt?'

He clapped him hard on the shoulder, so hard it shoved him into a mob grouped around a fire pit, jostling a man there in the act of lighting his pipe. He snarled, looked up at the two tall men, turned back with a muttered curse. Indeed, John heard that one low snarl under all the hubbub, one he'd heard so many times before – in the baiting rings, before the dogs were sent in to tackle the bear; in siege lines, just before a big assault. 'They are at a pitch, these men,' he murmured, shouldering through them. 'It would not take much to set them off.'

'Indeed. Combustible, as I said.' St Lawrence stooped, to whisper in John's ear. 'But do not fear – action is close that will set them afire. Sending them like the bullets they are into the hearts of all our enemies.'

They pushed on to the rear doors of the house. Two guards with halberds barred their way. 'Has he been searched, Captain?' queried one.

'He has,' replied St Lawrence, even though it was, for John, thankfully untrue. With this the blades parted and the captain shepherded him through, halting just on the other side of the entrance. 'I'll leave you here, man. You know the house, I warrant. You'll find him in the library – or the chapel perhaps, for few men understand so well their duty to their Lord on high. I must again to my post – though I've a powerful desire to see the prodigal greeted,' he said. 'Go with God.'

John gave him the 'amen' the big Irishman obviously craved. Then he crossed the room that faced the garden, moved down the unlit corridor beyond. He did know the house, but would have been drawn anyway by a laugh he knew even better.

The man he sought was in the library. John paused by the door to study him, and the path between them.

In Dublin Castle he had found a drunkard in the grip of the bloody flux and about an impossible task for which he had no solutions. Then, as often before, the earl had resorted to oblivion for an answer. Here, he looked different. There was colour in his face that fever had not put there, and a light in his eyes, which seemed less than usually clouded with debauchery. It was only on stepping closer that John's own eyes, whose cunning had lessened with his ageing, saw what they could not from afar – the pallor on a face drawn with new lines; the light in the stare that matched the note he'd heard in the laugh – a touch of mania to it.

There were a dozen or so men between John and his destiny. Several he knew – the younger earls Rutland and Bedford. The older lords Cromwell and Sandys. Gelli Meyrick, the man who organised the little Essex had and sought more, was muttering to two other equally red-haired fellows in Welsh.

He needed ease of movement for what he must do . . . and needs must do it fast. So leaving the door ajar, he slipped out of his cloak, laying it softly on the floor, then walked up to the table, unnoticed by men bent over a sketched map of London and Westminster. Several red crosses had been made upon it: Essex House, St Paul's Cross, the Tower. Whitehall Palace was circled and struck through.

When he was ready, he took a breath, cleared his throat and called, loudly, 'My lord of Essex.'

The men, deep in their whispers, started. Essex reared back and stared at John for several long seconds. When recognition came, it brought a smile. 'John Lawley! God's wounds, lad, but it's good to see you. Where have you been?'

It was ever thus with Robert Devereux. Before him you were his sole concern. When you left his sight you left his perception – unless he needed you. Inwardly John sighed. Outwardly he spoke. 'I have been in the Tower these fifteen months, my lord.'

'By my troth, have you? On what cause?'

This time John could not help the audible sigh. 'On yours, my lord.'

Gelli Meyrick leaned in, whispering urgently in his master's ear. The earl nodded and his eyes cleared a little. 'Of course I knew that, John. Mind's too full of . . .' He gestured vaguely about. 'We did add it to a list of grievances sent to her majesty and it was as ignored as the rest, alas!' He leaned forward, smiling. 'But did you get the pheasants?'

'The pheasants, my lord?'

'Aye. Gelli tells me I sent you a brace of them for your Christmas cheer.'

'Well, no doubt they heartily cheered the warder who intercepted them.'

Perhaps he spoke a little more sharply than he intended. There was a stir, and Lord Sandys, a man John had always marked out as the worst kind of bitter acolyte, suddenly spoke. 'Has this man been searched? Shows up on the eve of our great enterprise, re-leased suddenly from the Tower. Damn'd suspicious. Has he been searched?' he repeated.

There was a movement both away from John by some, and towards him by others – Gelli's Welshmen reaching beneath their cloaks. But a single voice stopped them.

'Search John Lawley? Search the man who has saved my life a half-dozen times, suspect him of wanting to . . . assassinate it?' That laugh came again, the hint of mania in it, as the earl continued. 'Master Lawley will have no weapon about him that means us harm but only one to use unswervingly in our cause. He is here as ever to serve only me. And he has come most happily upon the hour to do so.' He beamed. 'Is that not right, Johnnie?'

There was a promise he'd made. Not to Robert Cecil. To himself. Now was the time he acted upon it. This was the moment his life changed. The interim that had held him was over. No phantasm sat before him. The spectre was real. 'No, my lord,' he said, reaching back between his shoulder blades. 'For I do have a weapon here intended to do you harm.' And on the word, he drew the dagger from its sheath, kept it by his head, arm bent back for the throw, spoke again, quietly, clearly. 'No one move. The earl would be dead before you reached me. Tell them, my lord, the truth of that. For you will remember the Jesuit who tried to kill you in Flanders and his fate to die in your lap.'

All was stillness. Everyone stared at the man with the knife, who stared only at the nobleman three paces before him, who stared back and, after a moment, replied, 'It is true. And what is also true is that if John Lawley wanted me dead, then e'en now I would be greeting St Peter at the gates. So do as he says.'

They had been like this, the two of them, on several occasions over the years, one or both of them facing death. And for all his faults, there was one Robert Devereux did not possess, and that was cowardice. 'You know this, my lord. Your friends do not. So convince them to leave. You and I must have a private conversation.'

'I do not need to convince. I only need to command.' Essex did not take his eyes from John's. But his voice rose. 'Go. All of you.'

A murmur of protest, headed by the rising Welsh notes of Gelli Meyrick. 'My lord, we cannot leave you at a rascal's mercy . . .'

'No rascal. And no Brutus either. Leave us. Leave us now!'

He ended on a roar that sent the men scurrying. None came near John, arm raised and unwavering. And only when he heard the door shut behind him, and the shouted summons begin beyond it, did he guide the dagger back into his shoulder sheath. He went to the door, turned the key in the lock, returned to lean upon the table, so Essex did not see him shake.

'Well, John?' The quaver in his voice was the only sign that Essex was disturbed.

'Well, my lord. This first.' He shook his head. 'Trust no one. Not even those you think are closest.'

'Like yourself?'

'Even like me. For I have a new employer. He gave me this dagger. He gave me a bottle of an apothecary. And he gave me a bag of silver. Not quite thirty pieces, but not far short.'

The quaver had left the voice. 'So for whose service have you forsaken mine?'

'I think you can guess. Your most bitter foe. Master Secretary Cecil.'

The only change in Essex's face was a narrowing of the eyes. 'And yet I think, Johnnie, if that were true, you would not so readily declare it. You would use the knife, or the contents of your bottle, and then you would disappear. I can think of perhaps three men in the realm who could succeed in both. You are one.'

'Believe me, I considered it. My service to you over the years has cost me much. Liberty. Choice. A family. However.' He raised a hand against the earl's interruption. 'However, the chances of my life ending with yours would be great. The chances of me returning to the life I desire after such an act would be' – he shook his head – 'precisely none. So I have decided upon another course. It is a vow I made myself. One not taken lightly. I have had . . . much time to think upon it.'

Essex slowly leaned forward, till he too could rest his hands on the table. 'And what course is that?'

'I have vowed to see you triumph' – John tipped his head to the map before him – 'in whatever hazards you have planned.'

'And in return?'

'In return, good my lord, only this: that even were God himself to descend from heaven and beseech you to the contrary, you make this vow: to leave me completely, entirely and forever *alone*.'

The earl stared back, the mania in his eyes displaced by a watery sadness. 'I am sorry you find me such poor company, John,' he said at last, his voice mournful as a boy's. 'But I understand. I understand! It is hard for ordinary men to stand too long next to the fire of greatness!' Eyes that had briefly gazed above him on to posterity now returned. 'And to reward you for the offer of your sword in my great enterprise, this I vow – it will be the last time I call upon you. If I succeed, haply I will not need to. If I fail' – a shadow darkened the bright eyes – 'why then, I will not have the power – for my head will be spiked upon London Bridge.' The shadow passed and he beamed, continued, 'However, let us not consider that, John Lawley. Let us only think on triumph, all the more likely since you have returned to camp. Here,' he said, spinning the map around, 'let me show you what we have planned.'

'My lord, do not so!' John's shout was louder than he intended and he heard it echoed in rumblings beyond the door. He continued more quietly, 'I said before you should put your trust in very few – and tell even those few as little as possible. I have been a spy in my time and this is the rule: what your agents do not know cannot hurt you, no matter how tall they are stretched nor how compacted by the scavenger's daughter.' He shuddered as he thought of the many times his cell door in Martin Tower had opened and he thought he was being taken off to torment. 'So tell me only this: how soon do I muster, and where?'

'The where is here,' the earl replied. 'How soon?' He scratched his beard, then continued. 'I do not hesitate because I am taking your good counsel, John, but because I do not know the hour. Our plans are not firm set, our forces still mustering. For when we rise, we must rise swiftly and with firm intent.' He nodded. 'I can tell you this. It will be within days.' He lifted a different piece of parchment. John saw Greek letters, triangles, pentagrams inked upon it. 'Master Forman has drawn up a horoscope that clearly shows all the stars aligning in my favour.' He tapped a conjunction. 'Indeed, the next two days are filled with a power scarce seen since . . .' He smiled. 'Well, Johnnie, since the day we took Cadiz.' He laid the paper down. 'And my dear Henry is about some business now that may make a final difference.' He chuckled. 'Now I consider it, it is something that will appeal to you most particularly.'

'I wondered where the Earl of Southampton was, since he is ever at your side.'

'He is not far, man, not far.' Essex circled his wrist. 'He and several of our men have gone to the Globe.'

'Indeed.' It seemed an odd time to be seeing a play. John frowned. 'What business takes him there?'

'The rousing business. Three thousand lusty Englishmen and women gathered in one place to hear a tale to inspire them. Why, it's better than having one of my favourite divines preach a sermon for me at St Paul's Cross.' Essex's smile widened. 'For they will witness a very special play. And they will go forth and think of that, and talk on it, and perhaps, when the game's afoot, cry the name "Bolingbroke" upon the city streets.'

John flushed cold. 'Boling . . .'

'Aye.' Essex gave a huge laugh. 'On the morrow, if Henry has persuaded them, which I doubt not, the Chamberlain's Men will give a special performance of an old play.' He spread his arms wide and declaimed, ' "The most lamentable tragedy of King Richard the Second and the rise of that great monarch, Henry the Fourth." ' He clapped his hands together. 'God's wounds, man, it will be like the day we marched for Ireland and Will Shakespeare unveiled *Henry the Fifth*!'

God's teeth, man, thought John, I hope not. Yet he did not speak this, nor anything else, for he was already headed to the door.

'Where do you go, John?'

'To catch this play, my lord.'

'No hurry,' Essex called. 'Stay and dine with us. It plays on the morrow, not today.'

Not if I can help it, John thought. His dream of being left alone involved being left alone with the Lord Chamberlain's Men. And if they were linked to this treason? He shook his head. He could risk his paltry all in Essex's cause. He could not let Will do so.

The door opened to his tug. Two Welshmen fell through it. One was Gelli Meyrick. 'My lord,' he cried, 'are you safe?'

John did not hear the earl's reply, for he was halfway down the corridor. And it was only when he was standing again upon the water stairs of Essex House, buckling on his weapons and scanning the river for a wherry, that he realised something: his heart was beating at a normal pace. He was no longer cold. He had acted, as he had planned. His life was in motion again. But one action now led to another and that one required speedy transit across the Thames.

Richard the Second, Will? he thought. Bolingbroke? The death of kings? Are you quite mad?

XXXI

Eve of Destruction

Quite mad, it appeared. Or so Dick Burbage vouchsafed, when John found him at the Globe.

It had taken too long to reach it. He'd set forth when the theatres were about to give out, so there was not a wherry to be had as oarsmen all sought fares on the Surrey side. He had hotfooted it to the bridge, over which he made the usual halting progress, ducking and weaving through the mob, looking only ahead and not glancing up at Nonsuch House where he had been arrested, nor at the gatehouse where his head might soon be spiked. Progress had been only a little swifter along Southwark's back avenues, Clink Street and Rose Alley, for the crowds were exiting the playhouses and jamming these narrow ways.

When he finally reached the Globe, he ran through unattended front gates and passed the attendants in the pit, some of whom were sweeping the detritus of the groundlings into great piles of apple cores, nut shells and pie crust rims, while others scattered juniper to alleviate the stench of piss voided by spectators too idle or too enraptured to reach the jakes.

Though someone shouted at him when he mounted the stage, John paid no heed, passing across the boards and through the curtain into the tiring house. There he found at least one of those he sought.

Burbage sat at a table, his feet upon it, one hand around a tankard of ale, the other holding a roll at which he peered through spectacles. All were slammed down when John entered. 'Beshrew me,' he bellowed, 'if it ain't Clarence's ghost!' He rose and pulled John into a hug. 'Lad, we were sure that this time you were dead, drowned in a butt of malmsey. Or on a bender of such epic features that it had taken you round the world again.' He pulled back and stared hard. 'And yet you bear few traces of debauch. Where have you been these many months?'

'At her majesty's pleasure.' John frowned. 'Did Will not inform you? Nor Ned?'

'Nothing of that, no. I am sorry to hear of it now.'

John nodded, and fended off the player's further questions for a few minutes while he considered. He supposed his son would not talk of his latest incarceration. Innocent or not, a father in the Tower was not something to boast of. Finally, when Burbage drew breath, he asked, 'Is he about?'

'Aye.' The player sat again, took off his spectacles, rubbed his eyes. 'I meant to speak to you of something, when next we met. Your boy . . .' He tipped his head. 'Your boy does not seem to have the fire he once did.'

John frowned. 'What mean you? In his playing?'

'Aye. His comedy is fair enough – though he has found a way to conjure the lesser laugh. Did he watch Kemp much?' A slight smile came, faded. 'But we tried him in some things more serious. Lady Anne to my Richard Three, for example. He . . .' He hesitated. 'He could not grasp it. There was no threat, no . . . vulnerability beneath. He spoke the lines credibly, but . . .' He shrugged. 'It may be his age. Not quite fourteen, is he? A time for changes, sure. And perhaps worry for you, since you tell me your news . . .' He let the thought hang. 'Yet you know as well as any, John, in a company it is difficult to keep putting opportunity in the way that is not seized upon. There are others below him, rising fast, hungry.' Burbage shook his head. 'I am not saying he has not the stuff, mind. It is just . . .'

'. . . it may have been mislaid? Well, it *has* been a hard time of late . . .' John cut himself off. What could he speak of? His incarceration? The threat that Sir Samuel's return created? All true. Burbage would understand it too, nod in sympathy – yet in the end, all that mattered to him was the two-hour traffic of the stage. Players always had problems, perhaps more than other men, they went with the life. They had to leave them before they entered the tiring house. Nay, they had to leave them at home, howsoever disrupted. The life Ned sought was under threat here. On his behalf, John was being warned. 'I will talk to him,' he said.

'Do so. 'Twould be a favour to us all.' The player nodded. 'Shall I send for him?'

'In a moment.' He'd noticed when Burbage embraced him that he had pulled him into something yielding, a much-padded doublet. 'Have you been playing Falstaff?'

'Aye. *The Merry Wives of Windsor*.' He sighed. 'Though it seems in these turbulent times the taste is not for comedy. We were barely a quarter full today.'

John's voice lowered. 'Only tell me this, Dickon. That you embark not now on a stale tragedy.'

Burbage started. 'Which one?'

'*Richard the Second*.'

Burbage sucked in breath. 'How do you know already what has been arranged an hour since?'

'That does not matter. Only tell me it is not true.'

'It is.' The player continued fast as John hissed. 'Lad, I told you we are hard pressed. When the Earl of Southampton asked us to revive it, I demurred. "'Tis an ancient piece and may not now draw a crowd," I says. "Leave alone that it will tax this poor globe," he patted his head, "with trying to recall it." He picked up the roll he'd been conning, dropped it again. 'But then the rogue pulls out a purse of forty shillings and asks if that would help my memory. 'Tis not a ransom perhaps – yet it's twice what we took today. And of course the earl was ever Will's . . . dear companion.'

John stepped closer. There were other players moving about, and he wanted his warning to be for Burbage alone. 'You should find some way to excuse yourself, Dick. Return the purse. Plead illness. You yourself mentioned the turbulent times. Believe me, this is not a piece to be doing now.'

The player laughed, but uneasily. ''Tis only a play, Johnnie.'

'A play of regicide and revolt. The usurpation of a throne.' His voice dropped still lower. 'With people passing Essex House each hour and crying, "Bolingbroke!" Think, man!'

Burbage's volume matched his. 'Is this what has kept you from us this long time?'

'Never mind that. Just consider what I say.'

The player did, concern in his eyes. But at last he shook his head. 'I have no choice now, John. I have taken the purse, already sent to the printers for a playbill, assigned the roles to the players. Poor Heminges is near weeping, for he must try and remember the King. I will be . . .' He hesitated. 'Bolingbroke.' He looked around, then back, spoke again, more cheerfully. 'But your fears will be unfounded, I think. And perhaps this will be the best for us. You know how Will likes to reflect the times. This could be what we need to pull the crowds in, and take some away from the Rose. Henslowe's revived *Tamburlaine* this week, and Ed Alleyn's tyrant is drawing high and low. A tyrant falling here might do the same for us.' He frowned, and his voice sank again. 'If we had something new to offer 'twould be different. But your friend is stalled again, man. He won't play at all, he's not writing from all I can tell. He just sits in his attic, stares at parchment and mutters about ghosts.'

This was news. The last note he'd had from Will was a month before. 'Has he dropped into melancholia, then? He has so before. 'Twill pass.'

'Worse now. Far worse. Never seen him like it.' Burbage sighed. 'It is as if he is giving birth and the babe is breeched. 'Twill not come out, and I think that if it does, the child will rip all flesh away and kill the mother.'

'What is't that so obsesses him?'

'An old tale he would make anew.'

John scratched his beard. 'Not . . . *Hamlet*?'

'Aye. It obsesses him once again. Nay, it is beyond obsession now.' The player reached forward, squeezed the other's arm. 'Remember that day when I asked you to help prevent him writing it?' John nodded. 'Well, now I ask you the very opposite. By my holidame, by Christ and by the devil. By anything you can swear by! Get him to finish it. Get him to deliver it to us and perchance give us the success we need. Then we will not need to resort to . . . ancient tyrants.' He stepped back. 'And speaking of, I needs must study mine. No.' He smiled. 'Bolingbroke's the hero, is he not?'

'Only if he wins,' John muttered, then continued, 'Where is Will?'

'In an attic, hard by the Clink. It is next to . . .' Burbage frowned. 'It is hard to describe. I will send someone to guide you if you plan to go there straight.'

He had other people he needed to see, most urgently. Yet it sounded like his friend needed him immediately. And it sounded as if his son did too. 'Can you spare Ned?'

'I can. We did this play before he joined us so he has no role but groom and silent page. Holla, you!' he called out to a servant engaged in stacking properties from the performance. 'Fetch me young Lawley.' The man dispatched, he turned back. 'And, Johnnie, I will show my gratitude to you if you succeed here.' He held up his hand at the protest he could see coming. 'I know! I acknowledge it. I have promised before. But Will is in a greater crisis now than then. We all are. Be midwife to this birth, whether it be of monster or man, and I will make sure you are rewarded for it.'

If I survive the week, John thought, but received the hand Dick thrust out and shook it. 'I will do my best.'

'All I can ask,' the player replied, then added, 'And here's your boy.'

John turned, as did his heart inside him. Ned had grown, and not only up. He was beginning to fill the way the Lawleys did. Even in the pale winter sunlight that came through the open curtains of the tiring house, John thought he could see a shadow of hair upon the upper lip. Boy was shading into man, and he felt his heart give another lurch. How much had he missed of his son's life because men of power sought to use him?

What was not different was the look in Ned's eyes – the disdain of youth for fallible old men with not even the previous glimmer of relief at his freedom. And something else had changed . . . the voice, which had been pitched high before, now wavered, as if he could not command it fully. 'You sent for me, sir?' he said coldly.

Burbage blanched. 'Lad! Do you not see who is here?'

'I see very well, sir. It is Master Lawley,' he replied, without looking again at John. 'What do you wish of me?'

'Boy!' The player's face flushed with anger. But John stepped forward and grasped him by the forearm. Burbage looked at him, took a deep breath, then continued, his tone as icy as Ned's had been, 'I wish you to take your *father* to Master Shakespeare.'

'Must I, sir? I have lines to con.'

'You have your duty to me, whelp,' snapped Burbage. 'Do it and question me not.'

'Sir.' Ned bowed, then looked again at John. 'This way, then.'

Releasing the player's arm with a final squeeze, John followed his son to the tiring-house stair. They descended to the players' entrance and exited to the street. Upon it, Ned turned around the theatre and set off swiftly down the main strand.

'Hold, boy,' said John, catching up. 'I do not have your youthful legs.'

Ned nodded sullenly, slowed. His father fell into step and they progressed as fast as the crowds allowed them. John hesitated, not knowing how to breach the silence between them – then did, with what pressed him most. 'How is your mother?'

His son did not look up. 'You have not seen her?'

'Not yet.'

Ned shrugged. 'Well, she has been most busy since her affianced returned from the wars.'

His son said it with relish, with malice too . . . and with something less assured. 'And how is he?'

'Not as fat as he was – Ireland waned him, he says. Though he appears to be waxing again, judging from his actions at my mother's table.' Something was still there beneath the insouciance of the tone that undercut the boldness of the next declaration. 'He says also that now he has done his country's duty, he can tend to his own. So he had the banns read this Sunday last at St Mary Overies and thus, three weeks from now, he and my mother will be happily and forever joined in matrimony.' He glanced up briefly. 'I wouldn't expect an invitation to the nuptials.'

There it was. In the glimpse of eyes, even within the cheek of the comment. 'And you are not happy about this?'

'Happy? Of course I am. My mother will achieve her life's desire. She will be the village squire's wife her family intended her to be before . . .' He flushed, turned away.

'Before the player disgraced her,' John finished for him, and when he got no confirmation save a mutter added, 'So have you changed your mind? Are you reconciled to life as a village squire's son?'

'I told you before. I would hate such a life,' Ned muttered, his voice locked in its low register now and angry. 'And yet I am not of an age to defy my stepfather.'

'Are you not? And yet I recall that I was no older than you when I defied mine. And for the same reason.'

He could see Ned struggling between his pose of indifference and sudden interest. The latter won, grudgingly. 'What do you mean?'

'Only this: that at the age of thirteen, when a travelling troupe of players came through Much Wenlock, I decided that I was not going to be the scholar my parents wished me to be. They played, then left. I left with them.'

The conversation had taken them off the main thoroughfare, on to Clink Street, past the throng at the entrance of the prison, and down an alley that reeked of cess, halting before a door. John looked up. 'Is this where I will find him?'

That struggle continued on the innocent face. This time, indifference won. Ned shrugged. 'It is. I will leave you.'

He turned away. But John caught his arm in a grip that could not be broken, despite the boy's squirming. 'Listen, lad. Listen!' He jerked the arm, and Ned froze. 'I understand why you are angry with me. I do not seek forgiveness. Not now. Perhaps never. Yet this I know: your upset is affecting how you play. Nay, do not ask me how I know. Think only of this: you have a crossroads before you, and a choice to make, the same I made at your age. And one way will be closed off to you unless you—'

A shout interrupted him, loud enough to penetrate the oak before him, followed by a series of curses, ending in a moan. Both started, and Ned at last slipped his father's grip. Yet he did not run off. 'I have obeyed my tutor's command. Goodbye.'

'Oh no,' said John, seizing the hesitation and his son's collar at the same moment, 'for did not your master bid you take me *to* Master Shakespeare? This is only his door.'

With his free hand, John pushed and entered. A dank and gloomy stairwell lay before them. 'Youth before wisdom,' he said, shoving his son ahead of him.

'Pearls before swine,' muttered Ned, just loud enough to be heard as he stumbled forward.

John almost laughed – but as soon as he stepped over the threshold, a sound caught the laughter in his throat. It was a moan that could have come from a beast in a trap, if words did not punctuate the hum. Indistinct, the only ones he heard for certain were a piteous

'Christ have mercy!' 'Will,' he said, passing his son, taking the stairs two at a time.

The door was locked. He shook it, interrupting the noise within for a snarled 'Leave me be!'

'Will! Open here. 'Tis I, John Lawley. Let me in.'

A silence came, then the sound of a shuffling approach. The familiar voice hissed through the wood, 'Begone.'

'William,' John said softly. ''Tis John. Open for your friend.'

There came a muffled sob. 'I have no friends. I have . . . no one.'

John looked back at Ned on the stair. The boy shrugged, jerked his head towards the street. John looked at the solid oak before him, wondering if he could force it – and then he heard a bolt shot and feet moving away.

He entered, slowly opening the door before him. The stench hit him like a slap. It was composed of many things: unemptied chamber pots, an unwashed body, stale beer, and one scent that caught him in the throat, stuck there, enticement in the mire – whisky. 'Will,' he called, peering through the gloom, for no candle was lit and the one window was fogged with grime. There was a movement behind what John at last discerned to be a table. He stepped up to it, peered over.

Lying curled up on the floor, knees to chin, an arm flung over his face, was the Globe's premier playwright. 'What make you there?' John asked.

The figure did not stir. Words came from under his armpit. 'Begone. I know you not.'

'You know me, Will,' John replied softly. ''Tis your old friend Lawley. Come, now, st—'

'John Lawley's dead,' the figure below cried. 'Disappeared into the Tower, never to be seen again. Another ghost!'

'You sent me notes there, man, until recently. Plays, too. Come, you could see that I do not come from beyond the grave if you would but look up.'

As he spoke, he moved around the table, then bent, touching the playwright's arm, which flapped as if it would wave help away, then reached, caught. Bending, John took his friend's weight, lifted, needing to turn his face away. The stink in the room emanated mainly from the playwright's person. 'Ned,' John called, 'the chair.'

There was one on its side behind the table. Ned, eyes wide in fascinated horror, set the chair up and John lifted the body on to it. But when he went to let go and step back, Shakespeare clutched at him, feeling his arm as if checking for fractures. 'You are alive. You are not a ghost.'

'Not yet. Let me . . .'

Again he tried to disengage, again he was held. 'I have been visited by so many here,' Will whispered, his gaze moving into dark corners. 'They have all come. I thought you must be one of them, since I had no reply to my last letter. Broken like poor Thom Kyd upon the Tower's rack.' He began to weep. 'Yet you live and I did not visit you. Not once. I am a poor friend.'

He let go his grip to cry into his palms. John put a hand upon his shoulder, shook it gently. 'You would not have been allowed a visit, Will. Nor could you have risked it. And as for friendship? How many times have you come for me, when I was in your present state? How many times have you pulled my head from the jakes?' He patted. 'D'you remember in Bristol, the night we played *Oedipus* for the mayor and I puked within his worship's carriage?'

The snuffling halted. 'I stole the carriage, John. Hid it in the stables till it and you could be cleaned.'

'You did, old friend. And more times than I can count have you rescued me. So how if I tend to you now?'

He moved away, stumbled over a book upon the floor. Indeed, every board was covered with them, every surface too, those not filled with sheets of inked parchment. He crossed to the window, winter's pale light coming through the tanned skin across it. Reaching, he peeled the hide from the frame, light poured in, and the man behind him gave a piteous moan.

The room was the same catastrophe to sight as it had appeared to other senses. Papers and books scattered everywhere, bottles upon their sides, platters with mouldering remnants of food upon them. In one corner, a pot brimmed with excrement and vomit. Ned was staring down at his employer in disgust. 'Here,' called John, 'go you to the tavern hard by and fetch a bucket . . .' He considered. 'Make that two, of hot water. Bring scouring cloths too. Here.' He reached into the purse at his waist, pulled out a crown, threw it across. 'Fetch us also a quart of beer, the weakest you can find. And some bread.'

Ned frowned. 'I am needed back at the theatre.'

'You are more needed here, boy. Aiding the man who keeps the theatre in health. Go!' Ned stood for a moment, then sighed and left. John turned back. 'Now, let us see how I can help you.'

'This will help me,' the playwright replied, reaching for the one bottle that was upright on the table, knocking it, catching it, raising it.

But as he found his lips, John laid his hand on it. 'I'll have that,' he said.

The playwright scowled up – then smiled. 'Of course, man. You were ever thirsty – and after your stay in the Tower . . .' He released the bottle. 'First you drink, then I'll drink, and when we finish this one we will send your boy for more.' His forehead wrinkled. 'Your boy. Your fine boy. I had a fine boy once.' He gave a sob that rose into a miserable laugh, throwing his arms wide. 'Come, man. Let us get fantastically drunk together.'

John lifted the bottle. It was half full of whisky, the one scent in the room that did not nauseate. The reverse. He sniffed it, and felt the same pinch of longing he had felt standing at the door. He had hoped his stay in prison, where nothing was brought to his cell but weakest ale, despite some nights of pleading, would cure him of desire. It had failed to. His love was as strong as ever. His arm was raising the neck to his lips . . .

. . . and lowering it again. 'No,' he said, stepping to a corner to set the bottle down. 'Let us wait for the beer.'

Instead of arguing, Will nodded, and placed his head upon his arms. John again heard a soft sobbing. He sighed. There had been several times in their long acquaintance when he'd seen his friend thus. The bouts would last but a short while, he would retire to solitude, and soon return, his smile as sunny as ever – and usually with a new play or set of sonnets tucked under his arm. But John had never seen him thus prostrated. The scribblings upon the table showed a ferment of writing, the state of the room a prolonged gloom.

He espied a pipe on a shelf. He went to fetch it, kicking a pouch as he did. It contained tobacco, and John filled the one with the other. There was one glowing coal left in the grate, and he lit a nub of candle with it, and then the clay bowl. Sucking, he produced a steady glow then tapped the playwright with the stem. 'Here,' he said. Will looked up blearily, reached, took, inhaled.

There was a stool on its side nearby. John set it upright beside the chair. As the playwright puffed, he glanced down at one page amongst the many higgled upon the table; picked it up, peered, read it once, then once again aloud. ' "I have of late, but wherefore I know not, lost all my mirth." ' He looked at his friend. 'Have you, Will? Lost it all?'

Shakespeare inhaled deeply, then plumed the air with his exhale. 'All,' he replied. 'For what mirth can any man have who has lost what I have lost? Forsaken all that I have forsaken?'

'And what is that?'

'All that makes life worth the living.' He took another long pull at his pipe, coughed fragments of smoke, then swept the stem like a wand over the table. 'I have finished the play.'

'You are often saddened when you do.' John looked about the wreckage of the room. 'Yet why does this one make you more so?'

'This play . . .' Shakespeare wiped his eyes. 'This play would make a statue weep.'

'That good, is it?'

'Good?' Shakespeare let out a cackle that trailed into a moan. 'That will be for you to judge; you, who have been the first to speak a speech. Then my fellow players, who will take it, shrug, mutter and tear it to tatters for the groundlings to eat nuts and piss on the reeds while they mishear the shredding of my soul.'

'Your soul, is it now, William?' John couldn't help the smile. 'Is that what's lying about here?'

The other did not smile. 'No less than that.' He jabbed the pipe stem. 'Do you know what this piece is called?'

'I do not, except that Burbage said you were engaged . . .'

'It is called: *Hamnet, Prince of Denmark.* A tra . . . ge . . . dy!'

He waved his pipe in the air as if it were a viola bow and he was counting in the consort. 'Do you mean Hamlet?' John said gently.

'That's what I said, rogue!' the playwright snapped, half rising, pipe stem jabbed forward like a blade. 'Hamlet! Hamnet! Hamlet! Damnet! Damn! Damn!' His voice rose in a shriek, then, as John's hand fixed upon his forearm and gently squeezed, descended to a sob. His eyes, swiftly raised to John's, contained tears – and an appeal. 'Do you think he is damned, John?' he whispered, sinking down. 'Do you think he burns in purgatory?'

'Who?'

'My sweet boy. Hamnet! Hamlet! Hamnet!' His voice rose and fell again. Flipping John's hand, he squeezed it to the point of pain. 'I have seen him, John. He has visited me here. He cries out for mercy, for aid. And I could not give him life because I was here and he was in Stratford and I went home twice a year and missed his growing. Missed his dying!' The sobs rose, then fell again to a whisper. 'You and I were raised in a different faith. The Church today does not allow us to intercede for the dead. The Church today says they are gone for ever, beyond all aid. But they are not gone. They are here.' He slapped his head. 'They are here.' He slammed his hand down upon the pages. 'They are . . . here.' He flung an arm out towards the door. 'And I would help him!'

John snapped around, as if to see someone stride through it and to check that no one had. For it was true, they had both been raised with other beliefs. The Catholic Church taught that the dead were not gone, not entirely. The dead were at a different stage. And they could be . . . aided. 'Will,' he said softly, for what he was to speak was, in its own way, a form of treason, 'if you need a Mass sung for Hamnet's soul, I know a priest who could arrange . . . My stepfather . . .'

'I know many,' Shakespeare hissed, interrupting. 'For my father begged me to intercede thus for the dead son I hardly knew, that he had raised. So I paid some silver – for my guilt, for my absences, for secret intercession. Now my father lies dying and begs the same for himself. And I will do't – as poor a son as I was a father, the least I can do is that.'

He laid his head down again, forgetting the pipe, spilling embers on to a page, which John hastily extinguished. Only a few words were burned out and he wondered if they were lost for ever. But the little flames had reminded John of the bigger flames that his friend referred to, the place where sinners paid in fire for their sins. 'Perhaps what you have done here will be a type of Mass for your son,' he said gently, adding, 'For your father too, when his time comes.'

Shakespeare looked up. 'I had hoped it, John. If I could not gather

304

many to a secret Mass, perhaps I could call them to the Globe to partake of a different ceremony. Not the one I witnessed in Stratford churchyard, that short . . . dismissal.' He wiped at his streaming nose. 'I saw it with dry eyes. And now, five years later, I cannot stop weeping.' He blew his nose upon his sleeve. 'Do you think it may be so? Can I mourn him now as I failed to mourn him then?'

John shrugged. 'Perhaps. I'd have to attend the ceremony.'

'Then come. Indeed, I will need your help. You who understand something of lost fathers, lost sons.'

John frowned. He hadn't known his own father, dead before he was born. He'd seen him in dreams, conjured by his mother's tales. But was his own son lost? Not yet, he prayed. Not yet.

'There's something else you can do for the play,' Shakespeare continued. 'And perhaps there's something he can do too.' He raised his voice. 'For you love your father, boy, do you not?'

For a moment John thought his friend was again seeing his own son's ghost in the doorway. But when he turned, he saw Ned, who'd climbed the stair silently, and stood staring at the two men now, a bucket in each hand.

'Do you, Ned? Do you love your father?'

The boy lived in the theatre. He was used to drunkenness and maudlin feelings expressed. But John saw he did not know how to answer the playwright. 'All's well, lad,' he said. 'Just bring in what you have and wait below.'

'No!' Will lurched up from his chair, took a stumbling step towards the boy, who hastily set down the buckets, retreated. 'All is not well. Something is rotten.' He reached Ned, placed one hand on his chest, one on his back. He squeezed and the boy flinched, yet did not move. 'I ask again: do you love your father?'

John watched different reactions shade the lad's face. Fear of the man before him, disgust at his scented proximity, anger that he was being harangued by a drunk . . . yet when the expression settled, he saw something that made him sad, and strangely proud simultaneously. A calm honesty. 'I scarcely know him, sir. How is it possible for me to love him?'

Will slumped, his hands rising to fall again, on to the boy's shoulders. Ned staggered, then took the weight, his face turned from the man's sobbing. 'You do not know him,' he repeated. 'And my son did not know me. And John Lawley's father did not know him. And Hamlet . . . how well did he know his father, this father who shrieks for vengeance from beyond the grave? Is that not worse? Asked to atone for someone you did not know?' He turned and jabbed his finger at John. 'Could you?' He shook Ned. 'Could you?' Then he lurched back to the table, crying, 'Can I?'

As the playwright slumped again into his chair, John called, 'Go fetch the ale, boy.' Ned departed fast while John crossed to the buckets. They were filled with warm, if not entirely clean, water. Still, it was cleaner than the room and the man it was intended for. He picked one up, carried it across, found a scrap of cloth within, dipped, began with his friend's face, the encrusted food, the salt trail of tears. Shakespeare submitted, his eyes closed, lips still mumbling words. John moved on to his doublet, dabbed, rinsed.

After a while, Will opened his eyes. His hand gripped John's wrist. 'You have a chance that I did not,' he whispered. 'Do not lose it. Find your son if you can.'

'If I can,' John replied, daubing. And if other people let me, he thought.

It was as if his friend had read his mind. 'You can. Avoid those who abuse you. Return to what you love. Your family. The theatre.'

'Both are my only desire,' John replied, 'but there are . . . there are those who have different thoughts for me.'

'I know of whom you speak. My lord of Essex. The Master Secretary. They are both in here.' He waved at the pages. 'The ardent rebel. The scheming counsellor.'

It was then John remembered what was to happen at the Globe upon the morrow. Why he had hastened to Southwark. 'This is not the time to be writing of such things. Do you know what Burbage has agreed to? The company risks—'

'You are wrong,' Will interrupted. 'For when time is out of joint – and a nation itself goes mad . . .' His eyes were gleaming, fixed at some point above. Now his gaze met John's. He laid one hand over the pages on his desk, squeezed John with the other. ''Tis all here. A madness that is in the state and in the state . . . of man. In you. In me. A mad prince. Is he?' He smiled. 'A mad girl. Is she? Fine roles I have created – for Dick Burbage, sure. And for a girl . . . a player like . . .' The light faded in the eyes as he released his grip, looked away. 'Like someone.'

John saw it then, the first glimmer in the return of Will's wits. Saw it in the manager considering a player for a role, and dismissing him in the same moment . . . while looking in that player's father's eyes. In the look, John heard Burbage's voice again, his doubts. 'Ned can play it,' he blurted, then took a breath, continued more slowly, 'More than that, if this is the play about fathers and sons that you say it is, you *need* Ned to play it.'

The men stared at each other in silence for a long moment – one finally broken by another's voice. 'Need Ned to play what?'

His son had returned, again unheard, this time with a leathern bottle in one hand, a slab of coarse bread in the other. John cleared a little area upon the table, pushing the papers aside for his son to set down what he'd brought. 'Need me to play what?' he asked again, straightening.

The playwright peered up. 'What do you know of madness, boy?'

Ned did not blink. 'Madness? Something, I think.' He looked at them both. 'For am not I my father's son?'

There was a moment – and then both the sitting men were laughing. 'A fair answer,' said Will, leaning back, rubbing at his eyes. 'And one that might yet win you the prize. I will think on this.' He reached out, began to gather the pages before him. 'Go now, John,' he said. 'Nay, do not dispute with me. You have restored me enough, even unto the bounds of friendship.' He glanced around. 'The cleaning will be a form of penance.' He yawned widely. 'I will clean and then I will sleep. And you have matters to attend to, I warrant. You always have.'

John thought of what was being plotted across the river – and his own concerns upon the Southwark side of it. 'I do. So if you are sure I can be of no further help . . . ?' On receiving a nod, he continued, 'Then we will away. Send word how I can aid you in your' – he touched the papers – 'atonement.'

'I shall. Where can I find you?'

He'd forgotten, for the time he was there. He had committed to a course of action and a cause. It had no fixed address, no certain end. 'I shall find you, my friend. And until I do, keep well.'

'And you.' Shakespeare let out a huge sigh, then fell back into his chair. 'And your son also.'

They left him staring before him. As the door closed, Ned whispered, 'Can we leave him so? I have never seen him like that.'

'I have. And we can.' John was already descending the stairs. 'Poets are not like you and me, boy, mere players. They tread a different path to their creations. And from the look of him, Master Shakespeare's recent path has been rocky, perhaps the hardest he has ever trodden.' They reached Clink Street. 'While another lies ahead of me.' He laid his hand upon the boy's shoulder. 'Will you still be my guide upon it?'

There was a shudder under his palm; but whether from recent witness or present touch he did not know. I would like to find out, John thought. So he squeezed, lifted and, on receiving no answer, added, 'Take me to your mother.'

XXXII

Eruptions

There was always noise in Southwark. Especially at this hour, with higglers seeking to unload their goods before nightfall. From carts, trays or stalls exploded the competing cries.

'Mussels lily white, Wallfleet oysters!'

'Coney stew and pottage! Groat a bowl!'

''Umble pie and saveloy sausage! More guts than gravy!'

Men stood in the doorways of taverns and ordinaries, bellowing of succulence and warmth to be found within. Sixpenny queans called, siren-like, from alleys, while their half-crown superiors leaned from the windows of brothels and cooed. Everywhere wheels ground on cobbles, wagon drivers yelling and cursing, seeking passage through the throng, pedestrians giving back obscenity for obscenity, while the watchman's bass boomed out the hour: 'Give ear to the clock. Beware your lock. Four o'clock.' To some a prod to push through to bridge or boat. To others an invitation to linger somewhere snug and sinful.

The noise was at its loudest, the crowds densest, where the road funnelled before widening out to the churchyard of St Mary's. Yet if the cacophony was also at its height, one sound still managed to pierce it all, at least to the two Lawleys' ears. Perhaps they were attuned to it, like a viola's player picking out its note no matter the size of the consort. They looked at each other. 'Mother,' Ned said, and John swallowed, nodded, pushed the last and hardest paces to the door of the Spoon and Alderman. At it, they hesitated – for beyond its threshold, and beyond doubt, its landlady was going off on one.

Tess was ever gentle – until something riled her. Then, like the calmest sea swelled suddenly with a rogue wave, she would rise and roar. Father and son had both experienced it, and the look they shared said this: God mend me that I come not into this storm.

Yet come they had to, despite the warning in the eyes of the doorkeeper, six foot of English oak trying to make himself a twig in the tavern doorway. They had also to push against a tide of fleeing customers until, finally gaining entrance, they stopped to behold the scene.

On one side of the room, as far as they could get from the bar, stood Sir Samuel D'Esparr and his bodyguard Tomkins – stood, if their half-crouch could still be called standing. On t'other side, drawn up to her full height, was Tess.

She did not see the newcomers straightway. All her attention, and her mustered wrath, was focused entirely upon the cowering men; one especially. 'How is it possible, sirrah,' she exclaimed, 'that after an absence of a year, you return a greater fool than when you left? Were all your wits dispersed by bog vapour, Irish whisky and Dublin whores?'

'I . . . I assure you, lady,' Sir Samuel uncrouched enough to speak, 'I was chaste . . .'

'Chased? You were chased thence by a rogue, and chased back by the same one.'

'Sweet Tess, I only meant—'

'Don't "sweet" me, varlet!' she blazed. 'You have soured all sweetness with your decisions. Not a week – no, less, far less, a matter of days since you caused the banns to be read to announce our wedding, you then inform me' – she took a deep breath – 'you inform me that you will ride again under the banner of the man who so delayed our marriage before by stealing you away. More, that you will attend him in such a cause as this. May Christ give me strength,' she cried, stamping her foot. 'If I had that man here before me, I would say to him, I would say . . . "My lord, you may be her majesty's viceroy, but I know a traitorous dog when I see one . . ." '

John had heard enough. There were breaches in a besieged town's walls he'd stepped into with more relish. But though she had cleared the tavern with her roaring, it could still be heard outside, by ears

310

that might carry it elsewhere to others'. Dangerous ones. 'Tess,' he called, moving out of the shadows around the door.

It was enough to halt the tirade, though he knew it wouldn't be for long. And though he was blessed with a glimpse of relief in her eyes at the sight of him, it vanished all too fast. 'Oh, and speaking of fools, here we have the very prince of motley,' she cried. 'Let him tell you the consequences of following the man you seek to follow again. Let the whiteness of his skin testify to the cell he has only just come from, sent there because of the same man. Milord has led him into range of death, and away from love, more times than you have fingers and toes. See him and see a ruined life. See him and see what you will throw away if you now follow—'

'Tess!' John called again, louder, with a command in it. Coming forward, he said in a lower tone, 'I think I understand a little of your fury . . .'

'Oh? You do?'

'Aye. And I am sure it is justified . . .'

'You are sure? You who have given me more cause to weep than any man?'

He had deflected the storm on to himself. But at least her voice had lowered to near his. 'I admit it all, lady. And I would be happy to hear you number my sins again. Happy also for you to put Sir Samuel and myself in the scale.' It would not serve him to take all blame here. 'But I ask you to make the tally softly, lest someone hears who shouldn't. There are keen ears just beyond these walls, Tess. And the streets have never been more dangerous.'

'I care not . . .'

'Not for me, perhaps. Not even for this man who so richly deserves your wrath . . .' A squawk came at this from the other side of the room. 'But you do care about someone else who would be hurt if your words were whispered in the wrong ear. You do care about your son.' On the word, he reached back and dragged Ned out from where he cowered into the tallow light.

'My son. My son the player . . .'

John had been right. The danger of all whom she threatened came to Tess. John could see anger still in her eyes, see further words on her lips. But the flow was halted, and he stepped a little nearer.

'Come, love, let us all sit and talk of this. There must be a way to resolve it.'

'Don't you "love" me,' she grumbled, but stepped and sat heavily on a bench.

'Nay, do you not,' said Sir Samuel, also coming forward, sitting too.

John looked at the knight. Ned's report had been correct. He was no longer fat. Ireland had wasted him, as it had so many before him. But unlike a soldier made lean by exercise, Sir Samuel did not look well for it. Flesh hung from his face in loose folds from both jaw and eye, dewlaps on a hound, grey in tone. His rival for Tess's hand had only this advantage: he held the field. The banns had been read. For two more Sundays they would be read again, and on the third the wedding should take place. Should, if events did not intervene. Events that were unfolding across the river at Essex House; revels to which Sir Samuel had also been invited, it appeared. Good, John thought. I do not see why only one of Tess's suitors should hazard all in what is to come.

'Do I assume, lady, from your high colour, that Sir Samuel has done something to displease you? And that something is to do'– he lowered his voice still further – 'with Robert Devereux?'

Her colour deepened. 'You assume right. My life seems to be continually governed by his lordship's whims. Well, no more,' she said, looking hard at Sir Samuel. 'No. More!'

'My love,' replied the knight, 'you know that I seek only to please you in every way. Except honour.' He swallowed. 'I am Essex's man. He is my lord . . .'

'He holds your mortgage,' commented John.

'He holds my . . .' the knight glared, spluttered. 'That matters naught, sirrah! Only this does.' He gestured to the tangerine threads woven through his grey doublet. 'I wear his colours. How can I refuse his summons?'

The last was not asked rhetorically. An excuse was sought, the appeal clear in voice, in eyes. Tess answered it. 'You will send to say that you are sick.'

The murmur came from behind them. ' "Shall Caesar send a lie?" ' All turned – to look at Ned, who shrugged. ''Tis the scene I played in

Julius Caesar,' he explained. 'Calphurnia, disquieted by signs and portents, begging Caesar to stay home.'

'Ah ha! And when he refused her, he went to his death!' Tess slapped the table before her. 'It is an apt comparison.' She reached and took her betrothed's hand. 'So listen to your Calphurnia – and go not to Caesar's fate.'

The sight of her hand on D'Esparr's brought a rush of fury to John . . . which, with a deep breath, he swallowed down. Fury would not help him here. Yet something else might. So when he was ready, he spoke coolly. 'Not so apt, I think. For Caesar fell to conspiracy. Here *we* are the conspiracy.'

His hushed tone drew a nod from the knight. 'It is true, my love. We rise in support of our lord to overthrow the tyrant.'

Tess looked to speak. John cut in swiftly. 'It is not so much the cause, though I think that ours is just. No, it is a question of obedience – for the earl's last words to me were "Fetch me here your comrade in arms, noble D'Esparr." Obedience . . . and sense. For if a Titan falls, can we escape being crushed? We are known to wear tangerine whether we draw swords in the streets or no. So why not draw them and help him triumph? Why not ensure that he wins?' He turned to Sir Samuel. 'Marry, sir, it will be just like the day we vanquished our foes on the field of honour in Ireland.'

As John suspected, that event had been suitably gilded in Despair's memory. 'Will it not?' The knight turned eagerly to Tess. 'I have told you a little of that, sweetling. Of John and I, back to back, swords flashing, keeping scores of ambushers at bay.'

John smiled encouragingly to counter the obvious doubt on Tess's face. He suspected that she had a good grasp of her fiancé's short-comings. 'Besides which,' he added, 'this day will not be like that. Our enemy is clear before us, not melting into bogs. And their numbers are small, unlike the Irish – while their leader is no Tyrone but a stunted fellow the Queen openly calls her pygmy.' He leaned forward. 'A giant can crush a pygmy with a small step. And will, if I can aid him.' He shook his head. 'For truly, how can a man of honour, and a brother sworn to the noble earl's cause, do other?'

Tess was gazing at him sceptically. She knew how he had tried to avoid such antics before, recognised also, perhaps, a player's delivery. Not Sir Samuel – his face had that same adoration it had worn after

John had rescued him from his bludgeoning. 'By all the saints, sir, you are right, sir! We may have had our differences but . . . your hand!' He reached forward and seized John's. 'We two will help our noble lord to a triumph!' He turned back to Tess. 'And, love, think how it will be to have England's new hero at our wedding!'

'An honour indeed.' John clasped back. 'But, Sir Samuel, since you have been summoned there, I suggest you repair to Essex House immediately, to offer his lordship counsel and to hear how you may serve.' He stepped away from the table, drawing the man up. 'While I, who have just come from thence, will follow soon after.'

Tess stood too. 'You are both fools then,' she said. 'And, Samuel, I repeat, I forbid—'

'Enough!' Sir Samuel roared. 'I have listened to your soft pleadings. But like Caesar I will not yield to them.' Aware perhaps of the problem with the comparison, he coughed, then turned. 'Tomkins!' he commanded. 'My sword.'

His man, whom John had got to know a little in his brief time in Ireland, came forward with the weapon, giving John a look that spoke his mind: I know what you are up to. But it was not his place to question, simply obey. Tess had not those restraints. Fury had failed. Her concern was now clear. 'I appeal to you both. Do not get caught up in this folly. Lie low and await its passing.'

'Lie low?' Sir Samuel said disdainfully, buckling on his weapon. 'Such talk does not befit the affianced of a D'Esparr.' He held up a hand. 'No. Silence now, and let us proceed. Tend to your business – for the last few nights that it will occupy you. For when I return in triumph, you will no longer be an innkeeper, but once again a lady of the gentry.'

For a braggart, he swept quite impressively out the door, John thought. He turned. 'Tess . . .' he began.

'No, sir,' she said. 'I do not quite know what you are about. Though I suspect it is to once more interfere with my life. But know this: you will not climb into my bed over Sir Samuel's corpse.'

It stung, in part because there was truth in it. Yet not in the way she thought. 'Nay, lady, I do not seek his death,' he answered, 'but only this: to have it resolved once and finally between my lord of Essex and myself. Between Despair and me . . . and between me and thee.' He took her hand then and she did not give it . . . but neither did she withdraw it. 'Somehow, once again, it all comes down to mad Robbie Devereux and what he does now. All stakes are on that one hazard. And whether he throws it or does not, in the throwing he will resolve us all.'

He held her a moment longer, with his hand, with his eyes. And then he turned and marched out through the door. Sir Samuel awaited him beyond the threshold, a touch of suspicion within his eyes. 'Coming, Lawley?' he enquired.

'Not yet.' The suspicion grew and he hastened to allay it. He did not need Sir Samuel changing his mind. 'I have matters to resolve at the playhouse. Tell my noble lord that I will join him on the morrow.'

The suspicion did not truly lessen. But at least, with a curt nod, the knight strode off in the direction of Paris Gardens Stair.

John had taken a step back towards the Globe when a voice stopped him. 'You have not truly fooled her, you know. And whatever happens with the earl, she will never take you back.'

John looked at his son. Behind him, customers were again filing into the tavern. 'You think not? Well, we shall see.'

He began to walk away. Heard the following step, the voice. 'So here you go, Father. Ever treading the same route. To the playhouse to plead for reinstatement. To the earl's feet to do his bidding. And when both have let you down, to the tavern to beg for whisky.'

'And you, my son,' John said, without looking back, 'what route do you tread? For at the end of all this, if both of your mother's suitors survive it, and she chooses Despair over me, what is left for you? Only that same country life you claim to despise.'

Ned drew level, the look in his eye less challenging. 'Or to run away and join the players as you did.'

'That was different. In those days players were near outcasts and could be whipped from towns for loitering. We were always on the move and it took my mother and stepfather near a year to catch up with me. Then, when they saw that I was happy, they let me be. But if you wish to stay at the Globe' – he shrugged – 'you will not be able to hide. And Sir Samuel will not care if you are happy or not. Only that you do the correct thing by your new name, D'Esparr. Which will include not sullying it with the title of player.'

A stuck cart halted them, the crowd unable for the moment to flow around it. Ned studied the yelling mob, the carter plying his whip. When it came again, his voice was less harsh. 'Then what can I do?'

John looked at Ned's profile. Saw in it suddenly some of his own mother in the shape of the boy's eyes; saw again the darkness that they shared, in hair and brow, which came from his own father, the man he'd never known. It returned to him then, what Will had said about fathers and sons earlier; and something else too: Burbage hinting about Ned's shortcomings. All this, all he was feeling, made him seize the boy's shoulder, removing him from the jostle to a doorway close by. 'What can you do? You can make the Chamberlain's Men fall so in love with your playing that they will fight to keep you. They have influence and may be able to win out. But you have to prove yourself totally in their eyes. You need to seize this role of the mad girl my friend has written and eclipse every other boy player in the company.'

A fire came into Ned's dark eyes, blazed briefly, dampened. 'Yet to play madness well enough to do that?' Ned chewed at his lip. 'I have thought much on it, but . . . but what do I truly know about it? I know how to conjure a laugh, but that . . .' He shook his head. 'Perhaps it would be different if I had met one of the insane. But I have not.'

It came to John then, on the instant – he'd heard it in the snarl that underlay everything in that garden across the river, seen it in noble eyes. 'You wish to study madness, boy? Then would you like to go where you can observe it clear?' On his son's considered nod, he continued. 'Good. Then on the morrow, after the performance is done, I will take you to the centre of all madness in this realm.' He gave the slightest of smiles. 'I will take you to Essex House.'

XXXIII

The Stages of Revolt Part One

He'd seen the Lord Chamberlain's Men give far better performances. He'd played in a few of them. This old tragedy of Richard the Second had taxed the craft and memory of them all.

Yet few he'd seen had had such a powerful effect. From the drunken swordsmen in the pit to the earls in the minstrels' gallery, men drew their swords and clashed them aloft at any line that stirred them, punctuating every speech given by Burbage, as Bolingbroke, who strove and sometimes failed to ignore them. Indeed he struggled with a role he'd last played four years before. John could hear the improvisations required when lines went missing; all executed in formidable iambic, such was the player's skill. The crowd did not notice, nor care, and roared anyway.

It was as well that Essex himself had not been there, for the players could scarce have escaped the charge of conspirators. The wooden O felt like a giant fever boil; lanced, it threatened to gush out over the surrounding skin. Yet fever-pitched though the crowd was, John sensed they were not quite there, not yet. It was like the storming of any city, of which he'd partaken in a few. The petard had been laid 'gainst the gate. Packed with gunpowder and shards of metal, its fuse trailed back to Essex House . . . where the earl, hesitant as ever, held the only match.

It was time for the murder of a king – and so time for John to leave. He had taken a place on the gallery bench closest to the stairs. Slipping down them now, he left by the Globe's main doors and circled around it towards the players' entrance. He wanted to be away swiftly and on one of the first boats. Ned was already dressed in his street clothes, playing a servant. Once the clapping ended, he would be ready to go. John suspected there would be no closing jig. The conspirators had paid to be wound to a pitch, not released from it.

Halfway round the circle, he noticed something strange. Not the carriage drawn up there, for enough of them awaited the more noble of the audience; but the style of it. English carriages were in the main converted carts, covered in ornate trappings; mutton dressed as lamb and hell on the arse on the rutted tracks that passed for roads. This one was plainer than most, though the oak panelling was rich and polished, and John noted ribs below it, with leather straps that would allow some give over the bumps. Unusually also its windows had lace curtains – one of which was raised now by a gloved hand.

'Master Lawley!'

He hesitated. He knew the caller on the instant. Then he crossed and stood at the carriage's small door. 'Lady,' he said.

'Come in,' she replied and, flicking a catch and pushing the door out, she drew him inside.

He settled on to the cramped seat opposite her. 'Sarah,' he said, bowing his head.

They studied each other for a long moment. She had not changed since he had last seen her. Still pretty. Still dangerous. She was dressed soberly, in a plain if rich brown dress and matching bonnet. The only difference he could discern was in her face painting. The white lead base had been applied more thickly . . . and yet failed to quite conceal dark circles under her eyes – and the purple of a bruise high up on her cheekbone.

'So, sir,' she began, briskly, 'you do not look so ill from the effects of your incarceration.'

'I had friends within who took care of me.'

'And without? Did not your friends look after you there as well?'

John smiled. The nature of their conversations had always been thus – deceptively polite, whilst immediately probing; aside from their first, which had been entirely carnal and of which he wished he had a better – indeed any – recall. Yet he did not have time for the dance now. The play would end soon, the audience exit and he must beat them to the boats. 'If you are referring to my lord of Essex, Sarah, you should know that if you are out of his sight you are beyond his care – unless you are his enemy, and then you are too much dwelt upon.

318

And as for other *friends*, well, I suspect you are aware of my new relationship with the man who has befriended us both.'

'The Secretary?' She thrust out a lower lip. 'He has no friends, only slaves.'

As she said it, she did a curious thing – reached up and touched her cheekbone, where paint did not quite disguise a bruise. Ah, thought John, as she continued. 'And he has sent me to enquire after his latest.'

'He assumed you would find me here?'

'Of course. At the centre of treason, where a good spy should be.'

It was said with just a touch of bitterness, as half hidden as the bruise. Something was amiss with the lady. Something to be probed. 'And what does Sir Robert require of us, his minions? What has he sent you to discover from me?'

'The answer to the question that most concerns him, of course,' she snapped. 'Does Essex rise?' She glanced out of the window as another cry of 'Bolingbroke!' pierced the air, then went on in a lower voice, 'His followers gather in every tavern from Ludgate Hill to Westminster. They cluster around Essex House, which resembles a war camp now. They meet at the playhouse to witness regicide enacted.' She leaned forward. 'So answer me, and I will answer him. And then, perhaps, he will be quiet.'

She raised a hand towards her bruise again; realised it, dropped it – but John took it before it reached her lap. 'But will you be, Sarah?' he asked softly.

'I?' She tried to pull her hand back, but when he held it she let it go limp. Her eyes left his to look out the window. 'What matters my quiet?'

'It matters to you. And to me,' he added, squeezing slightly.

Her eyes came back to him, searching. 'Truly?'

'Lady, I suspect you and I are similar in this: we are tired of being used so. And we would find a way clear, would we not?'

'Perhaps.' A slight smile came. 'Do you know of one?'

'Yes. To let these two stags go at it one last time over the doe – and step from their course.'

'Is that what you do, John Lawley?'

He was not answering only her now, he knew. He was reporting to Cecil. 'I serve who I must serve – to serve myself,' he replied.

She stared at him for a moment, then looked away again, spoke. 'As do I. And I will best serve myself if I give the Secretary what he wants. Only then can I . . . keep from this stag's course.' He still held her hand, and now she returned the pressure. 'I once aided you, sir. Gave you a simple shake of my head to give you time to step off the path yourself. That you did not succeed is not my fault. I tried. Will you for me? Will you give me a nod or a shake and answer me. Does Essex rise this weekend or no?'

He thought back to all he'd seen at Essex House – the mounting fervour of the earl's followers, from nobles to rakehells, echoing in the cheers now erupting within the playhouse behind them. He thought of the maps upon the table, London marked for the seizing. Finally, he thought of Forman's horoscope, the favourable aspects of these two days. One had passed. Robert Devereux's faith had been clear as he spoke of it, invoking also his triumph at Cadiz. And on the sudden he knew – if the earl did not rise on the morrow, he never would. And if he did – as John would try to ensure he did – then the best chance for his lordship's success came with the Master Secretary believing the opposite.

John held her gaze, kept his own steady . . . and slowly shook his head.

Their hands slid apart. As he reached for the door, a trumpet sounded from the playhouse. The revels were ended. He pushed it open, stepped out. Her words slowed but did not stop him. 'Until the next time, Master Lawley.'

'Until then, my lady of cloves.' He bowed, then moved away fast and it did not take many steps to excuse his lie. It was up to her if she believed him and what she told the employer who'd struck her. Besides, of one thing he was certain – Sarah could look after herself.

Rounding the curve of the playhouse, he saw Ned awaiting him before its rear entrance. 'Ready for this, boy?'

Ned's eyes gleamed. 'Aye, Father.'

'Then let us to it.'

The next moment they were running for Paris Garden Stairs. They caught near the first wherry from the dock, sharing it with boisterous swordsmen; Celts in the main, red hair bared to the encroaching night, who had, like themselves, hotfooted it from the playhouse, afire to return and urge their hero on. Glancing back from mid stream, John saw that theirs was only the first of an armada, vessels of all sizes crammed with men, hallooing as if upon some hunt. He looked to the bridge, and though dusk light meant sight was dimming, the sounds came clear – of drums, bugles, huzzahs, along with cries of 'Bolingbroke!' and still more of 'Essex!'

Seeing the house approaching in the wherryman's strong strokes, a shiver passed through John that had little to do with river chill or February's deceiving sun. Well, he thought, I will be at his side soon enough. And I will do what I have always done with Robbie Devereux. Force him to the breach. Swing him over the ship's balustrade, a sword between his teeth. Lower his hand to the fuse. See him triumph or see him damned. And me with him.

He looked down at his son. Ned had stood upon the platform, as the crowd roared and surged. He had already experienced a touch of mob insanity. Now they were heading for the very heart of it . . . and John, for the fortieth time, questioned the wisdom of bringing the boy. Tess would be furious if she knew, and with reason. No, he thought, all will be well. The boil is not yet lanced. Only then will danger come. I will keep him at Essex House just long enough to witness what he needs and then dispatch him straight. An hour, two at most. A primer in madness to secure the role he needed to stay with the Chamberlain's Men.

There was the usual crowd at the gates. But Captain St Lawrence was at the postern again and speeded them in. 'Your son, i'st? Come to see history made, have you, lad?' He beamed, clapping each Lawley upon the shoulder. 'No, keep your weapons now, John. We only admit our trusted friends. Let us to it.'

He shoved them forward into the mob and straight into a crowd grouped around a fire pit. They were engaged in a canting song, the verse passed from man to man along with a bottle from which he swigged. John, catching the scent of whisky along with the words, felt a familiar clutch inside.

Bing awast to Romeville, then,
O my doxy, O my dell.
We'll heave a booth, and dock again,
And trining 'scape, and all is well.

The bottle passed close – but another shove sent him forward, beyond desire. 'Do not think that all is sinful drunkenness here, young lad.' St Lawrence appeared a little embarrassed. 'We are about holy work, remember.' He pulled them to another gathering. 'Hearken to this.'

This ring of men were also grouped around a fire. But no bottle passed here, and men did not rhyme on theft and copulation. John also knew he would have seen none of these men at the performance either – for Puritans decried the theatre as Satan's playground.

One young man was speaking, his lank blonde hair reaching to a plain white collar spread over a black suit. His hands were out and open-palmed at his sides, his eyes lifted to the sky, where all men stared. 'Remember ye!' he cried. ''Tis not enough to fight against God's enemies. Ye, his warriors, must first be cleansed of sin. Remember the words of Moses as we set out upon our holy work: "When thou goest out with the host against thine enemies, keep thee then from all wickedness."'

'Amen,' cried St Lawrence, along with every man in the circle.

John looked up at him. 'I did not take you for a Puritan, Captain. In sooth, I seem to recall two maids at Nonsuch . . .'

'Shh!' The man glanced at Ned, swallowed. 'I was a sinner, 'tis true, and a grand one too. But men like these' – he nodded towards the black-dressed circle before him, who had all joined hands and were now murmuring prayers, eyes shut, faces lifted into the snow that had begun to gently fall again – 'they have convinced me of my errors. God bless them and hallelujah!' Ned called 'amen', though John did not. The Irishman smiled and patted his arm. 'Ah, I understand, John. You have not seen the light yet. It will come to you as it does to all men. And yet.' He narrowed his eyes. 'Being a Cornishman, you are probably of the Catholic persuasion, are you not?' Before John could attempt to correct Essex's misapprehension as to his origins, St Lawrence went on, 'Yet do not concern yourself on that score. Though our glorious leader is himself the exemplar of the Reformed Church and its most strident defender, he is also tolerant of others' errors. He trusts that they, like him, will find the true faith.' He beamed. 'We have many like you here, John. You will be protected until you see the light of God.'

Whip me, thought John, but did not speak. He would not dim the fervent glow in the big Irishman's eyes. And he knew it all shone from 'the leader', as St Lawrence kept calling him. It was not surprising that Essex's twin idols – drunkenness and religiosity – had a near equal rule in his garden.

'Stay and listen to the word of God, John,' St Lawrence continued. 'Or claim a patch of ground before the playgoers return. 'Twill get crowded soon. I must return to my post.'

With a bow, he was gone. Father and son stayed in the garden for a short time longer, as it rapidly filled and swiftly assumed its former aspect – revel, riot, prayer meeting. When their wanderings had left the boy wide-eyed enough, John said, 'All forms of madness that can take men are here, are they not? Yet to further aid you in your study, let us to the beating heart of Bedlam.' He took Ned's arm. ''Tis time you met the Earl of Essex.'

He led his son to the rear of the house, where, recognised by the same guards, they were allowed through. The garden's din was part sealed off by the closed door, a different sound taking over – a hum that grew as they proceeded down the corridor, between a row of waiting servants, to the main hall. 'Here we go,' said John, hand on doorknob. He turned it, pushed in.

There was a circle of some dozen men in the centre of the hall. They were kneeling, their hands joined, their eyes shut. John saw immediately that the noblemen had made near as good time from the Globe as any low-born conspirator. Southampton was there, along with Blount, Mounteagle, Sandys; while a brace of earls – Rutland and Sussex – braced a third: Essex himself. Like them all he had his eyes shut. Like everyone he clutched the hands of the man to either side. And everyone was humming, save for one, the only man standing and that upon a chair. Gelli Meyrick, the earl's factotum, held a huge Bible in his hand. His clear, accented voice rang out, each utterance producing a corresponding surge of hums and repeated words in answer.

'Who made thee a prince and judge over us?'

'Who?' came the hum. Followed by someone calling, 'Not thee, Cecil!'

'And the Lord went before them by day in a pillar of cloud, to lead them the way.'

'Lead us, Lord!' came the response, with a different voice adding, 'Lord Robert!'

Then all the hands were lifted, a circle rising to the ceiling, and thence, John supposed, to heaven. It must have been something Essex's party had done before, as all men now followed Meyrick and chanted together:

Life for life.
Eye for eye, tooth for tooth, hand for hand, foot for foot,
Burning for burning, wound for wound, stripe for stripe.

John looked at his son. Ned's eyes had been wide in the garden. They were wider now. He felt his father's gaze, looked up. 'Yes, my boy. Random quotes from Genesis.'

For once, Ned was too stunned to look scornful. 'Exodus, Father. And one of the few they have left out is . . .'

Ned stopped as the missing quote came, the men shouting it as one, 'The Lord is a man of war.' And this time it was not a single voice that said it, but all. 'Our lord,' came the universal cry, all adding, 'Our lord of Essex!'

It was a signal. Men unclasped, only to clasp again in hugs, helping each other to rise. 'Is this it, sir?' said Ned, awe in his voice. 'Will they march now on the palace?'

'No.' John looked at the flushed faces before him – not quite flushed enough for that. There were other ways to bolster courage to be taken first.

'And the people sat down to eat and to drink . . . but they rose up to play,' Robert Devereux shouted. 'Is that not so, Gelli?'

'Aye, my lord.'

'Then we shall do the same as the other children of Israel,' Essex cried. 'Eat, drink . . . and then play a set shall . . . shall strike a crown into a hazard, mayhap?' His roving eyes fell on the two figures at the door. They brightened. 'Was that it, John Lawley? Was that not one of your friend's phrases in the play he wrote for me, *Henry the Fifth*?' He turned away. 'God's truth, maybe we should have had the Chamberlain's Men play that one tonight instead of unhappy Richard.' He looked now at Ned. 'Then all the youth of England will be aflame, do I not have it?'

John felt his son stir beside him. He had been in the play, knew the misquote. The boy was set to reply, and to correct, as was youth's way. John jerked him by the sleeve, shook his head.

Essex's butterfly attention had alighted elsewhere anyway, for Southampton cried, 'You would not say so, Robin, if you had been there. Three thousand fellows and their dames shouting: "Essex! Bolingbroke! Essex!" Christ's tears, if we'd had the pikes to hand we could have issued them to the audience and marched straight on Whitehall.'

Gelli Meyrick rang a bell. Poised servants poured in and John used the furore, as nobles fought for pieces of fowl and jugs of sack, to draw his son into the shadows of the hall. He was not so foolish as to think he would be invited to partake of the feast. The earl had obviously forgotten about his drunken knighting in Dublin Castle. Just as well, John thought. 'Be silent and make your final studies, for you will leave soon,' he whispered to Ned. When a servant passed close, John reached out, snagged a tankard of ale then settled, back to wall.

The play was not long in commencing. The preliminary was the feasting and drinking, with many pledges to the earl's health and cause, and damnation to his enemies at the court. The Queen was toasted, but with less enthusiasm than usually shown. John watched courage being gained by the bumper full – and wondered what might push it beyond liquored boast into action.

Then it came, as so often in a play, with an entrance. And John thought that if the nobleman entering had been upon the scaffold at the Globe, the groundlings would have hissed him. For he was from the group already being damned and liberally cursed.

Secretary Herbert was a member of the Privy Council and sat at Cecil's left hand. He was one of those men who appeared as wide as he was tall, a trick that his flounced mauve doublet, billowing pantaloons and serving platter of a ruff only emphasised. His air of self-importance puffed him still further, reminding John of a fish he'd seen in the Pacific Ocean that could inflate itself to thrice its size when confronting danger.

Herbert seemed unaware of the peril he was in. Essex House was a cockpit that night and Herbert a prime if outsized cock, with the odds seriously against him. 'My lord of Essex,' he declared, waddling to the centre of the room and planting himself, 'I bring you the Privy Council's warmest greetings . . .' He was surprised by a loud hiss, blinked, carried on. 'I also bring again the request made earlier when a mere messenger was sent. That is why they have sent me.' He contrived to puff up still further. 'So you should take most seriously their *request* to attend them forthwith.'

Silence followed the summons, long enough to feel uncomfortable. If Herbert had had neck feathers instead of a ruff, they would have now been rising. As it was, he looked uneasily down the line of blank faces raised to him, until one of them spoke.

'Shall I prick this bladder with my dagger and see if it pops?' ventured Rutland.

The hilarity that followed this remark was beyond the span of the joke, yet continued for some time and only subsided when Robert Devereux spoke. 'You may bear back to the Council,' he declared, 'the same answer the previous lackey must have failed to convey.' He drew himself up. 'I am not well,' he bellowed lustily. 'I will not stir forth. If I do, I fear mischief upon my person, and the harming of my followers, such as befell my dear Lord Henry only last month. And where is that accursed traitor Grey, who cut off our page's hand in that skirmish?' He glared. 'Free, and no doubt advising that same Council who commands me to appear before them now. No!' He stood, leaned down, still shouting. 'There are plots laid against me, sir. The Queen is bewitched by false advisers – and assassins lurk on every corner. And unlike someone here whose flesh would scarce notice the intrusion of a blade, I am not so well armoured.' Patting his own flux-shrunk shank, he laughed loudly, his cohorts joining in.

Herbert drew himself up to his full height – and girth. 'I will convey your . . . sentiments, sir. Yet let me warn you – 'twill be ill taken, I warrant you. Look for a different sort of summons, and soon.' Then, with a dignity impressive for a capon, the secretary turned heel and walked from the room.

Laughter died on the door's closing. 'God's body,' spluttered Southampton. 'Did you hear? The whoreson dog threatened us!'

''Twas not the dog that barked, Henry,' corrected Mounteagle, 'but his master.'

'The Toad!'

'Aye, that accursed Cecil.'

'Aye, Cecil! Cecil!'

Fury broke out at the name, vengeance summoned to fall upon that misshapen back. Daggers were drawn, fists slammed down upon the table that made the pewter jump. Eventually one voice pierced the tumult. 'But will the summons be to the Council . . . or to the Tower? Next time will they seek my presence – or my head?'

All fell silent, looked to the speaker, Essex. Whispers came.

'Truly, they seek your life.'

'The Toad will spit his venom.'

'Then what shall I do?' said Essex. 'Advise me, friends.'

'Flee!' shouted Christopher Blount. 'Downriver to Gravesend and a fast packet to the Continent.'

'For shame!' cried Southampton.

'Nay, stepfather,' answered Essex. 'I do not fancy the exile's road. Not when I have a sword half drawn.' He looked down the length of the table. 'What say you, Lord Sandys?'

'Draw it all the way, sir,' shouted the older lord. 'By God, you have three hundred men out there, all armed and sworn to your cause. The Queen in her palace cannot muster half that number. Let us send this answer.' On that he drew his dagger and drove it into the table before him.

Argument became general, a chorus of competing voices. Ned looked up at his father. John gestured with his eyes to the door. His son had seen more than enough madness this night to feed his forthcoming role. The result of it he could miss. John could sense now what had been absent before – that taper at last hovering over the fuse. Well, he was ready for the blast himself. But he would see his son well clear of the explosion.

They were at the door, his hand upon the knob, when one voice rose above all others. 'And what says my most loyal of retainers? What thinks an ordinary man from London's streets? What advice would John Lawley give?'

I was afraid of that, John thought, turning slowly to a room of suddenly silent men, all staring at him. They were, in the main, not a crew he would care to follow into battle. His lord, however? He saw him as he had seen him standing in the prow of the boat that bore them on to the sands of Cadiz. Poised. Ready. And old Lord Sandys was right – there were three hundred men outside made of hard stuff. Also he remembered what he'd promised himself – however strong his misgivings, for good or ill he was Essex's man, would be through the triumph or the disaster that was to come. He had promised himself that he would act. It began now.

'I think you should forgo all doubt, my lord,' he said. He thought of that same play that Essex had misquoted earlier. He knew it better than the earl. 'Follow your spirit, good my lord, and upon this charge cry, "God for Essex, England and St George."'

He felt Ned gape up at him. But it was on Essex that he fixed his gaze. 'By that saint, by all of them, you are right!' cried the earl, springing up. 'Tomorrow is the day. But what is the event?'

Cries came.

'Storm the palace.'

'Rouse the city.'

'Seize the Tower.'

Once again, a babel of voices. Definitely time for Ned to leave, John thought, grabbing the doorknob, opening the door. Halberd-iers, their weapons at port, peered in at the shouting nobility. John began to push through them.

A cry from behind, louder than the rest. 'Before we decide anything, we must secure our own doors so no one is forewarned.' John glanced back. Lord Sandys had left the table and was approach-ing the door. 'Bar all the gates,' he shouted. 'No man is to come or go without our express leave.'

'Fast,' John said, shoving his son ahead. And fast they moved – but not as swift as shouted commands. By the time they reached the garden's side wicket, five stout pikemen stood before it. Their officer, a large Welshman, put his hand in John's chest when he tried to pass. 'You heard the order,' he growled, 'no man in or out.'

'And what of a boy?' John asked. 'He has no part in this.'

'He looks man enough to me,' came the reply, accompanied by a shove.

John stepped back, gauging the opposition. But there were too many, and besides, this was no time for a brawl. It was time to think, bide . . . and seek another way out for his son. He had wanted to show him some madness, not immerse him in it.

Ned was looking up at him, fear clear in his pale blue eyes. 'What do we do, Father? I thank you for this instruction, but I believe now I have learned enough to pass the test.'

John forced a smile. 'You shall be off and soon. I shall find a way. Meanwhile' – he moved to an unoccupied stretch of wall, sat and put his back to it, opening wide his cloak – 'come and share a soldier's warmth while we await the opportunity.'

After a moment's hesitation, Ned knelt and John swathed them both. When he pulled him close, he could feel his son's heart beating fast. 'Did I ever tell you of the night I spent with Sir Philip Sidney?'

'The poet-warrior?' The eyebrows rose. 'I am . . . a great admirer of his verse and life. You knew him?'

'I lay with him even thus. Wrapped in one cloak in the siege lines at Zutphen. Alas, 'twas to be that noble gentleman's very last night upon this earth . . .'

XXXIV

'We Rise For Essex!'

The tale lulled his son. Ned slept fitfully against his father's chest. John did not, watching the gate for opportunity. None came, for none were admitted nor left – until Gelli Meyrick appeared accompanied by six cloaked and shrouded men just as the bell in nearby Bridewell's hospital tolled seven. The reforming whores who dwelt there must rise, and so, it seemed, must conspiracy. Meyrick's conversation with the captain was in Welsh, of which John knew not a word. But the upshot was clear. The gate was unbarred, six messengers were let out and some supporters who had gathered the other side were admitted before it was barred again.

He lay there, watching and hoping for another hour. But no more men came nor went. Finally he rose, stretching cramped and aching muscles and limbs. Too old to sleep in the field, he thought. Ned woke and John bent, wrapped him again in the cloak. 'Do not leave this spot,' he said. 'I will need to find you again, and swiftly.'

'I will not, Father,' Ned replied, the worry clear in his eyes.

John walked between rows of recumbent men, some snoring, some wakeful, seeking he knew not what. And found it, in the reassuringly large form of Captain St Lawrence. 'Good morrow, Lawley,' he cried, pumping John's hand with bone-cracking vigour. 'Did I not say you returned happily upon your hour?' He beamed. 'I cannot wait for my captain to lead me over the barricades, can you?'

'Hardly.' John looked around. Everywhere men were astir, shaking off night and dirt. 'So you believe that hour has come? What news?'

'We march upon the court!' The captain's brow furrowed. 'Or

upon the Tower.' It creased further. 'Or indeed the city. Rumour has them all.'

It was John's turn to frown. He had heard the same dispute within Essex's dining hall. 'Yet surely in the end there is but one choice, Captain? The court is where the Queen is. Seize her, seize the realm.'

'I'm with you, to be sure,' St Lawrence replied. 'As long as we also grab the hunchback and his cronies in the first scoop of the net.'

His rejoinder was delayed by another voice. 'Lawley.'

John turned. 'Despair.' The formerly fat knight stood there, looking too tired to even muster annoyance at the old joke about his name. 'So you are here?'

'And an uncomfortable time I have had of it too. The summons was not as urgent as you made out,' the man whined. 'His lordship had no pressing need to see me, it appears, and has not summoned me though I have sent him three notes.' The whine rose. 'I could have spent the night in my own bed and still been here for . . .' He faltered. 'For whatever is to occur this morning.'

'Or not,' John breathed.

'What do you imply, sirrah?' demanded Sir Samuel.

'I imply nothing, sir. I merely observe that your duty—' began John, but got no further, for loud banging interrupted him. It was the sound of a pikestaff striking wood, and it was accompanied by a bass voice bellowing, 'Open, I say. Open in the name of her majesty the Queen.'

The three men joined the surge to the back gate, which opened at the Queen's, and Gelli Meyrick's, command. The man who entered first was a head taller than the Welshman, and John recognised the face instantly. He had seen it only recently, for Sir Thomas Egerton, as Lord Keeper of the Realm, was in charge of all its prisons, including the Tower. He was also a member of the Privy Council. 'I come hotfoot from the court,' he declared loudly, 'bearing the Royal Seal of England as my warrant. So hence from my way, you saucy knave, and bring me to my lord of Essex.'

Meyrick *was* a saucy knave, a shepherd's son whom fortune had raised to knighthood. But he was in his dominion now and his warrant ran. 'Shut the gate,' he shouted, and was instantly obeyed. There were more in Egerton's party still to be admitted, but these were shut out to his loud protests. However, Meyrick's voice topped his. 'There are diverse plots afoot to murder my noble lord and master. No man but a friend may approach him. And you, sir, are no friend to Essex!' He turned to his guard. 'Take their swords!'

Despite complaints, all weapons were seized. Even the Great Seal was taken and only returned to its bearer, the one liveried servant to get in, on Egerton's strong objections. Yet his nobility did not stop him and his party being jostled as they progressed along the gauntlet of men that had rapidly formed, which led to the rear of the house – from whose doors now spilled another party, this one greeted by cheers, not jeers. John had heard whispered 'Egertons', and 'Great Seals' pass like the twittering of starlings from garden end's to house. They had drawn forth the conspirators.

'What, Lord Keeper?' Essex cried, halting. 'Are you come to arrest us?'

'Not so, my lord.' Egerton's deep voice rose above the cries of 'Shame!' 'Knave!' and 'Traitor!' 'I am come only to command what our former suppliants have merely asked before. That you present yourself forthwith to the Privy Council and explain what this gathering of fellows means.'

'Present himself to be murdered, you mean,' shouted Southampton, 'just as I was nearly murdered by the Council's creature Grey only last month. By God, my sweet page Christopher lost his hand defending me!'

'For which Lord Grey was imprisoned, good my lord . . .'

'And from which prison he was freed after less than a fortnight,' thundered Mounteagle. 'We know what treatment the earl can expect from you villains. A speedy condemnation and still speedier murder.'

Baying, the crowd surged against the halberdiers mustered to guard the visitors, threatened to overwhelm them. Shouts of 'Murder? Murder *them*!' and 'Treason!' rang out. Spittle flew.

Above the noise, Egerton struggled to be heard. But he was tall and lean, unlike the previous summoner, Herbert, and had a dignity that went with his title. 'My lord, you cannot be condemned if you have not sinned. And I know you have not . . . yet.' He glared with enough vigour at the men who pressed close to make them give back. In the relative silence he continued, 'So I urge you to come before the Council straightway. Let your grievances receive a hearing. If they are valid, you will receive redress. Those are the exact words the Master Secretary urged me to speak to you. He means you no harm . . .'

It was a mistake to mention someone so reviled. Egerton himself was reputed honest – yet the Lord Keeper had spoken one of Satan's other titles, and the abuse that came drowned out any reparation he could make.

Essex was one trying to be heard. His friends were shouting so he could be. But in the end it was the Lord Keeper's voice that again cut through the babel. He had taken off his hat as a sign of friendship when he'd approached. Now, seeing he was achieving nothing, he replaced it as a sign of his authority. 'Know, sirs' – he glared around – 'and all you that have assembled here, that I come on the command of the Queen herself. That I bear the Great Seal of England. And by the office given me I warn you all now: disperse. Submit your complaints to the Council – or take the consequences.'

John thought it a brave speech from a bear in a bear pit. But its bravery had as little effect as that beast's would have before a crowd hot for blood. 'Throw the seal in the river!' someone shouted. 'Throw the keeper in after!' came another shout, both surpassed by St Lawrence opening his huge mouth and yelling, 'Kill the traitors!'

Someone must have anticipated this, for now more halberdiers rushed forward, surrounded the party and hurried them up the terrace steps and into the house, right on the heels of Essex and his friends. It would serve no one to murder the Council's representatives. Yet.

But what *would* serve? This was the moment. John recognised it, for he had seen many such before; the one when talk turned to action, when courage and madness were screwed to the sticking point and burst their bounds – or when they did not. His men would have followed Essex to hell right then. All around him men were screaming, 'To the court!' John felt it too, though not from passion. From long experience. Do it now, Robbie, he thought, willing it through the walls of the house. Do it now.

The doors were flung open. A single man strode forth – the Earl of Rutland, youngest and handsomest of the conspirators. He was buckling on his sword, at the moment of pushing the pin into the final hole on the belt. Achieved, he looked up, flung his long brown locks back, his arms wide, and cried, 'To the courtyard! To arms and to horse! We rise . . . for Essex!'

The shout that came could have brought down walls. 'For Essex!' John already had sword and buckler affixed, but many men rushed for theirs. St Lawrence gave him a comradely slap hard enough to fell a tree and ran off. John looked behind him, seeking. But the garden was a maelstrom now, Ned somewhere in its midst. He could only hope that his injunction to remain in it would be obeyed. Unless he could escape, he would be better here than on the streets while this game played out.

John ran around the side of the house for its front. God's beard, he thought, he's going to do it. At last! A grin came. He could not help it. No matter how old he'd grown, how weary his limbs, he had lived for this kind of scrape once – and seemingly still. Rushed through streets or jungles, over besieged walls and the burning decks of galleons – for glory, for England, for gold; and for himself. Finally, no matter the cause, for himself. Now all questions were past, debate ended, now he could truly do no other, he felt as he ever had. Ecstatic. He was going to fight this day. It was something he'd always been good at.

In the courtyard, men lined up in rough ranks facing the house, some mounted, most on foot, some jabbering like crows, some silent, each man approaching the moment in his own way. John made his way to the bottom of the stairs and no one tried to stop him – not even Sir Samuel, jostling for position. Many there knew him, knew who he was – their leader's guard through all the years. Those who did not saw how he walked, the ease of it, the readiness. His hand rested on the pommel of his backsword, so lightly it appeared to float above it. No one there would grudge such a man his place.

He'd just settled when the front doors of Essex House were flung wide. Out marched earls and lords, booted, spurred, some with breastplates, some with plumes in their hats, all armed. They formed a rough V to the top of the staircase, paused there, waiting. Silence took everyone now, and John could only hear the breathing of men, the snort of horses – and the bell in the Bridewell tolling ten. On the tenth stroke he came, to a huge shout, wearing a tangerine scarf crossways over his chest, over an exquisite suit of ruffled black velvet. He strode to the head of the V, then passed on through the ranks below, cheered as he went. Before the gates he mounted, his horse frisked, as caught in the mood. But Robert Devereux was a superb horseman, and in a trice he had control. John saw no doubt in a face from which the years had dropped away. He had seen him so over the years . . . at Zutphen, at Cadiz. Fidgety as a cat before, cool as steel once decided.

The Earl of Essex stood up in his stirrups. He looked at his followers, silent again, ready. He drew his sword – a backsword, just like John wore. No foreign fancies for him this day. 'For Essex,' he cried, as John had cried before. 'For England. For St George!'

It was echoed. 'For Essex. For England. For St George!'

John shouted too, then took a deep breath. This was it. Rebellion. By day's end he would be a traitor or a hero. Sooner. For the Palace of Whitehall was less than a mile to the west, three hundred men could march there in twenty minutes, and in ten more overwhelm the palace guards and the Council's few followers. It would be over in moments. Essex would have done what he should have done fifteen months before at Nonsuch – seized the Queen's person. With her secured, his enemies imprisoned or fled, he would dictate terms, would again be Earl Marshal of England, the Queen's closest adviser and friend. Or . . .

Or he could be Bolingbroke and so he would be king.

The sword swung down in command. The gates were opened.

King Robert the First! Perhaps John *would* reclaim his misplaced knighthood then. He would have to give up the theatre. But he could also take Tess and his son, and Sir Samuel would never keep them from him.

John found himself smiling into a future. It would begin in the next moment. It would begin when Robert Devereux shouted, 'To the court!' and rode west along the Strand.

The earl was still standing in his stirrups, sword aloft again. Now he waved it above his head and cried out in that strong voice, 'To the City!'

And led his forces east along the Strand.

XXXV

The Stages of Revolt Part Two

'My lord! My lord of Essex!'

Because he'd been at the front to watch his lord come from the house, he was near the rear of those that squeezed slowly out of the gates. So it took John till they were halfway down Fleet Street before he reached the horse's rear. Even then he could not immediately get his lordship's attention, such was the volume of shouting that bounced between the house fronts and caught in the jutties that curled out over the way. Many were about, on their way to or from church, or having attended St Paul's pulpit for the Sunday sermon. More poured down from the alleys and lanes around, voices adding to the adulation. 'Essex!' most cried, making his own cry hard to distinguish. A few, 'Bolingbroke!'

With a last swivel and slide, he was beside the earl's horse. 'My lord!' he called up from the stirrup, to no response, for Essex was busy acknowledging his acclaim with slow circles of his wrist. 'Robert!' he finally bellowed, loud enough to be heard over gunfire.

It startled the earl's horse, which baulked and skittered to the side. It startled the horseman who, gaining control again, looked down. 'Eh?' His frown at the familiarity cleared when he saw who had addressed him. 'Johnnie!' he cried. 'Ever at the forefront, what? Good to be about them, eh?'

'About whom, my lord? Where are you going?'

Essex gestured ahead. 'To the City, of course,' he replied.

'Yes, my lord, but why?' John's footing slipped on horse turds, but he grabbed the earl's stirrup, stayed upright, ran on. 'It is the court you must seize. It lies at your mercy. By Christ's wounds, turn about.'

'By Christ's blood, I cannot!' The earl's eyes went misty. 'I burst once into my sweet Bess's chamber, all armed and besmirched. I cannot do so again. However, when she sees me at the head of the host of England – and that host has swept aside Cecil's puny defences – why then she will greet me as a warrior, worthy once more to kiss her neck!'

'The host of . . .' John gripped the stirrup again, lifted his legs, let the horse carry him over another brown pile. 'What host?'

'Sheriff Smyth has promised me a thousand men, with pike and arquebus. They will be assembling e'en now. We will meet them, turn about, and march on Whitehall.'

The crowds thickened as the way narrowed down the hill to Lud Gate. The stench of the Fleet river came clearly. John knew a foul smell when he scented one. 'Sheriff Smyth? Who is he?'

'I have not met him,' replied the earl, a smile for a lady of ample bosom who leaned from a window and blew him a kiss. 'Yet I've heard he is yeoman true, a stout fellow.'

'You've . . . heard?' John gasped. 'Then who has met him?'

'Oh, uh . . . Temple. No, Constable. I think. Anyway, he is vouched for, sure.'

John turned and spat. The vagueness of it all was typical of Essex. If a thousand men awaited ahead it would be useful to the cause. But it was uncertain – whereas a near-unguarded palace was not. 'My lord, I implore you. If you have ever trusted me, turn about now, make for Whitehall. Seize the Queen's person while it is unguarded.'

He said it with force and could see uncertainty at last enter the eyes. But as they crossed the Fleet and approached the City gate, another body of apprentices rushed through it and set up a halloo. 'No, Lawley. I trust you with my life, as ever. But you are, for all your virtues, a mere soldier. Strategy must be left to generals, eh? Besides, 'tis all arranged. 'Twill work for the best, you shall see. We will be turned about and making for Whitehall in a trice.' The brow furrowed. 'Yet if something goes awry . . . nay, you are right to advise some caution. A good general takes care of his line of retreat, yes? We learned that in Flanders, did we not? Now I think me, my castle is not as well looked after as it may be.' He looked down. 'I do not need you to rally the crowds, Master Lawley. As you see, I can do that myself.' He waved again to a further burst of cheering. 'Do you go back to Essex House. Prepare it as an armed camp for us to strike from later. Secure the prisoners. Here, take this ring.' He licked his finger, pulled off a thick gold band, a Tudor rose engraved upon it. 'Her majesty gave me this, when she was fond. Gelli Meyrick will know it. Tell him you have my command to erect breastworks.'

'Breastworks?' John was so stunned some turds surprised him, and he lost his grip on the stirrups. He just kept his balance, took a step . . . but Essex had kicked his horse into a canter as he and his party rode under the arch of Lud Gate and into the City of London. He watched the marching swordsmen bunch and push to get through the narrow entrance and then burst out like a cork on over-cellared ale. Apprentices and Sunday strollers followed, cheering, and the whole cavalcade disappeared up towards St Paul's Church.

John stood there, hand twisting on pommel. What could he do? Follow and see these pikemen? Try to persuade? That would be a hopeless task. Once Essex was finally set upon his course, John knew, from long experience, that he would not be steered from it. More often than not it led to disaster. Though once he had followed it and taken Cadiz.

Pray God this would be a time like that.

He turned about. There was nothing for him to do but obey his last command; and though the temptation to cross the bridge and seek refuge in Southwark was strong, he could not for two reasons: his son, still trapped at Essex House; and the earl's cause. He was no deserter. He would see it through. Yet as he turned about and picked his way back through the nobles' horse droppings, he could not shift the hollow feeling around his heart.

Essex House was strangely quiet after the previous furore. Some guards stopped him at the gates and an officer he did not know questioned him. Gelli Meyrick was summoned, recognised him, acknowledged the ring. 'I'm glad to have you here, Master Lawley, and that's a fact,' the Welshman said. 'I am more a warrior for the open field, do ye see? Never been in a siege, if it should come to that. Your advice will be most appreciated.'

'It won't come to it,' replied John, though he was by no means sure of that. Still, he was sure of nothing. Cecil and his crew could mount some sort of counter-assault before the earl returned. The least John could do was protect his property, his ladies who were within . . . and his prisoners. He realised now that the earl had meant Egerton and his party who had been seized. 'I will attend you,' he said to Meyrick. 'A moment.'

He went into the garden. It was near empty, its parterres smashed, its bowling lawn a mud field. A search revealed no Ned. He had been ordered to stay – but perhaps the lad had been smart enough to disobey and flee in the confusion. Perhaps he was already safe in Southwark.

Envying him if it were so, John set about organising some sort of defence. There was no question of the breastworks Essex had alluded to – no tools to dig them, no timber to be raised to line trenches. But he ordered wagons to be drawn up near the gates for a swift barricade, and the few arms and powder positioned near them and at the side wickets. The house was no castle, designed for long resistance. But with the forty assorted men and servants still within, John could contrive to hold it for a time, against a limited foray.

The first signs of which came within the hour. Gelli Meyrick called him to the gatehouse, and from there he observed a party of some twenty armed horsemen approaching from the west. 'Stand to,' he cried, and brought half his limited force to the walls with pike and musket. The horsemen reined in, gazed . . . then turned sharply about and rode back whence they'd come.

John stepped outside the gates, seeking along the Strand the opposite way, but saw only a town about its Sunday business, no Essex riding at the head of a thousand pikemen. He shrugged and went back to doing the little he could.

News came two hours later, borne by Captain St Lawrence. The man had run from the City and was sweating heavily despite the February chill. His story, blurted out between great gulps of air, made the sweat break upon John's forehead too. 'Let me be clear here, Captain,' he interrupted when the Irishman took another pause for breath. 'Are you saying that, instead of rousing the City to his cause then marching straight to take the palace, his noble Lordship sat down . . . to lunch?'

The Irishman flushed. ''Tis true. But I am sure the earl knows best. He is dining with Sheriff Smyth.'

'With Sheriff Smyth and his one thousand pikemen?'

St Lawrence scratched his chin. 'Aye, well . . . there were no pikemen, to be sure,' he replied, 'and no Sheriff Smyth neither for long. He was just leaving, he said . . .'

'I'll wager he was!'

'. . . but he was off to the Lord Mayor, he swore. Bound to fetch help there, eh?'

John turned away and cursed under his breath in terms that would have made the abbess of a brothel blush. Essex had done it again. Yet most of his invective was reserved for himself – for who was madder, the fool who led or the fool who followed that fool?

A sentinel's cry had him running up the stairs of the gatehouse, St Lawrence at his heels. They arrived in time to see a large party of armed horsemen gallop past, heading for the City. At a glance they could tell that these were not reinforcements for their cause. When their hoof falls had faded from the cobbles, other sounds could be clearly heard – a rallying bugle, a steady drum beat. 'The best thing you can do, Captain,' he said, turning to the Irishman, 'is to hasten back to his lordship and tell him that this day can only be saved if he returns now and does what he should have done this morning – charge the palace with all the forces that remain to him.'

For the first and only time in their acquaintance, John watched the big Irishman quaver. ''Tis . . . 'tis not possible, Master Lawley. I am spent.' He wheezed to emphasise his condition. 'Begod, can you not send someone younger?'

John opened his mouth to curse again . . . and then didn't. For down the timber-framed and cobbled canyons of Fleet Street and the Strand came, quite clearly, the sound of gunfire.

'Pistols and musket,' murmured St Lawrence. 'They go to it now.'

'Aye. Perhaps his lordship has at last discovered his only course by himself. Come.' John grabbed the Irishman by the arm and pulled him to the stair. 'Let us set about what further preparations we may.'

Yet there was little they could do. Few men, fewer weapons. Only in making a full reckoning of them did he see just how poor the preparations for the rebellion had been. What Essex had needed was a quartermaster and taskmaster, both. And the one man who may have been able to fulfil both those functions had been a prisoner in the Tower.

It was while walking the house a little later, hoping that he might stumble upon a cache of guns and powder that had been forethought – for the time for mere swords and bucklers had passed – that he heard someone singing along an upstairs corridor. It was a popular lament of Dekker's 'The plague full swift goes by'. There was something familiar to the voice. He followed it, disbelieving, and came to a door before which sat a half-dozen men with pikes. 'Who's here?' he asked.

'P-p-prisoners, my lord,' stuttered a corporal. 'And l-l-ladies too.'

'Ladies?' John exclaimed, then gestured. 'Open this door.'

The uneasy soldier hastened to obey. The door swung wide – to reveal a bizarre scene even for a day of them.

Seated in a semicircle of chairs, as if at a reception, were the party of emissaries dispatched by the Privy Council that morning. In the middle, as guest of honour no doubt, sat Egerton, the Lord Keeper. Either side of him were the two ladies of the house, the earl's wife, Lady Essex, and his sister, Lady Rich. All rose as John came in and halted, open-mouthed. 'What news, sir, what news?' cried Lady Essex.

But John could not answer for the moment, stunned as he was. For standing now behind those he'd just stood before was Ned. John had seen him act, but not heard him sing, so had not recognised the voice. Even in his surprise he realised that his son possessed a good tone which he himself did not.

Everyone emulated Lady Essex, shouting questions and, in Egerton's case, issuing commands. 'We demand our immediate freedom, sirrah!' he said. 'What means this rude treatment of her majesty's emissary?'

'Your pardon, my lord,' John said, coming forward, 'but until the earl commands it, I cannot release you.' He raised his hand against the uproar that came. 'I can tell you this. He is returning here forthwith and he will satisfy you all.'

From the corridor came the sound of boots. John turned to the door. Yet it was not their hoped-for leader who came through it but Sir Ferdinando Gorges, one of those new knights who hovered on the fringes of the Essex inner circle like a jackal seeking scraps. His thick curly hair was plastered on to his brow, his clothes in disarray. He had obviously been running hard.

'Your pardon, ladies, for the intrusion,' he blurted, heaving breaths, sketching a half-bow before turning to the men there. 'My lords, I have orders from the earl to escort you back to the palace.' Over the gasps that came at this, the knight stepped forward and actually seized the Lord Keeper by the arm. 'But we must be swift!'

Egerton shook the grip off. 'We will proceed as befits our station,' he replied coolly, and stalked slowly from the room, his party and Gorges following. There was something strange about such a sudden command, and John was about to step forward to question it when his own arm was taken.

'Father,' said Ned.

He gripped his son in turn and, with a shadow of a bow to the ladies, pulled him out the door. When it was firmly closed behind them, he shook the boy. 'What make you here? Did I not tell you to remain in the garden? And if you had to leave, why in the devil's name did you not just go?'

'I tried to, Father,' Ned replied. 'I was attempting the side gate when that red-haired Welshman recognised me from the playhouse and dragged me here to entertain the nobles.' He bit at his lip. ''Twas the strangest performance I ever gave. I could not remember half the words . . . of anything.'

John saw his son's shaking. His anger passed. He should not have caught his boy up in this. 'Come with me. Perhaps I can command you out of here.'

They were just approaching the side wicket when Gelli Meyrick ran past him. 'He comes! He returns to us! Open the gate.'

A crowd immediately prevented any exit – and then gave back before three men and their burden – a perspiring, prostrate Earl of Essex. 'Sanctuary,' he murmured as if in a fever and within the bounds of the abbey. 'Oh, sanctuary.'

The crowd surged into the garden. John tried to push Ned through to the gate . . . but it was slammed and locked before he reached it. He turned back to see Essex being laid onto the ground, leaning against a servant . His clothes were all askew, the black velvet suit besmirched, the tangerine scarf vanished. Around him, equally ditch-dragged, were the party who'd set out with such a flourish –

Southampton, Rutland, Sandys. All shivered, yet none so much as Mounteagle, whose clothes were soaking. Someone threw a blanket around him and he sank to the cold earth with a moan.

'My lord! My lord!' implored Gelli Meyrick. 'What's the matter?'

'Betrayal!' moaned Essex. 'The City did not rise for me. Sheriff Smyth cozened me. There were no thousand pikemen. There were no men at all.' He threw out a hand. 'Something warming, for mercy's sake!' He was handed a flagon, and between great gulps of sack he blurted out the story. 'We waited an age, drinking Smyth's execrable ale. But no one came, no messengers from the Mayor, no militia. We decided to return – but found Lud Gate chained against us and a force of pikemen holding it.'

He swigged, choked, a huge burst of wet coughing coming. Southampton took up the tale. 'We fought, of course. Sir Christopher Blount charged and we were preparing to follow him when . . . when . . .' he sobbed, 'when that gallant knight was gored in the face and fell senseless to the cobbles. What could we do . . . but take to the river?'

'And Sir Christopher?' someone called.

Southampton looked up, tears spilling. 'We had to leave him!' Over the gasps that came, the man's voice rose to a whine. 'We had no choice! We had to get back here. We had to reach . . . sanctuary.'

John turned away in disgust. He did not need to have been there to know what had happened. A milling of half-drunk, full-panicked lords abandoning the knight – the Earl of Essex's stepfather, God's wounds! – and heading pell-mell for the river, and a gate less guarded, to steal some boats, with Mounteagle in the confusion falling in. Of all the follies I have witnessed in his company, John thought, this exceeds anything.

There was further clamouring at the gate. It was opened and more fleers stumbled in – one of whom was Sir Samuel D'Esparr. 'God a mercy,' he cried when Ned went to him. 'What make you here, boy? What make I?' His voice rose to a wail and he sank slowly to the ground. 'We are all doomed! Disaster has befallen the earl and his cause!'

'No talk like that, you traitorous dog!' snarled a lean, much-scarred man. 'I'll gut you if you cry such treason.'

He had a dagger half drawn and was moving towards the fallen knight. John stepped between them. 'Easy, friend,' he murmured low, his palm on the other man's wrist. 'There's plenty out there to fight and your chance is coming soon.'

With another snarl the man sheathed, turned away, while John bent low over Sir Samuel. 'And you, man, keep your plaints to yourself.'

The knight subsided into private moans. Not so Captain St Lawrence. 'They are coming, begod,' he screamed, and as his shout faded, all there heard drums, fifes and the striking of metal-shod pikestaffs on the cobbles.

Cecil and his council, having failed to act before, were clearly acting now.

'To the walls!' Lord Sandys cried. 'And you!' He pointed to St Lawrence. 'No man else to come in unless you know them personally. And no man to leave, no matter how piteous their plea. We must secure the house! With me!'

He ran off, most of the bedraggled crew rushing for the front of the house and the courtyard. Sir Samuel lurched up and followed. But John stepped the other way, grabbing Ned by the arm, shoving him towards the gate where a few last stragglers were squeezing through despite the Irishman's efforts to push it shut. By the time he was five paces away, it was slammed, locked and bolted. Cursing, he looked down – and realised that the man lying still upon the ground was Robert Devereux. He was near enough to see the earl grab Meyrick by the collar, hear him hiss, 'My papers, Gelli. I must burn my papers.' His gaze left his steward's, found John. 'Lawley!' he gasped. 'Ever and absolutely faithful! Help me up.'

Once on his feet, some life returned to him. 'With me,' he cried, and with Gelli beside him, he ran for the house.

Ned, caught up in the event, looked to follow. But John held him back. 'Wait, lad,' he whispered, turning again to the gate. But there was no hope of getting out there now, not with soldiers standing before it, and St Lawrence with two pistols drawn. The garden ran a little further back towards the river, about thirty paces worth, and they walked halfway down it. But in organising the defence – and seeking a possible last avenue of retreat as any experienced soldier must – John had noted that the walls were twice as tall as a tall man, smooth and nigh impossible to scale; while even if Ned managed to do it, unnoticed, he would drop the other side into the company of the desperate men recently shut out or, just as likely, become a prisoner of the enemy's advance guard. A father could not send his son into either danger alone; and he could not go with him. For all his fury at the debacle Essex had once more engineered, he would not desert him, even now.

They halted in the last of the light spilling from the torches further up the garden. 'What are we to do, Father?' Ned asked. He was making an effort to keep his voice calm. Only the note of it, higher than he had lately used, gave him away.

John took his arm. 'I do not know . . . yet. War throws up chances, boy. We must be ready to act on one.'

They were about to go he knew not where when they heard the hiss from behind them. It was low enough not to carry to the gate but reached the two of them. 'Psssss!'

'What make you there, Lawley?'

He froze. St Lawrence was staring at him from twenty paces away. 'Checking the walls, Captain,' he replied, making sure Ned did not turn either. 'All seems secure here.'

'Good. Then . . .' A burst of hammering upon the gate interrupted, turned the Irishman back to the grille in it. 'Slowly,' John whispered, and he and Ned stepped back, one measured pace after another, until the shadows at the garden's end swallowed them quite. Then they moved more quickly until they could put fingers to stone.

'At last,' came the soft voice.

They recognised it. Actually, they had both recognised it from the hiss. The way one does if one is a son. Or a lover.

'Tess.'

XXXVI

Escape

Now he was looking hard, he could see the uneven darker shadow atop the wall. 'Tess!' he called again, softly. 'By my holidame! What make you there?'

'I have been waiting here these two hours hoping you would come. Now help me down, will you?'

'How did you get up there?' John knew the walls were as high the other side.

'There are fruit trees in the gardens here. I found an orchard ladder.'

John's heart beat a little quicker. 'Can you contrive to lift it, love, and pass it over this side?'

'I cannot.' A grunt of annoyance came. ''Twas my plan, but I kicked the cursed thing in climbing on to the wall. It fell and lies in a ditch below. Can you not help me? I am frozen here.'

Muttering a curse, John peered into the deeper darkness at the wall's base. But it was Ned who toed it. 'What of this?' he asked.

John joined him. In the corner, a gardener must have piled grass cuttings from the bowling lawn and leaves from the several elms. They were soggy after the winter's deluges but were waist height and softer than the ground. 'Edge along, Tess, to this corner. There's a shorter drop here.'

They heard her mutter, then her slide. Soon she was above. 'Try to lower yourself from your hands,' John called, 'then stretch till you . . .'

She did not wait, nor listen. She was above and then she was down, landing on her feet, tipping straight off the rakings, falling into his arms. He caught, held. 'Are you well?' he gasped, clenching her tight, her face an inch from his.

She swayed, steadied, stood. 'Aye, I think I . . . I am.' She left his embrace, stepped off the green pile. 'I am stiff, it is certain. Cold, but' – she shivered – 'hale for all that.'

John drew back to look at her. The shock came that the action had delayed. 'Why have you come, Tess?' he asked, incredulous.

'Why? You dolt! I have come for my son.' She grasped Ned to her, hugging him hard. 'Are you well? You are not hurt?'

'No, Mother, I am fine. My father has kept me safe.'

'Your father . . .' She turned back to John. 'What did you mean, sir, by bringing him here? Here, of all places? Have you lost the few wits you still retained?'

John flinched. 'I did not think . . .'

'Nay, that's certain. The one house in London where—'

A loud sound interrupted her. The bark of shot, followed by a shattering of glass. Someone screamed. All looked to it, then John laid a hand upon her arm. 'Tess, I am at fault, I know. I will answer for it hereafter in any way you see fit. For now, though, all I can do is try to keep you both safe.'

The shot had quieted her. 'Can we not climb back up?' she said.

He shook his head. 'If we could, Ned would have been over the wall ere now. The only way out is through the doors, and it is commanded that no man may leave by them.'

She looked back at him sharply. 'Did you say "no . . . *man*"?'

Her emphasis hung between them. John spoke to it. 'Aye, I suppose we could persuade yon Irishman to let you out. He might do it as a favour to me. But your son he will not allow.'

She turned her stare on Ned. 'Well then,' she whispered, 'how about my daughter?'

'Daughter?'

'Aye.' The slightest smile came. 'Perhaps some use can come of all your playing.'

Ned saw it – and blushed. 'Nay, Mother, I cannot.'

'Aye, son, you can and will.' She turned. 'Tell him.'

'I cannot see the way of it, but . . . Ned, if we can contrive an exit for you, then you must take it.'

'No, Father. I wish to stay here with you.'

John stepped close, put a hand on the boy's shoulder. 'Ned, if I could keep you with me, I would. But this escapade is going to end two ways – in battle or in surrender. Gaol or death are the only options here. If I am to survive either, I will need' – he glanced at Tess – 'the poor remnants of my few wits. They may suffice to keep me alive. They have done so before. Yet 'tis certain they are not enough to manage for us both.'

Ned stared at him a long moment. Then, to John's surprise, his arms came up and he pulled his father into an embrace. 'Do so then, Father. Live. And come back to us soon in Southwark.'

They parted. John looked at Tess. 'Yet I still do not see how this is to be arranged.'

'Leave that to me,' she replied, and reached to a button at her neck. He noted now that she was wearing the simple dress she wore to run the inn. As more buttons undid, he glimpsed her neck. Something more. Her fingers paused. 'Turn, sirs,' she commanded.

They obeyed. It did not take too long. She was wearing a long shift under her dress that could be buttoned high. She and Ned were near of a height now. It came to his ankles, though his boots poked out from beneath it. With his long hair loosened, her bonnet atop it, and John's cloak to cover all, he looked the part. But while the garb changed the look, his profession filled it. He was transformed.

John kept them on the dark side of the shadows until the mob around the postern thinned. Men were being vetted, some allowed in, none out. Those who were admitted were dispatched about the grounds. After a while, there was a lull. No hammering upon the door. Yet from beyond it other sounds came. Bugles called to muster. Drums beat. St Lawrence stood there, gazing towards the house, briefly alone save for his sentinel atop the wall.

It was the moment. 'Gently now,' said John, and the three advanced.

They were nearly by him before he heard their approach. He started. 'Lawley,' he said. 'What's this?'

'My wife and daughter, Captain.' The Irishman recovered enough to bow, and both Tess and Ned curtseyed. 'Maidservants in the house. Can you let them pass?'

'Alas, I cannot. You know my charge: no one to leave.'

'I heard the command: no *man* may do so. And I do not seek it.'

As St Lawrence made to speak again – to deny, John could see it in his eyes – he stepped closer, took the man by the elbow, led him slightly apart. 'You know that if it comes to a fight, we have but small chance. I am willing to die for my lord, as I know you are. But women are always threatened with a worse fate.' He let the words sink in. 'If I am to fight, let me not do so with half my care behind me.'

St Lawrence stared at him for a few seconds, then nodded. He looked up to the guard on the wall. 'How is it, Drummond?'

'Same, Captain.' The man peered left and right. 'They are not yet in the river gardens, only upon the Strand. No one near.'

'Good, then.' The Irishman stepped to the gate, shot the bolts, opened it halfway. 'Swiftly now.'

John put his arms around both Tess and Ned, guided them through the entranceway. On the other side, another house's wall and a narrow lane between.

'Thomas waits on the water with a borrowed skiff,' Tess said. 'We'll take that way.'

''Tis safest. Go.' John clapped Ned's shoulder. 'Look after your mother, boy.'

'I will, Father.'

Then Tess pressed close, startling him. 'Come with us, John. I can run as fast as Ned in this skirt. There's no one to stop us.'

She was right. St Lawrence had stepped back to give them the moment. It was so tempting. And yet . . . 'I cannot, sweetheart,' he said softly. 'While my lord lives, I owe him my service.'

'Robert Devereux? After all he has done to you? After all you have already suffered for him?' She stamped her foot. 'Out upon him, I say. He does not deserve such loyalty.'

John shrugged. 'Perhaps. But I made a vow: to stay this one last assay at his side. To see his triumph or witness his fall. I cannot break it.' He pushed her gently away. 'Now go.'

Still she did not obey. 'Have you seen Samuel?' she asked.

'Aye. He is within.' He sighed. 'And I will see him safe if it is in my power.'

The look she fixed him with was one he knew well. 'Really, sir,' she said, one eyebrow raised. 'Loyalty can be taken too far. Sir Samuel can fend for himself as well as any man.'

And with that, she turned sharply and made for the river.

He watched them till the darkness took them. Few torches moved in the gardens and orchards there. The Queen's forces would yet be mustering and, with God's good grace, they would make their waiting boat safely.

He stepped back inside. The bolts were shot immediately. 'A fine-looking wife you have there, Master Lawley,' St Lawrence said, turning back from his task. 'And a pretty daughter. Strange how you never mentioned her before. The twin of your boy, is she?'

The sparkle in the Irishman's eye was more than reflected torchlight. John smiled. 'I thank you, sir,' he replied.

St Lawrence shrugged – then both men started as a scattering of gunfire came from the direction of the courtyard. 'Each man to his duty, then,' the captain said.

'Aye.' John raised two fingers to his brow and flicked a salute. 'I will see you in the breach, sir.'

'You will.'

Shaking his head, John left. The sounds of a fight were growing ahead of him, yet he did not untie his buckler, nor draw his sword. He would kill no Englishmen this day unless he could not help it. All he could do was strive to give his lordship the time he needed to burn all incrimination – though he suspected it would do him little good when evidence of treason could be picked up on every corner between Charing Cross and St Paul's pulpit. But even as he went to check on gates and flimsy barricades, John knew he was rendering the earl a last service; for after today, if tragedy played out its regular course, there would be no earl to serve.

XXXVII

Despair and Die

John went first to seek his lord. He was not hard to find.

No skulking in a cellar or kneeling in a chapel now for Robert Devereux. He was in the dining hall, raging – and burning. Papers were scattered round him, in sheaves, leaning towers, chests. Men were bringing more all the time, threading through the clutch of women – his wife, his sister, their maidservants – and the dejected nobles who'd sallied with him. The room was filled with weeping, imploring, arguing, the maniacal earl ignoring all, flinging handfuls of paper and whole ledgers into the fireplace. Flames rose high and swiftly. 'Come, William!' Essex yelled, pausing to drag Mounteagle forward, the nobleman who'd been dunked in the Thames as they fled. Flinging him down, he laughed. 'Dry yourself before my hearth, why don't you?'

John stepped a little into the room, watching as both the earl and the fire roared. If only he'd been in this mood this morning – and used it to storm the palace, John thought.

The flames grew higher, the room uncomfortably hot. Then, underneath the crackling of paper, there came another, and one of the stained-glass windows exploded inwards.

The screams redoubled. Essex paused, papers held on high. 'Guns!' he cried. He looked above the heads of the women surrounding him. 'Master Lawley,' he commanded, 'defend me! Gain me another hour, I pray you. We are not warm enough yet!'

'My lord.'

At the door, John looked back. Essex was scrabbling at his throat, as if he was choking, which was possible considering all the smoke.

But then he pulled a string from around his neck, a velvet purse at its end. 'And we consign the King of Scotland to the flames,' he cried, flinging the purse into the hearth.

Shaking his head, John left the house and made for the courtyard.

On the instant, he could see that any delay would be far short of an hour. Yet the flimsy wagon drawn across the gates could be ballasted with books – Essex House might not possess much gunpowder, but it had an abundance of leather-bound volumes that could resist a bullet better than any fascine.

'You men,' he called to the swordsmen loitering near, 'with me.'

He broke one of the library's large windows on the side of the building, organised a line of men to run from it to the gates, passed books out. They filled the wagon and it occupied men who otherwise would just stand about and fear. But when it was done, he knew it would make little difference. From his vantage on the terrace he could see over the relatively low walls of the courtyard into the Strand beyond. It swam with troops. Various flags flew – he recognised the ensigns of Lord Burghley, the pygmy's elder brother; of the earls of Cumberland and Nottingham, the latter also being Lord Admiral of the Realm. There were others. The court had mustered its factions, far outweighing the puny ones within the walls.

He had a thought: to get the earl to boat and thence downriver to Gravesend and a ship bound for the Continent. But craning from the sentinel's perch at the side gate, he saw the enemy had now plugged the gap that had, he hoped, allowed Tess and Ned through. Flame light now glimmered on spear tip and helm down each of the side paths and throughout the gardens that filled the space between wall and water. A sudden sally of determined men might clear them away, but then what? John could think of no wherryman, howsoever desperate for a fare, who would come to the stairs to pick up the Earl of Essex this day. And what of the rest of them if one did? He did not desire another February swim. No. John shook his head. Cecil and his party had their rabbit trapped in his hole. Now they were going to dig him out.

The voice came from so near his ankle it made him start. 'Any hope there, Lawley?'

John looked down . . . at the quivering face of Sir Samuel

D'Esparr. 'None,' he said, stepping down, and continued, as bluntly, 'Prepare yourself for what's to come.'

He set off up the path, the knight at his elbow. 'But what is that to be, sir?'

He glanced at the man. With his watery eyes and his jowls aquiver, Despair looked as he must have done when the Irish set about him with farm implements. Piteous. But John had no time for pity. 'It may come to a fight. There's lords in the house who declare they would rather die sword in hand today than on a scaffold a week hence. And we, their servants, will be expected to die with them.'

'A fight?' The large lower lip began to tremble. 'You know, sir, it is not truly my . . . my . . .' He swallowed. 'What else may come?'

'Surrender, though I doubt we'll get terms. The lords will have relatives on the other side who may help them 'scape the axe.'

'And their ser . . . servants?'

'Newgate to start, and then . . .' John shrugged. 'Who knows?'

Their walk had taken them back to the main courtyard. John mounted the terrace, till he could see again over the walls to the forces there, which, even in the short time, had close to doubled. Lords were mustering to display their loyalty and a dozen new banners flew. 'Prison?' Sir Samuel's eyes overflowed now. 'I cannot go to prison. I could not bear it.'

'S'blood, man,' John hissed, 'master yourself, pray.'

But the knight's watery gaze and his attention were now fixed over the walls, to the ranks of the enemy. And hope suddenly chased despair from his eyes. 'Over there!' he gasped, clutching at John's sleeve. 'The ensign of Lord Compton.'

'What of it?' said John, trying to shake the man off.

Like a terrier, he held, even pulled John close. 'Get me to him, Lawley,' he whispered. 'I'll see you well rewarded for it. He is my wife's cousin. He is bound to help us.'

'Your . . . wife's cousin?'

It took a moment for Sir Samuel to realise what he'd said. He released the sleeve on the instant. 'She . . . she is an invalid, sir. Uh, immured in the country . . . She . . .'

He broke off, mainly because John had stepped close and seized him by the throat. 'You already have a wife? And yet you were going to marry my Tess?'

He loosed his grip just enough for words to dribble out. 'I was going to say . . . wife at death's door . . . going to tell . . . before the final . . .'

A shout came. 'Captain Lawley!' John did not instantly turn, but instead leaned closer. 'If we both outlive this day,' he said, 'I will see you in Newgate Gaol, Despair. And you and I will have a reckoning.'

'Captain Lawley!'

Throwing the man off, he turned now to see St Lawrence running towards him. 'Look out there, sir!' the Irishman shouted.

John looked, saw soldiers wheeling out a wagon laden with barrels, a timber lashed to the front of it like the bowsprit on a ship. The apparatus was dragged to a position opposite the gates of Essex House.

John vaulted the balustrade, crossed fast to the barrier he'd caused to be erected, St Lawrence at his elbow. Men with the very few muskets and pistols the defenders possessed were readying themselves. 'Captain,' he cried, 'books or no, this will not hold! Back to the terrace. Rally there.'

The Irishman did not hesitate. 'Back!' he cried, dragging the men closest to him away from the wagon. And indeed no one seemed reluctant to leave, running pell-mell backwards. John sent one lingering lad on his way, just as he heard the shouted command beyond, and the immediate sound of iron-rimmed wheels clattering over cobbles. Halfway to the terrace, he glanced back . . . and saw that one man had remained behind, indeed had scrambled over the barrier and was now tugging at the gate bolts

'Despair!' John cried, taking a step. Just the one, before the gates exploded.

The barrel-laden wagon smashed through the flimsy doors, destroying them in a moment and overturning the book-filled one beyond. Through shrieking wood and flying books, John sought . . . and saw Sir Samuel, or at least his neck and shoulders, sticking out from the wreckage. When momentum stopped, he ran forward, pulled smashed timbers aside . . .

He had seen enough dead men to know one instantly. D'Esparr's neck was twisted over at an impossible angle, and blood gouted from the chest, where a snapped spar had driven through. There was nothing to be done, and no way of extricating the corpse from the carnage. John rose, and walked back to the men mustered on the terrace.

'Did you know him?' St Lawrence jerked his head towards the destruction.

'Not really,' John muttered, and turned his attention to the enemy.

Their objective had been achieved; the gates were broken in. However, the combined smash of vehicles had erected an obstacle more impenetrable than John had managed to create. Still, soldiers were rushing to drag the wreckage back and the few shots were not dissuading them. Indeed, a far greater number of bullets were flying over the wall, striking the house, ricochets whining off stone. Glass smashed, allowing out a burst of female shrieking.

'Hold! For Christ's mercy, hold!'

Henry Wriothesley, Earl of Southampton, had regained the lower register of his voice – and mustered what courage he had left. He stood at a cabinet that gave on to the roof, waving the white flag of parley. He ducked as a tile exploded near him. Then a countering voice bellowed on the other side, echoed by many, gunfire eventually ceased and there came a near silence. Into it, the earl shouted again. 'Who is there who speaks for Cecil's party?'

John climbed on to a window ledge beside one of the shattered windows. A glance back showed him the hall – women and some men weeping, others still frantically feeding the flames with paper, though Essex himself was not one of them. Before him, over the wall, he had clear sight of a man stepping forward from the ranks. He was dressed in black armour, wore a Spanish-style helm upon his head. 'I speak for no party, sir. I am the Lord High Admiral, and I speak for the Queen. You are traitors all, and I demand your immediate surrender.'

Southampton did not have to answer – for Essex did. John saw that he had changed his suit, was no longer wearing smirched black but a dove-grey doublet with matching hose. He leaned out of the window beside his friend, his appearance cheered by the large number of spectators crammed into every space not occupied by soldiers. He acknowledged it with a wave before shouting, 'No traitors here, my lord, but only the most loyal and God-fearing of her majesty's subjects – unlike the atheists and caterpillars who have dispatched you on your mission. However' – he swept his arm grandly over the enemy forces – 'if you will but leave us some hostages here, a deputation that will include myself will happily go before my sweet Queen and make our case to her in person.'

'Hostages?' roared the Lord Admiral. 'Saucy knave! Your only choice is whether to surrender forthwith or be blown to pieces. We have cannon being brought up from the Tower e'en now for that purpose.' A man came forward and pulled at the Lord Admiral's sleeve. He argued sotto voce, shaking his head vigorously until finally he gave a brief nod. 'Listen, ye dogs. Though I am all for the fight, yet here's Sir Robert Sidney, an avowed friend of yours, who would talk of peace. He is willing to enter into the house and discuss terms. Will you admit him?'

'We will. The brother of the nation's hero and our good friend Sir Philip Sidney, whose sword I have here' – with some difficulty Essex drew his sword and waved it above his head, to more cheers – 'is more than welcome in my house.'

It sounded like an invitation to supper. Nevertheless, it was accepted, and the late poet's brother was allowed to scramble over the higgle of wrecked wagons and books that blocked the gates. He was escorted into the house and the earls descended from the roof to parley.

John sat upon the window ledge to listen through the smashed glass. Decisions were to be taken that would concern him. So he heard everything that was not conducted in whispers. There were many oaths, much vowing, as he suspected, to die fighting today rather than be butchered in a fortnight. Sir Robert Sidney left, conferred, returned.

St Lawrence joined him on the window ledge. He had somehow managed to scrounge a half-loaf of stale maslin and a flagon of sourish wine. John happily shared both with him and told him the news.

'It's surrender, then?' the Irishman enquired, drawing his cloak tighter around himself.

'Certain. The lords to be taken to some better-appointed prison, the soldiers to . . .' John shrugged.

'To the Clink, the Fleet . . . or worse, to Newgate.' The captain shuddered. 'Still, I doubt we'll remain there long. It'll be "whoops" and the Tyburn jig within the week, I warrant.'

'Perhaps not. The law comes hardest on those who lead not those who follow. It may cost you a hefty fine, though. Have you the money to pay it?'

The Irishman had half a grin. 'Do you think I'd be here on this fool's escapade if I did? Sure, all the boys from across the sea are here because it's the earl's larder or starvation.'

'Well, we can but await the outcome. Though I would not be him for all his red hair.' John was pointing at Gelli Meyrick, who had been in the negotiations and was just now accompanying Sir Robert Sidney back through the smashed gates

They watched the two men reach the huddle of officers stamping feet against the cold across the road. Words were spoken . . . and Gelli Meyrick returned alone. 'This is it then,' said John, descending from the ledge, stretching his cramped limbs. 'Will the earls be blown to the sky and us with them? Or is it prison for us all?'

They did not have to wait long for the answer. There was a renewed burst of women's wailing from beyond the shattered stained glass, followed by the sound of footsteps along the corridor. Then the lords emerged in much the same order they had that morning, if with distinctly less vigour. They did not form a gauntlet down which their leader marched. They formed a huddle, and first Southampton, then Essex strode into the middle of it. John heard a moment of murmured prayer, ending when Essex stepped from the group, stood at the head of the stair. He gazed at the ragged men in the courtyard for a moment and then, in a loud, clear voice, called out, 'Gentlemen of England, it is over. We have struggled gloriously but the odds were too great. Follow me, lay down your swords at the victors' feet. Trust in the Almighty and her majesty to look forgivingly upon us all. God save the Queen!'

With this last cry he descended the stairs. St Lawrence came to stand beside John, and together they watched as the noblemen left through the gates that had been immediately cleared for the purpose; then, as the remnants of Essex's pitiful army mustered for the last time, they joined them. The wreckage might have been swept aside, but no one had bothered to extricate the body trapped in it.

By the time they passed under the arch, the head of the straggling column had reached the conquering nobility. They halted, and by the dancing light of torches saw their leaders kneel before the Lord Admiral and offer him their swords. Essex was the first to pass his over – Sir Philip Sidney's sword, given on a field of honour all those years before from the dying warrior-poet's own hand. Now it was passed to that poet's brother. Sir Robert took it, kissed it, sheathed it.

The ragged band crossed the street. The nobility were done with their equals, and soldiers stood in their place to take soldiers' swords. John drew his, laid it down, stepped back, raised his hands. All of them were shackled around the wrist. Through the mob, he managed to get a last glimpse of Essex being shepherded into a carriage. A young preacher was at his side and both men were praying fervently. The roaring was over. His noble lordship would now be as docile as any lamb. There were no chains for him – though John suspected it was less his noble blood than this: at last, and truly, Robert Devereux had no place left to go.

A voice called him back to his own situation. An officer was at the head of the column. There was something about the voice John recognised – and when the man turned back to command them on, he saw his face.

It was the same officer who'd dragged him from Sarah's bed, the same who'd done a fellow soldier a kindness and brought him weak ale to his cell in Lollards' Tower, the one he'd fought in Nonsuch House. Cecil's man, Thomas Waller.

John smiled. It made what he had yet to do a little easier.

It was not a long walk to Newgate on a normal night. Down the Strand and Fleet Street, through the Lud Gate and left along the wall a little ways. But this night was far from normal. The city was as crowded as at midday, abuzz with the doings; and men and women who had praised Essex in his progress to the City now turned out in a mob to damn those who'd marched with him. The narrow streets were a gauntlet, and citizens stepped up to the shoulders of the guards that marched beside the prisoners to curse, to spit and to throw such vegetables as a February night could provide. Apprentices spilled out to block the way and display their ale-fuelled courage – for the taverns had reopened to profit from the event.

It was slow work, and despite the officer's roaring and his men's continual plying of their pike butts, it took half an hour, by the tolling of various church bells, to get across the bridge over the Fleet and to see Lud Gate beyond. The narrow entrance was blocked by a further shouting mob. Rather than force the gate, Waller decided on a less risky course – he ordered his men into the courtyard of a Ludgate Hill tavern, the Bel Savage. Strangely, John knew it, for its large yard often housed prize fights, organised by the Maisters of Defence to display their skills and attract students. He had fought there several times.

Waller commanded it cleared of revellers, pike points accomplished this swiftly and its gates were shut. 'We will bide here for an hour,' he told his corporal, 'till the watch has dispersed these idlers. Then we will proceed.'

His men hailed the solution – and the beer flagons that were immediately produced. The prisoners were allowed to sit but were given nothing to drink. Most lay on their sides and went to sleep. John noted St Lawrence among them. They'd become separated in the surrender and chaining.

John bided, keeping his eye on the officer across the yard. There were two guards close, but when these two had quaffed a flagon each and their sight was hazier, he began to move, as if he were not moving, taking a long time to cover the short ground between him and his quarry. When at last he was behind the man's chair, he spoke. 'Good sir,' he said softly.

Waller started, surprised that someone had got so close without him seeing; surprised more when he saw it was a prisoner; surprised most when he saw who that prisoner was. 'John Lawley,' he said, as quietly as he'd been spoken to.

'I seek a private word with you, sir.'

'I entertain no private words with traitors, sir.'

'And will not when you speak with me.' John rose up, leaned close, whispered, 'For I would talk to you on the Master Secretary's business.'

'Indeed? And what might you have to do with that, except by opposing it?'

'In private, sir.' John nodded towards the inn door. 'You will gain by it. On a soldier's honour.'

The man looked at him, narrow-eyed. But then he grunted, rose, walked through the entrance. In the shadows just the other side he stopped. 'Well? Tell me what business you have with the Master Secretary?'

'This.' With the difficulty of a manacled man, John reached to the edge of his doublet, broke and pulled loose some threads there. Eventually he was able to slide the folded parchment out. He held it up, and reluctantly Waller took it and went to sit at a nearby table where a candle flickered. He read by its light. His eyes went briefly wide, then hooded again.

'How do I know this is not a forgery?' he asked, lifting the scroll.

'I believe you know the Master Secretary's signature, sir, and his seal,' John replied. 'And perhaps also that of the Constable of the Tower?'

'Yet your name is not on here? Perhaps you stole it?'

'I did not. It was given me for . . . certain duties I was to perform for the Secretary.'

'And did you perform them?'

John glanced out into the courtyard, at the prisoners there. 'I think you can witness that I did.'

The officer stared at him for a long moment. 'So, you are both a traitor – to everyone! – and a damned double spy.' When John said nothing, Waller sighed, shook his head, then reached to the universal key at his waist. Leaning forward, he jerked the manacles off. 'There's the back door, Lawley. Take it.'

Rubbing his wrists, John took a step, then stopped. He looked at the carte blanche in the officer's hand. 'May I have that back?'

For the first time and only time, Waller smiled. 'You truly are a rogue, Master Lawley. I shall be watching out for you.' He shoved the paper down his doublet. 'Now on your way, man, before I change my mind.'

John stepped into the night. Beyond the yard's rear gate, he stopped in the narrow alley, leaned against a wall and, despite the reek, took several deep breaths. Only when he was steady did he move.

He was free. But he was not safe, that much he knew. Safety would require something else.

ACT FIVE

If it be now 'tis not to come. If it be not to come it will be now.
If it be not now, yet it will come. The readiness is all.

Hamlet

XXXVIII

Another Scaffold

The Tower of London. Ash Wednesday 1601

'Who's there?'

''Tis I, my lord. John Lawley.'

'John Lawley?' His name was groaned like the answer to a prayer. 'Come!'

Taking a breath, he pushed open the door.

It was not much of a prison cell compared to the many he had known. No instruments of torment lay about, no straw concealed the foul. The window was not even barred, but open to admit the chill March air. It was oak-panelled, a fire burned in the grate, and the furnishings were simple – a truckle bed, blankets piled upon it, some drawers upon which rested a jug and basin. The largest object was a table. It was completely covered in papers and ledgers. Behind that sat Robert Devereux.

'John!' he cried, rising. 'Cry you mercy, I took you for the headsman, come before his hour. Enter in, pray.'

'Good my lord.'

Essex came from around the table and enveloped him in a long hug. 'Of all men else, I wanted you here. Here at . . . the end. At the just reward for all my follies.' He pulled back but did not release, stared closely. 'You do not mind?'

Here, now, he didn't. The note had found him in Shropshire, Essex's servant also bringing the news that the hue and cry was over and no one had sought him. The lowlier traitors had paid the price on Tower Hill the preceding week. The highest one faced it this day. Ash Wednesday.

He had thought to send some excuse, had words written and sealed. But he had come in their stead. He was already tainted with the Essex cause and every man knew it. And looking in the eyes that searched his so eagerly, he was glad he had. He saw in them all he ever had – the melancholic, the ecstatic, the schemer, the politician. But mostly he saw beyond the years of debauchery, illness and arrogance to the boy he'd met near two decades before with his three-hair beard, an accent raw from the borders, afire to conquer the world and totally unprepared for the price it would demand of him. Here was the boy still, unblemished. Here was the man, spoiled. And John now felt nothing but a great pity. 'My lord,' he said softly, 'I will do you what service I can, as I have ever done, faithfully to the end.'

Essex gripped him hard again. 'I know you will. And yours will be the last face I see in this world before, with His grace, I see God's in the next.' The earl gave a laugh, wiped a sleeve across his nose and eyes, moved back around the table. He gestured to the mess before him. 'You see how my last hours are passed? With matters of estate so that my widow does not starve and my son has something to inherit. Trivial matters, when my mind should be focused on the redemption of my sins and God's glory to come.'

John looked down. Amidst the debris of the old ledgers and cracked property deeds, he noted a new book by its gleaming embossed gold leaf, recognised the title. 'And yet, my lord, not all your reading is duty.'

'Eh?' John lifted it clear. Essex squinted. Smiled. 'Ah yes, it's George Silver's book. Do you remember him from Cadiz?'

'I do indeed, my lord. He fought most gallantly beside us.'

'Indeed, a singular gentleman. Though he did not venture with us last month. Wise fellow.' His eyes clouded, then cleared again. 'Do you recall how he always so defended the superiority of the true English backsword over the devilish foreign rapier?'

'I do.' John thought of the two of them taking on the Ludgate Boys on Fleet Street. ''Tis a mighty obsession with him.'

'To the extent he has written a whole treatise on it. You hold his

Paradoxes of Defence. And the intemperate fool had the bravado to dedicate it to me. To me!' Essex smiled. 'That should damn his sales!'

'On the contrary, my lord – nothing sells like notoriety.'

'Well, I am pleased my death will oblige someone.' Both men laughed, perhaps more than the jest warranted. Eventually Essex coughed, went on more softly, 'Have you read it?' John nodded. 'What think you of the system?'

Well, thought John, why not discuss swordplay? Why not? There will be axe play soon enough. 'I think, my lord . . .' He was about to give out his usual – that he had tried them all and that the system that worked best was the one that allowed a long sleep in an un-holed skin. But then he recalled his latest times with sword in hand – in Nonsuch House. In the Irish ambuscado. Indeed, in the street with Silver and Shakespeare two years before, almost to this day. So instead he replied, 'I think he is right. The backsword and the blow has the vantage over the rapier and the thrust . . . six times out of ten. Those are English odds.' He shrugged. 'Or perhaps it is that I am merely, like Silver, an old English dog myself, and cannot be about these new, foreign tricks.'

Essex nodded. 'Well, I am of an older age too then, Master Lawley. It is what has put me within these walls, perhaps. Ushers me to what I go to now. The new men have it with their . . . new ways.' He sighed, pushed fingers through his thinning hair, then bent to rest upon the desk. His hand fell atop a satchel. Straightway his eyes gleamed and he rose from his slouch clutching the bag. 'And yet, why should the new men – Cecil and his crew – have everything their own way? Why should not old virtues be rewarded? I have secured one victory in the defeat anyway. Yours.' He thrust out the satchel. 'Contained within is the reward for a lifetime of loyalty, sir. Take it.'

Inwardly, John groaned. Rewards from this man had near killed him more than once. 'My lord, with your favour, you owe me nothing.'

'But I do.' Essex pulled back the flap. There were two rolls inside, sealed in tangerine ribbons. 'Open them. This one first.'

John placed the satchel under his arm, took out the scroll indicated, unrolled it. Placing it upon the desk, he weighted it down with small books at top and bottom and bent to study. It was a coat of arms, beautifully drawn and painted on fine vellum. One side of the shield was held by Essex's own hunting hound, the other by a unicorn, the fierce beast that could never be conquered except by trickery. Above them the usual broadswords did not swing but a backsword rested on a round buckler. There were bars and blazons in many colours. John did not truly understand the heraldic devices. But he could read the Latin motto well enough. '*Absolute Fidelis*,' he said aloud.

Essex had never enquired after his education. 'Absolutely Faithful,' he explained. 'As you have ever been, John. Or should I say, Sir John Lawley. This is for you. I had the College of Heralds draw it up but yesterday. Have a care, I think the ink is still wet.'

He chuckled, and so did John. It was a touching gesture from a condemned man with much upon his mind. But it could mean little more than the gesture. John knew that Elizabeth, furious that the earl had made more knights on campaign than she had in her entire reign, was trying to disbar them all – and conspirators made the easiest of targets.

The doubt must have shown on his face. 'Nay, do not fear it, John.' Essex thrust out that square-cut beard. 'I was her vice-regent in Ireland and it was my right to honour warriors so.' He shrugged. 'Yet I admit, some may struggle to get the College of Heralds to acknowledge them . . . which is why I decided to pursue yours myself.' He grinned, pointing to the parchment. 'Do you like it?'

John looked at it again, in wonder now. If it were true . . . then what? As ever, he did not have a pot to piss in. As ever, he would be living on his wits – and they were waning with his age. War and whisky had taken a toll.

Again, it was as if Essex read the book of his mind. 'There's something else,' he said, with unconcealed delight. 'It is under your arm. What could it be?'

John took the other parchment from the satchel, broke the seal, read. 'It is a grant of lands, my lord.'

Essex clapped his hands together. 'Aye! As I told you, I have spent my last weeks trying to sort out my estate.' He gestured to the table, awash with papers. 'Mostly I was selling what was not already mortgaged, which was little. And then I came across . . . that!' He pointed. 'An unmortaged estate I'd forgotten I owned. Do you read where the land is?'

John glanced down. The writing was tight-packed but he was able to discern a name amidst the scrawl. 'It says Zennor, milord. In the county of . . .' He squinted. 'Cornwall, is it?'

'It is!' Essex was shaking with excitement now. 'In Cornwall! Your native soil!'

It was the one great misapprehension Essex had always held of him. He would try again, this last time. 'Good my lord, I was born and raised in Shropsh—'

Essex, as ever, was not listening. 'Sixty acres. I did not know I owned it and so I could not sell it or I would have. And so I can bequeath it to you.'

He beamed. John thought to speak again, to explain . . . but it would serve no purpose, neither his nor the earl's. For it also struck him with sudden force. He did have a pot to piss in now. Sixty acres, even in a distant land such as Cornwall, would fetch some silver, sure.

And yet? A thought froze him. What would he spend that silver upon? Rent a slightly better hovel in Southwark? Purchase the first bottle of whisky that would inevitably come – not next week, next month, but within the year, certain, and a succession of them to follow? It might take a while to drink that amount of coin, but it would be gone eventually. Unless . . . unless there was something else to be done with this bequest? This must be scanned, he thought, looking up. Essex was staring at him.

'My lord, I . . . thank you.'

''Tis the least you deserve, dear Johnnie. I only wish . . .'

Footsteps down the hall. 'My lord, 'tis time,' came a voice.

John started but Essex waved a hand. ''Tis only Master Ashton, come for prayer. My last moments must be spent in that.' He lowered his voice. 'Will you wait? Will you accompany me on one last journey . . . Sir John?'

He nodded. 'As far as I am able to go with you, good my lord, I will.'

John allowed the Puritan preacher to pass him in the doorway, stepped out into the corridor. Its walls were hung with tapestries, its flagstones covered in rush carpets. Beauchamp Tower was where a special few of the condemned spent their last night on earth, and it more resembled a nobleman's house than a prison. He suspected that the Queen's mother, Anne Boleyn, had passed her execution's eve there. He then realised that his own grandfather must have visited her there . . . and begun that extraordinary tale.

The drone of prayer came from within the cell. John went to sit in an arrow-slit alcove. What would he think now, his French executioner grandfather, to see his grandson sitting there holding a knighthood and the deeds to land?

What do I think?

He began to work his thoughts – but had them soon interrupted by footsteps upon the stair. He looked up to see the officer who had but lately freed him, Thomas Waller. Close behind him came the man's master.

Sir Robert Cecil stopped dead when he saw John rising from his seat. 'Ha! So there you are, you naughty knave. I wondered what had become of you. And here I find you. Not where I expected at all.'

'Master Secretary.' John assayed the minimum of bows. 'Where did you expect me?'

'I know that you were at the siege. Yet you did not make the tally at Newgate. And I know how.' He glared. 'Yet whoever you showed . . . our bargain too did not retrieve it, as the paper instructed. I should never have given you such a liberty. It was a moment of weakness. I want it back.' He stepped closer, arm outstretched. 'Give it me.'

A loud shout of 'Hallelujah!' from the cell pulled Cecil's gaze away. For the briefest of seconds John was able to glance at Thomas Waller. The officer's face was as immobile as ever. Which made the small wink he gave all the more pronounced.

When Cecil turned back, John spoke. 'Sir Robert,' he said, as softly as before, 'I no longer have it.' He raised his voice just slightly as the other man stirred. 'Do not fear. It is sealed and lodged somewhere safe, guarded by this instruction: that it cannot be accessed even by me. By no one . . . unless, perchance, a certain event were to come to pass.'

'What event?' snapped Cecil.

'Oh, say' – John shrugged – 'that I was to be found, like Kit Marlowe, in a Deptford tavern with a dagger in my head.'

John could see the fury in the man's eyes, the words he would speak troubling his lips. Yet he mastered himself, breathed deep. 'Do you think such a device will protect you for long? I could deny it as a fraud. And who would be believed? The Queen's first minister . . . or a player, a noted brawler and a drunkard?'

John swallowed. Anger would not help him. Something else might. He reached into his satchel. 'They might, though, believe a knight of the realm.'

Cecil glanced at the scroll John held up. 'Do you think your knighthood will hold, sirrah? Oh yes, I know of it. Nothing the earl does within these walls goes unnoted. Indeed he boasted of his efforts with the College of Heralds on your behalf at our last interview. We have had several.' His lips curled into a grin. 'I should tell you that her majesty is even now at her palace of Greenwich, quill poised over the list of Essex's knights banneret, striking them off one by one. It gives her much delight, it is said.' He nodded. 'So you should consider the fate of one such: *Sir* Gelli Meyrick, my lord of Essex's steward. He believed the least *his* knighthood would obtain for him was the noble's courtesy of an axe on Tower Green. But it was stripped from him just before his bowels were torn from his body at Tyburn. The fate of all *ig*noble traitors.'

Though his sword and buckler had been taken from him at the Beauchamp's entrance, John stood straight now and placed his hands on his hips where his weapons would be. 'Is that what you threaten me with, sir?'

'I? Threaten?' The smirk widened. 'I do not need to threaten, sirrah. I need simply to remind. You are my creature still. Your fate in my hands. Note that, *Master* Lawley.' He leaned closer, spoke softer. 'For I *will* call on you one day. You may be certain of that.' He turned again towards the cell. 'And now to say a last prayer with the condemned. Forgiveness will always be exchanged' – he glanced at John once more as he swept past – 'between noblemen.'

Waller followed, his face as stony as ever. From the cell came murmured greetings, then louder prayer. John did not sit again. He just stared into the wall and considered the Master Secretary's words. Considered them well.

He was not left to his thoughts for long. Prayers ended, the cell door reopened and Cecil passed him and descended the stairs without looking at him again. Then there were more boots, ascending. Within the cell they must have heard them too, for the two voices rose from murmur to ecstatic appeal.

'Forgive me, O God, these my transgressions. Wash my sins away. Receive me into thy loving bosom. Amen. Amen. Amen.'

Six soldiers rounded the corner, kept coming. The captain of the guard halted before John. 'You are my lord of Essex's man?' he asked.

He had no desire to deny him now. 'I am.'

'And you are to accompany him to the scaffold?'

John nodded. 'So far, I pray, and no further.'

The guard nodded. 'So do we all pray. Will you fetch him out?'

'I will.'

As John entered the cell, amens rang out again. Essex was kneeling, hands clasped before him, eyes fast shut. Yet they shot open at John's tread and he could see in them just one moment of terror before a calm returned. ''Tis time?'

'It is.'

Essex rose, swayed, reached to the vicar at his side to steady himself. He leaned a moment, breathing deep, then looked at John. ''Tis not that I fear, you understand. All this praying' – he gave a little chuckle – 'is hard upon the knees.' The earl took another deep breath, then released his grip. 'Let us to it then,' he said, and crossed to the door. In the corridor the guard had formed and they took the earl into their midst. They descended, and as they exited below, on the captain's nod, a guard there returned to John his backsword and buckler.

It was not a long journey. Tower Green was a patch of snowy grass disturbed by the footsteps of the witnesses who had gone before. They swiftly reached the scaffold, upon which the masked executioner stood, leaning on his giant axe.

John followed the earl and his divine, the latter in continuous prayer, the former silent. He was focused not on the next world now, but on the moments that would precede his entry into it. A light snow was falling, melting as it landed, making the stairs they climbed slick; but Essex trod carefully, did not slip. The platform achieved, he peered down upon the small crowd, all men, each with bonnets pulled down and scarves raised high against the cold. They looked anonymous, like participants in a masque, only their eyes showing. They could have been enemies or friends – both, probably. John noted Cecil only because of the tall Waller beside him.

Whoever they were, Essex forgave them all and any that he had ever affronted. He blamed no one save himself – for his folly, his arrogance, his delusions. He was ever prone to self-chastisement, but here he made a simple tally, a last recounting of his sins. He was the foremost defender of the Church in England. He expected no forgiveness upon the scaffold, but he prayed for it in the kingdom to come.

'And this last I say to you: do nothing in this life save loyally serve her majesty. She was ever good to me and I her most ungrateful servant. May my foolish death serve her as a warning to other fools.' He stood straighter and cried out into the snow, falling heavier now, 'God save the Queen!'

There was a murmured response. Essex stared at the faceless crowd for a moment longer, then turned back. 'My cloak,' he said softly.

John reached to unclasp it, then untied the tangerine scarf, held that up. 'For your eyes, my lord?'

Essex took it, gazed at it a moment, then shook his head. 'Nay. I will look at God's world one last time. It will make a good contrast to His paradise that I am soon to see.' Yet he did not release the scarf, holding John there. 'There is one last favour I would ask of you. One that you may not be able to grant.'

'Ask it, my lord, and if it is in my power, I will do it.'

The earl pulled something from his doublet. When he held it out, John saw that it was a handkerchief. Indeed, it was *the* handkerchief that the Queen had given him to deliver to the earl in Ireland with her message of love. He had last seen it tucked into the earl's boot cuff when he burst into her bedroom at Nonsuch. 'If you ever get a chance, return this to her. Tell her . . .' He gazed above John, snow on his eyelashes. 'Nay,' he continued, 'tell her nothing. Just give it to her.'

He pressed it to his mouth, closed his eyes, opened them, passed it over. John nodded, made to step back towards the stair. But the earl reached again, caught the pommel of his backsword, drew it an inch, held him there by it. 'Shall we draw this good English steel, Sir John, and fight our way out of here?' He glanced at the masked crowd. 'Look at them down there with their bird-spit rapiers. Even Cecil

371

sports one. Could not a pair of bold Englishmen cut them all down, like we did our enemies at Cadiz? We two, against a hundred?'

John smiled. 'I am game if you are, good my lord.'

Essex smiled too. 'Aye, you always were.' The smile passed. 'Would that I had died that day upon such a cause,' he murmured. He shoved the sword back in, but kept his hand upon the pommel. 'Farewell then, Johnnie,' he said.

'Farewell, young Rob,' John replied.

A nod, a last smile and the earl turned away. John descended the scaffold, moved to its front, looked up in time to meet Essex's gaze a last time. Then Robert Devereux turned. 'About your work, sir,' he said briskly and, laying his head upon the block, he closed his eyes with a sigh.

The great axe fell – three times, such was the man's ineptitude. But when at last it was off, held aloft to the guttural cry of 'Behold the head of a traitor,' unlike the others there who gave back before the bright spray from the trunk, John stepped forward. Blood splattered him, his cloak, his hair and face. He was not concerned about that – only in seeing that the handkerchief was fully soaked in it. When it was, he turned and made for a postern he knew from his time there, the nearest one to St Katharine's Dock.

The wherry was tied up where he had left it. The wherryman rose when John approached. 'All done?' St Lawrence asked softly.

'All done.'

'May God have mercy on his soul,' said the captain, raising his eyes skywards.

'Amen,' said John. Shakespeare had lent him the money required to free the Irishman from Newgate. His traitor's fine was heavy, though, and he had decided on the swiftest way to pay it off – he would use his strength and size and ply the oar. Will had lent him the money for that too.

'Fancy a row?' John asked.

''Tis my trade now.' St Lawrence hefted his oars. 'Back to South-wark? We'll be against the tide, but . . .' He shrugged.

'Nay. With the tide.' John pointed downriver. 'Let's to Green-wich.'

XXXIX

Last Audience

It was an hour's pull to their destination, even with the tide and two men heaving lustily – for John took his turn at the oars, to let St Lawrence breathe; and to distract his own mind with exercise. When not rowing, he stared at the water, and tried not to think about what lay ahead.

Greenwich was one palace unknown to him – it contained no prison, after all. He could barely see the building for the falling snow, was only aware of a certain immensity of fluted gables and shining glass, standing in the midst of snowy fields and box-hedged gardens. The dock was just below these, the royal barge tied there. When the wherry nudged in just behind it, John climbed out, rope in hand to secure it. He had scarce straightened from that when he was surrounded by armed men.

'Your business?'

The officer who spoke had a cloak covered in snow and a hand upon his dagger. Three men moved behind him with pikes, their points levelled. Another held his over the boat.

John motioned for St Lawrence to remain seated. 'A message for her majesty, sir.'

'From whom?'

John did not hesitate. 'From Robert, Earl of Essex.'

There was a sharp inhalation, the pike points wavered. There was not a man in the realm who did not know what was happening, had happened, that morning. The officer put out his hand. 'Then deliver it to me and be on your way. We do not like men we do not know anywhere near the palace.'

'The message is not written. I must see the Queen in person.'

'She sees no one. Hasn't' – John saw concern on the man's face, swiftly mastered – 'for some time now.'

'She may see me. If you give her this.'

Reaching into the purse at his waist, he drew out the ring. It was the one given to him by the earl as he rode towards the City. It had authorised John to organise the defence at Essex House. The Queen, in a fonder time, had given it to her sweet Robin.

The officer regarded it for a long moment, as if he would not accept it. Then he did so with a snatch and a brisk 'Wait here'.

They waited. The pikes remained level with John's waist. He peered through the snow, coming in flurries that hid and then revealed the palace. Cecil had indicated a year before that the Queen was not always in her right mind. Perhaps she would not recognise the ring. Perhaps she would, and shun its bearer as the messenger of death.

A footfall squeaked on the new snow. He looked up. The officer returned and John did not breathe. 'You are to come with me,' he said, turning about.

He was hedged in, the officer before, two pikemen tight either side, two left behind to watch the Irishman. He was taken to the kitchen door and, just inside, had a few moments to enjoy the warmth and the scent of cooking food – when had he last eaten? – while his sword and buckler were once more taken from him, and hands roamed his body, seeking . . . finding the knife as ever in its sheath between his shoulder blades. That too was taken, with a small grunt of surprise. Then, when every inch had been squeezed and patted, his hat and cloak were placed aside. A different officer, who had stood by during the search, now beckoned him to follow. Two new soldiers moved each side of him. Together the phalanx walked down corridors and, finally, up a long flight of stairs, halting before tall oaken doors. A knock produced a barely audible reply. The officer nodded at the two guards. Each now tightly gripped one of John's arms. Without another word, the doors were pushed open, and he was shoved in.

The way, up corridor and stair, had been gloomy, an occasional gated lantern illuminating small parts of it. Yet that journey had been brightly lit compared to the room he entered now. He could not see to the walls, could not tell instantly if the space was large or cramped. Large, he decided, when light drew his eye, a flickering one, at a distance, doing nothing to relieve the dark.

They had halted five paces into the room. There was a deep silence, only man's breath disturbing it. Until a voice came, weak, and as if from far away.

'Bring him closer.'

John was moved forward again, halted five paces from the light. The candle was on a small table. There was a book upon it, open; a hand, palm up, atop it. On that, the ring.

'What is your message?' Elizabeth said.

He was there – and he did not know what to say. His plan had taken him so far, to the threshold. Now he had no idea how to step over it.

He could not speak. The other did, more sharply. 'Come, sirrah. You said that you had words for me. From my Ro . . . from my lord of Essex. Were they his last words? Tell me them.'

'Majesty,' John began, 'he spoke, at the end, most courteously . . .'

'Chh!' The sound was snapped out, halting him. The hand disappeared from the light spill. There came the creak of furniture. Then nothing for a few long seconds – until the voice came again, surprising because it was so near, just behind one of the arms the guards clutched now even tighter, preventing him turning.

'John Lawley.'

It was not a question, yet he replied. 'Aye, your majesty.'

'Strange. I was thinking of you e'en now.' The Queen moved as she spoke, crossing behind him to his other held arm. 'You were with him? At the end?'

'I was.' The memory came, more shocking now, somehow, than when it had happened before him, when he'd realised what he must do and acted. The three strokes. The head off at last. The eyelids flickering open as it was lifted. 'God help me, but I was.'

He could not help the slight sob in his voice. And the other voice, so soft before, changed also. 'Out! All of you, out! Out now!' Elizabeth screamed. He was wrenched back. Then her voice lowered. 'Not you, John Lawley. You alone are to stay.'

His eyes were growing a little more accustomed to the scant light.

He could see the officer's face before him, the hesitation clear upon it. But a further screech came. 'Out, I say! Leave us!'

The guards released him, moved back. The officer gave him a look, shook his head, then followed. The door opened, admitting a wedge of light. 'Close it,' the Queen barked, and they obeyed, taking the room again to the dark.

He did not move. The Queen did, footsteps shuffling once more till there was a creak of chair. The hand came again into the light, picked up the ring, twisting it this way and that. Now John could see her outline too, the wide sleeve of a dressing gown, a nightcap. The Queen was dressed for sleep or for rising, though it was the middle of the day.

'Tell me,' she croaked.

So he did. And when he was done, sparing only a few of the details that he would, in good conscience, not dwell upon himself, she sat in silence and with her eyes closed for so long he thought she might have fallen asleep. Until she spoke. 'So his last words were for me.'

'And for God, ma'am, yes. Though his thoughts in the end I believe were only of you.'

She looked up sharply at him. 'Why do you say so?'

It was time. It was why he was there. 'Because, ma'am, of the last thing he entrusted to me. He asked that I give it to you, if I got the chance. It is my last duty to him,' he said, stepping forward, 'so I decided I would discharge it straightway.'

With that, he held out the handkerchief. And he only remembered as he did the words she had spoken in Lollards' Tower, when she had given it to him to bear to Essex in Ireland: that if the silk was returned to her stained with a traitor's blood, so much the better.

This was not what she had meant. But it was too late now to take it back, for she had reached, grasped, gasped at the dampness, taken it into the light spill. And then she cried into the cloth, wetting it further, sounds wrenched from somewhere deep, a keening. And he stood where he had stepped to give it to her, did not move, did not turn away.

It continued for a while and then it stopped, suddenly, groans and tears wrenched back, judging by the steadiness of her voice. 'The kerchief was his – and mine,' she said. 'But the blood . . . did he ask you to do that?'

'No. I . . . I chose to.'

'Why?'

'I thought . . . I thought that perhaps, you would want something . . . of him. In the end.'

Another long silence – until she spoke. 'And you were right.' He was close enough, could see her well enough now, to note the tears among the folds of her skin, the light reflected and refracted through the water in her eyes. These pierced him. 'Why did you stand by him, John Lawley? The last one, even to the end?'

'Why? I am not entirely clear why, majesty. I had known him a long time, almost from his boyhood. I had known him sometimes at his best, though more usually at his worst. And yet,' he sighed, 'in the end there was no one else. Someone—' He swallowed. 'He needed someone there to bear witness. He did not want to die alone.'

''Tis true. None of us want that.' She swallowed. 'It is hard, is it not, to love someone who treats you so badly? Yet somehow we have both contrived to do so. I expected him to send me . . . to entreat . . . to beg . . . at the end . . .' she sighed. 'And yet he did not send any word before. Only this, afterwards.' She lifted the kerchief. 'Would I have tried to forgive him still? Would I have thrown the world into disarray again?' A slight nod. 'Perhaps I would. Perhaps that is why he did not send. Because he knew I might do so much, still. Do you not think it?' When John stayed silent, she studied him for a long moment and then her expression changed. 'Yet he did send you. Even though your duty ended when he died, still you are loyal even after death. But that is not the whole reason, is it? Are you not here also . . . for yourself?'

It was there, now, the opportunity. Essex may have asked for no last boon – but his servant might. 'Majesty . . .' he began.

Yet she interrupted him. 'You know why I was thinking of you before, Master Lawley? It was not because of what your family and mine have been to each other. It was not because I sensed you there this morning, standing in that place where your grandfather and my mother stood on a day like this. It was because of your name upon a list. A long list of names that I was striking out, one after another. It lies there, upon the table.' She lifted a hand to him. 'Help me to it. Bring the light.'

He bent, lifted the candle. She fastened upon his forearm.

Supporting her, they slowly crossed the room. A table was there, curling rolls of parchment upon it, some held open by stones. She pointed at one. 'Here it is – the list of knights my viceroy made in Ireland. Scoundrels, rogues, toadies. I deprived them of the honour with pleasure. But this name' – she tapped it – 'this name I paused long over and only this morning. Your name.'

He could see it under her finger, the familiar swoops making 'Lawley'. It had no line through it. 'Majesty, I . . .'

Her raised hand halted him. 'Pass me a quill, sir. Dip it first.'

He obeyed, then held his breath as she bent to the table. She quickly drew not a line, but a circle around his name. 'There,' she said. 'There . . . Sir John.'

He let go the breath. 'Good my lady,' he said. 'I thank you. You honour me. And yet . . .'

'And yet? You are confirmed with your knighthood and still you question?'

'Forgive me, ma'am. But this I know: the Master Secretary will not be pleased. His enmity will ever pursue me. And . . .'

The quill, raised, halted him. 'And Sir Robert knows how to hate, does he not? Today yields the ultimate example of that.' She licked her cracked lips. 'Well, you may leave him to me. He thinks because my powers decline that he may rule me. But I rule here! I am not in my grave, and the King of Scotland, whom he so assiduously and brazenly courts, is not here to confirm my pygmy in his title. It is yet in my power to see his wane.' She placed her gnarled fingers upon the table, forced herself up. 'You are my knight now. No man may touch you, except by my command.'

There were sudden shouts from the corridor, a voice he recognised calling, loud and angry. 'Ah,' said Elizabeth, 'as if summoned to enter by your friend the playwright's pen, he arrives on his cue.' Cecil's voice continued to rail, and a knock now came upon the door. 'Shall we admit him to hear of your confirmed ennoblement?'

'I think, ma'am, I would prefer not to be a witness to his discomfiture. He hates me well enough already.'

Elizabeth laughed. 'Indeed he does. And he also hates to be crossed. 'Tis one of my few delights left, doing so. Wait!' she called loudly, to more insistent knocking. She pointed into the darkness at the rear of the room. 'There is a back stair there, Master . . . *Sir* John.

You may take it. Yet before you do, know this.' She stepped closer to him, her head at his chest. 'We made what you chose to call a deal, once. I propose another.' She peered hard up at him. 'That all debts between your family and mine are now discharged. Both ways. We will have no further call, each upon the other. We will never meet again. Is that agreed?'

He bowed. 'It is agreed, your majesty.'

She held out her hand. This time he did not shake it on the bargain. Instead he bent, kissed. She stared a moment longer, nodded, turned away. 'You may leave us.'

He went. Yet as he reached the back door, even as he turned the knob, her voice came again softly from the dark. 'Do you love, John Lawley?'

'I do, your majesty.'

'And is your love requited?'

'I . . . I am not certain.'

'Then become so. Take a queen's . . . nay, take a woman's advice. Do not leave it . . . do not leave it until it is too late.'

The hammering had returned. Loud voices anxiously called. Yet as John took the stairs at speed, it was not those that echoed in his ear. A queen's last words did. A woman's.

He would be certain. That he knew as he hurried down the stairs and across the snowy gardens to the wharf. A question needed to be asked in Southwark, an answer given. When the tide turned.

XL

Proposals

The brewer, Matthew, told him that Tess was not at the Spoon but gone to the playhouse. Which seemed strange. The Lord Chamberlain's Men would have played for the last time there that season the previous day, Shrove Tuesday, before the Lenten closure. Unless they'd played at the palace again, as they had two years before – a night John remembered all too well. But no, the Queen was at Greenwich. And he doubted that she would sport on the eve of a day that would commence in such sorrow.

The Globe was not empty; indeed, it was abuzz. Labourers swarmed everywhere – thatchers upon the roof, patching; plasterers filling and smoothing the daub; painters on scaffolding, revitalising the faux marble of the columns. Coming through the main doors, seeing it, John felt an ache in his stomach. They were preparing at season's end for the next season. Wonders would be enacted there, men and women transported by words and actions. Tragedy would unfold, princes would fall, lovers would die. Comedy would make three thousand people laugh as one, buffeting the players with their raw breath. And he could have no part of it.

He looked from the gods to the pit – and there, standing in the very midst of it, hands on hips and staring up, was William Shakespeare.

John moved up beside him, settled, did not speak. The playwright's lips were moving. Even without a quill in his hand, his friend was always writing and John would not disturb him.

After a moment, the man muttered something, looked down, then glanced to his side. When he saw who was there, his eyes went wide, filling with joy. 'John!' he cried, reaching, pulling him into his arms. 'By Jesu, man! Ned told us that you were safe but then . . . you disappeared, as is your wont. When did you return?'

'A few days since. I have been . . . engaged.'

'Upon this other business?' Will's smile passed. 'The one concluded this morning?'

'E'en so.'

'Ah.' His friend's hands upon his arms squeezed. 'And all's well?'

'Well enough.' John slapped the other's arm. 'But what make you here, William? Are you not taking your season's triumphs on the road, to gull the dull and half-witted in the provinces from their silver?'

Will laughed. 'The company – and your son with them – set out this morning for Northampton. Though most lay in the wagons and groaned after the closing revelries of yestere'en. I remain behind to supervise this' – he gestured at the business around him – 'and to finish my play.'

'Which one?'

'I think you know.' He whistled between his teeth. 'It is said that an Afric elephant takes twice as long to give birth as any woman. Well, I have been an elephant with this one, sure.'

''Tis your reworking of *Hamlet* still?'

'Aye.'

'And it is not yet done?'

'Near. 'Twill be in time to open our new season next month.'

John considered. 'And do you play in it too?'

'I think this time I will. I think I will play . . . the father.'

John frowned. 'The ghost?'

'Aye.'

'I see. And your own father? You said he was ill.'

'Still lives.' Will looked away, up to the sky. 'Not for much longer, by report.'

Darkness had replaced the light that the reunion had brought. It was John who now took his friend's arm. 'You have been careful, William?' he asked softly.

'Regarding what?'

'This play. Its themes. The times are tender yet and it is only a month since you were called before the Privy Council to answer for

381

Richard the Second.' He lowered his voice still further. 'They let you off with a warning, I heard. You do not want to test that now.'

'This is different.'

'Indeed? As I recall the piece, it still features regicide, rebellion, usurpation . . .'

'All themes well established in *Hamlet.*' Shakespeare looked at the activity around him. 'I do but rework an old piece, truly.'

John looked into his friend's eyes. 'And ghosts, Will?'

'They have always been in the story too.'

'Not your own.'

The playwright looked sharply up. 'I do not know what you mean.'

'The night Ned and I found you . . . distraught. You spoke of fathers . . . of sons . . .'

'My father is dying,' Will said shortly.

'I know,' John replied, then lowered his voice. 'Will you have a Mass said for his soul?'

Shakespeare stared at him for a long moment, then spoke, loudly. 'Why would I do that, John Lawley? Our Church in England does not sanction it. And we are its loyal children, are we not?'

A workman, passing close with a timber upon his shoulder, glanced at them. John knew his friend spoke for other ears. He kept his own voice low. 'And if not for your father, what of Hamnet's soul?'

Will looked around. Labourers were still close. When he spoke again, his voice too was gentle. 'The play is called *The Tragedy of Hamlet*, John. Hamlet. Different father, different son. It is, in the end, but a play.' A smile came again. 'And one that could use you. I had thought, if you returned to us in time, to offer you a role. There is a scene where a certain gravedigger opines on fate and the world. I thought of you when I wrote it.' He looked more closely. 'Come, John, where is your delight? You ever have pressed me about joining us again upon the scaffold.'

Two thoughts jabbed him, equally keen: the lure of a return to his old life, with all its joys, dangled before him now; and the one that was conjured by his friend's last word. He felt them both, jostling in his guts. He took a breath, another, then shook his head. 'Nay. I thank you for it, truly. But my life . . . has changed. I have to change it further. And yet . . .' Words had passed upon that other scaffold. They came back to him now. 'And yet I would help you in this – I would set the fight for you, one last time. I have . . . an idea for it.'

'What idea?'

'Nay, let me show you when the players return. It is something you will desire, I think. It is . . . in keeping with the times.' John smiled. 'And as a parting gift, I will not even seek a wage for it. I will give you my labours for free.'

Shakespeare laughed. 'Well, Burbage would be thrilled at that. All this' – he nodded at the work around them – 'is expensive. Consider yourself hired. I will pay you in whisky.'

'No, my friend,' he replied softly, 'you will not.'

The two friends stared at each other for a moment. Then John remembered why he had come. 'I heard Tess was here.'

'Aye. She is in the tiring house. She insisted on sewing Ned's new costumes herself.' He shook his head. 'I know not what you did to him, but he is changed. As a boy. As a player. And your lady now makes for him a garb fit for madness.'

'Then, with your leave, I will to her.' John reached and took his friend's hand. 'I have more news for you, William. But it must await the hour.' He looked to the stage. The exit upon it led to the tiring house. 'And the event.'

'Find me later at my lodgings.' Will smiled. 'Good fortune, fellow.'

John left the playwright to his stares, climbed upon the platform, walked to the door, looked in. The room was filled with seamstresses, chattering, sewing. It took a moment to spot her, because she was almost hidden in a far corner, and silent.

He crossed to her. 'A word, lady, if you will.'

She looked up, and he was pleased to see that same relief in finding him safe, usually present after an absence, still there; pleased more that it did not fleet as fast as it had before. 'John,' she said, slipping the needle into the material she worked on, laying it down. She stood, still smiling, and stepped towards him – stopping when she noted that every noise in the room had ceased and all the seamstresses regarded them.

John stepped back. 'Come, lady – shall we walk?'

They did, out on to Maiden Lane, between the Globe and the bear pit – the mastiffs howling as they passed by – and thence into Paris

Gardens. The bowling lawns were covered in fresh snow and no man sported there. The fall had ceased, though clouds still loured, yet with the wind abated, they were warm enough as they made fresh tracks across the virgin white, crossing to the river in slow and squeaking steps. She took his arm, and he was content with that, and with the silence. Grateful indeed, for he was not sure how to begin.

So she did. 'Where were you since the fall of the house?'

'I thought it best to disappear. I went to Stepfather Lawley, in Shropshire.'

'Ah. And you returned . . . ?'

'Two days since. I would have anyway but I was summoned. By . . . by my lord of Essex.'

She halted them. 'You were with him?'

'Even unto the end.'

He said it, staring across the water. She pulled his arm tighter. 'I am sorry for it.'

'And I. Yet, truly, it could not have ended any other way. It was his fate. He found it in the end.'

'Found it?' She stared to the north bank too, as unseeing. 'Was it chosen for him by God, or did he choose for himself?'

'I do not know. Both perhaps? Neither?' He sighed. 'I will leave that to the priests and the playwrights to wrestle out between them.'

'Indeed, John? Put a bottle of whisky on the table and I reckon you will out-expound any priest, out-soliloquise any scribbler.'

She was smiling now. He was not as he turned to her. 'Lady, you know I do not seek that distillation all the time, though it oft calls to me. I think . . . I think it is this place that makes me answer. The playhouse. The taverns. Perhaps away from it I will find solace in other things.'

Her eyebrows – no longer plucked to a line, he noticed – rose. 'You are thinking of leaving Southwark? I thought you had coin down on a plot in the corner of St Mary Overies?'

'If I stay, I think it will be my bed soon enough.'

'But the Globe? I cannot believe you would forsake the stage. It is the life you love.'

'Once.' He looked away, downriver. He could just make out, over the gables of the bridge, the pennants atop the White Tower. 'But I have seen another life, ended on a different kind of platform. Look here!' he cried, squeezing his doublet where red stains besmirched it. 'I do not think . . . I would not find it . . . so *easy* to play again.' Tears came, flooding his eyes in the instant, running in hot streams down his cheeks. 'Sweet Christ!'

'Oh John, John.' She stepped close, took him into her arms.

He leaned on her and she held him up. He had not wept in decades. Perhaps that was why the reservoir was so full.

At last he subsided, gently shrugged free of her, stepped away. When he looked again, she had an eyebrow raised, a slight smile on her face. 'I thought it was the woman's role to woo with tears. Yet you have mastered it.'

He wiped an edge of cloak across his face. 'I do not woo. Not that way.'

'What way then?'

He hesitated. 'None,' he said at last.

'Ah, you would woo by seeming not to?'

'Nay, Tess.' He reached, took her hand. 'I know not seeming. A year in the Tower, a minute on a scaffold, it has taken all my seeming away. Everything else is false.'

'You think so now. You will think differently in two weeks when Will offers you a run of roles.'

'He offered me one, not one bell since. I turned him down.' He shook his head. 'It hurts me to say it. But I am done with it. That life is over.'

'Truly? Then you will need another position.' She looked keenly into his eyes. 'What say you then, sir, to assuming the role of protector of the most popular inn within the Bishop of Winchester's Liberty of Southwark?'

Now he laughed. 'Tess? Are you offering me a job? In a tavern? Me?'

'It is not a tavern, sirrah. It is the finest of inns, as well you know.' Her smile left. 'And I think . . . I think I am offering you more than that.'

'Tess . . .'

'Nay, sir, do not speak. Let me have my say.' She glanced upstream, her brow creased. 'We spoke before of fate. What is governed, what is chosen. I wonder now at Sir Samuel's fate, to die over there at Essex House that day. His death saving me from . . . well, not just being his second wife while the first yet lived . . .' She looked at him, went on a little more sharply. 'Yes, sir, I found that out when I went to claim the body and found it being claimed before me – something you chose not to send me word of!'

'I knew you'd discover it,' he protested. 'The news from me would have seemed . . . opportunistic.'

'Well.' She settled. 'His fate saved me from mine, at least. The one I'd certainly chosen. To be a *lady*? I do not think I could return to being a lady now.' She laughed. 'To speak truth, I do not think I was much of a lady even when I thought I was. My precipitous surrender to you would seem to show that.' She looked skywards, to flakes falling gently again. 'But to be married to a man universally known as Despair? God a mercy!' She shuddered. 'In Finchley?' Her gaze returned from the skies, to him. 'When the man I love lives in Southwark?'

Her eyelashes had snowflakes on them. He didn't think he had seen anything more beautiful. 'Tess . . .'

He stepped to her. But she raised a palm to him, held him off. 'Nay, sir. A moment more and then you may put my lips to a better use – if you still desire to. For you may wish to run instead.' She cleared her throat. 'I know there is risk in you being the landlord of an inn. But if you fall . . . well, at least you will fall close by. And when you stand – which is, as you say, most of the time – well then, sir, you will stand by me.' She nodded, then added, briskly, 'There, sir. I am done. What say you?'

Her hand dropped, no longer resisting him. Yet he did not enter in. 'Lady, are you proposing to me?'

She reached, took his hand. 'Do you know, sir – I believe I am. If you will have me.'

Then he did step in. 'Before I say aye or nay, there is something I have to tell you. However, since you have decided you can no longer be a lady, I give you leave to retract your offer. There were no witnesses to our hand-fasting.'

Then he told her. And when he had finished, and she'd still said yes, and just after they kissed, he raised his face into the now fast-falling snow and howled like a mastiff in a bear pit.

386

XLI

The Prince

The Globe playhouse. 2 April 1601

He'd thought himself too old a dog to be caught by such a trick.

How had it happened that he, John Lawley – an actor since he was younger than Ned – had been snared like any other groundling by such conjuring? When he knew the guile and the dodge of it – the artifice behind each gesture, the effort under the effortlessness of the players' every speech? He had always been able to distil the alchemy of the whole into its separate elements: verse and action, costume, music and scenery and the tricks by which the best players in the world took inked words from a page and sent them into the world as feeling.

He knew precisely what it was they did. He had done it often enough himself. Yet this day and from the very beginning – when a man upon a battlement hissed in terror, 'Who's there?' – John knew that this was different from anything he'd ever experienced, upon a platform, or before one.

It was the first performance of *The Tragedy of Hamlet.*

He had chosen not to read any of it, though Will had offered. He had considered only what he needed for his work. The players, Dickon Burbage and Bill Sly, had brought their characters to the fight and he left those to them. His desire was only to see the play as everyone else did, experience it as they did, for the first time.

Hard though it was, he looked away now from the stage, down to the people in the pit, along the centre gallery where he and Tess sat, above to the others. Three thousand of his fellow Londoners crammed into this thatched O under a spring sun which, due to the specific siting of the platform, warmed sections of them as it traversed the sky while leaving the platform largely in shade and the players upon it shadows within that shade. They'd come for entertainment, sure; but they'd come also for release after a month of Lenten restriction.

And the Lord Chamberlain's Men gave them that, with he and Tess as freed as any there. Caught by a ghost story, held by a family story, moved by a love story, by ambitions thwarted and obligations unfulfilled. Disturbed by a revenge drama that would not follow the customary course. Disturbed above all by this man standing there and asking them all – truly asking them, not telling them – why me? Why should I? What does it mean? What does my life matter, my duty, my honour, when I am this pitiable fellow, crawling between silent heaven and a noisy earth?

It helped that the man asking the questions was Richard Burbage. Yet a Burbage different than John had ever seen him, allowing that velvet voice to be shredded by the fate thrust upon him. It helped that the questions were framed by the playwright in a way he'd been seeking to frame them for years, experience, skill and his life combining now like alchemy, turning all the metals to gold.

Only for the brief moment when George Bryan began to speak the gravedigger's lines that Will had offered to him did John wish he'd accepted and was a part of it – until he remembered he was. For he was bound like everyone else upon the scaffold, above it, before it; a congregation caught in holiness, in devilry – and in something else too.

For there *were* fathers and sons, whatever the playwright had denied. The day quaked with them: Will's, for he acted the prince's dead parent; John's, for Ned entered, upon the stage and into the spirit, as caught and held as any. He'd known his boy to have some skills. He'd taught him some of them. Yet this, today, was beyond all tricks and practice; and when Burbage made an extraordinary speech questioning his very existence, that John could not remember a word of afterwards, only the feeling of desolation that it left, and when that desolation was doubled as Hamlet spurned his lover, spurned John's son, he felt again that rare prickle in his eyes. And he was not alone, it seemed. For the duration of the speech and scene, beyond it, those in the pit, in the galleries, barely moved, scarcely breathed. No bottle of ale popped, no cockle shell crunched under shifting feet.

It was not all sadness, though. This was a play by players – and about players too. A stage above a stage. And if Kemp's foolery was gone, the prince's bitter wit set the audience on a roar, undercutting the tragedy, releasing them for a moment only to enmesh them ever deeper.

On the platform, in the playhouse, there was rapt attention on a girl sent mad. Ned did not shed any tears – and so everyone else did. Resting his head upon his arms, John stared at his son, trying to discern with what bricks Ned had built the portrait, the props under the structure . . . and could not. His son had done what fine players did – taken the life he had seen, then released it as something newly discovered. He had become a fine player himself.

And for those who sought it, there were politics too – not least the scheming counsellor who sought to control everything. And when he died for his schemes, John smiled, hearing the audience gasp – for the style of the scene was a late addition to the piece Will had been working on so long, one as recent as two weeks before and the Earl of Essex's attainder at Westminster Hall. All London had heard the story – how Cecil had hidden to overhear proceedings . . . behind an arras. How he had burst forth to counter one of Essex's allegations. And after the gasp, many in the theatre that day cheered the stage fate of the eavesdropper, stabbed behind his arras.

A father and a child died – there, that day in London, that day in the realm, that day in everyone's lives. All who'd lost them did so again; and when both these were buried hugger-mugger, with rituals curtailed, as the Church in England demanded, many there felt that loss of ritual keenly, and mourned again.

They needed release. And so the skilful playwright gave it to them. Gave them a fight.

Tess gripped him now, as the challenge for the fencing match was announced. She knew what had taken him early each morning from their bed this last week since the players returned, with both Burbage and Sly prepared to work harder on this part of the play than usual. She knew that even John's fights followed a customary pattern, designed largely to thrill. But mere custom would not serve here.

John leaned again upon the rail, the spectator gone now, the participant engaged.

As the weapons were carried out, a thrill ran through the audience. Bill Sly's Laertes, in breastplate and steel gauntlet, chose a rapier – the audience hissing because all knew he'd already anointed it with poison to make certain his revenge – then added a dagger. Burbage's Hamlet made a show of studying what was on offer – before crossing to Marcellus with a cry of delight and drawing forth the man's backsword.

'This likes me well,' he said.

Tess reached to squeeze John's arm. 'Is this what I think?' she asked. 'The hero fights with sword and buckler against the villain's rapier and dagger?'

'Is he the hero? Does he fight a villain?' John shrugged. 'Aye, he'll fight the English against the foreigner. Native tradition against alien import. The old against the new . . .'

' . . . my lord of Essex against all who brought him down,' she finished for him, then looked at him hard. 'Oh, John. Even in a fight, do you and Will play at politics?'

'Nay, love, it is just a fight. Mark it.'

She did, along with the audience. There was surprise, and not just in the choice of weapons. The old play of Hamlet did not end with a bout of fencing but with bloody vengeance. All bent to it, eyes wide.

The players made him proud, were better than they'd ever been. And if there was the drama of the play within the fight, with its double-cross and poisonings, there were also the pure skills themselves. Old principles trumped the new techniques, backsword and buckler overcame rapier and dagger. Chivalry vanquished the modern – and yet succumbed anyway, as nobility will, to treachery.

The fight was over. The stage was covered with bodies. Hamlet summoned up the strength to say, with his dying breath, 'The rest is silence.' And John slumped back, as spent as if he had fought.

From one scaffold to another, he thought. It was not Robert Devereux who lay dead – his head was near picked clean of flesh by the crows on London Bridge not a quarter of a mile away. Those few who knew him as well as John did also knew that he had not the capacities and intellect of Shakespeare's Prince of Denmark. And yet? When a conqueror came at the end and claimed the throne, his words, almost the last of the play, honoured the recently slain. Both of them.

For he was likely, had he been put on,
To have been proved most royal.

A sigh ran through the playhouse at that. The bodies were removed, the play ending in loud shot. Yet if the audience was hoping for a jig to conclude, they were mistaken. Kemp's days were gone. A new age was upon them.

Through the curtains came Shakespeare. Still dressed as the father's ghost – Hamlet's, his own, all dead fathers – he held something white against his belly. Yet it was only when he laid it down, and as slowly departed, that all there saw what it was.

The skull. A skull spiked on London Bridge. Everyman's skull, resting now at the centre of a scaffold.

The Spoon and Alderman was crammed that night, though the doors were closed to the public and held by a large Irishman of soldierly bearing, one Captain St Lawrence. On John's suggestion, he'd been the first man hired by the new landlady – a former lady-in-waiting to the Queen.

Sarah had left the royal circle, lured by a note John had sent her – in a moment of inspiration prompted by the guilt of a memory: his deceiving shake of the head when he had sent her back to Cecil with word that Essex would not rise. She had swiftly gathered enough gold to put a down payment on the inn, its brewery and furnishings – acquired how, only she knew best, though John suspected that a certain Master Secretary had supplied much of it, recognising the potential for information to be obtained from a popular inn, especially one frequented by those shapers of opinion, the players.

He watched Sarah now, paused at a table; Burbage had his lute out, wooing her with a song. The tune ended, roars and applause greeting it, love's object departing to fetch more ales. She was not losing out in her first night in trade by not admitting all, for the place was filled with the denizens of the Globe, their friends and family. Sarah would learn what many a publican knew – actors drank more than almost anyone else, so to draw a regular crowd from the playhouse was to guarantee a profit. He watched her circle with tankards on her arm. Saw her pass Burbage a leathern bottle. Knowing what was in it, John licked his lips.

'Look.' Tess had appeared at his elbow and took it, pointing. Ned was in a corner, playing hazard. He was on point, and rolling. He must have hit it, for he let out a cry of triumph, and snatched up the winnings. 'As in the father, so the son?' she enquired.

'Mercy on him, I hope not.'

'Nay, sir, but have you fared so very poorly?'

He looked at her, smiled, shook his head. Taking all in all, and especially after these last two years – which, on consideration, were no more nor less hazardous than any other pair in his life – indeed he had not.

He turned again to study the crowd; noted the quips exchanged, the bursts of laughter, the detailed discussion of moments in the performance. They were remaking the play here, stitching together the whole from each man's experience – and woman's too, for wives and lovers were also there, adding what they'd seen and felt. It was already being woven into memory, the first performance, changing it from what it was, which could not be truly known, and certainly never recaptured. It was both the joy and the sadness of the art, the passing play. Yet there was joy in that too – for the next time they ventured it, something new would again be born. Different, perhaps as exciting, perhaps even more so.

He sighed. And then? he wondered. There would other plays. Will had some left in him, John suspected; while in this tavern he had the finest company of actors to play whatever he next chose to write.

Tess was studying him. 'Join them, my love,' she said. 'Enjoy the night.'

John looked around. He knew almost everyone there, would be welcomed in any circle. But he was outside them all now. Despite his fight, he was not truly part of the ritual nor its aftermath. 'Sweet,' he said, 'the tide will soon be turning. Shall we upon it?'

'Will you say your farewells?'

'Nay. I hate them. Always have.'

'To Ned at least?'

'What is left to say? Borrow the speech of Gus Phillips tonight: "To thine own self be true"?' He shook his head. 'He is playing that.

And living it. You say goodbye from us both. Tell him we will see him when we return at Michaelmas to collect our rent. I will await you outside.'

'As you command . . . husband,' she said with a smile, and moved away.

He watched her thread between the players, many bowing as she passed. Even when she was mistress here, she'd had the ways of a lady. And now she was one . . .

Smiling, John took one last look around the room, then went to the door. St Lawrence had a headlock on a large drunk and looked like he was happy in the work. John slipped past the fracas. He truly did hate farewells, and he was still bruised from the slaps of gratitude the Irishman had already given him.

It was crowded upon the street, so he stepped into the shadow of the alley to watch and wait. The pace in Southwark scarcely slackened, but on the first day after Lent, whorehouses, cockpits and gambling hells were packed with a frenzied crowd, and every tavern, inn and ordinary was fuelling the excess.

Smoke wreathed his nostrils. He looked up, saw a swirling circle of it pass from the alley. The gentle voice confirmed all. 'Will you miss it, do you think?'

The only man who needed his farewell was behind him. 'Now and again, surely,' he said, not turning, 'Yet not often nor for long, I suspect.'

Shakespeare emerged and passed the pipe across. John took it, sending his own rolling coil out upon the still night air. For a time that was all they did – smoking, refilling, competing, pluming the night with intertwining circles. Until Will spoke. 'I could not leave it. I have taken new rooms here now, hard by.' He lifted his face into the air, like a hound, scenting. 'All the better to fill my senses with it.'

'And yet your plays happen in Elsinore, Master Shakespeare. In fair Verona. In Athens. What need you of London?'

The playwright smiled. 'You know better than that, sir. My plays may happen elsewhere. Yet they all take place in the city I love and are filled with its citizens, high and low.'

'As tonight.' John tipped his head westwards, to where a darker thatched shape loomed. ''Twas . . . extraordinary, my friend.'

'Was it not? Sometimes'– he sighed – 'sometimes we simply get it right, don't we?'

'Aye. Sometimes we do.'

'And your fight, John. Your finest work. Did you mark how it was received?'

'I did. But I think that was less for my skills, or the players', than for the idea behind it.' John whistled. 'Who would have thought?'

'Many who were there. For the others' – he shrugged – 'they were entertained, as ever, and will continue to be. We may even stretch this one to ten performances. And the Lawley name will live on in each one.'

John sighed. 'William, you know that no one ever questions who makes the fight. They think it a thing of the players alone, and in the moment.'

''Tis true. 'Tis sad, 'tis true. But your son will also carry the name. With distinction – did you note him tonight?'

'Only a little.' John nodded. 'He has the stuff, has he not?'

'He has indeed.'

For a while longer the two men passed the pipe, relighting it from a lamp Will had beside him, making circles, watching the passing show in an amiable silence – until John broke it. 'I'll tell you something, William. You alone. I have been thinking much on names of late. What is in them? Mine is from my stepfather, Thomas Lawley. My real father was a savage, his name . . . well, near unpronounceable in English. So I have been thinking of changing mine. Find one to suit this new life I embark upon.'

'Oh?' Will looked at him. 'Do you need help? I am always making up names. I could write you a grand one.'

'And find myself a Feeble, a Bullcalf or a Wart?' John chuckled. 'Thank you, my friend. I have one already chosen.'

'And?' His friend turned. 'What makes a fitting conclusion to "Sir John"?'

'It came to me with the crest that my lord of Essex devised for me. Its motto is "*Absolute Fidelis*".

' "Absolutely Faithful"? 'Tis true of you, for you have ever been, to all your friends and causes. Even to the whisky that was so oft your downfall. How about Sir John Faithful?' The playwright laughed. 'No, zounds, that belongs to a character from a play by Dekker!'

'I was thinking of taking it as it is. Latin and English. What think you of . . . Absolute?'

William took a deep puff, exhaled long. 'Do you know – I like it. There is a line in the play we gave tonight. "How *absolute* the knave is!" And that's you, John. Not a knave but . . . absolute, in everything. Whatever you do, be it drinking or fighting or playing – or, may I say, loving – you do it . . . absolutely.'

'You are right in that, sir.' Tess joined them, taking her husband's arm. 'What conspiracies do you two make here now?'

John raised a hand. 'No more conspiracies. As I live and breathe, I am done with 'em. I hope to find none in Cornwall.'

'Then you will find a land without people. For where one man lives between two others, there is conspiracy born. But Cornwall?' Will shuddered. 'Are you both sure?'

'Come visit us. Perhaps you can tour a play when plague closes the London houses?'

'Tour? Is there a town worthy of the title to play in?'

The couple looked at each other a moment, then both laughed. 'We don't know,' John said, 'but if there is, we shall discover it.'

A silence came. 'Well,' said Tess, breaking it, 'we must . . .'

'And I,' said Will, tapping out his pipe upon his heel.

'Yes, you must return to your celebration.'

'Nay, John. You know I am not a carouser by nature. And as you know, a play's birth always leaves me a little melancholy. My child is abroad in the world and needs me no longer.' He smiled. 'But I have another one, shifting to be born, and I will go attend it now. So fair weather to your travels. Sir John. Lady Tess.' He bowed. 'Absolutes both.'

With a swivel, he was gone, unmarked, into the crowd. 'What did he mean by that?' she asked.

'I will tell you later.' John offered an arm. 'Lady Tess.'

'Sir John.' She took it. 'I wonder if I will ever get used to that.'

'More readily than me, I suspect,' he replied, leading her off.

There were two couples ahead of them at Paris Garden Stairs, but wherries circled just off the wharf. As they waited, John looked downriver to London Bridge, each house upon it glowing with torch or lantern. Only the bulk of the gatehouse was dark. Yet he still could see it, in his mind's eye at least. Knew what was spiked upon it. The crowds had waned that had come to gawk at the great traitor's skull. People would soon be passing without even looking up. Such was the fate of man.

'The rest is silence,' he murmured. He turned to Tess. 'Do you think that's true?'

'Silence? With you? I think it most unlikely.' She took his arm as a wherry ground against the wharf. 'Shall we?'

AUTHOR'S NOTE

When I look back at the writing of this novel, I feel slightly guilty. Am I supposed to have this much fun, indulging myself for over a year? The writing school mantra is 'Write what you know.' I've always amended that to 'Write what you love.' They often overlap, of course. And here was much of my knowledge and several of my passions combined. In no particular order: Shakespeare, sword-fighting, acting, theatrecraft, the Tudors, London . . .

. . . and *Hamlet*.

To say I am obsessed would be putting it mildly. It is an obsession born of experience. I played 'the Dane', as he is called (he is also known, less reverently, as 'Omelette'), in 1994 at Theatre Calgary, Canada. It was a strange production experience. I was the alternate Hamlet. This does not mean I did it with a funny walk and odd voice. It was just that the main actor – a star from Eastern Canada – didn't want to play Hamlet twice in a day. (Who does? Well, I do, but that's another story.) So I was brought in to do the matinees, which would mainly be for schools. I didn't mind at all – it was my chance at the dream role, to gain admittance to quite an exclusive club. I was promised plenty of rehearsal – which I did not get. A few runs of scenes, often in backstage corridors, a half-arsed dress rehearsal when the other players only did the Hamlet scenes so I never got an idea of the flow. Yet, to be honest, I was relieved. The director was making some . . . odd choices, in staging, in inter-pretation. For a start, he was obsessed by bringing in the show at three and a half hours, and when, in previews, it wouldn't conform,

397

he cut the entire first, brilliant scene. Sacrilege! So I was glad that I was largely left alone, with really just the text, and my determination.

I became a sort of warrior monk. Shunned company, gave up beer (which I love) and anything else, worked out a lot – riding the exercise bike to Olympian level – and dived completely into what Hamlet calls 'Words. Words? Words!'

I thought I was ready. I was in for a shock. When I walked out on to the stage the first time in my 'customary suit of solemn black' . . . I totally froze. Started hyperventilating. I had never been an especially nervy actor, but here I was in full panic mode. I thought: this is it, what you hear about: actor breaks down on stage and has to be carried whimpering off, never to act again. Then I thought: listen! What's he saying? What's my uncle saying? I took a deep breath, another, another. Then Claudius asked me a question, I answered . . . and stepped on to the rollercoaster. Three and a half hours later, I stepped off it. Or rather was carried off, because I was dead.

Aside from the birth of my son, it was probably the best single experience of my life. I was totally in the moment, each moment. I felt free. I tried new things. It was . . . beyond exhilarating. Oh, and it wasn't actually three and a half hours. When I came off, the stage manager told me I'd taken seventeen minutes off the running time. Seventeen! And this wasn't because I gabbled it. I believe I simply spoke the speech, as Shakespeare commands it in the play, 'trippingly on the tongue'. The director was ungraciously annoyed. He realised, I think, that he could have kept that first scene. The stage crew on the other hand bought me my first beer in six weeks – they were in the pub seventeen minutes earlier!

I played it seven times. Each time different, getting some bits better. Never as euphorically, though. That first time – what a trip!

Cut to fifteen years later. *Hamlet* has figured in some of my other books. (Those who have read the 'Jack Absolute' trilogy will know that Ate, the Mohawk, is as obsessed as I am.) The opening words of my *Runestone Saga* for teens are the opening words of Hamlet: 'Who's there?' But it was at the Art Gallery of Ontario at a theatre art exhibition, when I was wondering what to write next, that the thought hit – provoked by a particularly horrendous recorded recitation of 'To be or not to be' by some Stratford Ontario actor. It was accompanying a stage design. I know I am proprietorial, but I loathe it in a Shakespeare production when an actor walks on and tells me what he's figured out . . . *somewhere else!* Especially that speech. I want him to come on and seek meaning with us, the audience, his conscience, his co-conspirators. To demand: *What the hell am I to do?* Not blandly declaim: *This is what I already know.* Furious, I went to the café and, over a coffee, began to mumble the lines as I felt they should be said. And it came. The lightning bolt. I suddenly knew what I was going to write next. I took out my notebook and wrote these words:

Hamlet and swords, for fuck's sake. Hamlet and swords.

I was going to write a novel about William Shakespeare's fight choreographer!

Who knows if such a man existed? But as a former fight arranger myself, I know the expertise that is required. I realise that actors in Elizabethan times rehearsed far less than their modern counterparts and that they were also men versed in the use of weapons. Most men carried swords and knew how to use them. Which, I think, makes Shakespeare's fights most important – it was a discerning audience, unlike most people today. The players would be judged on their skill with a blade as on any other.

When I began my serious research into the period, I discovered I knew far less about the play than I'd believed. I knew the prince himself somewhat – but the time when it was written? Not much. Study informed me – and made the book, as good research does, giving me springboards for the imagination. I had not realised before how the specific events of the time shaped *Hamlet.* How much the Lord Chamberlain's Men were 'holding the mirror up to nature'. Reflecting back their audience and their concerns. Peeking under the surface of a rigidly controlled society – where satire had actually been banned. You could not mock the secretive machinery of state and its politicians – but you could, if you were clever, depict it and them in a play. Not to subvert – I don't believe Shakespeare was political in that sense – but to let your audience exhale.

These were most turbulent times. My research led me into them, into writing the lives of the players, on and off the various scaffolds.

The waning but still potent Elizabeth. The Machiavellian Cecil. The charismatically insane Earl of Essex, some of whose antics I have reported almost verbatim, such as his mad ride from Ireland to see the Queen near naked when he said, 'Though I have suffered much trouble and storms abroad I have found a sweet calm at home!' – to his turning right not left out of Essex House that fateful February day, to his yelling about 'atheists and caterpillars' from his roof. And I have also delved into the rapidly changing world that allowed Shakespeare and company, and theatre in general, to explode as it did – let's face it, the single biggest explosion in the form ever.

Part of that was to do with the new overtaking the old. And part of *that* was to do with styles of sword-fighting. Hence the novel's themes of traditional virtues overtaken by new fancies. In government, in theatre, in religion – and in the supplanting of the trusty English backsword and buckler by 'devilish imports' and 'foreign fancies', those tools of murder, the rapier and the dagger. Read George Silver's *Paradoxes of Defence*, published in 1599, dedicated to the Earl of Essex, already out of favour and heading towards his fateful, pathetic attempt at coup d'état. The changing world is summed up in those pages – and it will make you laugh out loud.

All this is reflected in the play. But I also believe it was a highly personal work to its creator, and filled with his life. If you look at my bibliography, you will see how much I endorse the theories of the brilliant Stephen Greenblatt in his *Will in the World* and of James Shapiro in his equally majestic *1599* (though I am convinced he gets the year wrong! There is much debate and no certain answer, but evidence points to the play first being performed in 1601). I believe Shakespeare's loss of his son four years before, the impending death of his father, his inability to bury and mourn them as he might have wished to do in the 'curtailed rites' of the new Protestant ascendancy, fills the play with parents and children. (I am not saying he was a closet Catholic as some believe, but I think it is possible to still be a good Protestant while missing some of the luxuriant ritual of the old faith.) As a father myself, and as a son (the actor who played Old Hamlet in our production had my own recently deceased father's eyes, bringing tears to mine on that first wild ride!), I see him as both, and try to understand the pain of loss he must have felt and how he fed that into the creation of the greatest game-changer in literature: *The Tragedy of Hamlet*.

I have said enough about it in my book. I will only add that each time I read, see or hear it, something changes. My wife complains that if I go away and haven't taken a copy with me, I invariably buy another because I have just reassessed some speech and need to verify. But it is so . . . malleable. I heard it once described as the ultimate straight role. I think that's true; each actor brings himself, his history and attitudes to it and that's why performances vary so widely. I have been changed by some great ones – on stage, Jonathan Pryce's, Derek Jacobi's, Ian McKellen's, my friend Simon Russell Beale's. On screen, Laurence Olivier's, Kenneth Branagh's majestic vision, Mel Gibson's (his pure talents as an actor so often submerged in his controversies). Each time, something in me shifts, something new is discovered.

It seems appropriate that I should be writing at least part of this note on 23 April 2012 – the anniversary of William Shakespeare's death in 1616. Quite likely the anniversary of his birth too, in 1564. As I write, England explodes with a Shakespearean Olympiad to precede the athletic one. All his plays are being done over the next few months, not only by British companies but by troupes from all across the world. I would love to see the Urdu *Taming of the Shrew*, the Belarusian *King Lear* or the Palestinian *Richard the Second*, to observe how relevant Shakespeare still is to people, their times and circumstances. Many of these will be staged at the extraordinary Globe Theatre in London. My several visits there took in the museum, some fight demonstrations and a quite wonderful production of *Dr Faustus*. This so helped me in imagining what the whole experience might have been like for a playgoer in 1599. I had an ale and a pie – though I was spared the smell of groundling piss. They have rather nice toilets there these days!

Shakespeare's words and visions thrive, continuing to be produced everywhere. There is something very special about the Bard of Avon that he is performed still, not as heritage theatre but as someone contemporary, holding the mirror up to this age's concerns, in whatever country, just as he did in London in 1601. I have no time for the Oxfordians (have you seen the abomination that was *Anonymous*? I nearly had to be escorted from the cinema!), or any other crew that would take his genius away from him and hand it to someone . . . smarter, better educated, higher class. To me, it's the worst of conspiracy theory allied to snobbism. For the point of genius and imagination is that they transcend limits. He may have been a glover's son, but he had a rigorous classical education in Stratford. Marry that to his imagination, feed that through the explosion in the theatrical form of the last two decades of the sixteenth century – another rigorous education – and consider the development of his work from the simplistic *Titus Andronicus* and *The Comedy of Errors* to the wonder of his later tragedies and comedies . . . there is no doubt for me. He was the man.

But *who* was the man? So little is known, not much written down. Great writers have extrapolated him and his preoccupations from his work and the very few biographical clues. He is something of a blank canvas – fortunately for the novelist. He could be any number of characters, from the litigious, penny-pinching scrivener, to the bisexual Catholic aesthete. I have taken a few clues, allied them to my sadly limited experience of playing him (a brace of Lysanders, Oberon, Don Pedro, Oliver, Salanio and, of course, the Dane) and then bent him, as any writer will, to my own purposes. He was 'sweet William' to me. He was not 'a carouser by nature' – as a writer myself, I know how hard it is to carouse at night and then produce the goods in the morning! He was also, I suspect, a pretty good actor.

I only get to practise that craft of theatre myself once in a while now. Whenever I do, I rediscover again the instant quality, the excitement of knowing that these people will never again be gathered in one place, that between them they must create the moments, actors and audience. When it works – and God knows it often doesn't! – it is like nothing else. Like any player – like my man John Lawley, with his limp! – I know some of the tricks. Yet I have also, occasionally, participated in the magic.

So that first phrase in a moleskin notebook – *Hamlet and swords, for fuck's sake! Hamlet and swords!* – has now expanded into the book, physical or electronic, you are holding. I've dealt with the *Hamlet* side a little – but what of swords? Well, I became an actor mainly because I wanted to leap around with bladed weaponry. I've been fortunate enough to do my fair share of it, on stage and screen. So when I discovered the whole 'backsword versus rapier' controversy of the late sixteenth century, it was irresistible.

I mentioned feeling very indulgent with this novel and its themes – extending into this, an indulgently long Author's Note! – but I do need to mention a last one – the link between my earlier 'French Executioner' books and my later 'Jack Absolute' ones. I have been inspired by Wilbur Smith and his Courtenay family saga. Like me, I doubt he set out to write about one family across the centuries. Yet there is something very satisfying in it, and I did sow that seed when I gave Jack the middle name of Rombaud in the novel *Jack Absolute*, with little further explanation. With John Lawley I have linked the two, and I have no doubt I will be able to create more Absolutes later in my storytelling life. For my readers it might add a little something. For those new to me – hie thee to a bookstore!

There's one last personal story here, concerning drunkenness. Not my own – though I probably supply details from a few examples! But I was delighted to discover the quote I use here at the book's opening, concerning the martin drunkard: '*when a man is drunk and drinks himself sober ere he stir . . .*' Because I met one such, in Clifden, Connemara, Ireland, a few years back.

He was Peter Fitzwilliam. (The names have been changed to protect the inebriated.) I was on a solo pub crawl there, and Peter was on the next bar stool. He told me he had been drinking for a month, 'on the whisky'. Apparently he did this once every five years, though between these binges he was teetotal. After a month he would pass several days drinking nothing but Guinness – till he had drunk himself sober again. It was touch and go, but if he stayed out much longer he believed his fiancée, to whom he'd been engaged for eleven years, would not take him back this time. I enjoyed many a rambling tale, and the odd snatch of song – which mainly concerned the drinking exploits of lads from a certain hilly part of Clifden. He had a very tall and equally intoxicated companion who he referred to as Peter the Poacher ('Yer man if you want a salmon'), who said nary a word but would grunt and raise both arms occasionally in support. When I got back to my hotel, I mentioned the encounter to the receptionist. 'Oh, Peter Fitz,' she said. 'Yes, I heard he was off on one.'

Little did I know I had met a martin drunkard. All I did know was that I filed him away – to be used, later, for John Lawley, who is 'yer man' for me to pursue one fantasy to the fullest. For I put him there, the place where I would set the time machine's dial for, were I given three hours. There, that afternoon in Southwark, standing in the pit of the Globe, a leather tankard of ale in one hand, a bag of nuts in the other, gazing up at the platform as someone asks, 'What's this new play called, then?' There, when a trumpet sounds and a sentry walks out, shivers and whispers, 'Who's there?'

I think I would even swap that first time I played the Dane for the opportunity to witness Burbage as the son, Shakespeare as the father, and the world changing before my eyes.

Now that would be indulgence indeed!

C.C. Humphreys
April 2012
Salt Spring Island, Canada

BIBLIOGRAPHY

My shelf groans with books. Before I begin I look at them and think how my novel is in them, somewhere. Here's where I hunted for it. Some I devoured, some just picked at. The most influential perhaps, for the times, Shakespeare's life and the influences on the play, were the Greenblatt and the Shapiro. I believe the term for them is 'magisterial'. My main *Hamlet* was the much marked copy I used to play him, the New Cambridge version. The introductory essay is brilliant!

SHAKESPEARE
Will in the World, Stephen Greenblatt
1599, James Shapiro
Shakespeare's Words, David Crystal and Ben Crystal
Shakespeare on Toast, Ben Crystal

THE TIMES, PLACES AND PEOPLE
Shakespeare's London on Five Groats a Day, Richard Tames
A Shakespearean Theatre, Jacqueline Morley
Shakespeare's England, ed. R. E. Pritchard
London, Peter Ackroyd
Religion and the Decline of Magic, Keith Thomas
The Elizabethan Secret Services, Alan Haynes
Sex in Elizabethan England, Alan Haynes
Robert, Earl of Essex, Robert Lacey
Wotton and his Worlds, Gerald Curzon
Roaring Boys, Judith Cook

THE PLAYS

Shakespeare, Complete Works, RSC, eds Jonathan Bate and Eric Rasmussen

Hamlet, New Cambridge, ed. Philip Edwards

Hamlet, Sourcebooks Shakespeare, ed. William Proctor Williams; series eds Marie Macaisa and Dominique Raccah

Henry the Fifth, New Penguin Shakespeare, ed. A. R. Humphreys

Julius Caesar, New Penguin Shakespeare, ed. Norman Sanders

THE FIGHTS

Paradoxes of Defence, George Silver

English Martial Arts, Terry Brown

The Complete Renaissance Swordsman, Antonio Manciolino, trans. and ed. Tom Leone

Sword Fighting, Keith Ducklin and John Waller

The Flintlock, Torsten Lenk

THE PHILOSOPHY

The Elizabethan World Picture, E. M. W. Tillyard

How to Live: A Life of Montaigne, Sarah Bakewell

'Hamlet, Duellist', S. P. Zitner, in *University of Toronto Quarterly*, 1969

ACKNOWLEDGEMENTS

As always, there are so many people to thank for their help in the creation of this book.

At my publishers, editorially there was as ever the super-smart Jon Wood, whose notes stimulated me to focus, and to expansion, not contraction (for 'edit' does not always mean 'cut'!). Also Jemima Forrester, who added a well-reasoned and welcome alternative perspective. While at William Morris Endeavor, Simon Trewin continues to skilfully – and amusingly – chart my professional course.

There is my family – my wife Aletha, who saw me play Hamlet in our courting days, still married me, and knows the level of my obsession enough to completely support me through this phase of it, as well as giving useful notes. And my son, Reith, eight now, whose talk and presence so stimulated my imagination about parents and their children.

Perhaps especially with this story, there are the swordmasters. I was fortunate to stumble into the extraordinary Academie Duello in Vancouver, a medieval martial arts school. These are serious and skilful people, exemplified by their leader and founder Devon Boorman, who crossed swords with me privately and whose brains I picked extensively. He also organised a Sword Symposium in February 2011 where I studied the sword and buckler techniques of the sixteenth-century Italian master Achille Marozzo, under the tutelage of the brilliant twenty-first-century Italian master Tom Leoni. *Grazie, maestro!* And I must also thank my fight partner during those days, Jennifer Landels, for her patience and skills – I am older and slower than I was, and, an excellent swordswoman, she coached me through it all.

One of the most extraordinary bouts I had was in the prosaic surroundings of a council flat above Boots the Chemist on Mill Hill Broadway, London. There resides *the* world expert on George Silver, Terry Brown, a superb martial artist who, well into his sixties, could destroy me with a breath. In his small front room converted into a *salle d'armes*, he took me through many aspects of the English master's work. 'Simplicity is efficiency's best friend,' he said that day, and I have tried to apply it, not only to John Lawley's sword-fighting but to my writing as well. Over a session sword in hand and another in the pub armed with pints, he generously shared his deep understandings.

Lastly there is the man to whom the book is dedicated. John Waller has always been an inspiration, from when he was my stage combat teacher at drama school through to today, decades later, when he will shoot crossbows with me in his Yorkshire garden. His knowledge of all things medieval is extraordinary: a master bowman, swordsman, hawker and hunter. And as a fight arranger for stage and screen, he always emphasised the principle I have tried to uphold in my writing: at any moment in a fight you should be able to take a still photograph of the action that looks great! Simple and sweet. Thanks, Master Waller, always!

To these, to all who've aided me, much gratitude.

C.C. Humphreys
April 2012
Salt Spring Island, Canada